Julietta stared down at him, mesmerised.

She watched his fingers toy with the fringe, and for a second she had a vision of that touch on *her*, trailing over her skin, lightly caressing the curve of her neck, the soft underside of her arm, circling a pebbled nipple that strained for his touch, his kiss…

She sucked in a sharp breath, closing her eyes against the alluring temptation. The air was filled with the scent of jasmine, smoke, wine, flesh. The drumming grew faster, deeper, thrumming deep in her stomach. Closing her eyes did not erase her desire; it only intensified it, sending images of their bodies entwining, rising and falling to the rhythm of the music, humid heat flowing around them. Perhaps *that* was what she feared when she was with him – that the tiny bud she pressed down so hard within herself would burst into full, ungovernable bloom as he touched her, and would never be suppressed again.

That she would lose all control, lose *herself*, within him. And that she could never allow.

A NOTORIOUS WOMAN

BY
AMANDA McCABE

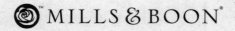

MILLS & BOON

All the characters in this book have no existence outside the imagination of
the author, and have no relation whatsoever to anyone bearing the same name
or names. They are not even distantly inspired by any individual known or
unknown to the author, and all the incidents are pure invention.

All Rights Reserved including the right of reproduction in whole or in part
in any form. This edition is published by arrangement with Harlequin
Enterprises II B.V./S.à.r.l. The text of this publication or any part thereof may
not be reproduced or transmitted in any form or by any means, electronic or
mechanical, including photocopying, recording, storage in an information
retrieval system, or otherwise, without the written permission of the publisher.

This book is sold subject to the condition that it shall not, by way of trade or
otherwise, be lent, resold, hired out or otherwise circulated without the prior
consent of the publisher in any form of binding or cover other than that in
which it is published and without a similar condition including this condition
being imposed on the subsequent purchaser.

® and ™ are trademarks owned and used by the trademark owner and/or its
licensee. Trademarks marked with ® are registered with the United Kingdom
Patent Office and/or the Office for Harmonisation in the Internal Market and
in other countries.

First published in Great Britain 2010
Harlequin Mills & Boon Limited,
Eton House, 18-24 Paradise Road, Richmond, Surrey TW9 1SR

© Ammanda McCabe 2007

ISBN: 978 0 263 88299 5

37-0210

Harlequin Mills & Boon policy is to use papers that are natural, renewable
and recyclable products and made from wood grown in sustainable forests.
The logging and manufacturing processes conform to the legal environmental
regulations of the country of origin.

Printed and bound in Spain
by Litografia Rosés S.A., Barcelona

Amanda McCabe wrote her first romance at the age of sixteen – a vast epic, starring all her friends as the characters, written secretly during algebra class.

She's never since used algebra, but her books have been nominated for many awards, including the RITA®, *Romantic Times* Reviewers' Choice Award, the Booksellers Best, the National Readers' Choice Award, and the Holt Medallion. She lives in Oklahoma, with a menagerie of two cats, a pug and a bossy miniature poodle, and loves dance classes, collecting cheesy travel souvenirs, and watching the Food Network – even though she doesn't cook. Visit her at http://ammandamccabe. tripod.com and http://www.riskyregencies.blogspot.com

Chapter One

Venice—1525

Oh, yes. He was really dead.

"Madre de dio," Julietta Bassano whispered, leaning close to examine the man's corpse, sprawled across the rich silk cushions of his gilded bed. It had not been an easy death, nor a pretty one. His face, so florid in life, was turned a dark, mottled purple-blue, his black beard matted with bile and spittle and blood. The wide, staring, sightless eyes were dotted with tiny spots of red, and his stiffening limbs were thrown wide in abruptly frozen death throes.

No—not an easy demise at all. She recognised the signs. She had seen them in her own husband three years ago, as he collapsed in the middle of their own bed, convulsing and heaving.

"Witch!" he had screamed. "Sorceress! You have

murdered me." And his clawlike hands had snatched at her gown, his blood and vomit spraying her flesh with death.

No! she thought sternly, closing her eyes and her mind to the memories. Giovanni was long dead; he had deserved his end, the pig. He could not hurt anyone ever again.

Unlike this man…

Julietta opened her eyes to stare down at the corpse of Michelotto Landucci, noble of the Most Serene Republic, high member of the Savio ai Cerimoniali. His richly brocaded robe hung open, revealing a heavy, hairy stomach, a flaccid, blue-tinged member. With a snort of disgust, she grabbed the edge of a silk sheet and drew it up over him, hiding him from view.

Behind her, she heard a soft, frightened sob, a stifled gasp. Julietta tried to take in a deep, steadying breath to calm herself, but the stench of death had grown too strong. It stuck in her nostrils, clung to her hair and cloak. Clasping the black velvet closer about her throat, she spun around to face the woman who huddled in the shadows of the palatial bedchamber. Cosima Landucci, wife—nay, widow—of the man beneath the sheet. Unlike her spouse, she was still fully dressed in an elaborate gown of gold-embroidered blue silk. Thick, dark red hair spilled down her back and fell over her white, unlined brow, proclaiming how very much younger than her husband she was. Just a child, really.

A child whose husband lay poisoned in his own

bed. *Well, well.* She would not have thought it of timid little Cosima. People were surprising. Ever surprising.

"What happened here, *signora?*" Julietta asked, as gently as she could. She knew this girl—Cosima had been a loyal patroness of Julietta's perfume shop for almost two years, coming in weekly to buy her special scent, jasmine and lily, and to talk to Julietta. And talk, and talk, as if she had no other friend in the world but her perfumer. And Julietta had been glad to listen. She felt sorry for the girl, who seemed so lost and unhappy despite her fine gowns and flashing jewels. She—well, she rather reminded Julietta of *herself* so long ago, when all her dreams of marriage and family were shattered in the face of cold reality.

But this—*this* was something else altogether.

"Well, *signora?*" Julietta prompted, when the girl just went on sniffling.

Cosima pressed a lace handkerchief to her face, her hands shaking. "I—I do not know what happened, Signora Bassano!"

"You were not here? You simply came in to find your husband dead?" Julietta gave a pointed glance at the dainty slippers and jewelled headdress discarded on the lavish Turkish rug.

Cosima followed her gaze and shook her head, the waves of red hair spilling over her shoulders. "No, I was here. We had just returned from a supper party, and he—he…" Her soft, little-girl voice faltered.

"Requested his conjugal rights?"

Cosima slowly nodded.

"Hmm," Julietta continued. "What else did he do?"

"D-do?"

Julietta suppressed an impatient sigh. *Dio mio,* but they did not have all night! Already it grew very late, and the Landucci household would be up and about in only a few hours. Julietta wanted only to discover what this girl wanted of her, why she had summoned her here, and then be on her way. She had her own business to attend to, business of far more import than a silly patrician woman and a dead husband who no doubt greatly deserved to be dead.

What was the point of this whole exercise?

Yet she knew she could not rush Cosima, or the girl would collapse entirely. Already she was trembling like a winter leaf in the cold wind.

"What did he do before he demanded to bed you? For you are still dressed, *madonna.*" Julietta gestured towards Cosima's gown, the sleeves still neatly tied in place, the gold lace on the high-waisted bodice smooth.

Cosima bunched the handkerchief in her fist. Her eyes were red-rimmed, her skin chalk-white. "He drank some wine, as he always does before—before… Quite a lot of it."

Julietta frowned. There were no goblets or ewers around the chamber. Cosima's tearful gaze flickered to the floor, and that was where Julietta saw it—the jewelled stem of a silver goblet, barely glimmering under the edge of the bed. She knelt down and drew it from beneath the heavy fall of velvet bedclothes.

In the very bottom of the cup rested the dregs of dark red wine, stagnant as blood, already drying at the edges. Julietta lifted it to her nose and sniffed cautiously. A faint hint of some green, grassy scent met her sensitive nose, along with the sweet headiness of the expensive wine. And something else. Jasmine and lily—Cosima's own perfume, mixed by Julietta's own hand and poured weekly into Cosima's vial of blue Murano glass.

Julietta set the goblet aside and peered once more into the black depths under the bed. Her nose wrinkled at the copious amount of dust—the maidservants were obviously not as diligent as they should be. Yet there was more than dust and dirt. There was the faint sheen of celestial blue glass.

She snatched it up, holding it to the light. The vial was empty, the silver stopper gone, but the scent of jasmine and lily still clung about it. Along with that strange touch of green grassiness.

It was a scent Julietta was all too familiar with.

"Poison," she whispered. It echoed in the vast chamber like a death knell.

"No!" Cosima shrieked. She dashed across the room, throwing herself to her knees beside Julietta. She clutched at Julietta's arm, her pretty face a rictus of despair and terror. "He cannot have been poisoned, and if he was *I* did not do it. Please, Signora Bassano, you must believe me!"

Julietta resisted the urge to shake off the girl's clinging hands, and instead held out the empty vial. "If you did not, *madonna,* then someone is at great pains to make it seem as if you did."

Cosima stared at the blue glass with wide, horrified eyes. "No. I did not—did not love my husband as a good wife should, you know that, *signora.* But I am a good Catholic! I would never imperil my mortal soul by…" Her expression crumpled, and she was in tears again.

"Basta!" Julietta seized the girl's arm and gave her a shake. "No time for that now. Your servants will be up soon, and we have much to do."

Cosima sniffled, and looked up at Julietta with hope writ large on her face. "You will help me?"

Julietta stared at Cosima, once again seeing herself as she once was. Young, alone, afraid. So very afraid. And with good reason. She wanted more than anything to walk away, to flee this cursed house and this troublesome girl. Yet she could not.

"I will help you," she said shortly. "But you must do everything I say, and quickly."

Cosima nodded eagerly. "Of course, *signora!* I will do whatever you say, if you will just help me again."

"Call my maidservant, Bianca, she waits in the corridor. The two of you must build a fire in the grate, a large one, as hot as possible."

Cosima nodded and scrambled to her feet, scurrying out the chamber door in silence, tears apparently forgotten. At least the girl could move fast when need be.

When Cosima was gone, Julietta also stood and

went to the window. No one was about so late at night, not even a boatman or street prostitute. The Feast of the Ascension, when Carnival would officially commence, was still days away. She pushed open the casement and stared down at the canal two stories below. The blue-black water was calm, barely lapping at the base of the palazzo in tiny, white breaking waves. The water knew how to keep its secrets— always. Julietta took the goblet and the vial and tossed them out as far as she could.

For an instant, the fading moonlight caught on the tainted objects, sparkling and dancing. Then they were gone, vanished with the merest splash as if they had never been.

"Madre de dio," she whispered, "do not let it begin again."

The sky was tinged the merest pale gray when Julietta finally made her way home from the Palazzo Landucci, Bianca trailing behind her as they slipped through the narrow *calli* back to their dwelling north of the Rialto. Julietta ached with exhaustion, every nerve crying out for rest, sleep, blessed forgetfulness. She would not sleep this morn, though, she knew that well, nor for many nights to come.

Not after all she had done.

The only sounds were the click of their shoes against the cobblestones, the creak of loose shutters in the cold breeze. No one was yet about, not even the vendors setting up their wares on the Rialto and in the fish market. The air was chilly, thick with mist and the sticky-sweet smells of the water. The pastel colours of the stucco houses, all pink and yellow and orange in the sunlight, were gray and white as the stars blinked off above them and the moon faded.

Julietta drew deeper into her cloak, pulling the hood closer about her face, hurrying her steps towards home and the illusion of safety.

"Signora…" Bianca began, drawing up beside Julietta in a rush of pattering steps. She sounded out of breath at their pace.

"Not here, Bianca," Julietta murmured. "'Tis not safe."

They turned into a narrow passageway which led to their own *campi,* a small, well-kept square with a large marble fountain in the centre, where all the residents could gather fresh water. A few nights more and that fountain would run with wine for the pleasure of throngs of costumed revellers.

As the bells of the church of San Felice tolled the hour, Julietta skirted around the fountain, pulling a key out of her cloak's secret pocket. At the blue-painted door of the dwelling that served as both shop and residence, she lifted the key towards the brass lock.

A sharp, clanging noise behind her stilled her hand, and she whipped around, every muscle tense and poised for action. Her hand flew to her side, where a serviceable dagger rested in her sash. Her gaze darted around the *campi,* from corner to corner, searching out any hint of danger.

Were they followed? She felt as if someone watched her, their stare like pinpoints of fire on her skin.

Yet there was nothing to be seen. Her neighbours' dwellings were all silent. As she watched, a cat streaked past the fountain, the only sign of any life.

Bianca let out an audible squeak of relief. "Only a cat, *madonna*," she whispered.

"*Sì*," Julietta answered, unconvinced. Yet, still, there was nothing to be seen. They were, to all appearances, alone. "We should get inside." She turned back to the door, and, as swiftly as she could move her trembling hands, opened the lock and ushered Bianca inside the dim dwelling.

Only once the solid wooden panels were closed and locked behind them could she draw a breath again. *Safe. For now.*

Chapter Two

So. That was the famous Julietta Bassano.

Marc Antonio Velazquez stayed in his hiding place in the narrow space between two tall houses for a long time after Signora Bassano slipped into her home and out of sight. He watched as a faint golden glow of light appeared in the window of the first floor, the floor where her perfume shop did business. Watched as the light faded, only to reappear above, a welcoming beacon in the mist-shrouded chill of a Venetian winter morning.

She was not what he had expected. He had expected beauty, of course, beauty of the fashionable sort demanded in Venice: golden hair, azure blue eyes, rounded bosom and hips. A canvas that Florentine Botticelli brought to glorious, feminine life.

Julietta Bassano would never be mistaken for La Primavera. She was tall and very slim in the plain black-and-white gown that could be glimpsed beneath her enveloping cloak. There were no soft curves of bosom, hips and belly, as was desirable in these demanding days. There were only straight lines, long legs, narrow shoulders. The hair that escaped from her hood was black as the night around them, not the gold that ladies spent hours sitting in the sun wearing a crownless hat to achieve. He had not been able to see her face clearly, but it seemed as slim as the rest of her, a pale oval, with sharp cheekbones, sharp chin.

For all that, though, there was something—something *enchanted* about her. She carried mystery and sadness about her like a second velvet cloak, something palpable and so alluring.

Marc could never resist a mystery, a complication. It was his great downfall in life. Yet he would never have thought her to be Ermano's sort of woman. There was not an ounce of giggling, golden softness about her. Just darkness, and hidden daggers.

No, not Ermano's sort. But very much Marc's.

Perhaps this task would be more enjoyable than he had ever anticipated. Enjoyable—until he had to destroy her. Very regrettable, indeed.

Chapter Three

Julietta set the last bottle into place on the gleaming shelf, balancing on her tiptoes atop a footstool to examine the array of sparkling glass, ethereal ivory, luminous onyx. Most of her patrons brought their own vials to be filled with their choice of scent, but a few liked to buy new containers and were willing to pay a great deal for the finest quality. This shipment, newly arrived from France, should do very nicely.

Julietta tilted her head to one side. "What do you think, Bianca?" she said. "Is the display enticing enough?"

Bianca left off polishing the long marble counter and came to scrutinise the sparkling bottles. She was typical of her people, the Turkish nomads, small, thin, dark, barely coming up to Julietta's waist when she perched on the footstool as now. But she had been as steadfast a friend as Julietta could wish for, ever since those bleak days when she fled Milan for the masks of Venice.

"Very fine, *madonna*," Bianca pronounced with a grin, reaching up to flick her rag at the shelf. "And certain to bring us a very handsome profit, now that they have arrived at long last."

"*Sì*, now that the Barbary pirates are driven away," Julietta answered. The pirates had plagued Venetian shipping for many months earlier in the year, harrying the trade convoys with their shipments of spices, silks, wine, sugar—and jewelled perfume vials. Julietta had missed her lavender from France, her white roses from England and the more exotic blooms and spices from Egypt and Spain. Then, the pirates were destroyed, in a tale so filled with adventure and danger it stirred even Julietta's rusty, unpoetic soul. The *salas* of Venice were buzzing with nothing but stories of *Il leone,* the brave sea captain who destroyed the wicked pirates and saved the sacred shipping of La Serenissima. Bianca herself, after seeing his triumphant arrival in Venice last week, had talked of nothing else.

"If I was a skilled poet, Bianca, I would write an epic about *Il leone,*" Julietta said lightly. She stepped down from the stool, brushing her hands on the linen apron covering her black-and-white gown. "It would make us a great fortune. Troubadors would vie to recite it, to set it to music and to play it in all the great *salas!*"

"You *have* a fortune, *madonna*," Bianca protested. Though she laughed, her dark, round little face wrinkled in puzzlement. And well might she be puzzled—Julietta rarely succumbed to whimsy at all, she was far too busy, far too cautious for that. After the night they had just passed at Palazzo Landucci, whimsy seemed even further away than usual.

Yet somehow—ah, somehow the daylight made things seem rather different. Even the city, so deserted, so haunted in the mists before dawn, was transformed by the pale winter sunlight, by thoughts of dashing sea captains and wicked pirates. In the small *campi,* people hurried by, intent on their morning errands. Laughter and jests rang out, blending with the everpresent bells of San Felice. Soon, very soon, it would be Carnival, the most profitable time of year for the shop. And, early that morning, after a mere two hours of fitful sleep, she had heard mass at San Felice, asking absolution of the night's sins.

If only absolution could mean perpetual concealment, as well. And if only Count Ermano did not make an appearance today. She had had quite enough of drama and danger without the count's ever-pressing attentions.

"You are right, Bianca," she said. "We do have a fortune, so the world will never be inflicted with my poor poetic skills. I must still be giddy from lack of sleep."

Bianca nodded slowly. "Of course, *madonna.* You should rest, go back to your bed for a few hours."

"No, no. It is almost time for us to open. Perhaps I will have a siesta at midday. Now, would you fetch some of the essence of chamomile from the storeroom? I will finish mixing Signora Mercanti's tincture."

Bianca nodded and hurried away, her brightly

striped skirts swishing over the freshly swept tile floor. As the store-room door clicked shut behind her, Julietta went back to tidying before they opened.

There was not a great deal to do—the shop was always kept immaculate, for fear dust or dirt could contaminate the sweet wares, wares Julietta spent hours blending and preparing. Every vial, every jar and pot and amphora, contained the toil of her own hands, the products of her own careful study. And the ladies of Venice, courtesan and patrician wife alike, flocked to buy them, to beg her to mix a magical scent for them alone.

Julietta stepped away from the counter, her back to the blue-painted door as she examined her little kingdom. It *was* small, true, yet it was all her own, from the mosaic tiles of the floor to the white plastered ceiling. It was the only thing she had ever had for herself, the only thing she had ever loved. And the small room, hidden in the corner behind its secret panel—that was most especially hers.

She reached out for a small bottle on the counter, a blue glass vial studded with silver and tiny sapphires that had strayed from one of her careful displays. She held it to her nose and smelled jasmine and lily.

Jasmine and lily. Hurriedly, she replaced the bottle, which was meant for Cosima Landucci, back on the counter, but the heady sweetness of it clung to her fingers, reminding her of her night's work. As she stepped back, she caught a glimpse of herself in the gilt-framed mirror hung behind the counter. Her hair was still neatly braided and coiled about her head, covered by a black lace veil. Her black-and-white gown, touched only by a hint of scarlet in the ribbons of her sleeves, was as neat and quietly elegant as ever after she removed her apron. But her face—her face was as pale as a phantom.

Or a witch.

The bell on the door jangled, announcing their first patron of the day. Julietta took a deep breath of sweetly perfumed air, trying to will colour into her cheeks, and painted a bright smile on her lips before turning to greet the newcomer. "*Buon giorno!* Welcome to…"

But the polite words faded from her tongue when she came face to face with her patron. This was not a golden-haired courtesan or a veiled matron here in search of a special perfume or lotion, or something else, something darker, something poured secretly beneath the counter. This was a man. And what a man, indeed.

He was tall, with powerful shoulders outlined by a fine doublet of dark red velvet, closely cut and un-adorned by lace or embroidery. A shirt of cream-coloured silk, soft and with the sheen of springtime clouds, peeked through the jagged slashings of the sleeves and the silk closures at the front of the doublet, rising up to a small frill framing a strong, sun-browned throat, a vee of smooth bronze chest.

Julietta's gaze moved inexorably, unwillingly, downwards to plain black hose and Spanish leather shoes buckled with shining gold. No elaborate cod-pieces shaped like a conch shell or a gondola to display and enhance his masculine equipment, no gaudy striped hose. No popinjay, him. Yet not a man unaccustomed to luxury, either. Her regard slid back upwards, past the narrow hips, the powerful shoulders, the muscled chest. His face was cast half in shadow by the brim of his red velvet cap, but she could see the large, blood-coloured ruby clasped in that cap, the teardrop pearl that dangled from his left earlobe. No—not unaccustomed to luxury at all.

Glossy, dark brown hair, streaked with the gold of the sun, fell in thick waves from beneath the cap, brushing his shoulders. And his lower face could be glimpsed, a strong jaw, close shaven, darkened by the sun, set off by the glistening white of the pearl. Not a soft merchant, then, or a banker who spent his days softly indoors. Not a churchman, assuredly, yet not a poor sailor or shipmaker from the Arsenal.

A man of power, certainly, of wealth and fine looks. Not a man who drenched himself in cologne, either; Julietta's sensitive nose told her that, even across the length of the shop. He smelled only of fresh, salty air, faintly lemony, clean. What would such a man need from her shop?

Ah, yes—of course. A gift for a lady. And here she stood, staring at him like a lackwit, gawking at his shoulders and chest and lovely hair as some alleyway *putta* would.

Julietta straightened herself to her full height, reaching up to check the fall of her veil. *"Buon giorno, signor,"* she said again, dropping a small curtsy.

"Buon giorno, madonna," he answered. His voice was deeper than she expected, rougher, with the hint of some strange foreign accent. Not a Venetian, then. "I feared you would not yet be open for custom."

"We are always open for such eager patrons, *signor,*" Julietta said, touching the tip of her tongue to suddenly dry lips. There was something strange about this man's voice, something that seemed to reach out and wrap itself around her with misty, enticing caresses. Something about his scent…

Could he be a sorcerer? A magician from foreign lands?

Do not be a fool, Julietta! she told herself sternly. *He is a man, like any other.*

A man who could be a very profitable customer, to judge by the ruby and the pearl, the fine velvet, if she did not drive him away with her gapings and gawkings. Julietta stepped even farther away from him, back behind the safety of the counter.

"And what can we assist you with today, *signor?*" she asked briskly. The pierced bronze brazier set on the tiled floor was warm now; she added small sticks of scented wood to the coals, filling the cool air with the smell of white roses. "Our selection of fine scents is unparalleled in all of Venice."

He moved closer to the counter, the short red velvet cape swung over his shoulders by a thin gold cord falling back to reveal sable lining, rich and soft. The bars of light from the windows fell across him, illuminating him like a stained-glass saint as he swept off his cap and lightly brushed aside the waves of his hair.

Julietta's lips, so dry, turned numb at the sight of his eyes. They were blue—nay, not blue, turquoise, like the waters of the Mediterranean, pure and bright, startling in that sun-browned skin. Piercing. All-seeing.

A sorcerer, indeed.

Il diavolo.

Her fingers tightened on the scented sticks still in her hand, and she felt splinters pierce the skin. With a soft cry, she turned to fling them into the brazier. Turned away from those eyes.

"That is what I have heard, *madonna*," the man said. She sensed him leaning lightly against the counter, watching her closely.

"Heard?" she muttered stupidly. *Sì*—she was behaving stupidly all round. She was a grown woman, a widow, a shop owner. She should not be unsettled by anyone.

Nay! I am not afraid, she thought fiercely. She swung around to face him fully, her head high.

A small smile played about his lips, lips as finely formed as the rest of him, full and sensual. He was younger than she would have thought; only the faintest of lines creased the edges of those sorcerer's eyes, lined his slightly crooked nose. Who was *she* to be made so nervous by such a young man, no matter how rich, no matter how fine?

"I had heard that this is the finest perfumerie in Venice," he said easily, "and that I must pay a call here."

"I am flattered, *signor*." Julietta moved slowly to the very edge of the counter, resting her hands flat on the cool marble surface, near the soft velvet of his sleeve. His body emanated warmth, and again she had that odd sense of unseen fingers reaching out to wrap around her, entice her. Yet she did not move away. "And what is it I may assist you with today? A gift for some lovely lady? No woman can resist a sweet scent blended only for her. In a jewelled bottle, perhaps? A pretty token of admiration."

His smile widened, and he leaned his elbows on the counter until he looked up into her face, beguiling and gorgeous. "Alas, I am a newcomer to Venice, and have not yet found the lovely lady who would accept my tokens of admiration. But I do seek a gift, for a very special woman, indeed."

Julietta felt her brow wrinkle in puzzlement. "A woman not of Venice?"

"Nay, a lady of Seville. I try to find her fine trinkets wherever I go, so she may know I am thinking of her."

The frown broke as Julietta's brows arched in a sudden stab of emotion hitherto unknown to her— jealousy. "Your wife, *signor?*"

He laughed then, a rough, musical sound, warm like a summer's day. The faint lines around his eyes deepened, crinkled in a mirth that seemed to demand an answer. Julietta pressed her lips tightly together to hold in a chuckle, even though she knew not what the joke could be.

"Nay, *madonna*," he said. "I am a seafarer, and have no wife. I seek a gift for my mother."

His *mother! Madre de dio,* but she did seem doomed to foolishness this day. "You seek a gift for your mother?"

"*Sì,* one, as you said, blended only for her. She is very special, you see."

"Very beautiful?" She would have to be, with such a son as this.

"Yes, and very sweet, very devout. Innocent as the morning. What would you suggest, *madonna?*"

Ah—here was something she could understand, rationally and coolly. The blending of the perfect scent. Julietta retrieved a tray from beneath the counter, a slotted ivory container holding vials of many precious oils, neatly labelled. Her fingertips danced over their cork stoppers. "Roses, of course," she murmured. "And—perhaps violets? Violets from Spain. What do you think, *signor?*"

She held out the vial, and he leaned close, inhaling deeply. Too deeply; he choked and sputtered.

Julietta laughed softly. "Not so much! This is pure essence of violet, very strong. Here, like this." She shook a small drop on to her wrist, drawing the lace frill back from her skin. She held the bare flesh out, the drop of oil shimmering.

He reached out in turn, balancing her wrist in his fingers, and Julietta caught a ragged, sharp breath in her throat. His fingers were long, warm, callused, bisected by tiny white scars. A gold ring set with a gleaming ruby flashed on his smallest finger. He held her delicately, but there was leashed power in his touch. His gaze was focused downwards on her wrist, his breath warm on her skin. Slowly, oh, so slowly, he bent towards the beckoning drop of oil, his lips moving closer...

"*Signora,* have you seen the lotion for Signora Lac—" Bianca's voice, familiar, prosaic—and shocked—burst whatever spell Julietta was under, whatever web the turquoise-eyed sorcerer wound about her. Julietta snatched away her hand and stepped back, shaking the lace back down over her wrist.

"I did not realize you had a customer," Bianca said slowly, stepping up to Julietta's side. Her quick, dark eyes were sharp and curious as she regarded her employer. "How do you do, *signor?* I hope you have found— Oh!" Bianca broke off on a breathless exclamation. She dropped the jar of lotion, which miraculously did not break, but went rolling away beneath the counter as her hand flew to her mouth. "*Il leone,*" she whispered.

"Bianca, whatever are you talking about?" Julietta asked irritably, leaning down to retrieve the jar. She felt suddenly bereft, chilled to be deprived of the sorcerer's touch—and angry at herself for feeling so!

As she straightened, jar in hand, Bianca moved away around the corner, gliding like someone under a spell.

A spell such as the one Julietta herself had fallen under.

"You *are,* aren't you?" Bianca breathed. "You are *Il leone?* I saw you last week when you arrived in the city. It was glorious! You are a hero. *Il leone.*"

Perhaps it was Julietta's imagination, but she fancied she saw a blush, of all things, a faint stain of dull red spread across his sun-browned cheekbones. *Il leone,* truly? The fierce sea warrior who drove away the plague of pirates? A muscle ticked along his square jaw. Embarrassment over his great fame—or anger?

"Ah, *signorina,*" he said, reaching out to take Bianca's hand and bestow a light kiss on her wrist. "You are too kind. I merely did what any concerned citizen would do. Pirates are such a nuisance."

"Oh, no!" Bianca cried. "You fought the pirate captain single-handedly, with only a dagger. You destroyed his fleet with your guns and lost no men of your own. You are—*Il leone.*"

"I prefer to be called by my own name, Marc Antonio Velázquez. And whom might I have the honour of addressing?"

Bianca stared up at him, enthralled. "I am Bianca, Signor Velazquez. And this is my employer, Signora Julietta Bassano, of course. We are honoured that you have come to our shop."

"Honoured, indeed," Julietta echoed. "I had no idea such a hero has graced us with his custom. You must allow me to give you the perfume as a gift, *signor.*"

"Ah, no, *madonna!*" he protested. "It is very valuable…"

"And we would have soon had no inventory at all, if not for your bravery. Please, allow me to give you this gift. In appreciation."

"Thank you, *madonna.*" He gave her a small bow,

watching her so closely she was forced to glance away or make a fool of herself yet again.

"Signor Velazquez has commissioned a scent for his mother in Spain, Bianca," she said. "If you would care to call again in two days, *signor,* the perfume will be complete."

"Two days," he murmured. "So very long until I can return?"

Julietta shrugged. "Art takes time, *signor.* It is delicate and cannot be rushed."

"Oh, *sì,*" he answered, "I do know that."

The door to the shop burst open, bells jangling, to admit Signora Mercanti, one of Julietta's regular patrons. Her wrinkled, powdered cheeks were red with excitement, her dark eyes bright. In the flurry of her furs and ribbons, the scurrying of her servants, the barking of her lap-dogs, Signor Velazquez slipped out of the shop, unseen by anyone but Julietta. She slid to the side, watching out the window as he crossed the *campi,* a splash of scarlet amid the pastel crowds. He joined another man, a tall, plainly dressed figure, by the fountain, and together they left the *campi,* vanishing down the narrow passageway, out into the great city.

Two days. He would be back in two days.

"Have you heard, Signora Bassano?" Signora Mercanti cried, grabbing Julietta's arm and drawing her into the bustle of the shop. She could scarcely puzzle after a man with such flutterings and flounces about her. "There is a great scandal abroad this morn. My maid heard of it in the market this morning."

Julietta shook her head, reaching down to scoop up one of the yapping dogs and hand it over to a servant before it could do its business on her skirts or her clean tile floor. "There is always great scandal in Venice, *signora*."

"Oh, but this is *very* great, indeed! Michelotto Landucci was found dead in his bed this morning, expired right beside his sleeping wife."

Julietta froze. The remembrance of Cosima Landucci and her dead husband was like a sudden splash of cold seawater, driving out the last remnants of hot lust for *Il leone*. How could word of it already be swirling down the *calli* and canals? But then, this was Venice. How could it *not* be?

"Indeed?" she said, as calmly as she could. "Is the manner of his death known?"

Signora Mercanti shrugged. "They say apoplexy, after too fine a supper and too young a wife. But is it not odd, Signora Bassano, that he is the third member of the Savio ai Cerimoniali to die since only November? Oh, Signora Bassano, I just thought of something! Is Signora Cosima Landucci not one of your patrons? She will be in seclusion, of course, but perhaps her maid-servant will come here today, and we shall know more."

Signora Mercanti plumped herself down in a cushioned chair and accepted a sweetmeat proffered by Bianca, obviously prepared for a long, cosy stay in the shop. The bell over the door jangled again, as more customers poured in, full of talk of the Landuccis, of the upcoming Carnival balls, and of *Il leone* and his heroics.

Il leone. Julietta tossed one more glance at the window before disappearing into the fray. She was filled with the most incomprehensible urge to run after him. To beg him to help her escape on his great, fast ships.

Escape. Yes. If only she could. If only he could vanquish her fears as easily as he had those pirates. But she knew that could not be. Her demons were beyond even the reach of the celebrated *Il leone.*

Chapter Four

"**W**ell?" Nicolai asked. "You have seen her?"

Marc paused to glance over his shoulder once more at the blue-painted door surmounted by the swinging wooden sign traced with the image of a perfume bottle. For just an instant, he imagined he saw her there. Julietta Bassano—tall, cold, proud, distant, yet not, he sensed, completely indifferent. Her pale cheeks had turned the most delightful of rose-pinks when he'd caressed her wrist. "I have seen her."

"And?"

Marc shrugged. "I am not sure what old Ermano sees in her," he lied.

Nicolai laughed, a loud, warm sound that caused two pretty maidservants to stop and glance at them with interest. It was hardly the time for attracting attention, though, as delightful as that would be later. Marc steered his friend into a near-deserted tavern, where they soon found themselves ensconced in a darkened corner with a pair of goblets of cheap ale and some meat pies.

"I would imagine he sees her fine villa on the mainland, her fertile fields there," Nicolai said, leaning back lazily in the splintered wooden chair. His brilliant Arlechino silks were put away in favour of plain russet wool, his bright golden hair pulled back tightly. Yet there was still the attention-seeking quickness of the born actor in his blue eyes, the impatient gestures of his long hands. Marc wondered again if his old friend could stay the course of this scheme.

But Nicolai was one of the few people Marc could trust, and as a travelling player he had been everywhere, knew everyone. He was intimate with every dark, dirty corner of La Serenissima, could coax free its secrets and its gossip in a way Marc, who had been away from Venice since he was six years old, could not yet hope to do on his own.

Not yet, but soon. Soon, this serene city would lie on its back for him and splay her jewelled legs like a two-*scudi* whore, and it would give up to him all he desired, all he demanded. All he had planned and worked for since he was a child.

And God help anyone who got in his way. Even a woman with night-dark hair and white skin scented with flowers and sadness.

Marc tossed back a long swig of the rough, cheap ale. "No villa or farm seems worth the fuss Ermano is making. One would think he had enough of those already."

"Perhaps the exalted count knows he is being made a laughingstock by his determined, and very public, pursuit of the widow Bassano," Nicolai said, his voice touched only at the very edges by the sound of his long-abandoned Russian homeland. "And it has made him more determined."

Marc remembered Julietta Bassano's eyes, as dark as black ice and twice as perilous. "I am sure that is true."

Nicolai took a long sip of the ale, his gaze constantly scanning the dim tavern. "What is your next step, my friend?"

"Why, to woo the beautiful *signora,* of course," Marc answered, with a humorless laugh. "She is the key to this entire affair."

"And with the freedom of Carnival upon us, who knows what will happen?"

"Exactly."

"Just take care, Marc, I beg of you."

Nicolai's tone, always so full of cynical merriment, was suddenly quiet and solemn. Marc tossed him a puzzled glance over the rim of his goblet. "I always do. How else could I survive the life of seafaring mercenary?"

Nicolai shook his head. "Ermano is well known for his treachery, even in a city as perilous and deceptive as Venice."

Marc had a quick, flashing memory, an image of golden hair spread across a marble floor, sightless blue eyes, a gaping red wound on a white throat. "Well, I know it."

"Yet you are still willing to bargain with the devil?"

Marc swallowed down the bitter dregs of the ale. "I must. I have come a long way to see this through, Nicolai. There were vows made, and I must fulfill them. It has been far too long."

"As I thought. You have always been a stubborn mule, ever since I met you in that filthy brothel in Germany."

Marc laughed. "But you needn't be a part of it any longer. I have no wish to be the ruin of the few friends I possess. It is my quarrel alone, after all." Even as he said the words, though, Marc knew he could not lose Nicolai's help; knew he had to keep it by any means possible. Nicolai had saved his life in that brothel, and Marc had saved his in return, threefold. He needed his friend at his back now, when it mattered more than ever.

Nicolai grinned, back to his merry Arlechino self. "And what else would I do to amuse myself in these dull days? The troupe does not move on to Mantua until after Carnival and Lent, when merriment will be wanted again. Until then, my meagre skills are at your disposal, *Il leone*." Something swift and dark flashed deep in Nicolai's eyes, quickly veiled by another laugh. "I doubt most of Venice would agree it is your quarrel alone, though. I think they would beg leave to share it."

Before Marc could question him, the tavern door opened, admitting a rush of cold air and pale sunlight—and Julietta Bassano's maidservant. The girl strolled over to the counter, her striped skirts and fringed shawl swaying.

"Signora Bassano's maid," Marc muttered. "I believe her name is Bianca."

"Ah." Nicolai nodded sagely. "A lady's greatest confidante is often her maid. And this one just seems full of—knowledge." Without another word, Nicolai slid out from behind the table and crossed the room to Bianca's side. In no time at all, flirtatious giggles echoed through the dusty air, like unfurled streamers of bright ribbon.

Marc dropped a few coins beside the empty goblets and took his own leave. Nicolai would be occupied for quite a while to come.

Outside the tavern the day was cold, but the early morning fog had burned away leaving pale, yellow-gray sunlight to light up the dark waters and pastel houses. Marc drew his short cape closer about him and melted into the crowds hurrying along the *fondamento*. With his cap pulled low, no one recognised him as *Il leone* and he was free to wander where he would.

Strangely, his feet desired nothing more than to return to Julietta Bassano's blue door. To lose himself amid the sweet, soft scents of her shop, to watch the tall, elegant lady as she moved behind the counter, proffering up violets on her fair skin. She was truly a glorious mystery, one he looked forward to unravelling one silken skein at a time.

But not yet. Even as he half turned towards her *campi*, he knew it was far too soon. He told her he would return in two days; two days for her to think of him, for her wary intrigue to deepen into the first blooming of need and desire. Two days for *him* to think of *her,* as well, to think of all he longed to obtain from her. Two very long days.

In the meantime, he had important work to do. He stepped forward to summon a passing gondola.

Julietta sat straight up in bed, gasping for air. Her skin felt cold, icy cold, despite the fire still smouldering in the grate and the thick coverlets piled atop her. She shivered and ran her hands over her face, shaking her head hard to rid it of the mist of dreams. It didn't work—she still felt as if someone was watching her, staring into her very soul until all her secrets lay bare.

She leaned over to light the candle on the bedside table, casting a flickering red-orange glow into every corner of the small chamber. There were no soul-snatching demons there, of course; she was alone, as always. Only stacks of books on every table and chair, a few pieces of clothing strewn about in black-and-white streamers, a half-drunk glass of wine.

"Just a dream," she whispered. Not even a dream she could remember. Only bright, flashing fragments of movement and colour remained. And a pair of searing turquoise-blue eyes.

Julietta tossed back the bedclothes and swung her legs to the floor, wincing as her bare feet touched the cold wooden planks. Her fur-trimmed dressing gown was tossed at the foot of the bed, but she ignored it, crossing over to the window in only her thin linen chemise. The cold was good. It shocked her into a waking reality where no dreams could touch her.

The moon, a glistening, silvery-yellow crescent, hung high in the glossy black sky. 'Twas hours until daylight, then. Hours until sunlight and work could distract her. Everything always seemed closer, more suffocating in the night. The past, the future, all inescapable.

But Venice belonged to the mysteries of night, to darkness and deep waters and shadowed doorways that promised so much. It made the night so tempting, ever beckoning her forth from the careful construction of her safe lies. "Come to us," the waters whispered. "Come to us, *belong* to us, as you know you do, and we will show you delights you could not even dream of. We will give you all you desire, all you seek, if you will just surrender."

Surrender. The one thing she could never do. Julietta Bassano was born to stand solitary, to fight always against who she was, who she feared to be. Yet on nights like this one…

On nights like this, Eros and Thanatos, love and death, entwined in the narrow *calli* of the city, and she had such sharp, sweet longings. She loved Venice, because she and the city were one in the night, neither of them ever what they seemed to be.

Julietta leaned her forehead against the cool glass of the window, watching the deserted *campi* below and remembering the man who had visited her shop that morning. *Il leone.* Marc Antonio Velazquez. By whatever name he went, he was dangerous. She knew that the instant he touched her hand, and her flesh came alive at the stroke of his.

Shrugging the heavy braid of her hair back from her shoulder, Julietta reached out to push open the window. She closed her eyes as the cold night air washed over her face and throat, along the curve of her breasts bared by the low neck of the chemise and, for one moment, she imagined it was *his* hand on her skin. His callused sailor's touch sliding roughly over her shoulder, tracing a crooked line of fire lower, ever lower, his breath cool and sweet, making her shiver in sweet anticipation…

Madre de dio! Julietta's eyes flew open, and she found herself alone, staring down at the emptiness of the *campi*. From a distance, echoing, she heard laughter and music from some merry gathering, but no turquoise-eyed sorcerer watched her. No caresses reached out for her.

Dangerous, indeed. Once, long ago, when she was young and foolish, she had thought her husband handsome and charming, had fancied herself in love with him like a maiden and a knight in a poem. She had craved his kisses, worshipped his voice and touch and glance. That had shattered in an unfathomable rush of hellish violence that killed the girl she had been for ever.

After Giovanni died and she came to start a new life in Venice, Julietta took a couple of lovers, gentle, unassuming, discreet men whose kisses were pleasant and sweet, but did not move her to the dizzying heights she felt when first with Giovanni. Neither did they ever cast her into black despair.

Marc Antonio Velazquez could do that. She sensed it, *knew* it. There was something hidden about him, concealed behind his good looks and fine clothes, his polished manners. Only one cloaked soul could recognise another. He was a complication she did not need. Her life was good now. Settled. Safe.

As safe as she could ever make it.

Men such as *Il leone* had no place in her world. She had to make sure of that.

Julietta shut the window and latched it before taking up her dressing gown. As she slipped it over her chemise, she left her chamber on careful, silent feet. Bianca snored softly on her truckle bed in the corridor, but Julietta just crept past her, down the narrow stairs to the darkened shop. The shutters were drawn tightly over the windows, the door solidly locked and barred; no one could possibly be spying on her here. Still, she glanced carefully over every inch of the room, every vial and jar, before creeping over to the hidden panel set in the wall.

Her fingertips quickly found the tiny knot of wood and pressed hard. The panels slid apart to form a fissure just large enough for her to move through. She lit a branch of candles before shutting the secret door behind her again, closing herself into her own private world.

There were no windows or skylights in her hidey-hole; the only light came from the soft flicker of the candles. It was a small chamber, yet held all she could need. Long, narrow tables were pushed against two of the walls, laden with scales, beakers, silver bowls, a mortar and pestle and a variety of spoons and knives. The other two walls held shelves piled with books: ancient volumes she had painstakingly and at great expense collected over the past three years or had inherited from her mother and grandmother. There were also several covered baskets and pottery bowls, rows of stoppered bottles. Suspended from the dark wood rafters were bunches of dried herbs along with other, stranger materials. Ones she would never want the patrons of the perfumery just beyond the wall to see.

Never.

Julietta quickly went to work, for the night was half gone already. She spread out her materials—a beaker filled with clear liquid, small scissors, the mortar and pestle—and lit a small bowl of oil. Narrowing her eyes, she gazed up at the herbs, gauging which ones suited her purposes tonight. Angelica, yes; nettle, rue, and marjoram—all of them held great powers of protection and wisdom. Using the little silver scissors, she snipped a sprig from each and put them in the silver bowl.

Her herbs gathered, she knelt beside the table, hands tightly clasped and eyes shut. "Oh, Great One," she whispered. "I pray that the mysteries will be revealed to me this night, and my place in the world restored. Help me to see the truth. Guide me in my actions. Protect me."

And help me to divine what this Signor Velazquez seeks here in Venice, she added silently.

"Amen." Julietta crossed herself, and stood up to reach for the herbs she had chosen, the mortar and pestle. These hours, deep in the secret cloak of night, belonged only to her, to the lessons she had learned so long ago from her poor mother, from her grandmother. They *had* to belong only to her—or they could mean her very death.

Yet somehow, despite the dangers she knew all too well, she was compelled to this. Compelled to use her knowledge to help other women whenever possible. Women like Cosima Landucci—women like herself. Not even the threat of the stake could stop that.

And not even a sorcerer's turquoise eyes could turn her purpose. It was set—and done.

Chapter Five

"*Madonna!*"

Bianca's voice, echoing amid the crates and boxes of the store-room, startled Julietta, nearly causing her to bash her head on the case she was unpacking. As it was, she stumbled backwards, a jar of oil clutched in each hand. She had been counting the new arrivals, completing the shop's inventory, but really, her thoughts were far away, drifting inexorably to the experiment that bubbled and fermented quietly in the secret room.

And trying *not* to drift to *Il leone*.

"Yes, Bianca, what is it?" she said, placing the jars carefully back into the padded case. "Do you need my help in the shop?"

Bianca closed the door behind her and leaned back against it, covering her mouth with her handkerchief amid a flood of giggles. "He is *here*."

Julietta knew immediately the *he* that Bianca

meant. She turned away from the maid to hide her suddenly warm cheeks, busying her hands with tidying the inventory ledgers on the floor beside her. She had to compose herself, to stop this absurdity immediately, or she would soon find herself giggling away, just like her silly maidservant!

This was business. That was all.

"Signor Velazquez?" she said.

"*Sì.* And looking even more lovely than before."

"Well, then, Bianca, the perfume he ordered is behind the counter, in the purple glass bottle. You can package it up for the 'lovely' gentleman." Yes, that was it—send the man on his way without even seeing him.

But life could never be so simple. "Oh, no, *madonna.* He is asking to see *you* especially."

Asking to see her, was he? Why should that be? If she had time to puzzle it over now she would, but that would have to wait for later, when he was gone and she was alone in her room. Right now, though, she had a business to run, and he was a very important customer.

An important customer who wished to see her. Especially.

Julietta pushed herself to her feet, removing her apron and brushing the dust of the store-room from her black skirts. A strange, cold apprehension fluttered in her stomach, but she ignored it and strode past Bianca, opening the door to the shop. Bianca slammed the door back into place as soon as Julietta was past her, leaving her alone in the shop.

Or rather, not quite alone.

They had been busy in the morning; so many people wanted their new scents for Carnival, and customers had crowded the shop to claim their purchases and hear the latest gossip of the Landucci death and the doings of *Il leone*. Now there was an early afternoon lull, and Marc Antonio Velazquez was the only person in the room.

He was half turned away from her, examining a display of the new French oil burners, which gave her a moment to examine *him*. She had begun to think that surely her mind had exaggerated his charms, painted him as taller than he was, stronger, darker, a figure of poetic fantasy. But, no—he was everything she remembered. He wore green today, dark forest-green velvet as subtle and rich as his red garb of two days ago, trimmed only with silver-edged slashings on the sleeves and a pale silver fox lining to his short cloak. He held his green velvet cap in one hand, turning it lazily in his long fingers, and the fall of his glossy dark hair gleamed in the sunlight.

The pearl still dangled from his earlobe, emphasising the strong, clean line of his jaw. A small frown creased his brow as he stared at the burners, yet she sensed that he did not see them at all, that his mind was very far away.

Just as hers had been these past two days.

She wondered what he thought of, what dwelled behind the façade of the elegant hero, the brave sea captain all Venice lauded. No, not just wondered—

longed to know. Her chest ached with the need, a need she had thought long dead and buried, a need to understand another human, to know she was not alone.

Yet why should that be, with this man, this stranger? For that was all he was, a stranger she had glimpsed only briefly and now fancied such dramas over. She was surely blinded by his beauty, as every woman in Venice was these days. She heard little else in her shop except the doings of *Il leone,* the ladies he danced with at balls, the honours the Doge showered on him. Julietta would have thought herself sick of him—if she had not so eagerly listened to every scrap of gossip.

Yes, that was all it was, a fantasy, built of sleepless nights and the growing excitement of Carnival. He was merely a man, as any other.

"Buona sera, signor," she said, stepping out of the shadows. "Welcome back to our shop."

He spun towards her, his thoughtful frown lightening into the charming smile she remembered. His eyes seemed somehow darker today, blue-green as deep seawater, not as turquoise. He took her hand in his and raised it to his lips for a quick salute. Quick—yet not unaffecting. Gentlemen usually merely brushed the air above a lady's knuckles, yet he actually touched his mouth to the skin of her fingers, soft as a cloud, warm as summer. His breath, sharply indrawn, swept across her wrist, then he released her, stepping away with a suddenly solemn expression etched on his face.

Julietta stepped away, startled. "I—your perfume is ready, *signor.* I bottled it in purple Murano glass, the colour of violets." She ducked behind the counter to retrieve the vial, taking a bit longer than was necessary to fetch it in order to find her serene centre again. She had felt *something* when he touched her hand so intimately. Not merely sexual attraction, though, of course, that was there, but something more. A quick swirl of something dark, hidden and vast.

It had been such a long time since her mother's gift visited her. Could it be coming back now, of all times and with *this* man? What could it mean?

Julietta rose from behind the counter, holding the bottle carefully in hands that longed to tremble. She wanted to run from the shop, to flee into the fresh, cold air and keep going until she left Venice altogether and found herself all alone in a country field. Yet she could not. Not yet. Not now.

He moved to the other side of the counter, his head bent to examine the gift. His hair fell forward in a shining curtain, hiding his face from her view for a moment, and she felt so very foolish. Had she not just told herself that he was merely a man? There was surely no magic here, no hidden darkness waiting to suck her down to its depths.

"It is beautiful," he said quietly.

Julietta turned the glass, the light from the windows catching at its perfect facets. It *was* beautiful, one of the finest pieces from her favourite Murano glass blower. It was the deepest of purples, set with tiny amethysts and stoppered in gold filigree. A fitting tribute for a hero. "I hope your mother will like it."

"She will love it, just as she would love all of Venice, if I could but show it to her."

"The city does, indeed, have many beauties, especially at this time of year," Julietta said. "The Piazza San Marco, the Doge's Palace, the glorious bridges…"

"The beautiful women?"

Julietta gave a startled laugh. "Those, too. The ladies of Venice are well known for their beauty and grace."

His gaze moved from the bottle to her face, watching her steadily with blue-green intensity. "One in particular, I would say. Lovely beyond any other."

The words were flirtatious, yet no light grin touched his lips. What lady could he mean? Julietta wondered with a sharp pang. "Ah, *signor,* have you now found a lady to accept your tokens of affection, as you said you had not when we first met?"

"Not yet," he answered, leaning against the counter with a smooth, catlike grace. She saw so clearly where he had earned his pseudonym. He was like a lion, indeed, sleek, beautiful, dangerous. "But soon, I hope."

"If you seek gifts for her…"

"I would, if I knew how to best please her." In one quick, gentle movement he caught her hand in his, running the rough pad of his thumb over the simple silver ring she wore. "She does not appear to care for jewels." His gaze slid over the plain black cloak hung on a hook by the store-room door. "Or rich furs."

Her? He meant to impress *her?* When every woman

in the city vied to strew flowers beneath his feet, join him in his bed? Julietta nearly laughed with disbelief, but his gaze remained steady, serious, never wavering from her face.

What was happening here? Surely she was no gullible girl to believe he desired her, no matter what guilty, secret hopes lurked deep in her heart. She remembered that brief swirl of darkness she had felt when he touched her hand. Something *was* happening between them, something she wanted so desperately to explain, to know.

Julietta drew her hand from beneath his, but leaned closer, until she could smell the clean ocean scent of him. "Carnival is a special time. Some say it is even— magic," she whispered. "Masks can set people free, can make them see the truth behind the disguises we all bear. Desire can come to reality then. Perhaps you will find what you seek in the nights of secrets, *signor*. Perhaps you can find what you always wanted."

They stared at each other in charged silence, not touching, yet close, so very close. Julietta did not know where her words came from. Her mother had always said that Julietta held herself inside too much, always thinking, planning. *Sometimes, my daughter,* she had told her, *you must simply say what is in your heart.*

Easier said than done, of course. And look where speaking her heart had got Julietta's mother. Yet Julietta knew that what she said was true. Carnival was a time out of time, a time when the truths of her life— the hidden room, Count Ermano, her past in Milan, everything—could vanish for a night. Behind a mask, anything was possible.

"Do you verily speak truth, *madonna?*" Marc said roughly.

Julietta nodded. *Follow what is in your heart,* a voice whispered in her mind.

"Then will you do me the honour of accompanying me to a ball in the Piazza San Marco tomorrow night, after the Marriage of the Sea?" He watched her very closely, his gaze unreadable.

Your heart! "Yes, *signor.* I will go with you to the ball."

Chapter Six

⧼━━━◌⟲◌⟲◌⟲◌━━━⧽

The crowds were thick on the *fondamento* along the Grand Canal, a living, pulsing mass of flesh, breath, velvet and linen, jewels, masks. The scents of perfumes and people blended with the strange, sick sweetness that always seemed to rise from the canals, twisting, twining with the sounds of laughter and chatter and music to form a golden net that hung heavy over all of Venice. It was the day of the Feast of the Ascension, the day the ancient ritual called the Marriage of the Sea would be enacted. No one wanted to miss *that*.

Not even Julietta. She pushed her way through a knot of people, using her unusual height to advantage in seeking a fine spot to view the procession before it moved into the lagoon and out of sight. Bianca followed closely behind, clutching at Julietta's sleeve so they would not be separated in the crush. At last they found a few empty inches at the edge of the canal, where they could watch and observe.

Julietta reached out to wrap her hand around a striped pole that would usually tether a gondola, but could today hold her in place, firm against the surgings of the crowd at her back and pressing on both sides. To her left stood a courtesan, henna-haired and perfectly rounded in her silver-spangled crimson gown, surrounded by a throng of admirers. The heavy perfumes of gardenia and bergamot rose from them, along with a copious amount of pungent wine. At Julietta's other side stood a young couple and their two small children, obviously artisans to judge by their simple garments and their scent of plain soap. All manner of people, rich, peasant, old, young, nun, courtesan, mingled on this day, as they would until Carnival exploded to a close and sent them all scurrying back to their own worlds again.

Julietta gave the two excited children a small smile and turned her attention to the wide canal before her. The Doge had not yet appeared, but there was no lack of spectacle even so. Barges and gondolas lined the inky water, black and gold and white, sparkling like an emperor's jewel case in the sun. Each craft was decorated with copious amounts of flowers and brightly coloured ribbon streamers. Music played from a few of the larger vessels, lively dance tunes from lutes and viols, mingling with all the laughter.

It had been many years since Julietta came to Venice; many times she had seen this pageant play out. Yet somehow it always awakened something deep inside her, her own laughter, her own mirth. It tumbled around in her heart like some unruly butterfly, reminding her of days when she was a young, carefree girl and longed for nothing so much as a fine festival, a dance, a song of courtly love. She never gave in to that wildness now, but it was still hidden there.

And she *did* like this day, the bright hope of it, the life that filled every corner, driving out death and decay even if only for a moment. Part of her high mood, she had to admit, had something to do with the thought of the evening to come, when she would see *him* again—*Il leone,* Marc Antonio Velazquez, whatever he wanted to call himself. She would see him, dance with him, and it filled her with an odd warmth she had no desire to analyse. It was dangerous, she knew that. He was a man of many secrets. Yet today she found it hard to take care, as she always should.

Thanatos was hidden by the crowd, the sunlight. Only Eros remained, full of mischievous romance. Or perhaps Dionysus, she thought, as she watched one of the courtesan's young swains reel drunkenly, saved from toppling into the canal when one of his friends grabbed on to his fine satin doublet and hauled him back on to *terra firma.* The woman and her admirers fell into great peals of merriment, leaning against each other, passing around a bottle that was sure to cause more such scenes as the day went on.

"Signora Bassano! Such a rare pleasure."

Julietta's smile faded, wiped away as if it had never been as she heard those words. A smooth, charming, elegantly accented voice, hailing her from the water just below her perch, dimming the brilliant day. She could have vowed that a gray cloud eclipsed the sun, but when she glanced up at the sky it was as cerulean and flawless as before.

She tightened her grip on the wooden pole and stared down at the canal, feeling Bianca press closer to her side. Count Ermano Grattiano—just as she feared. His grand gondola, glossy black edged with copious frostings of glittering giltwork and sprays of black-and-gold plumes, had come to a halt only feet away. The velvet curtains of the felze were drawn back, leaving its occupants revealed to view.

As always, Count Ermano was as gloriously capari-soned as his vehicle, in a doublet of gold satin edged in ermine and gold braid, his hose striped white and gold, his sleeveless coat lined with more of the rare white fur. A diamond the size of an egg winked and dazzled in his cloth-of-gold hat, mocking her with its glitter.

The gem was well matched to its owner, Julietta thought wryly. Though her senior by many years, Count Ermano was still a very handsome man, with thick white hair and a neatly trimmed white beard, cold green eyes bright and shrewd in a lined, chiselled lean face. He had a quick, wide smile, an easy air that belied the power and ruthlessness below the sparkling surface. He had made a great fortune in the Veneto, by means rumoured to be both fair and foul. He held an important position in the Doge's court, as a member of the Savio ai Cerimoniali, the committee which arranged state visits of foreign rulers, ministers, and ambassadors—the committee that had seen many of its members, including Signor Landucci, die so unfortunately of late. His home, Ca Grattiano, was one of the most glorious in the city. He had been married four times, all of them ladies of impeccable lineage, fortune and beauty, who passed away sadly before their time.

Now, he seemed to want to add Julietta's small villa and farm on the mainland—the settlement she had received from her husband's family when she left Milan—to his kingdom. Perhaps he even wanted to add Julietta herself, though she could not fathom why. He had every young, full-bosomed courtesan in the city at his beck and call, he did not need her tall, thin, dark self. Whatever he truly desired, he had been most persistent in seeking it. He came to her shop, sent small gifts, invited her to gatherings at his palace, ever since the day they met in San Marco.

Now he was even interrupting her jovial feast day.

But she had hesitated too long in answering his greetings. The people around her were beginning to stare in puzzlement, obviously wondering why she ignored such a very important man. Even the loud hum of laughter and talk had faded to a low buzz.

Julietta stared directly, boldly down at the count, who watched her with a narrow, patient smile on his finely drawn lips. Beside him, half hidden in the shadows of the felze, was his son, Balthazar, watching the proceedings with a scowl on his narrow, youthful face, arms crossed over his white velvet doublet. Balthazar was the heir to the Grattiano kingdom, Ermano's only child, yet he always seemed to behave like an unhappy prince, filled with some half-hidden, seething anger. But he was a handsome youth, with fine, high cheekbones, mossy green eyes and dark, silken straight hair falling to his shoulders. There was something odd about him today, something familiar she had never sensed in him before…

"Good day, Count Ermano," she called, giving a tiny curtsy of acknowledgement.

"Indeed, it *is* a good day, now that I have seen you, Signora Bassano," he answered. His words and demeanour were all that was courtly and correct, yet a mocking note lurked in his voice, as it always did. He seemed to sense the disquiet he awakened in her, and revelled in it. "Forgive me for not calling in your shop sooner. I have been visiting my estates on the mainland."

Ah, so that was it, Julietta thought wryly. And here she had thought her spell of repellence worked. Drat it all. "I trust all is well there."

"Impeccably so, of course." The count leaned over the side of the gondola, peering up at her with his bright emerald gaze. "*Signora,* would you care to join us for the procession? There is more than enough space for you and your maid."

Julietta's chest constricted at the thought of being confined with the Grattianos on that suffocatingly luxurious craft, and she clutched at the pole until splinters pressed into her palm. For an instant, darkness pressed in on the edges of her sight, and she wasn't sure if she was still standing by the canal or caught in a dream-vision. Surely that was no ordinary gondola, propelled by a mortal boatman, but a craft of Charon, waiting to ferry her to the Underworld.

She heard Bianca gasp, felt the maid clutch again at her sleeve. Those prosaic things brought her back to earth again, and her vision cleared. The count watched her closely, as if to compel her to agree. Such strange eyes he possessed…

"No, I thank you…" she began.

"Ah, Signora Bassano, you cannot refuse me." The count laid one beringed hand over his heart. "We are a lonely vessel of men, as you see, and ask only to be graced by your lovely presence for a brief while. I can offer you a fine view of the ceremony."

Before Julietta could answer—could refuse—a great cry went up around them, drowning out whatever Ermano said next. The Doge appeared in his great ceremonial barge called the *Buccintoro,* gliding into place at the head of the procession. Andrea Gritti, the Doge himself, was resplendent in a robe of cloth-of-gold and ermine, much like Count Ermano's own colour scheme. As the *Buccintoro* moved out to the lagoon itself, the other vessels followed. Music grew louder around them, growing to a celebratory denouement; flowers rained down in a shower of colour and scent. And standing just behind the Doge was— No! It could not be.

She peered closer, clinging to the pole, and saw that it was, indeed, Marc Velazquez, clad in rich blue velvet, jewelled cap in hand as he stared out to sea. His thick, dark hair tangled in the breeze, making him look like a pirate even as he stood in the most exalted company. He seemed every inch the dashing hero.

And she had agreed to go to a ball with him tonight! Should she really do such a thing, when she worked so very hard to be as inconspicuous as possible?

You will be masked, her mind whispered insidiously. *No one will know it is you. Just look at him. Can you really resist the chance to dance in his arms, just once?*

That blighted internal voice! Always tempting her. Yet she did take another glance. He was laughing, his head thrown back in mirthful abandon, strong and dark, a part of the sea and the sun. And she found she could not resist.

Count Ermano and Balthazar also turned to watch the procession, and Julietta took that split-second chance to slip away. Soon—all too soon—she would have to face her unruly passion for Marc Velazquez. But not just yet.

The private *sala* of the Palazzo Grattiano was echoingly quiet after the jubilant crowds outside, the dim firelight flickering on the white marble floors dour after the flash and colour of the festival. Marc was glad of the quiet, though; he could finally think, finally drop the façade of Great Hero, if only for a moment. And he needed to think. Badly.

He was alone now, as Ermano Grattiano had been detained below with another of the Doge's counsellors. Marc crossed the room to one of the tall windows looking down on the canal, his boots echoing on that cold, immaculate floor. Heavy, deep-green velvet curtains hung there, blocking out the dying light of day. He parted the fabric, drawing it back to let in a ray of orange-pink sun.

The *sala* was not very large, as the grand public rooms of the palazzo were. It was not meant for balls or suppers, but for private family meals, quiet conversation. But it *was* opulent, the walls covered in elaborate tapestries depicting scenes from the life of St Lucy, the furniture carved and gilded, upholstered in pale green brocade. The massive marble fireplace looked like nothing so much as a monumental tomb, supported by straining, Atlaslike figures, surmounted by carved saints and seraphim.

It had been a very long time since Marc had been in this room, longer than he cared to remember. Yet nothing had changed, not an ornament or a cushion, only a few different portraits on one of the walls. It was still the same cold hell.

Marc pushed the curtains back all the way, sending light rushing into the furthest, dimmest corners, and leaned against the marble sill, crossing his arms over his chest. Below him, the canal was thronged with boats full of pleasure-seekers, people masked and flush with laughter and wine and the promise of pleasures that would come with the night. Soon enough, he would be one of them. He would don his cloak and mask, seek out the lovely Julietta Bassano for an evening of music and dance and—well, whatever might come along.

Julietta Bassano. He had thought of her more than he would care to admit in these last days. Her image would appear in his mind when he least expected it, as he dined off gold plates in the company of great families, as he listened to music in grand *salas*—as he lay in his strange bed at night. He would picture her, tall, fair and dark as the night, serene as the Madonna surmounting this fireplace. Always so quiet, so elegant, always keeping her own counsel.

But the dreams of midnight—ah, they were very different. Only last night he had envisioned her there in his rented chamber, her black hair falling over her shoulders and down her slender back, her austere black-and-white gowns vanished, clad only in a chemise the colour and texture of moonbeams. She leaned over him amid the satin cushions, a tiny half smile on her rose-pink lips. Softly, slowly, her fingertips touched his throat, slid down over his shoulder and bare chest, leaving a ribbon of fire in its wake. She bent forward, her hair brushing silkily against his cheek, and she whispered strange foreign words into his ears.

He had known, even in the dream, that she told him rare and wondrous secrets, secrets that held the key to his deepest desires. Yet he could not concentrate on them, could not remember them. He only knew her touch, her magical touch, only longed to feel the honey of her lips on his, her breasts pressed to his naked chest...

"Maledizione!" Marc slapped his hand flat on the marble sill, relishing the sting of it against his callused palm. He reached up and unlocked the window, shoving it open to let in a gust of cool breeze. The high, jewelled collar of his doublet was choking him, so he unfastened it and ran his fingers through the loose, tangled fall of his hair.

The chilly air cooled his blood, yet still he remembered that dream, how very real it had been, how it had shaken him. When he awoke to find the courtesan who came to him for the night sleeping beside him, her pale red-gold hair spread across the black silk sheets, he snatched her into his arms and kissed her awake. Yet even her great charms, practised and perfect, could not erase the dreams of Julietta Bassano.

She was only meant to be a means to an end, a link in the careful chain he had forged over so many years. He could let nothing stand in his way.

And yet there was something in her dark eyes....

The door to the *sala* creaked open, drawing him out of his thoughts on the puzzle of Julietta Bassano. Marc turned, only to find that it was not Ermano Grattiano standing there. It was his son, Balthazar, poised as uncertainly on the threshold of that room as he was on that of life itself. He was tall, ungainly in his leanness, full of a fire, a yearning that he could not yet understand or control, angry and restless.

Marc knew this because he had been much as Balthazar was at eighteen, bursting with the heat and passion of life. Yet Marc had only been the adopted son of a Spanish sea merchant, with only his own wit and ambition to bring to the world. Balthazar Grattiano would inherit all of his father's vast holdings. Money, lands, fleets, jewels.

Women. Perhaps one in particular, a black-haired widow full of secrets? Marc studied Balthazar carefully for a moment. No, this slim youth could have no appreciation for the subtleties and mysteries of a woman like Signora Bassano. One day, perhaps, if he did not follow his father's path, his consuming desire to possess and destroy.

Marc had no quarrel with young Balthazar. He even felt rather sorry for him, despite his rich inheritance to come. But Marc would not allow him to stand in the way of what he had come so far and given so much to accomplish. *No one* would stand in the way of that.

"Signor Balthazar," he greeted, when the young man still hesitated in the doorway. "Good day to you."

Balthazar's jaw tightened, and he tilted back his chin to stare at Marc, a strange light in his pale green eyes. "I see my father has kept you waiting, Signor Velazquez."

Marc shrugged. "It is no hardship to wait in such a grand chamber, with such a glorious view."

Balthazar came into the room to join Marc at the open window, the last rays of the day's sun sparkling off the tiny diamonds sewn on his white velvet doublet. He wore a belt of more diamonds and deep purple amethysts, and another diamond hung from his ear, large as a thumbnail, set in an elaborate filigree of gold. Despite these great riches, he radiated only unfocused anger. Passion with nowhere to go.

Marc wondered briefly if he should introduce the young man to the pale courtesan of last night. She was beautiful and very skilled, but unfortunately he could not quite recall her name. And it seemed Balthazar had no trouble attracting female attention of his own. Below them, a silvery blond beauty who had been lounging in a gondola, her scarlet stockinged legs carefully displayed, sat up and gave him a dazzling smile and a wave. Balthazar in turn gave her a small nod. So, the thwarted passion was not of a sexual nature.

It had to be something deeper.

"They say you are much favoured by the Doge," Balthazar said, still watching the woman in the red stockings. His tone was careless; only the stiff set of his shoulders betrayed even an inkling of his real feelings, whatever those could be.

"I have been very fortunate since I came to Venice," Marc answered. "Many people have shown me kindness."

"Why should they not? You are *Il leone*. My father has also shown you great favour."

Marc studied the young man carefully, pushing down a flash of impatience with Venetian dissembling. "Your father and I have business together."

"Mutually beneficial business, of course."

"Does anyone conduct any other sort?"

"Indeed." Balthazar turned away from the blond

beauty to face Marc. His eyes were like sea glass now, almost iridescent. "Yet not everyone appreciates the favour you have been shown. They think you are merely a *condotierre,* hired sea power."

"I have certainly faced my fair share of jealousy before, Signor Balthazar. It follows any man of any consequence, great or small. But I appreciate the warning."

There was the sound of footsteps on the marble stairs outside the room, the faint echo of masculine laughter. Balthazar's gaze flickered to the doorway. "My father does not easily tolerate challenges to his position. Even from business partners."

"I have no desire to be a counsellor to the Doge. I will be gone from Venice soon enough."

Balthazar nodded. "Still, one can never be too careful in this life, Signor Velazquez."

He left Marc's side and crossed the room with his loping, youthful gait, passing his father in the doorway without a word.

"Ah, Signor Velazquez," Ermano said heartily. "I am glad to see that my son has been keeping you entertained while I concluded my business. I have sent for wine and refreshments."

"Your son seems a promising young man," Marc commented. He turned back to close the window, for the marble room had begun to grow chilly with the passing of the day. Below, torchlight shone on Balthazar's white doublet and diamonds as he climbed into the blond courtesan's gondola. She looped her arms about his neck, leaning into him as they glided away.

"Promising?" Ermano stared down at the canal with narrowed eyes. "You are very kind to say so and, of course, I have great hopes for him. He is my only son. Yet I fear he has too much of his mother in him. She was from an excellent lineage, but of little spirit."

With a beringed hand, he gestured towards one of the newer portraits on the wall, a depiction of a pale, plump lady overwhelmed by satin, sable, and jewels. The fourth Countess Grattiano. Marc pretended to study the painting, yet, really, he watched the count. Marc was much the same height as Ermano, taller than the average, but the count was wider, sturdier, his once well-muscled form turning slowly to fat. His white hair and beard were still thick, his gaze shrewd. He was an ageing lion, but powerful, alert, not yet ready to yield his glory to an unsatisfactory cub.

"I was married four times, you know?" Ermano said pensively. "All ladies of wealth and family, they served my fortune well, yet only one could give me a child that lived. A child of such surliness, such weakness. I fear for all I have built once I am gone."

"Many youths pass through such dissatisfied phases. Signor Balthazar is young. He may well yet grow out of it."

"I pray so." Ermano turned his gaze on Marc, his eyes as green in colour as Balthazar's, but more focused, less diffused with anger. "I would wager *you* never passed through such a 'phase,' Signor Velazquez. Your parents are fortunate, indeed, to possess such a son."

Marc nearly laughed aloud at the delicious irony. "I will pass on your kind words to my mother, Count Ermano. Perhaps they will help her to forget the days of my youthful rebellion, when I refused her plan for me to enter the Church."

"Your father is not living?"

Marc had a quick memory of Juan Velazquez, tall, swarthy, quick to temper, quicker to laugh. He had taught Marc all there was to know about ships and sailing, had imbued his adopted son with his own great love of the sea.

"Alas, no. Only my mother, who now resides in a convent near Seville."

"She is blessed, to have produced a son who can be called *Il leone.*" Servants came into the *sala,* interrupting their conversation to set out platters of sweetmeats. A tall, dark, silent Turk poured spiced wine, bowing out of the room as Marc and Ermano seated themselves on the brocade chairs beside the massive fireplace.

"I have not yet given up hope, though," Ermano went on. "It is true I am not a young man, but neither am I so very ancient. I could yet father more sons to inherit, perhaps even daughters who could marry well and bring further glory to the Grattiano name."

The count intended to wed again, to produce yet more offspring to rain anger down on northern Italy? Marc nearly choked on his wine at the prospect. "I wish you good fortune in such an endeavour, Count," he managed to say.

Ermano nodded thoughtfully. "Their mother would have to be strong, of course. No more weak-blooded *signorinas*. And intelligent, with a certain fire to her. I understand you have now visited Signora Bassano's shop. Twice."

Ah—so that was it. Ermano thought the tall, mysterious Julietta was just the woman to mother this great new brood. Marc could almost feel sorry for her. He placed his goblet of wine on the nearest inlaid table and faced the count. "I have. She seems a very—interesting lady."

Ermano chuckled. "*Sì,* she is that. And very difficult to get near. She is so very prickly, like the artichoke. Yet I am sure that once one gets to her core it is quite—sweet."

Marc felt a muscle tick along his jaw, tightening at the merest thought of Ermano putting his plump, jewelled hands on Julietta's "sweet core."

"Does she seem to like you?" Ermano continued, oblivious to Marc's anger. "Will she talk honestly to you?"

Marc took a deep breath, bringing in the scents of the sugary cakes and Ermano's mossy perfume. "It is difficult to say. She is, as you say, rather prickly. And very cautious."

Ermano waved his hand in a careless gesture. "Ah, well, she will come around. You are *Il leone,* hero of the republic! You must continue to visit her, gain her trust. Then we shall proceed to the next stage of our plan." He lowered his goblet to stare solemnly at Marc over its rim. "You will not be sorry you have agreed to help me, Signor Velazquez. I have much influence in Venice. I can be a great friend—or a terrible enemy."

Marc returned the steady regard, not flinching, not turning away. *As am I, Ermano,* he thought coldly. *As am I.*

Chapter Seven

"Well, Bianca, what do you think? Shall I disgrace my escort?" Julietta turned slowly before her mirror, gazing back over her shoulder to make sure the fall of her skirt was straight and elegant.

Bianca clasped her hands before her and nodded, black eyes shining. "Oh, *madonna!* It is beautiful. Where have you been hiding it?"

"In that clothing chest, of course." Where it had been packed away from her trousseau over all these years, unworn, unneeded. Julietta was not even sure why she had kept it. Most of her other grand clothes had been left behind in Milan. Elaborately embroidered silks and velvets were impractical in the shop, too obtrusive and ornate. Perhaps she had kept this one out of some strange sentiment. Or perhaps she had known that one day she would need it again.

Julietta turned back to face herself fully in the mirror. Her chemise was of ivory-coloured silk, thin, soft, shot through with glistening golden threads that echoed the bodice and skirt of gold lace over gold satin. Sleeves of cloth-of-gold were tied on with thin white ribbons twisted with tiny gold beads. It was a few years out of fashion; the sleeves were narrower and the skirt a bit fuller than was strictly desirable, the waist too high. But the lace was still sumptuous.

As Bianca took up a needle and thread and began to stitch up a tiny tear at the hem, Julietta fussed with her hair. Usually hair was not her foremost concern. She always brushed and braided it in the morning, pinning it up and covering it with a sheer veil so it was out of the way of her work. No trouble at all, and she did not miss the elaborate coiffures of her early married days, all twisted and oiled plaits and curls. Tonight, for some reason she could not even explain to herself, she had left it down like a girl. It fell in a straight black curtain to her waist, entwined with gold and white ribbons.

Bianca broke off her thread and stepped back. "You look like the sun itself, *madonna*."

"Let us hope I do not look like mutton dressed as lamb," Julietta muttered, repeating a long-forgotten favourite saying of her old Scottish nursemaid.

"Madonna?" Bianca asked, her face creased in puzzlement.

"It means I hope people do not think I am an old widow trying to recapture my vanished youth."

"Oh, no! You are not so very old, *signora*. And you will be masked, anyway."

"To hide my crone's wrinkles!" Julietta laughed, and reached for the mask resting on a nearby table. It was of fine white leather, carefully trimmed with gilt, fashioned in the shape of a cat's features. She held it up to her face, and it did, indeed, seem to have a transformative quality. She was not herself, not Julietta Bassano, sensible shop owner, respectable widow. *Yet who was she?*

Only the night could tell. And what would Signor Velazquez think of her new aspect? Would he be proud to take her hand, to lead her into the crowd, into the dance? Or did he regret already the whim of inviting her tonight?

Julietta slowly lowered the mask to find her own brown eyes staring back at her in the mirror. What *had* possessed him to invite her to the ball? She did not understand, particularly after seeing him with the Doge today. He was greatly favoured in this city, much sought after and courted. Any woman would be proud to be seen with him at the festivities. Yet he had chosen to invite *her*.

Why?

Her heart had been full of suspicion for so long she hardly knew any other way to be. People always had hidden motives to their words and actions; there was always so much swirling just below the calm, dark, quiet surfaces—much like the waters of Venice themselves. Nothing was ever what it seemed, not really. Marc Velazquez was no exception, she knew that just by looking into his opaque blue eyes. As turquoise as the sky, and just as vast and changeable. Clear skies in the morning could mean violent storms in the evening, and a wise woman—a woman with her own secrets to hold—would avoid storms of the sort produced by men such as *Il leone*. They could prove deadly.

And yet, and yet…

There was that strange feeling when he held her wrist in his hand, when he leaned close to look into her eyes. It was a storm of a different sort, warmer, more alluring, yet every bit as dangerous. And it would not be denied. Secrets and deceits—yes, there were those in abundance. But she was being pulled along by this new swirl of emotions, and they would not let her go just yet.

Nor did she *want* to be released. Not right now. Carnival had obviously entered her blood, spreading a lust for life she had imagined long buried. The mask, the gown—they all conspired to make her forget herself this night.

She slipped on her shoes, a new pair of high-heeled gold-brocade slippers fastened with white ribbons, and wandered over to her open chamber window. The crowd was thick tonight, not as aristocratic as the gathering in the Piazza San Marco would be, but just as merry. They were masked and cloaked and costumed, dancing on the cobblestones, drinking the wine that flowed from the fountain.

Tonight began a time out of time, a moment when the cares and griefs of life could all be forgotten and joy snatched at like a bright jewel. Every person in

Venice was caught up in the whirl—why should she not be? She had been careful for so very long. She just wanted to laugh, to dance, to drink wine until she was giddy with it.

"It is only one night," she whispered. "What could happen?"

As if in answer to her query, a delicate missile landed with a crack on the bricks by her window, and the sweet, heady scent of roses wafted through the air, along with a shower of bright confetti. Julietta gave a startled laugh, and leaned over to watch the paper and bits of shell float to the ground below. A perfume egg, one of the hallmarks of Carnival, an eggshell carefully emptied and refilled with perfume, had just been lobbed at her head! The laughter grew in her throat, bubbling up in an irresistible flood. She clapped her hand to her mouth, yet it would not be held back.

As Bianca came up to her side to see what was funny, Julietta scanned the area for the culprit. She did not have to search far. He stood near her very doorstep, a tall figure clad in a black velvet doublet and silver hose, his black cloak covered with iridescent silver stars and crescent moons. Though he wore a mask, a silver sliver of moon, and his dark hair was tied back, she knew him at once.

Marc Antonio Velazquez. *Il leone.* He grinned up at her, his teeth white even in the torchlight. A pirate's smile, filled with wild glee as he prepared to board an enemy vessel.

Julietta shook her head wryly, and leaned out of the

window to touch a smear of the perfume with her fingertips. She brought it to her nose to smell, and found the roses touched with a strange musk. "An inferior product, *signor,*" she called.

He laughed, a deep, rough sound that made her shiver. "*Madonna,* your own perfumes are much too fine to waste on mere bricks and mortar! Yet I would happily spread precious myrrh and lilies beneath your feet if it would please you, along with the finest pearls of the Orient, amber of Russia, sapphires of India…"

"Then you would be a fool, indeed," Julietta answered, her laughter threatening to bubble up again. "Crushed pearls never did benefit anyone."

"Then permit me to enter your dwelling, *madonna,* and I will drape the pearls about your white throat, carpet your very chamber with the sapphires, twine emeralds in your hair, if you will but smile at me like that again."

Julietta felt an answering smile tug at the corners of her lips and next to her Bianca was giggling into her apron. But she would not give in. It was far too early in the evening for such ridiculous flirtations. Later in the evening, after more wine and music, perhaps…

"You are a silver-tongued devil, Signor Lune," she said.

"I have learned from the best, Signora Sol," he answered. "Poets and players who are the finest of their craft."

"Ah, then, you must not waste it on such a one as I," Julietta said. "I have no need of pearls and sapphires and I allow no one admittance to my dwelling. Not even poets."

"Alas, my sun, I am wounded!" He clasped one hand to his heart. "Have I nothing to offer you? Nothing that may tempt you?"

Julietta pretended to ponder this, tapping her fingertip to her chin. "A dance, perhaps."

"Then I am at your disposal! I have also been taught to dance by the best. A fine pavane, a galliard, a *moresque*…"

Julietta slammed the window shut, laughing. As she locked the clasp, two more eggs hit the glass, leaving streaks of oil and bits of shell behind.

I must be moon-mad, indeed, she thought. If she was truly sensible, she would stay home on this night, safe in her secret room. But it was an enchanted night, after all, and she did not feel at all herself. She slid her mask over her face, tying the golden ribbons before dashing down the stairs, destined for a sorcerer's embrace.

The Piazza San Marco was glorious in its festivities, ringed thickly on all sides by torches that cast their glittering red-gold light on the equally bright throngs of revellers. The usual booths of merchants and bankers were moved out to make room for the dancing, for the crowds. Everyone was masked, clad in everything from plain black *bautas* to elaborate costumes of jewelled silks and gauze. They swirled in the patterns of a giant wild *volte,* faces of gold, silver and ivory white whirling past in a dizzying cavalcade. A multitude of musicians played their lutes and recorders and tambours, the tune rising faster and faster, ever more frantic, as the dancers called out *"La volte!"* and the men swung the women high in the air. Acrobats and players clad in tight, bright, beribboned garments gambolled at the edges of the dance, tumbling, miming, loud with bells and rattles.

Julietta drank it all in, standing in the shadows, holding on to Marc's arm as the grand pageant played out before her like a scene from some pagan fresco. She feared her mouth might be hanging open in astonishment, as if she were a mere country farmer's wife, but at least her mask hid it from the passers-by. It was just all so—so wondrous. An enchanted dream.

She had been part of Carnival before, of course. If a person lived in Venice, they could hardly avoid it, the gaiety just burst out of every corner. But usually she stayed close to her home, dancing in her own *campi,* perhaps going to a masked supper at the home of a customer or friend. She never attended grand events such as this.

Especially not in the company of such an escort. Julietta glanced up at Marc, studying him in the torchlight. His face was expressionless beneath the silver mask, yet she could tell that he watched the crowd intently. The muscles in his arm were tense and coiled beneath her arm.

As if he sensed her regard, he turned to her, a smile hovering at the corners of his sculpted lips. He leaned down to murmur in her ear, "It is like something out of Ovid, is it not? The pagan hordes celebrating their feast of the gods."

Julietta smiled in return. "That is the sort of thing I was thinking," she said. Just then, a couple danced past disguised as Apollo and Aphrodite in swirling white-and-purple draperies, wreaths of golden laurel leaves on their heads, purple masks concealing their faces. "Perhaps that is an even more apropos comparison than we thought, Signor Velazquez."

"Oh, come now, my sun. You can call me Marc, can you not? For this one night."

Julietta still watched the dancers, but she was all too aware of his regard on her, of the feel of him under her hand, the warmth and strength beneath the velvet of his sleeve.

It seemed a small thing to ask, calling him by his given name, yet somehow—it did not feel small at all.

"I—suppose so," she murmured.

He leaned even closer, until she felt a cool, gentle breath stir the curls at her temple, and she shivered. "I suppose so—Marc," he prompted.

Against her very will, her desire to always remain cool and aloof, safe, she swayed towards him, inclining for the merest instant against his shoulder. "I suppose so, *Marc*. Just for tonight."

He chuckled deeply. "*Va bene*. And I will continue to call you the Sun. Just for tonight." He straightened the arm she held, until his hand caught hers and their fingers entwined. His were roughened, a bit callused, and she was again reminded that beneath his rich velvets he was a sailor, a man of the sea and the wind. And man who was less and yet more than he appeared.

A man who suited this night of masks.

"Come," he said, tugging at her hand, "let us dance."

Julietta had not danced, *really* danced, for a long time. A complicated arrangement like a *volte* was very different from twirling along a simple line. But she followed him, her feet moving of their own inexorable volition until they found a space in the midst of the crowd.

The music was louder, the air hotter, scented with a multitude of fragrances: rose, lily, bergamot, orange blossom, the musk of human skin. Marc shrugged his short moon-and-stars cloak back from his shoulders and slipped his arm about her waist, turning her in time to the music. He was a good dancer, she found to her surprise, smooth, practised, gentle yet strong, sure of his steps and able to guide her neatly. Why she should be surprised, she did not know—thus far he had proven expert at everything he did. Defeating pirates, politicking at the Doge's court, charming perfumiers and their maidservants—why should dancing be any different?

"La volte!" the crowd shouted. Marc's arm tightened on her waist and he swung her high into the air, holding her there as he turned her around, faster and faster until her head spun giddily and the crowd was a mere blur.

Julietta threw back her head and laughed helplessly,

holding on to Marc's shoulders as he twirled her around yet again, as easily as if she was a feather.

No sooner had her slippers touched the earth than the cry of *"La volte!"* went up again, and she was borne aloft, even higher, held there by Marc's strong embrace.

It was intoxicating! Not since she was a girl had Julietta felt so light, so free, so dizzyingly wonderful. Nay, not even then had she ever felt quite like this. Never until this moment. And all from a mere dance, a tangle of music and light and people. It was incomprehensible.

Or, perhaps not so very incomprehensible as all that. The music crescendoed and slowed, and Marc lowered her to the ground. Julietta clung to his shoulders, feeling his body pressed against hers for just a moment, all hard, muscled angles and planes. So young and strong, warm and alive, so perfect in her embrace. So very dangerous.

He watched her closely through his mask, the torchlight turning his blue eyes luminous. A lock of dark hair had escaped from its black ribbon tie, falling over his brow like an inky question mark. Julietta's lips felt suddenly dry, and she touched them with the tip of her tongue.

"You are a very fine dancer," she whispered.

"As are you, my sun," he whispered in return.

People pressed them on all sides as the music ended, causing Julietta to stumble against him. He caught her, holding her steady, pressed against his velvet-covered chest. She could smell his own clean, seawater scent, and her head spun anew, even as she stood on the earth.

"Would you care to dance again?" he said against her hair. She was a tall woman, yet he was even taller, his chin resting atop her head.

"I think I would like some wine," she answered.

He clasped her arm, leading her through the crowd, adroitly steering her past stumbling, embracing couples. "The *moresque!*" someone called out, and rings of bells flew through the air, caught in outstretched hands as laughter rose like a bright cloud.

At the edge of the crowd, a marble fountain flowed with wine, thick and red and sweet. Marc tossed a coin to a page, who dipped two goblets into the liquid and handed them over to him.

Marc pressed one of the silver vessels into Julietta's hand and held his own up in a salute. "*'Durmiendo, en fin, fui bienaventurado, y es justo en la mentira ser dichoso quien siempre en la verdad fue desdichado,'*" he said, his Spanish golden-liquid from his throat.

Julietta sipped at her wine, finding it spiced with cinnamon on her tongue. "And what does that mean?"

"It is from a poem. 'For while I slept, in short, I was in bliss, and it is right that one be blessed in lies who's always been in truth unfortunate.'"

"'In truth unfortunate.' I like that."

"I have made something of a study of the poems of Juan Boscan. His words on the purpose of our lives, the meaning of love and illusion, truth and lies. It is very moving."

So—not such a simple sailor after all. A politician, a dancer, a poet. What else lurked deep in his soul?

"Yes," she said, "it is moving. I fear I know little of the Spanish poets. I do love our own Italians, though. Petrarch, especially."

"A most discerning choice, Julietta, I must say. I would love to hear your thoughts on his use of the myths of Daphne and Actaeon." Suddenly, a wide grin lit his face, and he tossed his goblet to the page for a refill. He drained the wine and set the vessel down again. "But not tonight, my Signora Sol! That is far too serious a topic for a ball. Come, let us dance again."

Julietta laughed, letting him draw her along by the hand. The wine had gone to her head, and she felt full of laughter suddenly, dizzy and silly and happy. Absurdly happy.

The *moresque* had ended, its Oriental bells and flourishes given way to a fast-paced *bransles*. The steps were not ordered or mannered, but free flowing, quick. Julietta and Marc twirled into their places and she clung to him, still laughing. He laughed, too, a deep, joyful sound more intoxicating than the wine, holding her close as their steps moved faster and faster.

Beyond the crowd, the Basilica glowed in the torch flames, golden, immense, eternal. It was a reminder of God, of the fact that all actions had consequences, yet it did not seem to condemn. "Have your merriment tonight, and enjoy it," it seemed to say. "I will still be here tomorrow, waiting for you. Always waiting."

Julietta's real life would still be there tomorrow, too. It would never be lost. Yet tonight—tonight was something apart. A dream.

They danced to the edge of the crowd, ending against a marble pillar along a palace terrace. The laughter and music still reached out for them, beckoning, but for the moment they were a circle of two, quiet, hypnotising. Suddenly warm, flushed, Julietta pushed her mask away from her face, letting it dangle down her back by its ribbons. She tilted her head back against the cold stone; it was the only thing holding her up.

Marc loosened his own mask, easing it atop his head. He stared down at her, holding her only by the hands, yet it felt as if they embraced skin to skin. His face was half in shadow, his expression inscrutable. But she feared that her own emotions, a tangle of fear, defiance, attraction, need, was writ large on her face.

Slowly, he raised her hands to his lips, pressing a kiss to first one, then the other. His lips lingered over her knuckles, warm, embracing. As they trailed away from her skin, leaving heat and fire in their wake, he did not release her, but pressed her palm to his cheek. His skin was smooth, only slightly roughened by evening whiskers. A lock of loosened hair brushed her wrist, an alluring contrast of cool silk.

"Who are you, Julietta Bassano?" he muttered. "Where did you come from? For I would vow you were not born of this earth at all."

Julietta's heart fluttered wildly in her breast, and he softened a kiss into the pulse of her wrist. What was happening here, wrapped in the embrace of this night? She did not understand her feelings, did not understand *herself*. She had never felt quite like this before, and there was no mirror of divination, no cards to help her. She had only her confused, lust-ridden self.

"I—came only from Milan," she managed to whisper.

He laughed gently against her hand, and the sound echoed to her very core. "Oh, no, Signora Sol. You came from the land of the Duende. I can see it in your eyes. They are not the eyes of a mortal woman. And I am hopelessly under your spell."

He was under *her* spell? No, no—it was quite the other way round.

Marc's arm slid around her waist, drawing her closer to him, ever closer, until there could not even be a sigh between them. The lace of her gown rasped and caught on his velvet doublet, and his lips were so very near. Julietta's eyes fluttered closed, her head tilted back…

"'Twas a lover and his lass, with a heigh and a ho and a hey nonny no!" a voice sang in their ears, and a tambourine rang sharply above them.

Julietta jerked away from Marc, her hand automatically flying to the dagger that wasn't there. Every nerve and sinew hummed and vibrated, her skin flushed hot and then ice-cold, screaming of danger. After such sweet, heady lust, it was as cruel as a sword.

Marc's arms loosened around her, and she pressed tightly against the stone pillar, pivoting on the balls of her feet to face their attacker. Yet the attacker was no soldier or bravo, it was a player, an Arlechino clad in multicoloured silk motley that fit close to his tall, lean body. Shimmering golden hair fell halfway down his back, and a black mask covered half his face, but a mischievous grin curved his full lips. As she stared at him, he laughed and proceeded to cavort around them, shaking that tinny tambourine.

Julietta finally caught her breath. She longed to strangle the player with her own hands for dragging her out of the mist of dreams and Carnival and into reality, yet truly she should thank him. Losing herself in the bonfire of her desire for Marc Antonio Velazquez seemed a fine idea in the midst of a wild revel, but it would not appear so wise in the hard light of day. Her life was a walk on a fine wire, just like those acrobats in the Piazza. One misstep either way could prove fatal.

She peered up at Marc, who watched the Arlechino with narrowed eyes. A faint flush of anger touched his sculpted cheekbones, the only sign of any emotion. He reached out again to clasp her arm, drawing her protectively close.

"I have seldom seen an actor with such an abysmally poor sense of timing, Nicolai," Marc said, his voice deceptively quiet.

The Arlechino—Nicolai?—merely laughed and danced to a halt, the bright ribbon streamers that fell from his shoulders undulating in the flickering lights. "You know this knavish fellow?" she asked.

"Sadly, I do. I think his own mother would not know him, though, after I help him to a swim in the canal."

His free hand shot out as if to seize the mischief-maker by his ribbons, but Nicolai merely danced out of the way.

"Oh, come now, is that any way to treat a friend, *Il leone?* I merely feared it was too early in the evening for such licentiousness and sought to save your energy for later endeavours." Nicolai spun towards Julietta and gave her a low, elaborate bow filled with many flourishes. "And this must be the lovely Julietta Bassano. An unparalleled delight, *madonna.*"

Julietta could not help but smile at his antics, even though they had cost her a foolish, longed-for kiss. "You have the advantage of me, *signor.* You know my name, though I do not know yours."

"Oh, *madonna,*" Nicolai said softly, his voice touched with the strange lilt of the frozen north, "I doubt anyone ever has the advantage over *you.*"

Julietta frowned in puzzlement, as Marc reached out and gave Nicolai a hearty shove. "This knave, as you so rightly called him, is Nicolai Ostrovsky, the leader of that gambolling troupe over there." He gestured towards a set of tumbling acrobats nearby, a Columbine in white-and-black silk who tried to pretend not to be watching them, a tightrope-walking dwarf, a slim man in a dottore mask, among others.

"The finest set of players in all of Italy, *signora,*" Nicolai said, with yet another bow.

"I'm sure," Julietta murmured.

"You have taken up enough of our time, *testano,*" Marc said, reaching out to give Nicolai another shove. "I brought the lady here to dance."

"Ah, well, is that not why we are all here? But this ball has become paltry and colourless. We were just on our way to a celebration of a different, far more desirable sort. Do you care to join us?"

The two men watched each other carefully, still and poised as if on the brink of—something. Julietta was suddenly seized with an undeniable curiosity about them, about what might be going on just below this merrymaking surface. What schemes would a sea captain and an actor be concocting?

"Oh, yes," she said, before Marc could answer. "We would enjoy that very much, Signor Nicolai. Lead the way."

Chapter Eight

⁓❧⁓

The *calli* Nicolai led them down were narrow and dark, crowded closely by damp walls of cracked and peeling stucco, the cobblestones slick and uneven beneath Julietta's shoes. Even here, deep in the bowels of the city, far from the grand palazzos, they could hear the echo of laughter and merriment, music and shouts. But there were no balls here; the doors were barred, the window shutters closed and locked. All was dim, ominous quiet. The only light came from a torch Nicolai bore as he walked ahead of them, his bells jangling.

She tilted back her head, staring up at the tall, silent buildings to where pale laundry on their lines fluttered in the starlight. So, there were inhabitants here after all. People who wore shirts and skirts and hose, not gnomes who dwelled in tree stumps clad in skins and furs.

They emerged briefly into an open space, a narrow *fondamento* trailing beside a canal. In the distance, she saw the bridge that led over to the Jewish ghetto. Lights twinkled there, and she could hear faint strains of music, yet it might as well have been on another planet.

Nicolai glanced behind him, his smile flashing in the flickering light of the torch. "Still with me, are you?" he said, faintly mocking. Or maybe it was his Muscovite accent, filled with primitive mysteries so far removed from Italian sunlight. "Don't worry, we are not far from our destination."

Julietta's fingers curled tightly for just an instant into Marc's arm, crushing the soft velvet of his sleeve. Was she a fool to follow these men? It would not be the first time her curiosity led her into trouble. She had learned to master the impulses that made her long to *know* about the world, every part of it, every idea and emotion and experience. Such impulses could only mean danger and trouble, even death, for people who dwelt in a world such as theirs. Julietta knew this all too well, and she had no desire to repeat the past.

But sometimes, like tonight, that curiosity bubbled up hot and quick, undeniable. She had only drunk the one glass of wine, yet it felt she had imbibed a flaskful. Her head was light, her skin warm and tingling, her stomach fluttered with anticipation of what might be just around the next corner.

It seemed she was not herself tonight—not the self she had built so carefully over the last few years. She was possessed by the spirits of her mother and grandmother, the force of the moon and stars, of Carnival.

By the heat of Marc's body beside her, leaning into her as they made their way down a narrow *sortoportego*. Tomorrow, she would find herself again.

That would be soon enough.

She realised then that her fingers were kneading Marc's sleeve, wrinkling the soft velvet. He glanced down at her, a tiny half smile on his lips below his mask. "Are you well, Julietta?"

She nodded, not looking at him. "Quite."

"I have known Nicolai for many years. He would never lead us into danger. But he *does* always know where the most interesting gatherings are to be found. His friends are never dull."

"I do appreciate *interesting*," Julietta murmured. "Most of the time."

Marc laughed, causing Nicolai to pause in his pathway and glance back at them. "No jesting, my friends—unless you share the joke." He took another few steps and stopped before a door, holding his torch high. In the daylight, the door was probably a bright yellow colour, but the paint was peeling, a tiny window set high in the wood covered with a grille of bars. "Here we are!"

Only silence followed his quick, staccato knock, stretching so very long that Julietta began to shift on her feet. Visions of retracing their steps on the long journey back to the Piazza San Marco, without even glimpsing what was behind that door, flashed through her mind, leaving a chilly disappointment behind. At last, there was a creaking sound, a click, and the window above their heads slid open. There was a flash of pale skin behind the grill, a soft whisper. "What is it you desire?"

"*Salto portego,*" Nicolai answered. The window slammed shut, the door opened.

Julietta shivered as she peered past Nicolai's shoulder into the dark dwelling. She could see nothing but candlelight on a whitewashed wall, a gloved hand that beckoned them forward. It was like a poem, a dark tale where a princess is imprisoned for mysterious purposes or mystical ceremonies, until she is rescued by a virtuous knight. It was like...

Like tales her grandmother told her when she was a child. Tales the old woman had sworn were true. Yet Julietta had never seen such things for herself, never dreamed she could. What would happen to her tonight?

She let go of Marc's arm and stepped eagerly over the threshold, following Nicolai and the black-clad figure that granted them entrance. She felt Marc close behind her, warm and strong, his hand resting lightly at the small of her back to guide her, keep her safe. For this one moment, this flashing instant in the strange procession of her life, she was not alone in her quest.

She was not certain *how* she felt about that, what she thought about Marc—if she could even begin to understand him. Yet there was not time to puzzle it out now. Their guide led them down a steep flight of stone stairs, the air around them dank and damp, as if they travelled below the level of the city, down into the water itself. Even Nicolai's bells were muted.

At the foot of the stairs was yet another door, one that was quickly unlocked and pushed open by their guide. Marc's hand flattened on her back, ushering her through the portal into another world.

Julietta had thought the ball in the Piazza was a dream. This was—she knew not what. A vision induced by drug-laced smoke, perhaps a universe conjured by a sorcerer to tempt her into ways she knew she must not follow or she would be lost.

She turned to look at Marc who stood behind her, his face and demeanour completely still, impassive. Yet he seemed somehow expectant, poised on the edge of some sharp precipice, just as she was. When she had first met him, she compared him to a sorcerer, with enchanting eyes and spells in his very fingertips. That feeling only intensified now, as he stood there clad in dark moons and silver stars, his eyes glowing from behind the slits of his mask.

What was happening to her?

"You see, *madonna*," Nicolai said close to her ear, drawing her away from her tempting magician. "I told you our celebration is of a more desirable sort than that colourless event in the Piazza. Do you not agree?"

He stepped back, giving her a full view of the room. It was a large, square, windowless space, the walls thickly whitewashed and hung with tapestries to ward off the damp. Flickering torches set in sconces illuminated the woven clothes, showing that they were not the usual scenes of Biblical tales or classical mythology. These showed strange creatures, huge cats, dragons, unicorns, wrought in brilliant colours and bordered with twisting, twining patterns of exotic flowers and plants.

Music played, lutes and brass finger cymbals, deep drums that sent a rhythm deep into her stomach and toes. Just as in the piazza, couples danced, a swirling tangle of colours in the middle of the flagstone floor. Yet they did not move in any ordered pavane, they merely followed the rhythm of the drums, hands and bodies meeting and parting, skirts swirling, feet flying. Some of the women wore bells on their wrists and ankles or sewn to their hems, and the silvery strains blended with the music.

In the corners of the room, pierced brass braziers emanated sweet-smelling smoke, dispelling the faint dankness of the air. There was no furniture, but large cushions were set about the edges of the room for people to lounge upon. Julietta's gaze slid over them, along the walls, up to the low ceiling, made even lower by draperies of red-and-black cloth. Everyone was masked, disguised, but a sense of lightness, of ease and good fun, hung about the room, an aura of comfort Julietta had never sensed before.

Slowly, the tension banding her shoulders eased, and she smiled at Nicolai. "Oh, yes, *signor.* You were very right."

"I knew you would enjoy it here," he answered. "And I am seldom wrong about people. Just ask our friend *Il leone.*" The Columbine from the Piazza appeared at Nicolai's shoulder, pressing her delicate black-and-white-clad body to his side.

"We have been waiting for you, Nicolasha," she murmured, trailing slim fingers along the ribbons on his shoulder.

"So sorry to keep you waiting, *ma doushka*," he said, sliding his arm around her waist. "Enjoy your evening, my friends!" he called, as Arlechino twirled his Columbine into the dance.

Julietta turned back to Marc, to find him still studying her carefully with his turquoise eyes. She had become rather adept at reading people over the years—every patron who entered her shop desired something, and she knew how to read what it was before they even spoke. But she could not read him.

It was very irritating.

He smiled, and held out his hand. She slipped her fingers into his palm, and his clasp closed around them, lifting them to his lips for a quick, sweet kiss against her skin. "Would you like to dance?" he asked.

Julietta swallowed hard. The drunken feeling she had out in the street had only increased, a quick, dizzying blend of his kiss, the feel of his skin against hers and the scented smoke from the braziers. "Not yet," she answered. "I think I would like to sit down."

Marc nodded, and led her to one of the cushions along the wall. It was thick and silken beneath her as she lowered herself, tucking her legs neatly under her skirts. For an instant, she longed to lie down fully, letting her body sink into the feathery softness until every bit of fear and constraint melted away. She could not quite let herself go so completely, though, not when she was so uncertain of the people around her.

Marc had no such qualms. He stretched out on the cushion next to hers, his long legs sprawled before him, his head resting on the edge of her lace-covered lap. One hand idly toyed with the fringed trim of the cushion, drawing the wool through his long fingers. Behind his mask, his eyes drifted closed, and she half expected him to purr in sensual satisfaction, like the lion he was named for. A cat of prey, back from his hunt, reclining in glorious abandon to enjoy his victory and claim his spoils.

Julietta stared down at him, mesmerised. She watched his fingers toy with the fringe and, for a second, she had a vision of that touch on *her,* trailing over her skin, lightly caressing the curve of her neck, the soft underside of her arm, circling a pebbled nipple that strained for his touch, his kiss…

She sucked in a sharp breath, closing her eyes against the alluring temptation. The air was filled with the scent of jasmine, smoke, wine, flesh. The drumming grew faster, deeper, thrumming deep in her stomach. Closing her eyes did not erase her desire, it only intensified it, sending images of their bodies entwining, rising and falling to the rhythm of the music, humid heat flowing around them. Perhaps *that* was what she feared when she was with him—that the tiny bud she pressed down so hard within herself would burst into full, ungovernable bloom as he touched her, and would never be suppressed again.

That she would lose all control, lose *herself,* within him. And that she could never allow.

"Wine, *madonna?*" a soft voice said above her. Julietta opened her eyes to find a masked woman holding out a tray filled with goblets of iridescent Murano glass.

"Grazie," Julietta murmured, accepting a vessel of blood-red glass. As she sipped at it, the server moved away, threading her way through the teeming crowd.

The wine was unlike any she had tasted before, a light, white brew that was dry on her tongue, touched with the sense of amber and apples, faintly buttery. It was also strong, whirling through her veins with a giddy heat. Julietta rested her head on the wall behind her, her free hand trailing almost of its own volition to the head resting in her lap.

She released the ribbon tying back his hair and sifted her fingers through the loosened strands, spreading them over her skirts. It was soft, almost silken, but thick and waving, tangling and clinging to her fingertips as her eyes drifted shut again. That light, seawater scent of his rose to her nostrils, mingling with the wine and the sweet smoke. Lightly, she pressed her touch to his temple, through the bone and pulse of blood.

How *alive* he was! Warm and strong and young. She craved that life. She had been half-dead for so long, safe and careful in the world she made for herself. Never had she met anyone as vital as this man, so full of the movement of the sea and planets and stars. She opened her eyes to find him watching her. The pupils of his eyes were dilated in the dim room, making his eyes darker, more opaque, unreadable.

"What are you thinking of, my sun?" he said softly.

What *was* she thinking of? How could she say that she thought of *him*, of the very life flowing through his veins, the life she longed to absorb into herself and possess for ever? She never could. "I am thinking how glad I am that we encountered your friend Nicolai tonight, that he brought us to this place."

"You like it here, then?"

"Very much." She shifted her gaze back to the dancers, away from his disconcerting, steady stare. The music was even wilder, the drumbeats rising and rising until surely even the slumbering dead on their funeral island could hear it. She saw Nicolai in the midst of it all, his doublet open and ribbons flying, Columbine in his arms. He sung along to the beat, strange words in his own lilting language. Julietta did not know those words, yet they called to her, echoed in her own confused emotions.

Her fingertips slid slowly down Marc's cheek, slightly roughened with whiskers, and along the clean, sharp line of his jaw. Gently, she pressed a touch to the sensual curve of his lower lip. It was slightly chapped from the sea air and sun, yet softer than she expected, almost like a flower petal. He swallowed hard, yet did not move. His breath flowed cool over her hand.

Her touch came to rest on his shoulder, finding the

muscle and sinew that twisted beneath the velvet. He moved finally, reaching up to unfasten the jewelled closures of his doublet. The lacings of the fine linen shirt beneath were loosened, and Julietta saw glimpses of smooth, sun-browned chest between the stark whiteness of the cloth, only lightly sprinkled with pale brown hair. She could imagine him on his ship, perched high in the crow's nest, leaning into the wind and the salt spray...

She gulped down the last of her wine and placed the glass on the floor beside her. No sooner had it touched the flagstones than the server was there again, taking up the empty goblet and proffering a full one. Quite against her better judgement, which was shrieking to be released from the cage she had locked it in for the night, she drank it.

It was as dry and dizzying as the last dose, and it made her giggle as she sipped at it. *Demon wine.* Yet she knew very well it was not merely the wine that made her feel this way.

"Do you have a sip to spare for a thirsty sailor, *signora?*" Marc said, reaching up to lightly touch her wrist.

Julietta peered down into the half-full glass. "Perhaps, since the sailor was so kind as to bring me here tonight."

She held the vessel to his lips, and he raised his head to drink, the strong muscles of his throat tensing. When the wine was gone, he lowered himself back to her lap, reaching out to toy with a fold of the golden lace.

"I am glad you like it here," he said. "Nicolai can search out the most hidden places in every city."

Julietta relaxed against the wall, curling both hands into the fall of his hair. She closed her eyes, and swayed gently to the music. "You have known him a long time?"

"A very long time," he answered lazily. "We met in a brothel in Germany. A—dispute broke out, and Nicolai saved my life. He also showed me some of the, shall we say, less savoury establishments along the Rhine."

Julietta laughed to think of the two of them, sailing up and down the Rhine in search of whores who would not start "disputes" and try to break their patrons' heads.

Marc grinned. "Aye, I know. Foolish of us. Youth was our only excuse. We were very young and stupid."

"And now?"

"Now, I am older and slightly less stupid."

Julietta traced his brow with her fingertip, the taut skin only slightly creased beneath her touch. "You are surely ancient, Marc. But what was a sea warrior doing in Germany?"

"I did not always use my ship and my fighting skills for whoever can afford to pay for them. I once worked for my father."

"Your father?"

"He was a merchant, and a very successful one. He owned many ships, which sailed into every port in search of rare and exotic wares. I was just a child when he started taking me with him on his voyages, started teaching me of navigation, how to read the sea and plot a course according to her whims. I saw many corners of the world with him—Germany was but one."

Julietta listened in silence, enthralled by this tiny glimpse into the soul of *Il leone*. So he *was* a man, after all, born of mortal parents! How she envied his childhood of travel, of adventures. He had seen the world, while she had seen only her family's palazzo in Milan, her soul fed only by her grandmother's tales. "It sounds wonderful."

Marc laughed. "Oh, *sì,* it was that. And also rough at times. The sea is a mistress who is beautiful beyond compare, but she is also a capricious goddess who will caress you one moment and turn your ship to kindling in the next. My father had a saying he always repeated: the sea knows its own."

"And what does that mean?"

"It means that if you were born for the life of the sea, you cannot fight it, cannot escape it. And he was right. I love the life of the sea and ships, and I can never be free of its hold. Not entirely. Yet…" His voice trailed away, and as Julietta watched him the corners of his lips turned down.

"Yet, what?" she asked, longing to know what he would say.

"Yet it is a hard life. My father knew that well, and in the end it was the sea that claimed him. My mother wanted me to enter the Church, and I think my father would have been somewhat relieved to see me follow that path, as well. Safer, you see, more steady. But he knew I had the sea in my soul, just as he did, and there was naught to be done."

Julietta almost laughed to envision him with a tonsure, clad in a rough black hassock, elevating the Host before a crowd of enthralled female parishioners. "And would you have made a fine churchman, *Il leone?*"

"Do you doubt I would?" he said, his frown dissolving into that wide pirate's grin. The hand that pleated at her skirt flattened against her leg, lightly caressing, moving in gentle, alluring circles through the cloth. Julietta gasped at the feelings, at the shiver his touch raised.

"I think you would have made a fine cardinal in Rome," she whispered, closing her eyes as she let herself be carried away on a wave of sensation. "Even a fine pope."

"Aye. I would have liked being pope. But I like being a sailor even more, especially at this very moment." She felt him sit up on the cushion beside her, his hand sliding along her waist, drawing her into the curve of his body.

"And why is that?" she murmured, her head spinning with the wine, with his touch and the scent and warmth of him.

"Because if I was a churchman, I would not be here in Venice, in this room, with you."

"Nay, then you would be in your Papal palace with a woman far more beautiful."

His lips touched her temple just above the edge of her mask. "Impossible. There is none more beautiful than the sun." The hand at her waist slid down, grasping the hem of her skirt and drawing it up slowly, ever so slowly, until she felt cool, scented air on her leg. One of his fingertips toyed with the ribbon tie of her garter, at the sensitive point just above her knee.

"Are you trying to seduce me?" she whispered.

He laughed against her hair. "Is it working?"

Julietta opened her eyes, staring up at him. He was just as beautiful as before, with his tousled hair, and the smooth, bare skin of his chest, rising and falling with the force of his breath. A quick pulse at the base of his throat, the hollow there shining with a crystalline drop of sweat that she longed to catch on her tongue, to taste him, feel him become part of herself. Ah, yes, she wanted him, with a powerful force she had never felt before, never even imagined existed in the world. An inexorable force poured through her, urging her to grab him and pull him down onto the cushions with her, taking him into her until she did not know where she ended and he began. It was almost unstoppable.

Almost.

For, as she studied his face so close to her own, his beautiful lips only a whisper away, a chill crept from her very core up to her heart, spreading its ice out to her fingertips and toes.

This moment was not real. It was not to be trusted. This man was not to be trusted. It seemed a simple thing to have sex with him, to take her satisfaction in him and be done with it. Yet she knew, knew in her very soul, it would not be like that. It would not be a simple thing at all.

Julietta reached down and caught his hand in hers, gently drawing it away from her leg. "Not this eve, *Il leone,*" she said. Her voice was thick and rough, but at least it did not tremble or waver, giving away her uncertainty, her need.

Most men would have been angry at such an abrupt rejection, perhaps even would have turned to violence, as her husband had. Yet, once again, Marc showed that he was *not* "most men." He was unlike anyone she had ever known. He merely sat back, moving away so even their breath no longer touched, and held his hands up.

"Alas, my sun, you do wound me," he said lightly, if a bit breathlessly. "Is there nothing I can offer that would please you?"

"You could offer me more wine," she answered. Her throat was achingly dry, her skin cold. Perhaps wine could warm her again, yet she doubted it.

"Whatever you wish." He stood up on legs that did not even tremble, unlike her own poor limbs. His hand was steady as he swooped up their empty glasses. Yet she noticed that he drew his cloak closely about him, careful to conceal his codpiece.

Julietta would have laughed, if she had even an ounce of energy left. But the chill had receded, leaving her tired and heavy. Whatever the warning was, it had left her, and she sat still and watched Marc as he disappeared into the crowd.

The smoke was thick in the air, swirling around the dancers. Even their steps were slower now, moving in an almost stately pattern to a lower, more primal drumbeat. Several couples lounged on the cushions, entwined in embraces, kisses—much as she and Marc had been, unheeding of anyone around them.

Julietta's head suddenly ached, and she watched the room with an odd sense of detachment, distance. It had been a glorious night, indeed, but perhaps it was time for her to go home. To be alone in her secret room and puzzle out what all of this could mean.

She slowly rose to her feet, leaning on the wall for support as the room tilted. She ran her gaze over the crowd, but she did not see Marc, nor did she see Nicolai and his Columbine. The people were a whirl of masks, of wild visages both beautiful and frightening, strangely distorted. Her head was swimming from the wine and the smoke. She closed her eyes for a moment, taking in a careful breath.

When she opened them, she saw a doorway cut into the wall across from her, shielded by a red curtain painted in exotic golden symbols. She had not noticed it before, yet now the curtain fluttered slightly, beckoning her forwards.

Julietta pushed away from the supporting wall and made her way around the edge of the dancers. Her feet seemed to move of their own volition, carrying her forwards, impelled by the force of her wretched curiosity—just as she had been led forwards all night. It was that deep, undeniable need to *know* that brought her here in the first place. That, and a wild, foolish attraction to Marc Velazquez. Now it carried her to this room which contained she knew not what.

She reached the red curtain, and slowly stretched out her hand to touch the thick fabric. It was rough, warm velvet, thick and stiff with the painted symbols. She only touched it with her fingertips, but the fabric slid easily to one side, as if to welcome her.

Julietta stepped carefully into the doorway, peering into the room beyond. It was small, square and dark, the walls completely covered by heavy tapestries. The only light was from one candelabra, set atop a low, red silk-covered table in the corner. Behind the table, a woman sat on a pile of cushions, and as Julietta studied her she could not fathom what had made her so hesitant to enter the room. The woman was no dragon or serpent, but only an ordinary mortal, small, thin, neither old nor young. Dark hair lightly threaded with silver was twisted atop her head and tied with white ribbons; a white mask half covered a smooth, olive-complected face. Her white, lace-trimmed sleeves were tied back so as not to interfere with her task.

Spread on the table before her was a suite of cards, but not just any cards. Narrow rectangles of paste-board, gilded at the edges and painted in opulent colours with fantastical scenes of courtiers and fools and creatures. Julietta leaned closer, and recognised the Visconti-Sforza deck of tarot cards—cards just like the ones her grandmother had once possessed, kept locked away in a carved ivory box. They were not often used for divination, even in Milan where the designs had originated, but her grandmother preferred them so.

The woman glanced up to find Julietta staring, and gave her a sweet smile. "Good evening, *madonna*," she said, her voice as serene and soft as that smile. "Would you care for a reading?"

It had been a very long time since Julietta sat for a tarot reading. She remembered standing across a table from her grandmother, barely able to peer over the edge, watching as the silver-haired woman laid out her cards. "Ah, *ma petite*." She had sighed, as she studied the cards closely. "I fear you will never tread an easy path in this life."

How true those words had proven to be! And other things her grandmother saw revealed in the cards— things Julietta did not care to remember. But that was many years ago. Perhaps things had changed?

And perhaps she was a fool to have such hopes, even now.

"*Sì*," she answered, and moved to sit down on the cushions across from the white-clad lady. "I would very much like a reading."

"*Va bene.* I am Maria, *madonna*." The woman gathered the cards up, folding them into a neat stack. She handed Julietta the pasteboard rectangles, watching as she reshuffled the deck and divided it into three stacks.

"You are familiar with the tarot, I see," Maria commented.

"Yes," Julietta answered shortly.

"You have a question tonight?"

Just one? Her mind whirled with so many doubts and confusions, she could not even begin to sort them out.

"You have many emotions, I see," Maria said. "Let us do a simple seven-card spread, perhaps that will lessen your confusion."

She drew seven cards and laid them out on the table, face-up. Her expression was serious yet completely unreadable, impassive as she traced her fingertips over the painted and gilded pasteboard. "You know Dante's dark wood?" she said.

Julietta nodded, puzzled. Surely there was nothing about Dante in the cards? "'Midway upon the journey of our life, I found myself within a forest dark, for the straightforward pathway had been lost.'"

"So it is."

"You see something about—forests in the cards? Or darkness?"

The woman shrugged. "Who can say, *signora?* I am merely an interpreter. Yet there comes a time when we all must journey through the underworld, and find our own magician." She pointed to the first card. "You see here—the Magician. You have the ability to make your own reality, to forge a new direction. You have the power in your own hands, if you will only use it."

Her gaze slid to the next card. "The Devil, reversed. You must let go of fears, move into the future free of chains. The next card is the High Priestess, also reversed. The truth, you see, is dropping away from her; she is not entirely honest with us tonight. Something is not right."

Julietta thought of Marc, of how dark his blue eyes were as he stared down at her tonight, of how his arms felt strong and safe, yet more dangerous than any dagger, when he held her. *Not right*—yet she could not resist him even as she could not resist breathing. But perhaps the card indicated herself, not him. "The next card?" she asked hoarsely.

"Death, upright. There is a reversal in your life cycle. The past is gone, if you will let it rest."

Gone? Julietta gave small shake of her head. The past was never gone, it was always close on her shoulders, reaching out for her with icy fingers, trying to drag her back. Just like the painted, grotesquely grinning spectre on that card.

"Then we have the Hierophant, reversed," Maria said. "Unorthodox behaviour, *signora,* an unconventional way of living."

Julietta had to smile. Just by being here tonight, by sitting across from this woman, she could be called *unorthodox*. As for the rest of her life… "Very true, *signora.*"

"And the final card—the Chariot, upright. It is an auspicious card, *madonna.* You will have success through your hard work. You have a kind nature, but perhaps you are too intensely focused on your goal."

"Is that not a good conclusion, though?" Julietta said. *Success*—sometimes she thought she could almost taste it, feel it within her very grasp, but then it slithered away yet again.

Maria nodded slowly, her gaze still bent on the cards.

"If we can trust the High Priestess…" she murmured. She reached for the third stack of cards and held it out to Julietta. "Choose one more, please, *signora*."

Julietta stared at the proffered cards in surprise. Her grandmother had never thus ended a reading. "Choose one?"

"Please, *signora*. Indulge an old woman."

Julietta slowly reached out and drew a card from the top of the stack. She placed it carefully on the table, face up, above the row of seven.

"Ah," Maria said, "the Ace of Cups, reversed. A great rush of emotion is taking place, and soon the cup will be empty. Your heart is not open to new love. It is closed, cold. Empty."

Julietta stared down at the formation, studying the painted images carefully, as if she could change their position, their messages. "It cannot be otherwise?"

The woman shrugged, yet her smile was not unsympathetic. "I am merely the messenger, *madonna*. Our fate is—what it is. Yet I have seen a strong will turn back many a tide. Evil *can* be transformed into good, hatred to love—a cold heart to one aflame with emotion. With God's help, anything is possible. I tell this to all I give readings to, though some do not choose to listen." She tapped her fingertip on the Ace of Cups. "Always remember, *signora*—the reversal of this card is up to you, and you alone. You have the will. Do you have the courage to use it?"

Did she? Sometimes Julietta thought she had used up all of her courage in coming to Venice, starting this new life, and she had none left to spare. And some-times she felt she could conquer the very secrets of life and death. At this moment, she was simply weary, her head aching from the wine. She needed rest. Perhaps in the morning this would all seem clearer—or more like a dream.

"Grazie," she murmured to the woman, and stood up to take her leave. A shadow shifted in the doorway, and Julietta's breath caught as she saw it was Marc standing there, watching her. He said nothing and did not move from where he stood, one hand holding back the curtain and the other balancing a glass goblet. For an instant, he seemed a sombre stranger, not the man who had danced with her, flirted with her, kissed her with such heat. Julietta had always been unsure of him, ever since the moment he first stepped into her shop. Now, she felt the tiniest flickerings of fear, and she did not know why.

Did he disapprove of what she was doing? Did he think the cards to be the devil's handiwork? Many of the nobility enjoyed the tarot, but there were a few who were beginning to look askance at it. She remembered the way Marc looked on the Doge's *Buccintore,* the way he mingled so easily with men of power and in-fluence—men like her own father, her long-ago father-in-law. She remembered what the cards said—a cold heart can be set aflame with emotion, but only if the will was strong enough.

Beware, she thought she heard someone whisper. When she glanced over her shoulder, though, she saw no one. Even Maria, the woman in white, had vanished with her cards.

"I brought you some light ale," Marc said quietly, moving at last to press the cool glass in her hand. "It will quench your thirst better than the rich wine."

"Yes. Thank you." Julietta took a careful sip. It was buttery and slightly bitter, but she tasted no undertones of anything unwholesome. "It must be nearly dawn."

"So it is." A hint of a smile touched his lips, making him seem more the Marc she knew—or imagined she was beginning to know. "Time for the night's revels to be ending."

"So very soon?" she murmured. In truth, it felt as if she had just arrived in this strange place—or mayhap had lived here all her life.

"I fear so. But there is always tomorrow night and the night after that. I would share them all with you, my sun, if you would allow me."

Julietta swallowed the last of her ale, and looked up at him to make some teasing remark in return. Something in his eyes stilled her voice, something dark and serious, as if he was in complete earnest with his plea.

"We should take our leave," she murmured, bending down to place her empty glass on the floor. When she rose, Marc took her arm in the lightest of clasps and led her out of the small room and back through the gathering. The embers of merriment had cooled considerably, the drumming ceased, leaving only the soft strum of a solitary lute. No one danced, but many people lounged on the cushions. Smoke hung still and heavy in the air and empty glasses and ewers littered the floor.

Marc steered her carefully among the sprawled bodies and detritus of gaiety until they emerged out of the room on to the steep staircase that led up and out into the real world of the city. Marc's fingers entwined with hers, and Julietta felt as Eurydice must, being taken out of the illusory underworld by her Orpheus.

The narrow *calli* outside was deserted, and Julietta tipped back her head to draw in a breath of damp, sweet air. The sky was deepest blue, touched at the edges with a grayish pink that heralded the dawn of a new day.

"'Tis chilly," Marc said, and she felt a soft weight swirl over her shoulders. His cloak, surrounding her, capturing her in his scent and the heat of his body. The sun wrapped in the moon.

"But you will be cold," she protested, reaching up to push the cloak away, though truly she wanted nothing more than to sink into the velvet, wrap herself into its starry protection.

"Nay, *madonna*," he answered wryly. "My blood burns all too hot." He took her hand up again and led her down the slick stones of the street, taking her home as the sky flamed pink and orange and lavender above them.

Chapter Nine

Marc's room was so silent and, still, it almost rang with it, as he locked the door behind him and dropped his cloak and mask to the floor. His blood and nerves still throbbed to the beat of the drums and finger-cymbals; his skin smelled of the exotic, pure jasmine that scented Julietta's hair.

Julietta. Marc tore off his doublet and shirt, crossing the room in only his hose to where a basin and ewer of cold water waited. He splashed its chilly drops over his face and chest, pouring it over his heated flesh, yet it did nothing to cool him. He still saw her in his mind, lying beside him on the silken cushions, her black hair spread beneath her, her lips parted for his kiss, eager for his caress.

But not half as eager as he was for hers! When first they danced the *volte* in the piazza, when he held her against him, lifting her high in the air and slowly lowering her to her feet, feeling every inch of her slim, supple body, every nerve had come achingly alive. He wanted her, *needed* her so, as if there was no other woman in all the world. Perhaps he could have blamed it on the wine—yet he had drunk none then. Perhaps the spirit of Carnival, the atmosphere of wild revelry, was at fault.

Nay. He knew that was not so. It was *her.* When he was not with her, he could think coldly of his plans, his careful plots. Of what an important part she played in them now. But when he was with her, when he looked into those dark eyes that seemed to see so very much, when he touched her silken skin, smelled her perfume—no rational plans could stand. No coldness.

"Maledizione," he muttered viciously, and raked the flat of his hand through the basin, sending a silvery shower of water to the wooden floor. He should stay far away from her, even from her cursed shop. There was surely a kind of sorcery in her eyes, in her touch, a magic that lured his thoughts away from what he owed the past, what he had vowed on the souls of his dead.

She made him forget himself. Yet truly he knew that it was no sorcery on her part, only his own weakness that drew him to her mystery and her strange beauty. A weakness he must overcome if he was to fulfill his vows in Venice and return to the lure of the sea.

"In truth unfortunate," he murmured, staring up into the small glass mirror hanging on the wall. He did not see himself there, his face and hair dripping with the rivulets of spilled water. He saw Julietta, pale and serious as she rose from the tarot table and turned to face him, her eyes widening in a sudden flare of suspicion.

Julietta Bassano—what is your secret? he thought. What is it you hide? What does Ermano seek from you?

Aye, he *should* stay away from her, yet he could not. He needed her too much, she was the missing piece in his puzzle box. They were connected now, bound together inexorably until his vow was fulfilled. Such was their fate, a fate surely to be read in those gilded cards. If he had met her somewhere else, in Spain perhaps, or France, or even on faraway islands, if they were different people…

But "if" was a futile game to play. He knew that all too well. He was no longer a mere sea merchant; she was not a young *señorita* he could marry and settle into his Seville hacienda to await his return from voyages. They had to play out their own fates. The sun and the moon, trapped in their own worlds.

He reached for a piece of towelling that rested beside the basin. As he ran the canvas over his face and chest, his gaze fell on the objects arrayed on the table. Soap, his razor, a locked leather case and the purple glass bottle of scent he had purchased for his mother.

The bottle was not where he had left it, carefully aligned with the case. It sat on the edge of the table, its amethyst facets glittering innocently.

Frowning, Marc picked it up, holding it to the light to examine it more carefully. Julietta had sealed the filigree stopper with a thin ring of wax. The wax appeared to be intact, yet there were two tiny nicks in the hardened purple circle, a small scratch in the glass he would vow had not been there before.

Marc placed the bottle back on the table and took up instead the razor, a straight, flat, shining blade he used to remove his beard every morning. It could be just as useful in slitting throats.

He spun around on the balls of his feet, his gaze darting over every inch of the room. It seemed just as he had left it. The heavy red-velvet bed curtains were tied back, the bedclothes smoothed up over the bolsters. The chairs and table were arranged before the cold fireplace, the curtains thrown back from the window. It appeared deserted and chilly, anonymous, as rooms always were in such inns. A man could be whatever he chose in such a room—if he was careful.

His trunk, a battered oaken chest carved with swirling mermaids and serpents on long afternoons at sea, sat at the foot of the bed, its lock still in place. Marc took the tiny key from inside his discarded doublet and unlocked the chest, pushing the lid back. Like the perfume bottle and the objects on the table, all seemed to be in order. His clothes were neatly folded, his papers rolled into scrolls and bound with ribbons and seals. But the thin piece of blue string he had placed between the lip of the trunk and the ledge lay atop a pile of folded shirts—and he had not been the one to dislodge it.

Whoever it was, they were long gone, leaving no footprints in the dust or lingering perfume in the air.

Yet he had to increase his vigilance, always be wary. Even when he held Julietta Bassano in his arms.

Especially when he held Julietta Bassano in his arms.

Chapter Ten

"*Signora! Signora,* wake up." Bianca shook Julietta's shoulder persistently, even as Julietta shrugged her hand away as she would a buzzing gnat. "Wake up!"

"Er, erm," Julietta muttered, and rolled deeper under the bedclothes in search of a peaceful place where people with pounding headaches could finish their slumber. Alas, it was not to be. Bianca's hand merely followed, reaching out to pull at the sleeve of her chemise.

"Is it time to open the shop?" Julietta said, pushing herself up against the pillows. Her hair, which she had forgotten to braid before she fell into bed, drooped before her eyes in a hopeless tangle. She brushed it back and observed Bianca through bleary eyes.

The maid, unlike her employer, looked as if she had spent the night sleeping the sleep of the innocent in her own blameless bed. Her wiry black hair was neatly tucked beneath a spotless white cap; her striped skirt and pink bodice were clean and carefully pressed. Her eyes were clear, her smile bright as she held out a small tray.

"I thought you might be hungry," Bianca said, or rather chirped, annoyingly. "And water is heating for your bath."

Julietta's stomach gave a lurch as she glanced down at the pitcher of ale and small loaf of bread, golden and fragrant as if just baked. She wasn't sure she could bear food again, but if she was to go about her day's business she would need sustenance.

As she tore off a corner of the bread and chewed slowly, Bianca bustled about the room with quick, tidy movements, picking up the remains of the night before. She smoothed Julietta's lace and silk between her hands before folding it away in the clothes chest, untangled the ribbons of the discarded mask and the now-scuffed brocade slippers.

"How was it last night, *signora?*" Bianca asked, perching at the foot of the bed once her tasks were complete. "Was it very grand?"

Julietta took a sip of ale before replying. Bianca had added her own sweet herbs to the brew, ones guaranteed to banish headaches. "Yes, very grand, indeed. And very crowded."

"Was there glorious music?" Bianca persisted, her raisin-dark eyes shining. "And beautiful clothes?"

Julietta felt a sudden pang of conscience. How had she never seen that Bianca longed for merriment, too?

That she must tire of being always here at the shop, always working? She just seemed to be so happy, so eager to help, to learn about the making of fine scents, the running of a business. Very soon, Julietta would have to insist that Bianca take a night out, go and enjoy Carnival. Perhaps even this very night!

Or perhaps Julietta merely wanted an excuse to hide herself away, to hole up alone in her room and not think about Marc Velazquez and all that had happened last night.

Later. That was all something to ponder later, when she was bathed and brushed and dressed and felt more like herself again, not this wild, wanton creature lying late abed. Julietta reached for the comb that rested on the bedside table, and as she dragged its ivory teeth through the tangled snarls of her hair, she described some of the night's costumes and jewels for Bianca. She told her of the hundreds of lights in the piazza, how they made San Marco glow; of the music, the dancing, the fountains of wine.

Of that other gathering, the one deep in the underworld, she said nothing. She was not entirely convinced it had been anything but a dream.

"And *Il leone?*" Bianca said, with a sly, sideways smile. "Was he a fine dancer?"

"Very accomplished," Julietta answered shortly. She remembered suddenly exactly how it felt to be lifted high in his arms, balanced as if her tall figure was a mere feather, their bodies sliding against each other in heat and friction and need. How she wanted to wrap her legs about his hips, her arms around his neck, and never let go. Her hand faltered on her hair, the comb fumbling to her lap.

"I would wager so," Bianca continued. "So strong, he looks! You must have been the envy of all the women there, *madonna*."

Julietta scooped the comb up, dragging it hard through the tangles until her eyes watered and she could no longer see their dance in her mind. "We were masked. None could know who he was."

Bianca snickered. "Oh, I would wager many would know by his figure alone! Those broad shoulders, those narrow hips, that—"

"*Sì*, Bianca!" Julietta firmly interrupted.

"I wish I could have been there," Bianca went on, unconcerned, "to see what a glorious pair you made, to hear the music."

"Why don't you go out tonight?" Julietta said. She made quick work of her braid, tying off the end with a bit of black ribbon and shrugging the heavy rope back over her shoulder. "I can watch the shop."

"Perhaps I shall, *madonna*," Bianca answered. "Or perhaps tonight you will have to go out again." She reached into her apron pocket and drew out a vellum scroll. "I nearly forgot that this came for you early this morning. Is it another invitation?"

Julietta glanced at the neat, ribbon-tied tube, sealed with a blob of green wax, and her heart gave a strange lurch. Could it truly be from Marc, already? Yet even as she reached for it, she knew it was not. The scent

on the rich vellum was not of clean ocean water, but
of bergamot and roses.

Count Ermano. Suddenly, her stomach felt
queasy again.

She broke the seal and unrolled the message,
quickly scanning the neat words printed there in heavy
black ink. "It is, indeed, an invitation," she said drily.
"Yet not the one your romantic heart craves, Bianca."

"Nay? No love letters from *Il leone?*"

"No love letters from anyone." Praise be to San
Giovanni for that. She did not think she could face the
count's flowery protestations so early in the morning.
"It is an invitation from Count Ermano, to a banquet
at his palazzo this evening."

Bianca gave a disappointed frown. "Shall you go?"

Julietta did not *want* to go. Time spent in the
company of Count Eramno was always wearying, and
a long, formal evening at his home was sure to be
doubly so. Yet she read further in the missive, and saw
that Ermano was careful to inform her that many important nobles and wealthy merchants were to attend,
names she recognised as loyal patrons of her shop—
or people she would like to have as loyal patrons. She
and her small shop were very small fish, indeed, in the
great sea of Venetian politics, and she liked it that way.
She had lived the life of a member of an Important
Family before, and it did not suit her. But she *did*
enjoy having many customers who wanted their own
special scents and were willing to pay a great deal for
them. She wanted them to keep coming to her little es-

tablishment, and not those of her many rival perfumiers.

Thus, a certain amount of socialising, of conversation and laughter and a few well-placed compliments
would not come amiss. Even if it was in Palazzo Grattiano.

Julietta laid the letter aside with a sigh. At least
there would be a goodly crowd at this banquet, and she
would not be alone with the count.

"Well, *madonna?*" Bianca prompted.

"Yes, I suppose I will go," Julietta replied slowly.
"I must. But you should still go out, as well. The house
can be unattended for one evening, surely." She pushed
back the blankets and swung her legs out of bed,
stretching her toes towards the floor to face the
morning. "Come. We must open the shop."

Ca Grattiano was lit from the rooftop to the gondola
poles as if for a glorious festival. Torches blazed on the
roofline and the dock, born aloft by pages clad in rich
green-and-silver livery. Every window glowed pale
gold, welcoming beacons to the crowds alighting from
their vessels and making their way to the inner courtyard. Pennants fluttered in the evening breeze, more
green and silver that flashed and crackled.

Julietta sat on the edge of the cushions in her hired
gondola, waiting for her turn to disembark. Her skin
tingled with wary anticipation, her feet twitched in
their velvet slippers as if urging her to flee when she
had the chance. The palazzo was the grandest, largest

dwelling along the canal, crafted of dark and pale pink marble set in an elaborate criss-cross pattern. The windows were surmounted by intricate cupids and strange demons, staring down at the well-dressed hordes ascending upon them.

The entire place spoke strongly of great wealth and power, of the desire to overwhelm by impressive awe. Most people would feel honoured by an invitation to dine in such surroundings. Julietta longed only to leave, to be free of the suffocating sumptuousness. She remembered the gathering of last night, remembered the drums and silken cushions, the smoky air, the wine, the wild abandon.

Such a place seemed a million miles from this one, and she wanted so much to be back there again, free to laugh and dance, to kiss Marc Velazquez with impunity.

It was too late to flee, though. Her gondola bumped against the dock, signalling her arrival, and the boatman held out his hand to help her alight.

Most of the guests had already arrived, and the inner courtyard of the palazzo held only a few people making their way up the wide stone staircase to the public rooms on the second floor. Here, too, there were so many torches that night appeared to be day, a strange orange glow that ushered her upwards to a glittering, artificial world.

Inside the open double doors, a page waited to take her cloak and lead her into the fray. Tall, silver-framed mirrors hung on the walls just outside the grand *sala*, and Julietta paused to glance at her reflection.

Compared to some of the other ladies' elaborate garments, her red velvet gown was stark, with only a bit of gold embroidery on the bodice and the hem. She wore the same cloth-of-gold sleeves from last night, tied on tightly to reveal small puffs of a white-and-gold chemise. Her dark hair was braided, twined with red ribbons and crowned with a small gold cap trimmed with seed pearls. No, she was not the most fashionable woman there, but the crimson colour flattered her, and her jewels, a pair of pearl earrings and a long strand of pearls and rubies that once belonged to her mother, were quite fine. She would do.

Fortified with this small dose of vanity, she stepped into the crowded *sala* and gazed steadily about her at the other guests, at the powerful, the wealthy, the great, the ones who might wonder how a perfume-shop owner came to be among them here. They gazed back, but none challenged her yet; they stayed in their same large groups and small knots, placed carefully about the room as if in a scene of *commedia dell'arte*.

And what a room it was. Julietta accepted a goblet of wine from one of the pages and strolled to a quiet corner to absorb it all. She had never been inside Ca Grattiano, had only heard tales of it from customers in her shop. None of the breathless descriptions were exaggerated. This room was as glorious as any in the Doge's Palace itself, with soaring ceilings crowned by a fresco of gambolling gods and shepherds. The walls were hung with massive tapestries, the floors made of polished, gold-veined marble. The air was thick with the scent of thousands of wax candles set in dozens of gilded sconces and candelabra. It was a fit setting for the silks and jewels of the guests, more of whom poured through the doors every second.

Julietta sipped at her wine and regarded the pageant as she would a play staged for her amusement. It was always fascinating to observe people, to watch how they spoke to each other, how they flirted, how they smiled—or did not smile. How they oh-so-subtly gained the upper hand over one another. It was an intricate dance, a never-ending one.

She felt so very detached here in this grand *sala,* not at all as she had at Nicolai Ostrovsky's strange gathering. There, all of her cool regard fled as she stared into Marc's magical turquoise eyes, felt his touch on her skin. There, she plunged directly into the swirling tides of life, buffeted by its waves and eddies. That was where danger lay. *This*—this was safe. Even as she stood in the midst of her enemy's home, she was safer than she had been with Marc Velazquez.

A cluster of people in the very centre of the room parted, revealing their host. Count Ermano wore purple tonight, embroidered with silver gilt thread and trimmed with shimmering silver fox fur that echoed his waving hair. The jewels on his thick fingers flashed as he gestured in laughter at some joke. The crowd surrounding him watched raptly as he spoke, as if he held their fortunes and fates in his hands, while he did not appear to see *them* at all. He flattered the women, kissing their hands; he jested heartily with the men. Yet his gaze flickered over them in an instant and then was on to the next prey.

That sharp gaze now moved ever closer to Julietta's hiding place. She edged back towards the tapestry-hung wall, but it was too late. Ermano glimpsed her there, his eyes widened and he called out, "Ah, it is the lovely Signora Bassano! How happy I am you have graced my home this night."

The people surrounding him also turned to look at her. If they were surprised that the count would so single her out, they gave no indication. They merely went on smiling the same bland, charming smiles, smoothly gliding out of his path as he made his way towards her.

"Count Ermano," Julietta said, giving a small curtsy. "I am honoured by your invitation."

"Not at all," he answered, reaching for her hand. He pressed a brief kiss to her fingertips, then held them tucked within his own. It took every ounce of strength to not snatch her hand away! Yet her own social training was too strong, even so many years removed from her girlhood in Milan. She smiled stiffly, and stood very still.

"It is I who am honoured that you came here, though I wish you would have allowed me to send my own gondola for you," Ermano continued. "What do you think of my home, Signora Bassano?"

"It is beautiful, Count. I am sure there is no place to equal it in Venice."

Ermano shrugged carelessly, but there was a

pleased light in his cold green eyes. "It needs a woman's refining touch, I fear. The decorations are sadly out of fashion. But come, let me introduce you to some of my other guests. You already know many of them, of course. I have seen Signora Mercanti many times in your lovely shop...."

Julietta allowed him to escort her around the room, making polite chatter with the richly clad throngs, commenting on fashions, shops, the newest artists. Her face ached with the force of her smile and her stomach fluttered with the urge to flee into the night. These were not her people; this was not where she should be!

She could not run, of course. Ermano was always close beside her, his strangely possessive clasp on her arm, his perfume clinging in her nostrils. She did not understand his behaviour, did not understand this entire evening. The palatial marble walls seemed to edge closer and closer, the crowd swaying before her eyes.

Luckily, before she could faint, the doors to the *sala* were thrown open and a trumpet herald sounded, echoing off the marble floor, the soaring ceiling. She spun away from Ermano, grateful for the noisy interruption.

The Doge himself, Andrea Gritti, appeared under the arch of the horns, his gold-and-white robes glistening. He took in the assembled crowd with cool eyes as his train followed him into the room, creating a tableau of opulence and power. Directly behind the Doge was Marc Velazquez.

Julietta froze in the middle of easing away from Ermano. Her skin tingled, cold and then blazing hot as a summer sun. She shivered, and her gaze fluttered to the floor. She felt like an utter fool, a silly young girl who would giggle and blush when faced with a handsome man. But her body wouldn't listen to her admonitions to stop acting so ridiculously. It shivered again, startled to see him, longing to run to him, rooted, frozen, into place.

She sucked in a breath, and the thick, warm scents of candle wax and perfume helped bring her back down to solid earth. She took a goblet from another page and took a deep sip of the rich wine as she glanced back to the Doge's group. To Marc.

For an instant, she could only see him as he had been last night, sprawled across her lap, his hair loose and doublet open, regarding her with slumberous, sensual eyes. She blinked, and her lusty pirate was gone, vanished inside the polished courtier who stood across the suffocatingly palatial room. He wore black, as he had last night, but there the resemblance ended. His doublet and hose were stark velvet, unadorned except for a strip of silver embroidery at the high collar, silver clasps along the front. His hair fell to his shoulders in glossy waves, and that single teardrop pearl glistened in his ear.

His face, still beautiful and hard as an angry god, was expressionless as his dark-ocean gaze swept over the crowd. As if they were assembled only for him, to be held for his pleasure or his dismissal. And, indeed, they might as well be. *"Il leone,"* the whisper went up around her, a wave of awe and fascination. The woman who stood behind Julietta, a lushly gowned and richly bejewelled noblewoman, tittered and giggled.

Much as Julietta herself longed to do. But she did not have the luxury of being silly, as those pampered women did. She could not afford the attention she would attract by throwing herself at Venice's new hero, by rushing to his side, clinging to his sleeve, sighing up at him. She couldn't afford any more gossip, speculation.

Julietta's fingers curled into a fist as she watched a cluster of those ladies approach Marc, curtsying, laughing softly behind their feather fans. A whisper of a smile finally touched his lips, and he bowed over their white hands, responding quietly to their simpering sallies.

No—she did not want to be a part of their group. One of many. She remembered how his fingers felt on the bare skin of her thigh, hot and hard, how his kiss tasted under her mouth, of wine and cinnamon and dark, needful things.

She trembled at the blurry, heated memory, and her stare slid of its own accord to his hand. It was folded now over the gilded hilt of a dagger in his gold belt, the long, sun-browned fingers loose and casual. She saw them caught again in gold lace skirts, drawing the fabric up to bare her flesh for his avid eyes....

She took another desperate gulp of her wine, seeking forgetfulness in its heady potency. Only to find, as she peered over the golden rim, that Marc watched her now, his turquoise eyes a deep midnight blue as they stared into hers, steady, solemn, knowing. As if he divined her lustful thoughts.

Julietta could not tear her gaze away, could not turn or move or even smile. She was firmly caught by that blue stare, trapped like a hare in a cage, unable to thrash free or scream out.

His fingers tightened on the dagger. *Julietta,* he whispered silently, his lips forming her name, and it was as if a slow kiss slid along her throat. Her eyes narrowed, and he smiled, the mere ghost of a grin. *Later,* that smile seemed to say. Later.

There was no time to ponder this troubling puzzle now, though. Count Ermano clapped his bejewelled hands, the sharp crack bringing sudden silence to the echoing room.

"My friends," he announced, "our banquet is served."

Count Ermano was renowned in Venice for the luxury of his table, for his devotion to bringing rare delicacies to his guests, for the vast variety of his removes. Julietta saw that none of the reports were exaggerated.

His dining hall was as palatial as his grand *sala,* a long chamber of cold white marble and arching, frescoed ceiling, warmed by tall fireplaces at either end. Rich tapestries depicting the wedding feast at Cana muffled the echoing stone of the walls. The polished expanse of table was lined not by mere benches or stools but by cushioned, velvet-upholstered chairs, one for every guest.

A carved, thronelike seat at the head of the table was reserved for the Doge, with their host at his right hand and Marc at his left. Julietta, being of less importance, was seated midway down the table, but Balthazar Grattiano sat beside her. The young man was quiet, as always, sullenly handsome as he offered her choice morsels of meat and fruit.

Julietta scanned the offerings laid out on silver and gold platters. Ermano's generosity, as well as the vastness of his mainland greenhouses, had surely not been exaggerated. Her father's table was renowned in Milan, and her husband's had not been ungenerous, but she had never seen such variety. There were leeks swimming in almond sauce, chicken amarosa, *biancomangiare,* trout stuffed with lemons, pumpkin tortelloni, marinated anchovies, vast basins of zabaglione bobbing with plump strawberries, *fave de Morti,* boiled beef, capon, as well as many dishes she could not identify. Majolica bowls overflowed with glistening rare fruits, sugared almonds teetered in silver cones and wine flowed freely.

Julietta merely sipped at the heady brew. Her head felt light, and this was no place for giddiness. She had to keep all her wits about her.

"A strawberry, Signora Bassano?" she heard Balthazar ask, and she dragged her gaze back to her dining partner. He held a fat, dark pink berry out to her, still so serious and unsmiling.

"Grazie," she murmured, and plucked the fruit from his grasp. It was sweet and juicy as she bit into

it, a rare treat in the midst of winter, but she could not fully enjoy it. She felt so tense and alert; this whole evening set her every nerve on edge. She remembered the tightrope walker in the Piazza, teetering on the thinnest of wires, staring down into an unknowable abyss. The Doge, Count Ermano, Balthazar, Marc— they were all dark mysteries, and they pressed her on all sides.

She studied Balthazar as she munched on the strawberry. That strange sense of familiarity, which she had first felt on the day of the Marriage of the Sea, haunted her yet again. She couldn't figure out why, though. His thin, youthful face promised great beauty, his cheekbones sharp, his nose straight, full lips so often set in that thin, angry line. His dark hair was long and straight, a shining curtain. He had his father's green eyes, but where on Ermano they sparkled with the hard, cold edge of emeralds, on Balthazar they were dark and mossy, as a primeval forest.

Julietta frowned. She did not understand this young man. At his age she had been giddy with naïve hope and enthusiasm, a wild romanticism her marriage killed out of her. He always seemed so wary and watchful, dissatisfied. Yet what did he have to be dissatisfied with? All Venice waited to unfurl itself at his jewelled feet.

Julietta did not like puzzles. They always led to trouble.

"What do you think of our grand hero, Signora Bassano?" Balthazar asked. His gaze fell on Marc, who spoke quietly with the Doge. Balthazar's solemn expression did not alter, but Julietta saw the fine-grained skin along his jaw tighten.

Julietta also gazed upon the little group, the centre of all power in Venice. She did not see that power, though, nor the glittering trappings of politics. She saw only the beautiful man whose caress she craved beyond all reason. The object of all her foolish, reawakened desires.

What did Balthazar see? Something to envy, to emulate? To hate?

"He is—very handsome," she answered carefully.

"So, you wish to join the ladies who flock around him like pigeons on the Piazza? To clamour for his attention?"

"No," Julietta said truthfully, "I do not wish to do that. It is possible to admire something for its beauty without wishing to fight for it, to possess it."

Now, *there* she lied. She longed to possess Marc, to take him into her body, her soul, and know he was hers. But she was too proud, too selfish—too cautious—to "flock" with the others.

She had no desire to compare her tall darkness with their golden delicacy, to bring such negative notice to herself. But she could tell none of that to Balthazar.

"Then you are truly unique," Balthazar said, quiet bitterness underlying his tone. He stabbed at a morsel of gingered veal with his eating knife. "All of Venice worships *Il leone,* even my father."

Julietta glanced at Ermano, who sat back in his chair with a satisfied smile on his face, a king surveying his realm. "I doubt your father 'worships' anything. Except for God, of course, as all mortals must."

"Very tactful of you, Signora Bassano, and you are quite right. My father is far too secure in his own power to be in awe of anyone else's. Yet he *does* admire Signor Velazquez, he confides in him. Perhaps he wishes *Il leone* was his true son?"

Confided in him? Julietta had not known Marc was so very acquainted with Ermano. It chilled her to think of their "confidences". Truly, was there not an ounce of trust to be had in this city? Power came first, and Ermano had power in spades. She was a fool if she ever forgot that.

Julietta toyed with the stem of her goblet, slowly absorbing his words. "And what do *you* think of our guest, Signor Grattiano?"

Balthazar lowered his tone, his voice a mere scratchy mutter in her ear. "I think he is a great fraud."

Julietta's gaze flew up to his face, startled. This was plain speaking, indeed, and rarer than rubies in this world. Was he intoxicated? But, no—his goblet was only half-full, his forest eyes clear. "A fraud?"

"Do you think he is all that he says? A merchant sea captain who just happens to be able to defeat ruthless Barbary pirates? A Spanish businessman who is the consummate courtier, who can worm his way into the highest echelons of our society?" His hand suddenly shot out, grasping her wrist in a hard clasp. "Do you not wonder what he *really* wants here?"

Julietta gasped. At the touch of Balthazar's skin, her

mind was bombarded with dark bursts of colour and emotion. Pain, fear, anger, envy, longing, dark passion, thwarted love. How could her mother's "gift" come upon her again here, now? She had suppressed it so ruthlessly over the years that it usually only came to her in small, easily banished spurts, as on the day she met Marc and he touched her wrist.

Now, she felt sucked into the morass of Balthazar's mind, a tangle of danger and passion. It was an ugly place, and she felt it catching at her soul. She yanked her wrist back from him, her skin cold and clammy. Trembling, she reached for her wine, raising it greedily to her dry lips.

"Forgive me, Signora Bassano," Balthazar muttered. "I did not mean to burden you."

"What do you know about Signor Velazquez?" she whispered. "What have you discovered?"

"Nothing concrete as of yet," he answered. His brooding gaze slid back down the table, not seeing the throng of ever-more raucous guests, flushed with the fine food and drink, sparkling like diamond heavens. He saw only the quiet, intent group at the head of the table. "But I soon will, I promise you."

Julietta was saved from answering as the Doge rose from his seat, bringing silence to the room. He raised his goblet high and said in ringing tones, "We must all drink to the health of Signor Marc Antonio Velazquez, the saviour of our shipping, the very life-blood of our fair city. We give thanks for his strength and bravery, and offer every reward we can lift up."

Goblets were raised all along the table in answer, a murmuring wave of praise and thanksgiving. Marc himself bowed his head in dignified thanks, but Julietta could not help but notice that Balthazar did not truly drink of his wine.

"To *Il leone,* indeed," Julietta whispered. Yet she feared all her good wishes, all the simpers of the ladies, the envious glances of the men, could scarce stand him in good stead in the face of such jealous enemies.

Chapter Eleven

Julietta was utterly exhausted. The cacophony of conversation, the rich food and wine, the brief glimpse into the deepest secrets of Balthazar Grattiano's mind, it all dragged at her senses. Her limbs felt heavy, her brain whirling, as she sat near the door of the grand *sala,* half listening to the music Count Ermano arranged for his guests' after-dinner entertainment. The madrigals were lively and light, a beautiful counterpoint to murmured conversation, to the sweetmeats being passed around, but she could barely hear it.

Balthazar was truly a strange, bitter young man. But his words to her made a certain sense. They were nothing Julietta herself had not thought. What *was* Marc doing here in Venice? What was his sorcery that drew everyone to him—even Julietta?

She rubbed at her temples, staring out over the gathered company. Marc was nowhere to be seen, nor was their host. The Doge sat upon his throne, listening to the music, closely attended by his counsellors. Balthazar was seated in a window embrasure, next to a young blond beauty. She smiled up at him shyly, and he nodded to her in return. Yet, still, there was that strange tightness around his jaw, the wary set of his shoulders.

Julietta remembered the force of his anger, and she shuddered. That poor little blonde.

Suddenly, it was all too much. The crowd, the heat of the air, the perfumes, the wine, the constant dissembling. She was dizzy, overwhelmed. No one was watching her, half-hidden on her stool near the door. She slid to her feet and crept silently from the room.

The corridor was dim in comparison to the brilliant *sala,* lit only by a few flickering sconces casting their glow over the rare Turkish carpets and Florentine paintings. From behind the closed doors of the dining hall she could hear the clink of glass and metal, the splash of water, the chatter of the servants as they cleared the table, no doubt sampling the leftover delicacies. As she tiptoed past, the music from the *sala* faded behind her, leaving only the heavy silence of the house itself.

The silence of a prison, or a tomb.

Julietta found a half-open doorway near the sweeping curve of the marble staircase, and she peeked inside to find a small, deserted withdrawing chamber. There was little furniture, only a table, a low couch, a few chairs, but there was a large window. The clear glass let in a stream of milky moonlight, a glimpse of the healing concealment of night.

She edged inside, drawing the door shut behind her. The solitude enfolded her like a velvet cloak, soothing her taut nerves in the quiet. No one watched her here, no one tried to discover her secrets—or conceal their own. She crossed the room in a few quick strides and unlatched the window, throwing it wide.

This side of the palazzo faced a narrow canal, quieter, yet still a part of the Carnival revels. A few boats floated in the purple-black waters, carrying couples entwined in the shadows. Laughter and murmurs, heady sighs and cries, a low moan, floated up to her, creeping up the stone walls.

Julietta leaned against the window frame, closing her eyes to draw in a breath of night air. The breeze was heavy and moist tonight, thick with the sickly sweet smells of the canal, of perfumes and passion. How she longed to be out there in the night, amid the concealment of masks, the easy desires of the body. Lust was honest, easily answered. Perhaps if she gave in once to her desire, it would be finished. Done. And she could get on with her life.

Yes. Lust was simple. And she did desire Marc's body, his flesh, his kiss, his smell, the hot weight of him on her, inside her. But there was—more. More to *him,* to her feelings for him, to what she saw deep in his fallen angel eyes. And that was what scared her, what held her back.

Balthazar was right. Something was going on, something strange and dangerous. She could not afford to be caught up in it. Yet she very much feared she already was, that the net was already tightening around her.

The door clicked softly behind her, and her eyes flew open. Her hand tightened on the window frame, but she did not turn around. She didn't have to. She knew who stood there, watching her.

Marc.

"What are you doing hiding in here, Julietta?" he asked, his voice low and rough.

And the door slid closed behind him.

What mischief was his sun concocting now?

From his hidden spot in the curve of the staircase, Marc watched the scarlet-clad figure as she slipped away from the party and crept down the corridor. She glanced back over her shoulder, dark eyes narrowed, before she disappeared through a shadowed doorway.

His blood hummed with the thrill of a mystery. His entire body felt taut, drawn up like a bowstring, on edge, as it had ever since he first glimpsed Julietta in the grand *sala*. He had thought—hoped—he had driven her out of his thoughts since they parted in the hazy predawn after Nicolai's party. Thought the memory of her jasmine perfume, the satin feel of her skin, the siren allure of her kiss, was buried in his work. In the victory of edging ever closer to his goal.

But that was not so, and he could no longer lie to himself. The woman he thought to use as a tool, a piece of his puzzle, had wrapped herself around his senses so that she was always with him. Even as he bowed and charmed at the Doge's court, or practised at his sword-play in his deserted room in the afternoon siesta, lunging and feinting until the sweat poured from his back and his mind clouded with battle-lust—even then she was with him. In his bed at night he dreamed of ropes of her hair, of the intimate way she smelled, tasted.

It was lunacy. She was only a woman, a woman full of her own secrets and lies. He was close, so very close, to the realisation of all his plans. He could not let her ruin them, could not let her near. Not that she would permit him to come near at all. He remembered the way she pushed him away at Nicolai's party, her face turned away from his kiss.

Nay—they were not for each other. Yet still he lusted, still he dreamed.

Marc glanced up the dark corridor above the winding staircase, to the room where he was lately closeted with Count Ermano in quiet conversation. It was all silence, only faintly pierced by the music and laughter of the gathering. Then he turned back to the closed door, the carved wood Julietta hid behind.

What could it hurt if he just took one glimpse inside, just to see what his mystery woman was doing?

Of their own volition, his feet carried him down the marble steps to that door. He could not turn away, not now. Leaning close, he listened for any hint of sound. There was none.

Marc twisted the door latch and stepped inside.

She stood framed in the open window, one hand on the frame, limned in amber light, her face turned in profile as she watched the canal below. Her pale skin was striped in shadows, her heavy braid of black hair, twisted with gleaming pearls, glossy over her shoulder. Her lips were parted, her eyes downcast. She was stillness itself, as serene and self-contained—as untouchable—as a frescoed saint.

Somehow her very remoteness made Marc long for her all the more. Made him want to bend her willow-slim body in his arms, kiss her, touch her, until her chill melted away, her façade vanished, and she showed him the very core of her being.

"What are you doing hiding in here, Julietta?" he asked, his voice hoarse and rough even to his own ears. He closed the door behind him and leaned back against it, his arms crossed over his chest. He felt as he so often did before a battle: nerves taut, senses singing with vivid, sharp-edged life.

She was his foe in real life—he should never forget that truth. And she was becoming one of the most formidable he had ever faced.

Julietta gasped, her spine stiffening. He watched, fascinated, as her white fingers tightened on the window frame. "Should you not be with the others?" she murmured.

"I could ask you the same thing," he answered.

Slowly, her hand released its grip and she turned to face him. With her back to the window she was thrown even more into shadow, her tall figure outlined in moonlight. She shrugged her hair back over her shoulder. "I am far too insignificant to be missed," she said. "But you—you are *Il leone*. The guest of honour. Our host will want to show you off."

Marc pushed away from the door and strode towards her, drawn to her by some inexorable, undeniable force. It had drawn him in the banquet room, as well, even across the crowds.

"I think Ermano would be far more likely to miss *you, querida,*" he muttered. He reached for her hand. The skin was cool with the night air, scented with summer roses. His fingers entwined tightly with hers, and he raised their joined hands into the opalescent light. She went very still, yet she did not pull away. Her breath quickened, matching his.

"What do you mean?" she said quietly.

"Our host is in love with you. All of Venice can see that."

Julietta gave a small snort, making him smile. "Ermano is only in love with himself—all of Venice knows *that.* I denied him my property on the mainland, now he is like a child told he cannot have a sweet. Now it is all he wants."

Marc shook his head. He had seen the feverish fire in Ermano's cold green eyes when he spoke of Julietta Bassano. It was the same flame that ignited in the eyes of the Barbary pirate captain when he fancied Marc's ship an easy conquest. "There is more to it than that, and you know it, Julietta."

She gave a low, frustrated sob, and suddenly tugged hard on her hand, trying to free it from his clasp. "I don't want to talk about him!"

Marc merely tightened his hold and reeled her closer, until they stood mere inches apart. Her breasts caught on a breath, their pebbled, velvet-covered tips brushing his chest. His other arm snaked around her waist, drawing her even closer. Her breath was cool and quick against the skin of his throat. She was still, yet he could feel the tensile strength of her aching to break free, like a wild sea-bird caught in a fisherman's net.

But he could not let her go. Not now. Not yet. The need of her was grown to a raging fire in his veins.

He leaned his head close to hers, nuzzling the fine sweep of hair at her temple, inhaling deeply of her jasmine scent. *Maledizione,* but she was intoxicating! "Then we won't talk about him," he whispered closely in her ear. She shivered under his touch. "Let us leave this place."

Her lashes swept down to cover her eyes, lacy spiderwebs against her white cheeks. "The count, the Doge…"

"You said it yourself—we are too insignificant to be missed. Come, this party is dull, anyway. We will find a better one, a more private one."

Those lashes swept upwards, revealing the dark, unreadable pools of her eyes. Their edges crinkled with hidden laughter. "Shall we find your friend Nicolai again? You said he knows all the merriest gatherings."

Marc laughed roughly. "Oh, my sun, we don't need him. We shall make our own merriment."

She shook her head hard, as if shaking off any hesitation. "Very well, then. Let us depart—if we can find our way past our host."

Marc's gaze flashed to the open window. Drawing Julietta with him, he hurried over to lean outside, peering down. As he suspected, there was a narrow flight of stone steps leading down to the *fondamento*. A secret exit for Count Ermano, when he did not want the pomp and attention of his front door.

"This way," he said, swinging himself out of the window. He reached back for Julietta, clasping her around the waist to lift her down, but she stiffened.

"It is a very long way down," she murmured.

"I will always catch you if you fall, Julietta," he answered. "Always."

She studied him closely for a long moment, as if gauging the worth of his vow. The worth of he himself. Finally, she nodded, and he lifted her out of the window into the night.

Chapter Twelve

Julietta held tightly to Marc's hand as he led her down the narrow, slippery staircase. The couples who had occupied the canal earlier were gone now, leaving only the soft sound of water lapping up over the edges of the passage, the click of their steps. There was a dark, oily puddle at the foot of the stairs, and Marc lifted her up to swing her over its foulness.

He did not let her go when the danger to her shoes was past, though. Instead, his hold on her waist tightened, and he spun her in a jubilant circle, as if they were prisoners who just made a daring break for freedom. Julietta laughed, twining her arms about his neck. She pressed tiny, quick kisses to his cheek and jaw, breathing deeply of that seawater scent that was his alone.

It was heady! She felt, indeed, like she *had* broken out of a prison, both the stultifying, formal atmosphere of Ca Grattiano and her own doubts and fears, her own secrets.

They were still there, of course, lurking just behind her desires, ready to leap out again. For this one moment, though, she was free of them all. She had broken free of them, shoved them back into their own prison.

Slowly, Marc lowered her to her tiptoes, still holding her in a loose embrace.

"Where shall we go now?" she asked, sifting her fingers through his fall of hair. It clung to her skin like rough satin.

"First, we find a gondola," he said. "And a bottle of wine."

"And simply drift?"

"Of course. Drift for ever, if my lady so commands it. Or stop wherever her fancy lands."

He turned and hurried out of the narrow canal passage, drawing her with him until they emerged in the light and noise of the crowded Grand Canal. It was the height of the night's revelry, and laughter hung in a brilliant cloud, as thick as the brightly coloured streamers that floated down all around them.

Rather than cross before the lurking behemoth of Ca Grattiano, Marc paused and glanced about until he found what he obviously sought—an unoccupied gondola.

As he hailed the gondolier and leaned down to negotiate with him, Julietta hung back in the shelter of the wall. Torch-bearing pages lined the façade of Ermano's house, and she had no desire for any of them to see her. It was doubtful any of them would report to their master that two people were seen running away from the party, but she did not want to take any chances.

A brightly clad peasant woman sauntered past, a basket over her arm filled with cheap masks. Julietta touched her own cheek, bare for a formal banquet, and called out, "*Scusi, signora!* Two masks, please."

Thus suitably disguised, Marc in a plain black mask and she in shining gold, they settled in their escape gondola and were quickly borne away. They melted into a sea of vessels, hidden by the rising tide of drunken gaiety all around them.

Julietta sank down against the velvet cushions, sighing with pleasure as she tilted her head back to stare up at the night sky. Every nerve in her body relaxed as they drifted away from the treacherous banquet into their own private Carnival.

Marc retrieved a bottle of wine from beneath their seat and opened it. The heady scent of cheap wine floated out, blending with the waters and Marc and her own perfume. "I fear there are no goblets," he said.

"It doesn't matter," Julietta answered. She reached for the bottle and took a long sip. It was rough and strong, not spiced like Ermano's expensive, sweet blends, and its warmth spread right to her toes.

Marc laughed, and tipped his head back as she held the bottle to his lips. As she tilted the drink into his mouth, a tiny rivulet inched its way down his chin, and she did the one thing she *could* do—she licked it away.

His skin was taut and hot under her tongue, slightly

scratchy, the tartness of the wine blending with the slight saltiness of his flesh. The small taste only whetted her appetite for more, and she slid closer, spreading kisses along his jawline, the arch of his throat.

Marc groaned and dragged her against him, his hard arousal pressing tight to her skirts. It awoke an answering need deep inside her belly, a flood of hot, hazy desire. She snatched at the front of his doublet with eager fingers, tearing open the jewelled clasps, untangling the lacings of his silk shirt so she could at last touch the smooth, sweat-damp expanse of his chest. His heart pounded against his skin, and she pressed her palm flat to it, fascinated. How *alive* he was! She craved that life, needed it. Needed *him*.

He covered her hand with his, entwining his fingers with hers. "Julietta," he growled, and she felt the rumble of his voice, the uneven cadence of his breath. "I tried to fight against this…"

"I know," she whispered. "Oh, but I do know!"

"What is this strange sorcery you possess? I have never known a woman like you."

Julietta rested her forehead against his chest, surrounded by the moist, male heat of him. *Strange*—that was exactly what she thought of him. That he was a sorcerer, a sensual sorcerer sent to beguile her away from her purpose, to entrap her in hot pleasure until she could think of nothing else.

"I am just an ordinary woman," she murmured. "And you, Marc Velazquez, are my prince, who saved me from an evening at Ca Grattiano."

He gave a harsh, low laugh. "I am not feeling particularly *princely* right now."

His clasp tightened on her waist, dragging her over his lap until she straddled him, her hands braced on his shoulders. She felt his open palm slide over her hip, pressing the thick velvet of her skirts tight until he grasped the embroidered hem. Slowly, so slowly, he drew it up until her left leg was bare. His rough sailor's fingers slid beneath her ribbon garter, caressing the naked skin of her thigh.

Julietta could not think, could not breathe, could not do anything but *feel*. This was a terrible idea, the very worst, but she was beyond all rationality. If this led to her downfall, her doom, so be it.

For tonight, anyway. This one perfect night.

Julietta tightened her thighs over his legs, feeling the smooth cloth of his hose abrade her bare skin. As he trailed a fiery ribbon of kisses along her throat, pausing to lick at the tiny hollow of her pulse, she let her head fall back, freely offering him all she had. His tongue trailed the line of her low neckline, dipping into the hollow between her breasts. Her nipples ached, straining for his kiss, his touch.

She uncurled one hand from his shoulder to tug at the fabric of her bodice, releasing one pale breast. They were too small, she knew that, particularly compared to the plump peaches of fashionable Venetian courtesans. But she didn't care now, she only wanted to feel his kiss on her skin, the aching fire of his caress.

Marc groaned deeply, a sound so laden with need that it echoed her own. "Julietta—so beautiful."

She stared down at him in the starlight, at the angel's face, the fall of his glossy hair. "Not as beautiful as you."

"The *most* beautiful, *querida*." And he leaned forward to capture her nipple between his lips, rolling it, nipping gently before taking it deep into his mouth to suckle.

Julietta moaned, her very core flooded with hot need. *"Mon amour,"* she whispered in her mother's half-forgotten French language, twining her fingers through his hair to hold him even closer. *"Mon ange."*

His lips slid away from her taut, aching nipple, leaving it glistening, and he blew gently on it. Julietta trembled deeply, and tightened her legs even more over his.

"Julietta," he muttered, holding her close. "You're so—beguiling. But I can't make love to you in a gondola."

She shrugged her bodice back up to her shoulder and glanced around. In another gondola, very near theirs, a couple was doing just that, her satin skirts tossed back as he pumped between her stockinged legs.

Julietta laughed. "Why not? *They* are."

Marc gently set her off of him, and reached down to adjust his hose. "Perhaps my sensibilities are more finely honed than theirs."

Julietta laughed even harder, curling close to his side. She trailed her fingertips down the exposed vee of his chest, tracing the muscled contours, the sharply etched abdomen. "Oh, you are so very sensitive, my pirate."

He caught her hand and raised it to his lips. "I thought I was your angel, your prince."

"And so you are. For tonight." She leaned close and whispered, "We can go to my house. Bianca is gone for the evening."

He glanced down at her sharply, his eyes gleaming in the darkness. "What are we waiting for, then?"

The shop was silent as Julietta closed the door behind them, shutting out the waves of laughter and music from the piazzetta. Only vague shadows drifted over the walls and the polished counter, sparkling off the displayed bottles and oil burners. She pulled off her mask and leaned back against the blue-painted wood for a moment, still breathless from their careless dash along the *calli*. Her body felt heavy, weighted, but tingling with lightning life, glowing with sparks wherever Marc had touched her, kissed her. She wanted *more* now, wanted everything!

She tilted her head back, watching the black outline of his silhouette as he moved to the counter, removing his own mask, bracing his hands on the cold marble. Yes, she desired him; every inch of her being cried out for them to finish what they started in the gondola. Yet she felt strangely shy now. They were alone in the dark quiet of her own home, he stood mere feet away from her. She had only to reach out for him, call his name, and he would be hers. For now. Jungle lions could no more belong to any person than the sun and stars could. The force of his passion told her he would give his all to his lover as she lay in his arms, then vanish with the dawn.

That was what she wanted, was it not? A lover to bring her pleasure, excitement, but not one who would invade her life and secrets. The palpable force of her desire for Marc Antonio Velazquez was a living thing within her, a rising flood not to be denied. Why did she hesitate?

Marc swung towards her, a ray of torchlight from the window falling over his tousled hair, the clean lines of his lean face. "Julietta," he muttered hoarsely, "you are truly not like anyone else."

Julietta gave a strangled laugh at his exasperated words. Of course he would not give her honeyed lies about her celestial beauty, her angelic gentleness. That was for men like Count Ermano, polished and smoothly dishonest. Not for her sea captain, her pirate. "I could say the same about you."

"Then we must be meant for each other."

"So we must," she answered. As if drawn by an invisible golden thread, Julietta pushed away from the door and glided towards him. He held his hand out to her, and she slid her fingers within his warm, strong clasp. He drew her into the circle of his embrace, his other arm circling her waist to hold her fast against him. "For tonight."

"Just tonight?" He bent his head to kiss her throat, his hair trailing silken fire across her cheek. His mouth was open, wet, greedily tasting of her skin.

Julietta looped her arms about his shoulders,

holding him ever closer. She longed to climb inside of him, to lose herself in his very essence, to forget everything else but the way she felt now, this moment. Adrift in a turbulent sea of sensation and emotion, where only the two of them mattered.

She arched into him, rubbing against the iron hardness of his erection. His kiss trailed lower, to the edge of her bodice, his tongue tracing a hot line over the top of her breast.

"Marc!" she cried. "I feel—I'm falling."

"I'll catch you, *querida*," he whispered. "Just as I promised."

Julietta threw her head back, staring up at him in the shadows. His eyes glowed an unearthly pale blue, as if he was turned into the sea itself, roiling with instinctual passion and need, a force never to be denied.

She was beyond denial. Julietta edged away from him, until only their hands were entwined. Without a word, she led him up the narrow stairs to where her chamber waited.

She released him only to open the shutters, letting in filmy, silvery light, the distorted echo of merriment from the square below. For an instant, she pressed her forehead to the cool, wavy glass, letting the chill edge around the fire of her desire. She could scarcely breathe, hardly think! Things were moving so very fast, a flooded river that could not be turned back.

You have the ability to make your own reality, to forge a new direction, she heard the tarot reader whisper in her mind. Could it truly be as simple as that?

There was a hint of sound behind her, a rustle of velvet, and she felt Marc's arms encircle her from behind, drawing her back against his body. His lips lowered again to kiss her temple, her cheek, drawing a ragged line of heat to that tiny, sensitive spot just below her ear. The rush of his breath made her shudder, and she knew that it *could* be that simple. For now.

Anything could happen under the masks of Carnival.

Marc spun her around in his arms, swinging her up until their eyes were level. He studied her closely for a moment, as if to read her thoughts, her very soul. The only sound was their mingled, laboured breath, and, Julietta feared, the deafening drumbeat of her heart.

"Who are you, really?" he said, finally, his voice a jagged whisper.

Julietta touched the very tip of her tongue to her aching lips. "I am only Julietta."

Marc shook his head, a muscle in his jaw working as if he longed to say more, to find the magical words that would draw out the very essence of her.

"No more," Julietta demanded. "No more talking." She clasped handfuls of his slippery, silken hair in her fingers and drew him towards her, claiming his lips with her own.

Marc groaned deep in his throat, his tongue sweeping over her waiting lips into her mouth, a kiss to end all kisses. One of desperate need that had been growing ever since they met, a passion to be lost in and happily never found. There was no art or artifice to it, no calculated method, only desperate seeking, a consuming fire.

Julietta was barely aware of the coolness of the sheets under her back as Marc lowered her to the bed, his body covering hers. She only knew *him,* the smell and feel of him, the delicious weight pressing her down. As their kisses grew ever deeper, more wet and needful, she reached out with clumsy, desperate hands and pushed his velvet doublet off his shoulders, roughly tossing the expensive fabric to the floor. His thin silk shirt, damp with sweat, clung to his shoulders and chest. She trailed her mouth down from his, tracing her tongue over his throat and chest, tasting the heady, salty pungency of his skin.

Marc reared back from her caresses, reaching down to grasp the hem of her gown. He dragged it up, his avid gaze following the line of her silk stockings, her bare thighs above red garters—the black thatch of her womanhood, glistening with her moist need.

He stared down at her, his lips parted, his eyes unreadable. Julietta watched him, panting, her flesh trembling.

"But who are *you?*" she murmured, even as she stretched her arms up to him.

"Who do you want me to be?" he answered, sliding into her caress.

Julietta reached down to the lacings of his hose, freeing the heavy, throbbing, veined length of his manhood into her hand. It tightened under her caress, lengthening from hard and hot to implacable iron. He shuddered deeply as she traced the hot, satin flesh, catching a tiny drop of semen from the tip with her finger. She lifted it to her lips, licking the heavy musk of it from her own skin.

Marc groaned, dropping his head to the hollow between her neck and shoulder, his breath warm on her skin. He lowered himself between her welcoming legs, his thumb searching out the wet centre of her. Julietta cried out at his touch, tracing her wet seam, easing over the tiny, hard pearl hidden in the swollen folds.

"I need you *now,* Julietta," he groaned.

"Yes," she agreed. Only that one word seemed left in her hazy mind. *Yes, yes.* She spread her legs wider, letting him fully inside.

The rough cloth of his hose gently scratched at her bare thighs, but it only drove her need higher. He reached between their bodies, gently parting her with his fingers as he sought entry. Julietta's eyes closed, her head falling back against her pillows as he drove himself home, their bodies joined as one.

He drew back, one slow, tantalising inch at a time, almost sliding out of her wetness. Julietta cried out in protest, and he lunged back inside.

His thrusts were quick, desperate, pounding into her with delicious force. Julietta wrapped her legs about his pistoning hips, keeping him close as her world turned dark at the edges. A humming started deep in her ears, growing ever louder, a rising chorus of ecstasy. Never had her climax started so quickly before! Usually it needed care and coaxing; sometimes it refused to come at all. But now all her senses flew apart, fragmenting in a vast explosion of stars.

She felt like the sun in truth, a great expanse of sizzling heat, of feelings and incoherent sensations.

Above her, Marc cried out, a torrent of Spanish words and syllables of desire. His muscles tensed under her clasp, and he arched back as she felt the hot spurt of his seed deep inside her.

He collapsed beside her to the mattress, their legs still entangled, their hot, laboured breath mingled. Slowly, weightless as a feather, Julietta sank back down to earth. Never had she felt so replete, so relaxed, so confused, so—so tired.

Her desire, denied ever since she met Marc, for the moment was fulfilled, and her very veins felt weighted down with delicious, aching exhaustion. Next to her, Marc's own breathing grew slower, more even.

Julietta eased up to a sitting position, staring down at him. His eyes were heavy-lidded, half closed, and he gave her a lazy grin that made her heart leap anew. He reached out to trace a light caress along her arm, tugging loose the ribbon ties of her sleeves.

"Before you go to sleep, *Il leone,*" she whispered, "unlace my gown."

"Anything my fair lady desires," he answered, his voice heavy with sensual laughter. She turned her back to him, letting him release the thin cords of her lacings. His hands smoothed the velvet of her gown, the silk of her chemise down her body, baring her skin to the night. His tongue followed his hands, a trail of light tastes along the hollow of her spine.

As he cast her garments to the floor with his

doublet, his kiss pressed to the spot just above her buttocks. Julietta shivered, falling back into the curve of his body. He yanked off his ruined shirt and they reclined against the cushions, skin to skin.

As she drifted off to sleep, she felt his gentle touch unplaiting her hair, smoothing the long strands over his chest and throat. Slumber tugged at her, leading her inexorably down into blessed darkness. Still, she could not quite give in to its lure. Never had she allowed another person into her home while she lay in helpless sleep! What about her secret room?

But she had brought the perils of the world into her home, into her very bed, by her own power. Was it only a matter of time until everything dissolved beneath her feet and she vanished into the abyss?

And if she did, did she even care? Julietta had known very well, from the first moment she saw Marc in her shop, the first instant he touched her hand, that making love to him would shift her entire world, sunder all she worked so hard to build. She knew that—and yet still his lure was too great. She reached out and grasped at the fire, knowing it would burn her, consume her.

Her gaze eased over his body, the muscled contours naked and gleaming, dark against her white sheets. She shivered as she remembered the slide of his hands over her skin, the heat of his kiss, how his body filled and stretched hers, completing her so perfectly. *"Querida,"* he had whispered in her ear. *"Mi vida, mi soledad."*

Oh, yes—it was worth it. Julietta had learned long ago that in this life mortals chose their actions, chose their sins, and thus chose to face their consequences. When she left Milan she chose her path, chose to follow her mother's lessons the best way she could. When she took Marc into her bed, she knew there would be a price.

Would she be strong enough to pay when it came due?

She did not know, could not know. But she did have this moment, and she intended to make the most of it. She leaned over his body, relaxed, coiled, damp with their lovemaking. One of her fingertips reached out to circle the flat, brown disk of his nipple, and she heard the sharp intake of his breath.

"Are you awake?" she whispered. Her unbound hair fell around them in a silken curtain as her mouth followed her fingers, her tongue darting out to lick at the pebbled flesh, surrounding it with moisture before blowing on it gently. He tensed beneath her.

"I am now," he growled, grasping handfuls of her hair, pressing her closer against him.

She laughed, scraping her teeth delicately over his chest. Her lips slid down his abdomen, pressing soft, quick kisses that left him groaning for more. "There are still a few hours before dawn," she whispered. "However shall we spend them?"

Her palm slid up until she grasped his turgid manhood, her fingers twisting to gently balance his balls on their tips. His clasp tightened convulsively in her hair. "I can think of a few ways."

"I thought you might," she murmured. And her lips closed around his straining length, warm and pulsing, earthly paradise.

They were as close as two people could be, and it was enough. For the moment.

Chapter Thirteen

The large antechamber of the Doge's Palace was crowded but strangely, eerily silent. The people collected there did not cluster in gossiping knots, as they did at almost every other gathering in Venice. They stood alone along the frescoed walls, faces tightly closed, hands clasped tightly as if in prayer. Occasionally, a pair of lips would move, silently practising a petition, but no sound emerged. There was only the rustle of fine cloth, the shuffle of shoes on the parquet floor, the crisp sound of parchment folding and unfolding.

Marc stood in his own corner, next to a statue of a classical goddess clad in flowing drapery and twisting vines, watching the crowd of supplicants with close interest. Though he had been summoned here by the Doge himself and had no petition to present, he still had to wait patiently. And time hung heavier in this room than anywhere else, an oppressive, humid weight that held them all in the purgatory of politics.

There was no furniture in this waiting room, but the walls were elaborately painted with scenes of the Last Judgement. Brilliantly coloured views of heaven and hell, of serene saints, implacable angels, smoking, red-skinned demons, and tormented, damned souls twisted all around him. It was as if the art illustrated what bliss could be theirs if their requests were granted—and what horrors awaited if they were denied.

Marc turned his back on them, facing instead a scene of St Mark blessing Venice, a golden-haired woman swathed in white silk and crowned with gold and emeralds. Easier on the eyes by far.

Marc did not know why he waited there, why he was awakened this morning from his uneasy slumber in his rented room to be presented a heavily sealed summons to the Doge's Palace. He had only returned to his own lodgings a few hours before, stealing through Venice in the predawn glow after reluctantly rousing himself from Julietta's warm bed. He smiled now to recall how she had looked as he'd kissed her one last time, her tall, elegant body wrapped in rumpled sheets, hair tangled over her shoulders. Her eyes were heavy, slumberous as she'd held him against her.

"'Tis not yet near day," she'd whispered. "Don't go yet."

And, by St Mark, but he was tempted! Tempted to deepen his kiss, to lose himself again in her arms, her body, until reason had no place yet in the world.

Even still, in this formal place, he thought he smelled the perfume of her hair, heard her low, soft laughter in his ear....

Marc shook his head hard. Memories of the night before, of the wild, sweet eroticism he found in Julietta Bassano's bed, had no place in the hard light of a new day. The Doge's Palace was a luxurious, palatial pit of vipers. Distraction was dangerous.

He dragged his gaze away from Venice and her white silks, dragged his mind away from Julietta clad in nothing but her own pale skin, and studied the others who waited. There was only one chair in the vast chamber, a tall-backed seat of carved wood cushioned in dark blue velvet. The lady who sat there did not appear as the others, who were either frankly tense and nervous, or covering their tension with haughty pride. She looked—angry.

Once she must have been a rare beauty, but now her oval face bore heavy jowls, deep lines around her eyes and nose emphasised by thick white powder. Her substantial frame was swathed in matte black satin; a floor-length black lace veil covered her white hair. Her only jewellery was a large jet-and-amethyst cross clasped around her neck, but its dull gleam was nothing to the burning fire of her dark eyes. They peered out at the world from the snow-white rolls of her face with a malevolent glare.

Until they landed on Marc—and lingered in speculation. He gave her a bow, and she rose creakily from her seat, moving towards him with a crisp rustle of silk, like a ship in full sail. "Do you know me, young man?" she said. "I am Signora Landucci."

Marc felt strangely like a deer caught in the sights of a carnivorous lion, yet he could not seem to move away. He was caught in the trap of his own cursed curiosity. Who was this woman, and what did she want?

Scarcely had she spoken to him than the great double doors at the far end of the room swung open. A page, clad in the Doge's white-and-gold livery, stepped forward to call out, "Signor Marc Antonio Velazquez, the Doge will now grant you an audience."

"Excuse me, *signora*," Marc murmured, sliding around the woman's dark bulk.

But she reached out and grabbed his arm as he passed her, her plump, white hand like a vise on his green velvet sleeve. "Beware the perfumier, *signor*," she hissed. "She killed my son, Michelotto. And I will prove it."

Marc merely nodded to her and continued on his path to the doors, but his heart thudded heavily in his chest. *Beware the perfumier.* What trouble was swirling around his lover? He knew she held secrets in her heart he could not begin to fathom. Yet they were hers to hold or to reveal, as she would.

Unless they encompassed him, as well. A scented miasma that would wrap them both in disaster.

The page led him up the wide staircase, past various servants hurrying on their errands, and clusters of petitioners leaving their own audiences and making their way out into the daylight. To Marc's surprise, he was not led to the immense council room, but into a smaller, windowless *sala*.

The chamber was dim, shadowed, the walls hung with dark tapestries. It took a moment for Marc's eyes to adjust to the gloom after the dazzling brightness of the white marble staircase. He blinked, and saw that the Doge sat on his throne at the far end of the room, surrounded by his counsellors in their black robes and red sashes, and Ermano Grattiano. He gave Marc a small, secret nod.

"Signor Marc Antonio Velazquez, your Excellency," the page announced, and backed out of the room as Marc made his way forwards to bow low.

"Ah, greetings, Signor Velazquez. I have been looking forward to seeing you again after our interesting conversation aboard my *Buccintore*," the Doge, Andrea Gritti, called. Though Gritti, once a great military hero and commander of all the Venetian armies, was now well into his seventies, his eyes still glowed with sharp intelligence. His body beneath the red-and-gold robes coiled with burly strength. He was no mere puppet, as so many Doges before him had been. Even Marc could see that.

The question was, what did the great Gritti want with *him* on this day?

"Your Excellency," Marc greeted.

"I apologise for the delay," the Doge went on. "There are always so many appointments to grant, but we know that your time is very valuable while you are in our city, and we will not keep you for long this afternoon."

"I am happy to be of assistance in any way I can," Marc answered.

"You have been of great use to us since your arrival," the Doge said. "And we are most grateful. Yet now we have a new threat to our fair Republic."

Marc frowned. "Pirates again, your Excellency? My ship can be quickly readied...."

"No, no. Something rather closer to home now, I fear. You know of the deaths lately of some of my counsellors, men of the Savio ai Cerimoniali?"

Of course Marc knew of them. They were whispered of everywhere, the suspicious ends of those powerful men—including that black-clad lady's son, her "Michelotto". But he had to admit he had not paid a great deal of attention to the tale. It was mere gossip, peripheral to his own task. "Yes, I have heard of it. I am sorry for your losses, your Excellency."

The Doge waved away the condolences, his ducal ring flashing. "At first it appeared their deaths were only linked by their positions, yet now it seems that the manners of their demise were similar, as well. We have spoken to their servants and their families, and each man perished in much agony. There was blood, vomit, the death's rictus."

Marc's skin turned cold. "Poisoned?"

"It could well be. Poison is sadly not unheard of in our fair city. Those men were all involved in very delicate foreign negotiations, and their loss is a heavy one for the Republic, as well as for their own families." The Doge drew in a deep sigh. "Signor Landucci's mother has been particularly persistent in her demands for justice."

Marc could well imagine, after his own brief but vivid encounter with the lady. "How can I be of help? I am a sea captain, your Excellency, I have little knowledge of poisons and murders. I also know little of the residents of Venice."

"Yet you do know one." The Doge held out his hand, and one of the ministers gave him a small sheaf of papers. "These anonymous accusations were placed in the lion's mouth. They state that there is one common link between these dead men—their wives or mistresses are regular patrons at the perfume shop of Signora Julietta Bassano."

Julietta? Marc's entire body froze at the sound of her name, nerves singing as if for battle. His fingers automatically reached for his sword, but he had been forced to surrender it at the palace portal. "You—believe Signora Bassano to be a poisoner?"

The Doge pressed his fingertips together, studying Marc over the steeple. "Perhaps the provider of the poison? Perfumes are often a convenient way to convey foul substances."

"Signora Bassano is not a native of our city. And it is very easy to conceal the poisons in the oils," one of the counsellors commented. He and Ermano exchanged a glance.

"And an easy thing for ladies to purchase and utilise," said the Doge. "All of Venice knows that the Landucci match was not as—harmonious as one would wish." He held up the papers. "These are anonymous, of course, and cannot be acted upon without witnesses. But they do make a great deal of sense. We have seen this sort of thing too many times before. What do you know of Signora Bassano, Signor Velazquez?"

What did he know of Julietta? Everything—and nothing at all. He knew her taste, her scent, the rake of her nails across his naked shoulders, the twist of her legs around his hips. All the secrets of her body—none of her heart.

"I know that she owns a perfume shop," he answered carefully. "That she has an important place in this city, a wide clientele. That she has far too much honour to betray the Republic, her home, in such a foul way." That she could never devise a murderous poison and give it to a dissatisfied wife—could she?

The Doge slowly nodded, his ministers impassive and watchful around him. Even Count Ermano merely studied the floor gravely, as if he scarcely knew Julietta Bassano and her fate was of little interest to him. As if he had never asked Marc to spy on her. "You appear to have a high opinion of the lady," Andrea Gritti said.

"I do, your Excellency. Though I fear I do not know her as well as I would like."

"Of course. You only met a few days ago. Perhaps she has told you she did not always live in Venice?"

"Yes," Marc answered. "I believe she came from Milan."

"So she did. Her husband, Giovanni Bassano, was from one of the great old families of that city, well known for their service to the Sforza. A man of much power and renown, Bassano was. There was some surprise when his widow chose to establish herself as a shopkeeper in Venice, though, of course, the Republic welcomes anyone with useful skills to offer."

And with much coin to offer, as well, Marc believed. "Signora Bassano has expressed to me her great gratitude to Venice for providing her a new home, her joy at living here." While that was not quite true, Marc *did* see that Julietta belonged here, in this city of masks and dark waters, that she fit here. "I am sure she cannot be the murderer you seek."

The Doge nodded, and handed the papers back to the counsellor. "I am sure you are right, Signor Velazquez, but we must follow every clue. Justice must be served. We merely wanted to seek your opinion of Signora Bassano. I am sure you will inform us if you discover anything that forces a change of opinion."

"Certainly, your Excellency," Marc replied.

"*Va bene,* Signor Velazquez. We take our leave of you, then."

Marc gave one last bow and left the oppressive chamber. He passed the black-clad Signora Landucci on the stairs as she was led up to her own audience. She gave him an imperious nod, but Marc scarcely saw her. His mind was full of nothing but Julietta.

She was in danger, he could feel the intense heaviness of jeopardy all around, as if a storm approached and they lay vulnerable on open seas. He was no good defending her with words; he was no courtier, like

Count Ermano, able to smoothly turn every tide to his benefit. He was a warrior, a man of the sword and the cannon. But he could not turn his ship's guns to rumour and whispers.

Julietta, Julietta, he thought darkly, as he took his sword and cloak from the page. *What have you done?* If he could only snatch her up, carry her to his ship and bear her far away from this place, to a land where they could be safe.

Yet there was no such spot, no country where they were safe from themselves.

Outside the palace, the Piazza bustled with life and movement, ordinary daily business amid the merchants, the beggars, the bankers. High up over the entry he spotted a stone lion, propping up a book with his massive right paw. "Rest here, Mark my evangelist" was carved there. But Marc knew he could find no rest.

As he turned his steps instinctively towards her shop, he was stopped by a voice calling after him.

"Signor Velazquez!" he heard Count Ermano cry.

Marc glanced over his shoulder to see Ermano emerging from the palace, escaped somehow from the darkened audience room—and from Signora Landucci. The emeralds sewn to the trim of his black cloak sparkled and winked. "Count Ermano," Marc answered.

"I am sorry you had your day interrupted for such a matter," Ermano said. "You and I both know that Signora Bassano will soon be cleared of any such suspicions, particularly if she has your help."

"I am sure of it," Marc said calmly.

Ermano drew him aside, into the shadows of the portal where they were away from the noisy crowds. "But what of my own errand with the lady? Do you sense that success will soon be at hand?"

Marc studied the man carefully in the half-light. It was hard to read Ermano; the man was far too practised in concealing his true thoughts behind dazzling smiles and a cold green gaze. But his shoulders were taut with eagerness as he leaned towards Marc, reaching for his arm.

Marc fended off his touch by raising his hand. The ruby ring on his smallest finger glowed, giving him strength.

"It is difficult to say," Marc said. "Signora Bassano is not one to tell her deepest business."

"Indeed, she is a most alluring mystery. Yet surely she likes you—you are *Il leone!* And if you help her in this most dire matter she will be even more certain to follow your counsel. She is only a woman, after all, reliant on a man's better sense." Ermano glanced away, touching his lips with the tip of his tongue as if anticipating a delectable feast. "Her lands will surely be mine before the summer."

Marc drew away from him, his skin clammy with sudden repulsion. "Perhaps she will have much more to worry about than her estates—like her neck."

"No, no," Ermano said dismissively. "You must continue as you have in befriending her. No one else I sent had any success at all. Now, I must return to the Doge. We will talk again very soon."

As the count hurried away, Marc turned from the palace. The Basilica glittered, all gold leaf and glowing bronze in the pale winter sun. The throng was thick in the Piazza, teeming with laughter and quarrels and life. It was beautiful beyond belief—and it suddenly looked rotten, ominous. He longed for the clean purity of the ocean, where the dangers were vast yet impersonal, where the elements and even the pirates could be battled honestly.

He had been on land far too long. He needed to finish this.

Marc swung away from the crowd and strode off through the *calli,* his steps carrying him towards Julietta's shop. The blue-painted door was open, and he could hear the rising rhythms of feminine chatter and giggles, the high-pitched barks of lap-dogs.

He had no desire to be drawn into such flutter and flurries right now. He was taut with anger, with hot battle lust—and with lust of a more amorous sort, for the absolution of Julietta's passion, the glory of her body and her mouth.

Cautiously, he stepped up to the window, peering inside. She stood behind her gleaming counter, holding up an ivory tray of oil bottles for a patron's inspection. She was dressed again in stark black and white, but her hair was uncovered, a glossy coronet of black braids unadorned by jewels or ribbons. She looked so elegant, so solemn, so intent on her work— so far from the wild temptress she was last night as she boldly climbed astride his body.

His chest tightened as he watched her, his beautiful, magical lover, and he knew he would protect her with everything he had.

Everything.

Chapter Fourteen

It grew late. The sun was sinking below the horizon, reaching out tendrils of pink and orange and lavender, as if to cling to the remnants of the day. The *campi* outside the shop was abandoned after the bustle of the afternoon, as everyone had vanished into their homes to prepare for the evening's festivities. Only one page boy was still there, filling a bucket from the bubbling water of the fountain.

Julietta paused to take in the scene as she drew the shutters closed, to watch the sunset turn the pale gray stone of the houses to a liquid gold. It was surely the most beautiful part of the day, so fleeting and precious, so quiet and pure after the rush of the day. Before the wild dissipations of the night.

She rubbed at the ache at the small of her back. It had been such a busy afternoon, filled with patrons and gossip. There was to be a grand, glorious ball at the Doge's Palace to close Carnival, and everyone wanted to order a new scent for the occasion. Something unique, something no one else would have. She and Bianca were kept running, filling out the orders, and supplying more commonplace demands for lemon water and rose musk. As quickly as she could bottle the ingredients they were sold.

But the rush was a good thing. It filled her coffers with coins—and kept her from thinking of Marc all day long.

Not that he was truly ever far from her thoughts. He was still a favourite source of gossip and speculation among her patrons, of laughing feminine observations and shy blushes.

Once, when his name was mentioned and a young courtesan made a shrewd comment about how vigorous his "mast" must be, Julietta nearly dropped a precious blue glass vessel. It was all she could do to keep from giggling and blushing just like the others!

But truly she had never known anything like last night, never lost herself so into the force of passion and need. All she knew, all she saw, was him, and even her work could not save her.

Julietta leaned her forehead against the window glass, watching as the steely-gray edge of night crept across the courtyard. Soon it would be full dark, the masks and cloaks would appear and the cares of real life forgotten. But would she see Marc again? Or had he gained all he wanted from her, and would now vanish back to his true love—the sea?

Her heart gave such a pang at the thought, a sour

ache. Such longings were dangerous. It surely meant she began to care, and that could only lead to pain. To trouble. Better if he did *not* appear tonight. She could start to forget him all the sooner.

Yet even as she slammed and locked the shutters, closing out the temptations of the night, she knew it would never be so easy to forget him. Something inside of her had changed at his touch, and it would not be changed back so simply.

Julietta hurried back behind the counter, busying herself with straightening the array of bottles there, wiping up a few spilled drops of oil. Perhaps she should leave Venice for a time after Carnival was finished, go to her farm on the mainland and rest in quiet as she contemplated her sins for Lent. She could study, work—forget about blue-eyed pirate. Perhaps in one of her mother's books there was a recipe for a memory-loss potion.

But even as the whimsical thought crossed her mind, she knew it would not work. Marc was too strong a presence for such spells. A part of him would merely hide away in a corner of her mind, linger there for ever, refusing to be banished.

Bianca emerged from the store-room with a pail and sponge and set about scrubbing at the floor. Dozens of feet had left tracks of dust and mud, and Signora Mercanti's lap-dog paid them yet another visit. Bianca muttered about dirty mongrels as she scoured away, her striped skirts spread about her like flower petals.

"What would you think about closing the shop for a few weeks after Carnival, Bianca?" Julietta asked. "We could go to the mainland for a while. We do no business here while people are intent on their penance, and we could use the rest. You especially; you have worked so hard these last few weeks."

Bianca slowly sat back on her heels, brushing aside a loose black curl with the back of her hand. For an instant her eyes flashed with something strangely like dismay. Then she glanced back down, emotions hidden. "It is true that our patrons usually don't return until after Easter, but there is always work to do, *madonna*. Stocks to replenish, orders to fill…"

"True, but we could do all that from my farm. But if you wish to stay in the city, of course you can."

Bianca looked up again, eagerly. "I could run the shop for you while you are gone! You have taught me so much, but there are still things I need to learn for myself. You could trust me, *madonna*—I would be the best caretaker! You could rest and not worry about a thing, I vow."

Julietta regarded her maid with some surprise. It was true that Bianca had always been a hard worker, an eager pupil. She did all that was asked of her, observed all of Julietta's lessons on the creation of fine scents. She was a good companion, as well. Julietta just had not realised that perhaps Bianca wished for more, might like more responsibility, more autonomy.

And she found she was most reluctant to give the

shop she had built so painstakingly into the hands of another. Even Bianca.

"It is true that I could not run the shop without you, Bianca," she said carefully. "We will see what happens in the next few days."

Bianca nodded and went back to her chore, but Julietta could tell she was a bit disappointed by the answer.

"You should go out tonight," Julietta went on. "I can keep a watch on things here."

Bianca slanted her a sly, teasing little smile. "Will *Il leone* be paying a call later?"

"Nay!" Julietta snapped, sharper than she intended. "I expect no one."

Bianca shrugged. "As you will, *madonna*. Perhaps I will go out. There is to be music and feasting in the Turkish quarter tonight. It has been a very long time since I tasted *baba ganoush*."

Her voice sounded wistful. "Do you ever feel homesick for your land, Bianca?" Julietta asked, going on with her task of straightening bottles.

"It has been many years since I saw Turkey," Bianca answered. "My life here is better than it ever could have been in Constantinople. But there are certain things I miss, yes. The smell of cinnamon in the air. The sounds of the marketplace. The call to prayer from the minarets. The taste of baklava! I should have listened closer when my mother tried to teach me how to make it."

Julietta laughed. "I, too, miss things from my child-hood home, though I would never want to live in Milan again." And she had tried hard never to look back. The past would tear at her heart if she let it.

"What do you miss, *madonna?*" Bianca asked.

Julietta opened her mouth to answer, to tell Bianca of the women's quarters of their home, the domain of her mother and grandmother, where there was always laughter and perfume and books. She was interrupted by a short, sharp knock at the door.

Her hand automatically flew to her hair, to be sure it was tidy; her heart leapt in her breast. What if it was Marc, come to whisk her away into the night?

Bianca sprang up to go answer the door, pulling back the bar to swing the panels open. It was not yet so late that they had to be very cautious.

For an instant, Julietta thought it *was* Marc, and she reached out to grasp the edge of the counter for support. The man was tall, draped in a long, dark hooded cloak, standing back in the evening shadows. Then he stepped forwards, throwing back his hood, and Julietta's heart sank. Far from being the man she longed to see, it was one she would rather never lay eyes on again.

Ermano Grattiano.

He gave her a charming, cold smile, his eyes gleaming as he came towards her. "Signora Bassano," he said, his voice low and intimate. He swept back his cloak to reveal a yellow satin doublet, trimmed in glossy sable fur. He untied the cape and swirled it away, handing it off to Bianca, who promptly scurried away into the store-room.

Julietta could scarcely blame her, even as she cursed her for the abandonment. Ermano seemed—different tonight. Even more intense, more on edge. He fairly glowed with some strange inner tension.

Julietta curtsied, and said, "Count Ermano. What a surprise. Have you come for more perfume? I fear our supplies of bergamot are rather low at present…."

"No, no, Signora Bassano. I merely have come to return this." He held out a length of red velvet—the cloak she wore to his banquet. "You left so hastily last night you forgot it."

Julietta felt her cheeks heat as she recalled *why* she departed Ca Grattiano so hastily. *"Grazie,"* she murmured, reaching for the heavy fabric. "I apologise for departing before taking my leave. The hour had grown so late, I was weary."

"I confess I was rather disappointed." He leaned closer, carefully studying her face as if to read her inner emotions there. Julietta held herself still, cool and remote. "I wanted to introduce you to the Doge."

"That is most kind of you, Count Ermano," she replied. "But surely I am far too insignificant to be brought to the attention of the Doge."

"Not at all. I am sure you have the potential to become the most significant woman in the Republic. If you wished it."

Julietta frowned in puzzlement. "I am happy with my own station, Count."

"Of course. For now." He leaned back, his gaze roving restlessly over her empty, darkened shop. His hands rested in fists on her counter, opening and closing, his gold signet ring flashing. "Tell me, Signora Bassano, what did you think of my home?"

"It was very beautiful. Your hospitality is surely without equal in Venice," Julietta said, a bit taken aback by the quick changes of subject. Ermano *did* seem frantic tonight, a mania hidden beneath his fine clothes and manners. Julietta was half tempted to touch his wrist, to read his emotions—but she feared she did not want to see what was happening there. It would surely overwhelm her.

"I do enjoy seeing my friends in my house, giving them the finest food and entertainment I can," Ermano said. "Of what use are riches if we cannot share them? But how much more glorious such evenings would be if there was a proper hostess at the foot of my table."

This was not the first time Ermano hinted of such things to her. He spoke of how his home's furnishings were outmoded and needed a lady's soft touch. How the rooms of his palace required the laughter of strong children to bring them alive. She would have thought he was attempting to woo her, if such a thing was not unfathomable. She was a foreigner, a shop owner; he must marry a patrician. That was her only comfort when he spoke so strangely to her.

Tonight, though, a twinge of disquiet sounded deep in her soul. Something was very amiss.

She stepped back. "Your banquet was perfection itself, Count Ermano."

"Except that the most important guest left far too

early," he said, his voice filled with smiling charm. "Please, Signora Bassano, allow me to arrange for a private presentation to the Doge, in the ducal palace. Then we will dine quietly in my home. There is much I long to say to you, much you must hear."

Now Julietta *knew* she was in danger. She curled her hand around one of the taller perfume bottles, prepared to smash it and use it as a weapon of she had to. "This—is very sudden."

Ermano shook his head. "You must know of my great admiration for you, Signora Bassano." He took a step closer, allowing no distance, and her free hand automatically came up. He paused, his smile widening. "But, yes, it *is* sudden. Forgive me. I will leave you now to ponder my invitation, and will expect your answer within a day or two. Please believe me, *signora,* my admiration is most sincere. I wish only to persuade you of the advantages of sharing my life."

"If this is about my property…"

Ermano's face took on a wounded cast. "Certainly not! At first I did want only to buy your land; it would add much to my estate. Then I saw that you yourself could add far more." He reached for her hand before she could stop him, raising it to his lips.

Julietta shuddered at the touch of his mouth to her skin. It was smooth, practised, romantic—and repulsive. She slid her hand away from his clasp, tucking it into the folds of her skirt.

"Bianca!" she cried. "Count Ermano is leaving."

He gave Julietta an eerily gentle smile, as Bianca dashed out of the store-room with his cloak. "Until later, then, *signora*." At the open door, he suddenly turned back towards her and said, "I hope you know I am completely sincere. I will eagerly await your answer." He reached back for his cloak, forcing Bianca to step into the doorway to return it.

After the door closed behind him, and Bianca shot the locks into place, Julietta sagged against the edge of the counter, uncurling her fist from the bottle. She shivered as if she stood out in a snowstorm, and she wrapped her arms tightly around her waist. How she longed to run, to flee! To disappear into the night.

This could not be happening. Not now.

"What did he want, *madonna?*" Bianca asked.

Julietta shook her head. She hardly knew what to say. "To return my red cloak." She spun around suddenly and dashed up the stairs as if demons chased at her heels. She needed the silence, the solitude of her chamber, until she could think calmly again. She needed to rid her skin of Ermano's perfume.

"Boil me a great quantity of water, Bianca," she called back over her shoulder. 'With lemon and lavender."

Alone in her room, she shed herself of her clothes and removed the pins from her hair, shaking the heavy black strands loose over her shoulders. She took in a deep breath, then another and another, until serenity settled around her like a cloud.

Yes, Ermano's sudden suit was an unlooked-for

difficulty. He was not a man to accept rejection grace-fully—or at all. Yet if there was one thing she had learned from her grandmother, it was that no problem was insurmountable. There was always a solution.

One way or another.

The door to Julietta's shop opened, spilling out golden candlelight to the stones of the courtyard. Marc paused in his steps, his eager stride to her home, and slid into the darkened shelter of an archway, where once he and Nicolai had spied on that very building. Gossip was unavoidable in Venice, an inescapable part of life; it was nearly impossible to keep a secret in the close quarters of a water-bound city. But he saw no need to flaunt their new affair to every patron of the perfumery!

He adjusted his mask, the cloak hood that covered his hair, and watched as a tall shadow broke through the bar of light. The man half turned to take his cloak from the maid, and called out, "I will eagerly await your answer."

Ermano. Marc shrank back even farther into the concealing gloom, his fingertips resting on the hilt of his dagger as he watched the man bow and reach out to teasingly flick one of the maid's wiry ringlets. As the count made his way across the *campi,* marching through the gathering crowds as if he did not even see their curious stares, the door slammed shut and the shop was encased in darkness.

What was Ermano doing there with Julietta so late at

night? What answer did he await from her? Perhaps he had come to inform her of the accusations made against her, to offer her "protection" in these dangerous days.

Marc's jaw tightened, a wave of fury rushing through him at the thought of Ermano touching Julietta with his soft hands, drawing her body close to his. Never mind that Marc himself had planned to use Julietta, use her gifts, her passion; had coldly calculated what part she could take in his schemes. Those chilly ideas were swept away now in a burst of flames, of anger towards Ermano and his reptilian ways.

He longed to run after Ermano, to leap on him in the dark *calle* and plunge his dagger into the man's throat. He would have his revenge at last, though not in the carefully precise, delicately plotted way he had thought. Ermano would have paid with his blood, and Julietta would be safe from him for ever.

Yet even as he turned towards the archway, watching as Ermano was joined by Balthazar and two other sword-bearing *bravos,* Marc knew such an improvised murder would do no good. Ermano might be dead, yes, but then so would Marc. No one would know the truth of the exalted Grattiano, and Julietta would be left vulnerable to enemies who would attack her through the lion's mouth.

Not much longer, he told himself. Then he would have all he had worked for.

He swung back in the direction of the shop, hurrying across the flagstones. The crowd, rather sparse only moments before, had grown thicker, a tangle of masks

and laughter. Torches flared into life around him, wine
flowed red as blood in the fountain. Yet Julietta's
dwelling had grown dark, the only light a square of
amber from her chamber window. He stood beneath
that glowing beacon like a heartsick swain, watching,
straining for even a glimpse of her.

What a fool I am, he thought wryly. Worse than the
characters Nicolai played in his *commedia dell'arte,*
trailing around after Columbine as she led her clown
on a merry, futile dance. He was caught in some
ancient witchcraft, a spell that wrapped him in hot,
silken pleasure and made him forget all else. The
future—the past. And yet he found he did not want to
break free. He *could* not break free.

A flicker of a shadow passed behind the glass, a silhouette of a woman, her arms raised as she combed
her hair. Marc reached inside his cloak and withdrew
the perfume eggs he bought before coming here. He
remembered her laughing contempt of the inferior
scent that filled the delicate shells, and wished he
could replace it with her own jasmine perfume. Still,
it was better than breaking her glass with stones, or
inviting a dagger in the shoulder by climbing through
her window uninvited.

He tossed the egg towards her shadow, and it splat-
tered against the window frame. It took two more, all
he had, before she came to throw open the casement
and peer down at him. She frowned as her gaze
searched the doorstep, her hand clutching her brocade
robe close about her throat. Her hair fell free over her

shoulders, damp from a washing, as black and opaque as the night.

"Who is there?" she called, her voice tight. "Show yourself!"

"'Tis only me, *querida*," he answered softly, stepping into a square of light. He pushed back his hood. "I did not mean to frighten you."

"Marc!" A smile eased over her face, softening its tense contours. "You came."

"Did you doubt that I would? My sun has little faith."

She waved her hand in an impatient gesture, and said, "Stay there, I will let you in."

He watched as she withdrew back into the chamber, pulling her window closed behind her. He glanced back at the square, but no one appeared to be watching them. Musicians has struck up a lively *branle,* and there was the thunder of dancing footsteps, the roar of merriment.

It was a mere moment before the scrape of a door unlocking met his ears, and the wood swung open to admit him. He slid inside—and found himself in Julietta's arms.

"Marc," she whispered, pressing him back against the closed door. Her quick, elegant fingers, still scented with the oils of her bath, reached for the ties of his mask. The black strip of cloth fluttered to the floor, leaving him utterly exposed.

"Julietta," he groaned, reaching for her. Her robe was loose, and he slid his arms through the fur-trimmed opening, around the soft warmth of her naked body. Her skin was still damp, slick with lavender oil, and the feeling of her flesh, the narrow span of her waist, the weight of her breasts, so familiar yet so mysterious, heated his blood until it sizzled in his veins.

"It has been too long," he muttered, burying his face in her hair, his lips seeking the curve of her neck. She tasted of lavender and lemon, and, too, of clean water and Julietta. *So beautiful.*

She laughed, the sound low and rough on his skin. "We only parted this morning."

"At dawn. It has been hours. An eternity."

Her arms tightened about his shoulders, her head falling back for his kisses. "And we have another eternity until the next dawn. How shall we fill it?"

He raised his head, staring down at her. Her eyes gleamed in the darkness, her lips parted enticingly. He *should* fill it with warning her of the danger she was in, of making his confessions to her and begging her for absolution. But when he kissed her, his mind whirled like a drunkard's, his world upended, and words would not come.

"I want to show you something," he said impulsively. There was only one place now where he could find words, where he could truly be his deepest, most hidden self. He had never shown it to a woman before, yet he wanted to show it to Julietta. To let her see his soul, just this once, before he lost it for ever.

Julietta laughed, leaning into the edge of his body. "That sounds most promising. Shall you show it to me here, or must we go to my chamber?"

The tips of her breasts, pebbled berries begging for

his touch, pressed against his thin linen shirt. Marc moaned deeply, his engorged manhood screaming at him to lower her to the floor, to couple with her then and there! He set her back, though, his hands gentle and firm on her shoulders. As he sucked in a lungful of much-needed air, she stared up at him with a puzzled little frown.

"It isn't something like that," he said raggedly. "Go get dressed, my sun. We have to go out."

"Out where? Would it not be better to stay here? Bianca will be leaving soon…."

Marc shook his head. "It is too large for me to bring to you."

Julietta smiled, obviously puzzled yet intrigued. "What should I wear to see this—large object?"

"Something warm."

She studied him very carefully for a moment before slowly nodding. "Very well. I will only be a moment."

She tucked her robe around her nakedness, turning towards the stairs. Suddenly, she swung back, her voice reaching out to him in the darkness. "Will I be sorry I went with you, Marc?"

"I hope not," he answered, as honestly as he could. One day soon, they would probably all be sorry he came to Venice at all. But not tonight.

She made no reply, just dashed up the stairs, her foot-steps softly pattering on the smooth wood. Above, her chamber door closed and he was alone in the deserted shop. The smell of her skin and hair surrounded him, an intoxicating brew he feared he would never be rid of.

Marc pushed away from the wall and crossed over to the counter. The marble was wiped clean, polished to a high gleam in the moonlight from the window. A few clear glass bottles lined the edge, but the precious faceted, coloured containers with the jewelled stoppers his own vessel had carried to Venice were locked away. Jars of lotions gleamed on high shelves, and oil burners lurked in the corners. All was tidy, quiet, beyond suspicions of poisonings—or witchcraft.

He glanced towards the stairs. There was a murmur of feminine voices that floated from above, but he was still alone. If only he could discover her secrets here…

But there was no time. The chamber door opened above, a burst of laughter spilling out, and Marc backed away from the wall. When Julietta appeared, wrapped in a heavy black cloak, he stood idly by the counter.

"All right, *signor,*" she said. "I am ready for my adventure."

The whore in Balthazar's arms giggled and sighed, wriggling with pleasure as his hand slid up her split red satin skirt. They stood braced against the rough stucco wall along the side of Julietta Bassano's shop, within sight of the teeming courtyard, yet half concealed in the shadows.

This was perhaps not exactly what his father had in mind when he commanded Balthazar to guard the widow's house and watch her comings and goings, but a man had to have *some* amusement. Julietta Bassano seemed a strange and mysterious woman, yet in truth she appeared to live a most dull life. The shop was dark and tightly shut since his father left, and surely Balthazar had missed nothing in the few moments it took to follow this luscious piece into the alleyway and lift her skirts.

"Ah, *signor*," she breathed, her thighs spreading wide for his seeking hand. The upper part of her face was masked, but her carmined lips were full, her teeth white and even. The hair that trailed in long tendrils down her back was a pale red-gold. She was no ordinary street *putta*, surely. Despite his father's low opinion of him, he did have *some* standards.

Balthazar grasped her slender waist and lifted her up against the wall, leaning into her hard as her legs came around his hips. Her moans were low and breathy in his ear. They were possibly practised, learned from her "abbess" in her brothel, but the wetness he felt against his fingers was real enough.

Sì—at least he was useful for *something*, despite the contempt his father showed for him every day. Even if it was just pleasuring sluts.

He reached down to unlace his codpiece, his penis straining for release, when suddenly the door to Julietta Bassano's shop swung open. A low murmur, a whisper, a laugh carried to him on the night breeze, and then the lady herself emerged. She was muffled in a hooded cloak, but Balthazar knew it had to be her. The figure was too tall and slender to be the little Turkish maid. And with her was a man, also cloaked and masked.

"Merda," Balthazar cursed, stepping back abruptly. The girl slid to her feet, mewing like an abandoned kitten.

The man must have crept in while Balthazar was not looking, after all! His father would have his testicles for this. Balthazar tugged his own hood up over his head, watching as the couple made their way across the *campi* hand in hand. They paused by the fountain to dip into the wine, and as the man drank his hood fell back for an instant. He wore a half-mask, yet Balthazar recognised the sleek fall of dark hair, the gleaming pearl earring.

Marc Velazquez. So the widow, his father's chosen one, had taken up with *Il leone.*

This was a precious piece of information, indeed, one Balthazar could surely use to great advantage. Perhaps it would even take him a step closer to his father's respect—and possession of his father's fortune.

"Signor," the girl whined, her white hands reaching out for him.

"I must go," he snapped. Her protests abruptly ceased as he shoved a handful of coins at her. "Perhaps we will see each other again here tomorrow night."

He left her there, following Signora Bassano and her lover as they made their way out of the courtyard and into the crowds of the city. Yes, this was his fortunate night, indeed.

Chapter Fifteen

Julietta was not sure what she expected when Marc led her from the shop, but surely it was not this. He stood in a waiting boat, his hand outstretched to help her down from the quay. A *boat*—not a gondola or a raft, but a solid wooden skiff built for longer journeys than a quick jaunt down the canal.

"Come along, *querida,*" he said coaxingly. "'Tis safe. I can steer any vessel."

"I know you can," she said. "You are *Il leone,* are you not? What I want to know is where you are steering us."

"I told you, it is a surprise." He gestured with his hand. "Come, I will keep you safe."

"Oh, very well," she answered. "I did say I was ready for an adventure." She took his hand and stepped down into the gently rocking vessel.

It was surely no luxurious gondola; there were no velvet cushions or gilded woodwork. It was a vessel made for serious work, for withstanding the waves. But Marc had put soft pillows down for her, along with fur lap robes and a basket filled with wine and sweet-meats. As she settled back into the soft warmth, he sat down across from her, shedding his heavy cloak to take the oars.

His black velvet doublet was unlaced, and his white linen shirt gleamed in the night, drawing her gaze in-exorably to his bare skin, to the play and ripple of his muscles as he steered them out into the traffic of the canal. Truly, she had become a lascivious woman, a veritable Delilah, since he came into her life! It was hard to think of her business, her work, when all she could see was his skin, his eyes, his hair, all she could hear was his voice. She almost understood the bards' songs now, the words of the poets, as she never had before. And never wished to.

This was dangerous.

Julietta leaned against the cushions, watching Marc as he steered their craft adroitly among the indolent gondolas full of merrymakers. His face was etched with intent, but his muscles rippled smoothly as silk. It was obvious he did this often; he was no soft courtier, he was a man of action and of deeds rather than words. After her encounter with Ermano, she revelled in the honesty of Marc's physicality.

"Where are we going?" she asked again. Their vessel slid to the edge of the crowd, past palaces and churches and monuments, towards the mouth of the city, and her curiosity reared up sharply. Were they

going to another of Nicolai's hidden gatherings, this
one so secret it must be held on an outer island? Or a
bower where they could be alone all night, without a
hint of the city's revelry to mar their passion?

She frowned, remembering the way Ermano kissed
her hand, his cold green eyes watching, implacable,
unmoving, intent on his desire no matter what she
said. Marc was not Ermano, he was nothing like him.
But her instincts, always those of a skittish, freedom-
craving bird fluttering against bondage, rose up in her.

"Are you kidnapping me?" she whispered.

Marc laughed. His voice was not at all breathless
or strained, even as he laboured at the oars. The wind
picked up as they slid into the lagoon itself, the breeze
toying with his hair and the cloth of his shirt.

"Aye," he answered, his voice raised above the
whistle of the breeze. "To hold you for ransom,
signora. A whole case of your finest rosewater. And
the command of your delectable body, of course."

"I always knew you were secretly a pirate
yourself," she said.

His face was unreadable in the darkness, yet she
knew he watched her. "And you, *madonna?* What are
your secrets?"

Julietta shivered, and drew her cloak close about
her. "Me? I have no secrets," she lied.

"None at all?"

She hesitated for an instant. "None interesting
enough to speak of."

He was silent for a long moment. They had left the

crowds far behind, and the only sounds were the soft splash of water against wood, the creak of oars. The black hulks of outer islands lurked nearby, the cottages of Burano, the high walls of San Michele, the funeral island, yet it seemed that the two of them were suspended in their own world. Solitary, silent, wrapped in the heat of their two bodies, their desire—and the force of what was unsaid.

"I do not think any part of you could be uninteresting, Julietta," he murmured.

That sense of battering against cages flooded through Julietta again, yet she did not know why. All that held her—her shop, her work, Ermano's strange imprecations—they were all left far behind tonight. Her craving for Marc Velazquez was a trap of a different sort, one of her own making.

"Very well," she said lightly, "I will tell you a secret."

"I am all attention, *querida*."

"But you must tell me one in return."

"All right. Fair is fair."

"When I was a girl, I hated my figure. I grew so tall so quickly, I hardly knew what to do with my legs and arms, how to move. All of my friends were so lovely, so small and round, while I was nothing but sharp elbows and ribs. My grandmother tried to help. She ordered gowns made from voluminous yardages of fine fabrics, with padded chemises. She made me drink cream and eat cakes and fatted calves' livers until I thought I would be ill. Nothing helped. If anything, I *lost* weight. I looked like a gondola pole, not a woman."

Marc laughed, and the sound made her smile, too. The horrors of the cage lifted, and the night suddenly sparkled with a million stars. "Is that your secret? That you are tall and slender? Forgive me, my sun, but I already divined that for myself. Your beauty is impossible to disguise."

"My—beauty?" Julietta feared she blushed like a girl, her face hot in the cold breeze. She was not fool enough to believe she was beautiful, but it was nice to hear it all the same. When the words came from *him*.

He paused for an instant in his rowing, suddenly still and intent. "I have never seen any to equal your beauty, Julietta."

She shook her head. *He* was beautiful, with a glory to rival the classical statues of Greece and Rome. Every woman in Venice desired him; they would cut off their own hair to be in her place now. Yet she—well, she was still tall and dark. But in the night she could pretend they belonged together.

He went back to pulling on the oars, carrying them deeper into the lagoon. "So, what is the secret?"

Julietta laughed. She could scarcely remember now what the point of her tale was! "Ah, yes. Well, you see, there was this handsome boy, whose family was rumoured to be looking for a bride for him. My father was to give a ball, and this boy's family was invited. I so much wanted him to admire me, so with the help of one of our maidservants I devised a plan."

"A gypsy love potion?"

"Of course not. Those never work, anyway. No, this

plan was much simpler. We sewed stockings into balls and stuffed them into my bodice. *Et voilà*—I finally had a lovely bosom."

"Such rare ingenuity."

"I know. We certainly thought so."

"And was this boy impressed? I am certain I would have been."

"At first. He asked me to dance a *moresque* with him. I was overjoyed to be the envy of my friends—until tragedy struck."

"Never say…"

"Yes." Julietta sighed at the memory. "The stockings came unmoored right in the midst of the dance. They fluttered down to my feet and my bodice was quite flat again. I was humiliated for life in front of all Milan."

Marc threw back his head and laughed, the rich, dark sound echoing up to the moon. It made Julietta laugh to remember the agony of her fourteen-year-old self. "I ran up to my chamber, and not even my *grand-mère* could coax me out."

"So, *querida,* that is the secret of your exquisite bosom," he teased.

"Well, they did grow a bit after that, though not as much as I would have liked. I have no need to pad my bodice any longer."

"So I have noticed. Much to my delight, I assure you."

Julietta leaned closer to him. "Now, *Il leone,* you owe me a secret."

"I have nothing to rival yours."

"Nevertheless, a bargain is a bargain. Come, one secret. And don't think to imitate mine. I know you do not stuff your codpiece."

They slid around the ragged edge of an uninhabited islet, and outlined against the starlit sky was a great Spanish *nao,* sails furled, masts skeletal in the moonlight. On the side were the gilded words *Elena Maria.*

"There is no time, my sun, for we are at our destination now," he said, drawing them steadily closer to the silent ship.

"Your ship?" Julietta asked, staring up at the deck high above her head. The vessel seemed deserted, almost a ghost ship. As if it would vanish once they were too close.

"My home," he answered. Then he shouted out, "Ahoy, there! Mendoza, you lazy arse, wake up and lower the ladders."

Immediately, the vessel Julietta took to be a ghost came to life. Torches flared along the railings, and faces peered down at them.

"Captain Velazquez? Is that you?" a man's voice, accented in rough Spanish, called.

"Aye, 'tis me. And I bring a guest, so tell everyone to put their hose on and hide the whores."

Ribald laughter rippled, echoing on the wood and the wind. "Aye, captain! It's good to see you, we began to fear when we had no word from you."

"I've been busy."

"So we see." A rope ladder dropped over the side, slapping against the planks.

Julietta eyed it with some trepidation. It swayed precariously in the breeze, and she did not see how a person could get a safe foothold on it. But Marc leaped from the small boat on to the first rung, leaning down to hold out a hand to her.

He smiled at her. "Come, Julietta. Did I not say I will keep you safe?"

She glanced from the narrow ladder to his face, masked and hidden even in the light of the torches. "You did say that, *Il leone.*"

"And have I ever disappointed you?"

"Not yet."

He clicked his tongue chidingly. "So suspicious, *madonna.* Come, let me help you aboard, and I will give you *two* secrets."

Julietta laughed. "How could anyone resist such enticements? Very well, my pirate captain, take me aboard your ship."

She clasped his hand and stepped up from the rocking boat to the swaying, twisting ladder.

"Just don't look down," Marc said.

"Apt instructions—for life *and* ladders," she muttered, and commenced climbing in his surefooted path. In only a moment he was lifting her over the railing to the deck, and they were surrounded by men. Grinning, bearded faces peered at her, their laughter and greetings flying around her.

Marc held her close to him, his hand warm on her arm as he answered questions, returned jests, his gaze quickly scanning the clean lines of his ship. Julietta looked, too, fascinated by this glimpse of his true world, a universe of creaking timbers, polished guns, layers of canvas and coils of rope so very different from the Oriental opulence of Venice.

Finally, he took one more glance around, and, seemingly satisfied with what he saw, said, "I will be here until dawn, Mendoza, if you would like to take some of the men and row into the city. You've kept an excellent watch here these last few days, it is surely not just to ask you to forgo the pleasures of Carnival altogether."

The black-bearded Mendoza, Marc's second-in-command as Julietta gathered, grinned, revealing two front teeth replaced with shining gold. "Indeed, *señor le capitan,* we have missed the soft company of fair ladies out here in the lagoon, the taste of good wine. But we would endure much more to serve the Velazquezes. You know that."

Marc nodded solemnly. "I do know that, and I am deeply grateful. Soon you will all have your reward."

As the boats were lowered to bear most of the crew away to their revels, amid many shouts and jokes, Marc steered Julietta along the polished deck. It was not vastly spacious, but so perfectly organised and efficiently laid out that not a square inch was wasted. Marc ran a caressing hand along the inlaid railing, a narrowed gaze cast up into the weblike riggings, and Julietta knew that this was his true home. He belonged here, on his deck. It was his destiny.

Just as hers was amid the secrets of Venice.

"Your ship is beautiful," she said softly.

He smiled down at her, and for an instant the veil was lifted from his glorious eyes. She saw only pride there, a quiet delight. "The *Elena Maria* was my father's gift to me," he answered. "Keel length of fifteen *rumos,* thirty-two guns. She is a valiant vessel, and has served me well in commerce and in battle."

"This is where you defeated the pirates?"

He nodded. "They had us outgunned, with their carrack, but they rode heavy in the water, having just pillaged an English galleon and taken on her cargo. Also, they did not expect us. It was a foggy day. We came hard about to her port and opened fire before they could heave off their drunken revels and answer us with their own cannon." He leaned slightly over the railing, drawing her with him to point out a long, neatly mended gash along the hull. "She was wounded, though."

"She seems healed now."

"And so she is. While I have been masking in Venice, the men have been hard at work making repairs. No captain is more fortunate in his crew than I am."

Julietta clasped the satin-smooth railing, peering down at the scar that had once been a splintered gash. She frowned, imagining the blast of cannon fire, hot as the flames of hell, the stinging smoke, the stench of blood. The shouts and screams, the ring of steel on steel. The ominous thud of bodies collapsing to the slick deck. "Were any of your men wounded?"

"Nay, by the grace of Our Lady."

"Yet they could have been." *He* could have been. Julietta shuddered, imagining his turquoise eyes glassy and sightless, blood spreading across his chest as he lay in the ruins of his beloved ship.

Was it only her own fear, or a premonition? Her mother's cursed gift?

"Perhaps." Marc wrapped his arms around her waist, drawing her close to him. She felt the gentle press of his lips to her hair, and she closed her eyes tightly, willing the visions of blood and death to disappear, willing this moment to be all there was. "We are merchants, true, but we are also men of the sea. We must be prepared to face whatever dangers befall us. But my father taught me well, Julietta. I can always protect myself—and those who put their faith in me." He kissed her temple, and slid away until only their hands were touching. "Come with me."

He led her to a short flight of wooden steps, trailing down into a narrow passageway, a stoutly bound door. Here the scents of pitch and wood were stronger, overlaid by the salt of the sea. Marc pushed open the portal and drew her inside, leaving her only to light a branch of candles.

As their glow multiplied, Julietta saw that they were in a cabin. It was small and narrow, yet not really as she would have imagined a ship's cabin to be. There was no hammock, no sludge of dirty water coating the floor. A wide berth was tucked against the wall, neatly spread with a black velvet counterpane and bolsters. A desk along the opposite wall had a neat array of shining, mysterious brass instruments, rolls of maps. An oval mirror surmounted a tall *toilette* stand, and starlight glimmered from a porthole set high in the varnished wooden wall.

It was spare, neat, scrupulously clean—and told her not a thing about Marc.

Julietta leaned her hand against the polished frame of the berth, watching as he removed his mask and swirled off his cloak, letting it rest on the chair beside the desk.

"Welcome to my home," he said, turning to face her with a grin. She saw then what this place said about him—he was relaxed here, at peace, his eyes glowing. None of the wary watchfulness of Venice hung about him now. This truly *was* his home, his refuge.

What was it like, to have a place that brought such comfort, such peace? A place to really belong. It was so long since she had that feeling herself, that surety that she was safe, that she was where she should be. Not since she was a child, since she lost her mother. Ever since then, it was as if she floated free in the sky, blown by the winds of chance, trying to anchor herself with her work.

Perhaps she should have anchored herself to the sea, instead.

"It is not the Doge's Palace," Marc said. "I fear I have neglected the frescoes and the gilding. Yet it has everything I need."

"I think it is a beautiful ship," Julietta answered. "Though I fear I know little of nautical matters."

"Well, a *nao* has two decks, you see, one bow to stern, for cargo, water barrels, ropes, sails, ammunition. One made up of bowcastle—" Suddenly, he broke off with a wry laugh. "I did not bring you here to bore you into a stupor, Julietta! Here, have some wine."

He reached into a cabinet tucked beneath the desk and removed a bottle and two plain silver goblets. As he poured out the burgundy liquid, Julietta wandered over towards the *toilette* stand.

"You could never bore me at all, Marc," she murmured, staring into the wavy glass of the mirror. She still wore her half-mask, and for an instant she thought she saw a stranger there, a visage concealed from all the world. She untied the satin ribbons and let the scrap of cloth flutter to the table, and then she found she was just herself.

He brought her one of the goblets, the battered silver cool in her hand. She sipped at the sweet Rhenish blend, her gaze sweeping over the contents of the stand. They were as sparse as the cabin itself, just a wooden comb, a shaving set in an inlaid box, a ceramic bowl for washing. And two small portraits, framed simply in wood and propped on delicate stands. They were two women, and females more different from each other could scarce be imagined.

One was dark, her mahogany-brown hair parted in the centre and drawn back sleekly beneath an embroidered cap and sheer black veil. Her eyes were large and deep brown, lustrous in a round, olive-complected face. She wore a high, frilled chemise beneath a black satin gown, her throat encircled by a heavy garnet cross on a silver chain.

The other woman was golden, pale blond hair caught up on the sides by jewelled combs and then falling free down her back. Her smile glittered with mischief, and her eyes—her eyes were a radiant turquoise blue. She had the elfin, pointed face so fashionable in Venice, with fair skin lightly dusted with pale freckles over the bridge of her narrow nose. Her gown was carmine velvet, cut low to reveal her white breasts and one pouting pink nipple, the fabric sliding off her shoulder as she reached up one hand to hold it. A gold ring set with a large ruby glittered on her finger. A ring Julietta had seen many times before.

"I see you have met my mothers," Marc said quietly, right behind her.

Julietta jumped, startled. She had forgotten he stood so near, in her fascination with the portraits. And he always moved so quietly, as if he was a lion in truth. "Your mothers?"

He laid a gentle touch on the frame of the first painting. "This is Senora Elena Maria Velazquez, my mother in all the truths that matter. You chose well in making her perfume, *querida*—she is truly all goodness and sweetness."

"Violets and roses," Julietta murmured. "And the other?"

"She gave me birth, right here in the Serene City. Her name was Veronica Rinaldi."

"Rinaldi?" The name echoed in her head. She had heard it before, she knew it, but where? Venice was a thicket of romance, gossip, intrigue, stretching back decades. Even old tales were ever present, ever needful. "Was she not a courtesan, a..." Then Julietta remembered. Her fingers tightened painfully on the stem of the goblet. "She was murdered, by a gang of thieves during Carnival. After a ball at Ermano Grattiano's palazzo."

"Yes," Marc answered tightly. "Murdered by thieves."

His words were short, but they held a wealth of pain and fury. Anger she understood—oh, by all the saints, she *did* understand! To lose a beloved mother in a cruel and violent way tore a person's world to shreds, and it was never put right, not completely. The wound became a ragged scar, like the one tracing the hull of this ship.

She reached for his hand, to comfort him, to try to see deeper, but he stepped away from her, turning his back to stare out the porthole.

Julietta gulped down the last of her wine, staring into Veronica Rinaldi's painted blue eyes. If she hoped to read something there, some clue to the woman's sad end, she was disappointed. There was only the old sparkle of laughter and flirtation.

"You must have been very young," she said.

"I was six," he answered, and she heard a soft splash as he finished his own wine.

"Was Ermano her lover?" Julietta asked.

"Of course, though one of many. My mother was beautiful, cultured, full of merriment and intelligence, the most sought-after woman of the city. He had to have her, at any price."

Julietta could well believe that. Ermano always craved

the best, always wanted what he did not have. "What happened after she died? How did you get to Spain?"

"I saw her murdered, but the killers did not see me. I hid behind a screen, and when they left after their vile crime, taking her jewels with them, I fled. I ran through the night, stricken with a blind panic, until I found a boat to hide in near the Arsenal. When it went out to the lagoon the next morning, I stowed away on a Barcelona-bound ship. It proved to be Juan Velazquez's vessel. He took pity on me, took me home to his wife. They were sadly childless, and raised me as their own. I always remembered Veronica, though…"

Suddenly, like a crack of thunder, he slammed his palm against the wall. The stout glass of the porthole creaked. "I was a coward! A craven deserter to abandon her like that. I should have gone after her murderer, then and there."

"No!" Julietta cried. She dashed to his side, catching his arm in her clasp. He tried to draw away, but she held him fast. "You were a *child*. What could you have done?"

He stared down at her, yet she feared he did not really see her. He was trapped in the past. "I could have avenged her."

Julietta shook her head. "They would surely have killed you, too, and your mother's sacrifice would have been for naught. You did the right thing in running, in living to grow up and become the man you are."

"A coward?"

"Nay. Any man who can defeat Barbary pirates,

who can captain a ship and command the loyalty your men obviously have for you, can only be a person of great strength. Of courage." She smiled up at him teasingly. "You have certainly proved your bravery in involving yourself with *me*."

He rewarded her with the wisp of a grin, with the slight glow that kindled again behind his eyes. "She deserved to have her revenge, Julietta. Yet I, her own son, abandoned her to lie in her own blood in Grattiano's *sala*."

And where was Ermano when all this happened? Julietta mused. Why did *he* not avenge his lover? Why had Marc never said he knew Ermano before? But she wanted to ease Marc away from this precipice of guilt and old pain. She knew so well how easy it was to topple over and be lost for ever.

"She knows what you have done to bring honour to her over all these years," she said. "She can look down on you now and see that you are the great hero of her city. As for her killers—they were surely given their punishment long ago. Such *bravos* do not live long, and they do not die peacefully."

Marc suddenly caught her in his arms, dragging her hard against his body as his lips found hers. They were hard, desperate, and Julietta met him with equal need. There was no artifice, no practice to their kiss, only the fervour of their passion, the slide of tongue against tongue, mouths bruising, full of all the emotions of years and grief.

The past was gone; it could not be changed or

mended, yet it was never completely dead, either. It haunted all their moments, altered the glory of what could have been for ever. She bore her ghosts with her always, as did Marc. Only in the sun-flare of sex could the ghosts be banished for even a moment—only in *his* arms could she forget.

And she wanted to forget! She wanted them both to forget the scars and know only each other. She could give them that.

Julietta stepped back from Marc, tearing at the ribbons of her cloak until it fell away. She wore only a simple woollen gown beneath, but she fumbled at the cord fastenings, her hands suddenly shaking and clumsy. She sobbed in frustration, longing to be free of the bindings of cloth and thread.

"Here, my sun," Marc whispered, reaching out for her. He gently turned her around and unlaced the back of her bodice. His own hands trembled, his breath was quick and urgent on the nape of her neck, stirring the tendrils of her upswept hair, making her quiver with desperate desire.

Her gown fell away into a puddle at her feet, and she kicked it away, pulling her chemise over her head in a flurry of snow-white muslin. It, too, fluttered to the planks of the floor, and she spun around to throw her arms about Marc. His velvet doublet was deliciously rough against her naked skin, and she jumped up into his embrace, wrapping her legs tightly around his waist. Marc laughed in surprise, holding her in his arms, burying his face in her hair.

"I think you are wearing far too many garments, *signor capitan*," she whispered. She tossed back her head, giving him free access to her throat, her breasts, the line of her shoulders.

"And you are also wearing too many," he growled against her skin.

"Too *many?*"

He raised his head from her collarbone to grin down at her. "The heels of your slippers are digging into me, *querida*."

Julietta spluttered with laughter. "Then you had best carry me to the bed quickly, *signor*, for I refuse to let you go for even a second."

He followed her instructions with great haste, crossing the small cabin with her body still wrapped around his. He reached down to snatch back the counterpane, and lowered her into the cool welcome of linen sheets. But he did not follow her. Instead, he stripped his own clothes away, tossing them to the floor to join hers before edging himself along to kneel at the foot of the berth.

Julietta levered up on to her elbows to watch as he took off her shoes. They were fashionable satin slippers with high, curved heels, buckled in etched silver. "Oh, yes," Marc said darkly, throwing them out to land with a thud on the floor. "These must go."

She laughed, sprawling back against the soft sheets so stare up at the beams so close above her head. "I know of men in Venice who would pay good coin to be kicked with high-heeled shoes," she said. "That is one of the specialties of a courtesan who frequents my shop. She tells the most fascinating tales…."

"Alas, I am not one of them. I am a man of—simple pleasures." He still held her foot, the ankle delicately balanced on his palm. Slowly, he raised it to his lips, his tongue tracing the instep, the curve of her ankle bone.

Julietta sucked in a sharp breath, her entire body arching at the lightning-hot sensations.

"Pleasures like a woman's skin," he muttered. His tongue edged up her calf to the sensitive spot just behind her knee. His kiss deepened there, pressing hard to her pulse until Julietta thought she would weep with the pleasure of it. "You smell like jasmine."

"And you smell like the sea," she whispered, closing her eyes tightly as he slid higher between her legs. He eased her calves back along his shoulders, his kiss soft on her inner thigh. "Like freedom."

"I can give you freedom, Julietta," he said, and she felt the rasp of his roughened cheek against the tender skin just below her womanhood. A womanhood that wept for his touch. "I can give you anything you want."

"I only want *you!*" she cried out. And it was true. Nothing mattered but the two of them, alone on this ship, entwined until they were as one.

"And you have me," he said. "Always."

Then his mouth touched the very core of her, his tongue tracing her damp seam, once, twice, before plunging inside. Julietta screamed at the crashing wave of ecstasy, spreading her legs wide over his shoulders. Her fingers twined in his hair, pressing him closer. He reached between them, his skilful fingers easing inside of her, playing over her swollen folds as if she was a lute, meant to sing only for him.

With one more rough sweep of his tongue, she fell among the stars, tumbling into a maelstrom of pleasure. Golden light exploded behind her eyes, and for a moment she could not even breathe. She could only whisper his name, over and over. "Marc, Marc, Marc."

"I am here," he answered. Her eyes fluttered open, watching as he slid up her body, his skin a delicious friction against hers, hot and sweat-slicked. He kissed her shoulder, the arch of her throat, open-mouthed and wet. She could smell herself on his lips, their scents mingled in a humid, intoxicating blend she could never capture in a bottle. She tightened her legs about his waist, his engorged, iron-hard penis pressed to her.

His lips closed on her straining nipple, circling with his tongue, drawing on it hard as if he was starved for her, would consume her.

I love you! her mind shouted. *I love you, Marc.* But she dared not voice it, even in the throes of their passion. Love was always dangerous. Love was never to be trusted.

Still, she wept with the force of her feelings, every time he kissed her hearing that word. *Love.*

"So beautiful," Marc whispered against her breast. "My Julietta."

"I need you, Marc," she groaned. "Come inside me now."

"Anything you command." He held himself above her, his arms rigid, limned with hard muscles as he slid slowly into her welcoming wetness. Stretching her, filling her until there could be nothing else. He eased inside, deeper and deeper until he touched her very soul, it seemed. Then he drew back and drove inside again, harder, ever deeper.

He groaned, his head thrown back, throat corded with tension, his hair clinging damply to his brow.

Julietta raised her hips to meet him thrust for thrust, pleasure building up again inside her, an unbearable pressure. Surely she would explode with the force of it! No one could feel like this and live.

"Julietta!" Marc shouted, his body taut as a bow string above her. As she felt the warmth of his release flood her, deep inside, she rose up to answer him. The stars exploded around her, purple and gold and green, and she lost herself in their glories.

"Julietta," he whispered, collapsing beside her. He slid out of her, but their legs and arms were still entwined, binding them together. For always.

The creak of wood, of oiled rope, awakened Julietta from her dreamless stupor. Her eyes flew open, and for an instant she did not know where she was. The candles had sputtered low, casting only a shadowed, flickering glow over the room. Over the heap of abandoned clothes and empty wine goblets, the faint, fuzzy starlight glowed at a porthole.

Of course. She was aboard Marc's ship. In his arms.

She closed her eyes again, stretching her limbs experimentally to discover that she lay on her side, pulled up into the curve of Marc's body, his arm heavy over her waist. The musk of their lovemaking, their bodies and wine and candlesmoke, hung heavy in the close air. She wished she could bottle it, capture it in a perfume and have it with her for ever. To take out and inhale, and remember, after he sailed away.

Her body felt soft, boneless, still tingling with the delight she found in this man. The pleasure was enormous, yet she knew it was more than that. It went deeper. In him she found an answer and a solace to old sorrows, a soul as filled with secrets as her own. A man with magic in him that he could not even see or acknowledge. A magic she craved, far too much.

She traced a gentle caress over his hand. It was strong, with long, elegant fingers that could equally steer a ship, wield a sword, or bring delight to a woman. The back was lightly dusted with crisp brown hair, the palm laced with tiny scars. The pads of his fingers were callused, yet he never lacerated her skin with their roughness.

She still did not know very much about him. Did not know why he came to Venice in the first place; perhaps to seek his mother's murderers, after all these years? She did not know why he lingered, what he wanted with people like Ermano Grattiano. Or even with her. Yet surely, in the deepest essentials, she *did* know him. For they were alike. Two lost souls set adrift, seeking a shelter the world could not hold for them.

A sudden chilly panic seized Julietta, a knot of ice in her belly. She could not breathe! The air caught in her throat, choking her, and she had to be away from his touch. Careful not to wake him, she eased out from beneath his arm and climbed from the berth. She found her rumpled chemise in the tangled garments and pulled it over her head.

Air. She just needed air, to breathe, to think. The flash of realization—that she needed Marc, that they were two of a kind—had bludgeoned her with its suddenness. She was still caught in the drugging joy of their lovemaking, and could not make sense of anything.

She dragged a small wooden footstool over to the porthole and climbed up to fumble at the latch. It gave way, and the stout glass swung open, bringing a fresh, salty breeze into the stuffy room. It was cold and crisp, clean with the smell of the open sea, untainted by the sickly sweetness of the city. The mutter of voices came from above her, signalling that some of the crew were still aboard, keeping watch.

Julietta stared out over the purple-black expanse of water, the tides laced with the silver sprinkle of starlight. How beautiful it was here, how deceptively peaceful and alluring. She could see why Marc loved it so.

She did not want to need him, a man of secrets, a man already wedded to the sea. To need anyone was merely to invite pain and grief. But one could never fight fate.

Julietta closed her eyes and inhaled deeply of the

cold sea air. She did not know, truly. It would take time for all to become clear, time that grew desperately short. It was at moments like this that she longed for even a fraction of her mother's powers of divination.

She heard a rustle behind her, the landing of a soft footfall on the wooden floor. Marc was awake. She did not move, only waited as he came to her, naked, his embrace sliding around her body from behind.

He kissed her temple, inhaling deeply as if to draw her inside of him. "How long have you been awake?" he said, his voice hoarse.

"Not long," she answered. "I wanted to see the water, the open horizon. It is so beautiful."

Marc rested his chin on her shoulder, peering through the porthole. "Almost as beautiful as you."

Julietta shook her head wearily. She wanted to weep. "Don't tease, Marc."

"I'm not. You *are* beautiful, Julietta. The loveliest thing I have ever seen."

"Is that why you brought me here tonight?"

"What?"

"You said earlier you did not bring me here to bore me into a stupor. Did you bring me here to flatter me?"

Marc was silent for a long moment, perfectly still, his breath on her hair their only movement. Finally, he reached up to swing the porthole wider, pointing outside. "I brought you here to see this."

"The water?"

"Yes. Do you know what the sea means, Julietta?"

"Waves, fish. Seaweed?"

He laughed harshly. "That is what it *is*. What it *means* is—freedom."

It was so close to what she was thinking of, longing for, that she swung around to face him, startled.

He watched her closely. "On this ship, we are all free, bound to no state, no master. We can go wherever our desire takes us, we can see everything the world has to offer. Our names, our past, our wounds, they are as nothing."

A wave of pure, aching longing swept over Julietta. How did he know her deepest desires? To be free, to see all the wonders of the world. She swayed towards him, and he caught her tightly in his embrace. The salty wind curled around them, and for an instant they were one with the sea, with each other.

"I can give you that, Julietta," he whispered. "I am not a wealthy man, I can give you no palaces or titles, but I can give you freedom. If you are ever in danger, ever need me, I will be by your side." He slid the small gold-and-ruby ring from his little finger—the same ring his mother wore in her portrait—and pressed it into Julietta's palm. "Wear this; if you have need of me, send it. I will hear you."

Julietta stared down at the ring, its glow blood-red in the waning night. "Marc…" she said, stunned.

"Nay," he answered. He took the ring back and slid it firmly over her finger. It fit perfectly, the gold band still warm from his skin. "Do not say anything now. It grows late. I should take you back to the city."

* * *

Marc's shoulder muscles ached as he drew on the oars, rowing them ever closer to the lights of Venice. He was glad of the old, familiar pain, though. It kept him from thinking too closely of all that had transpired tonight.

Julietta sat in silence across from him, cloaked and masked again, surrounded in thick darkness. The decision to take her to his ship was made in haste, when he saw Ermano emerging from her shop. He wanted only to carry her some place far away, a place where they could be alone. Could be themselves, could be honest.

Or honest up to a point. He had not told her of what he learned at the Doge's Palace, of the anonymous forces of hatred and greed that swirled around them, a poisonous fog licking at their heels. Julietta was clever, but she was unpredictable. He knew she was used to living amid danger disguised under an antic mask. Yet what would she do if she discovered the trap Ermano had laid for her?

Would she lay waste to his own careful plans, force his hand too early? He could not take that chance, not yet. Not now, when it could be both their necks in the noose.

And yet—and yet he meant it with all his heart when he vowed to her that he would keep her safe. Carry her to freedom, if only she summoned him. He had come to Venice with the coldest of souls, prepared to give everything to avenge past wrongs, fulfil old vows. It was what he had prepared for, worked for all these years, and now it was within his very grasp! He could taste the coppery tang of revenge. Then he walked into Julietta's shop, and all changed. The world tilted, and he could not set it right.

Not even making love to her, tasting her, feeling her in every way, could assuage his appetite for her. Not just for her body, but for her mind and heart. Even as she wrapped him in her arms, surrendered to him in his bed, there was a part of her she held back. A part that was completely unknowable. He wanted her secrets—but he still did not want to give up his own in return.

Her presence in Venice was an unexpected gift, dropped into his hands in the very midst of a dark time, a time of fulfilment and utter destruction. He did not want to lose it. The more he was with her, the more he craved her. Yet neither did he know how to hold on to her.

Marc shook his head, pulling harder at the oars. The water clung thickly to the wood; they were getting closer to the city, farther from the peace of the sea. Julietta shifted in her seat, adjusting her cloak around her, and he smelled the heady scent of jasmine released from the woollen folds. Her perfume dizzied him, made him feel drunk on its sweetness.

He must be mad! He loved the Spanish poet Juan Boscan, loved his sublime language, his words on religion, nature, romance, duty. Yet never before had he truly understood their most common metaphor— love as a fiery sickness in the blood, an insanity that can never be cured except in death. Now he saw it was all true. His passion for Julietta had no rhyme or reason, it just *was*. How it would end, he could not say. In their union, in the end of all secrets, or in the cold grave.

"Thank you for showing me your ship," she said quietly. "And for giving me this ring."

"I meant what I told you, Julietta," he answered. "If you ever have need of me, you need only call."

She nodded, staring down at her folded hands. His mother's ring glinted there, as if it had found its true home. "I only hope I can give you as fine a gift one day."

Marc shook his head, stung by a twinge of sharp guilt. "You owe me nothing. My gift is having met you."

She lapsed back into silence, curling her hand into a fist as if to protect her ring. The watery passage grew narrower, and they were no longer alone as they left the openness of the lagoon. More and more vessels crowded around them, private gondolas, barges bearing entire banquets. Music rang out. The real life of the *Elena Maria,* of the freedom of the waters, was left behind, replaced by the dream of Carnival.

Or was the sea the dream? He no longer knew.

Julietta did not speak again. All too soon they slid alongside the dock near her piazzetta, the oars still at last. They sat across from each other for a long moment, not talking, not moving.

"When can I see you again?" he muttered, suddenly setting aside the oars and reaching for her. She moved into his arms as if she was meant to be only there, their bodies fitting together like a puzzle box.

She kissed him softly, her fingertips tracing his cheek, the line of his jaw, with the most infinite tenderness. "Not today, or tonight," she whispered. "I have work I must do. Tomorrow night. Come to the shop after dusk."

He nodded, and she slid away from him, clambering up on to the *fondamenta* before he could move to help her. Without even a glance back, she disappeared into the drunken crowd, leaving only a hint of jasmine in the air around him.

Marc slammed his fist into the side of the boat, splinters driving into his bare skin. He did not even notice the sting.

Tomorrow night. He had until then to find a solution, to devise a way to end their untenable situation. He would break this web of lies—somehow.

Chapter Sixteen

The new perfume was not coming together as it should.

Julietta stirred at the sticky mixture, which had been so carefully brewing for weeks, but it just lay heavily in the bottom of the beaker. It was dark green, not pale as it should be, sticky and liquefied.

She sighed, and reached for a parchment that was covered in her mother's spidery handwriting. She had followed the recipe so very carefully! It was to be the triumphant culmination of all she had worked for, her finest creation. What could have gone wrong?

There was nothing she had missed, not that she could see, anyway. Perhaps she was simply distracted today. Distracted as she had been ever since Marc Velazquez first walked into her shop. Distraction was very dangerous, even if it *was* delicious.

Julietta put the cover back over the mixture and set it aside. She would let it sit a day or so more, then, if it still had not brewed properly, she would add another measure of rue. Perhaps then it would work.

The shop outside her hidden room was quiet. It was Sunday, and the city slumbered after its long revels of the night before. Only the sonorous toll of church bells broke the hush of the streets.

Alone but for the whisper of Marc's voice in her mind. "When will I see you again?"

She put him off until tomorrow in hopes that a bit of time without his intoxicating presence would clear her senses, allow her to think again without being caught up in the whirling, disorienting maelstrom of desire. It was of no use, though. Even when she was solitary he was with her.

Last night changed things, in some indefinable, ungraspable, yet undeniable way. By taking her to his ship, sharing his world with her, he had showed her a part of his hidden heart. A glimpse of his true world. And it made her care for him all the more.

She had found him in the tangled concealments of her own world, but it was not who he *was*. Despite his success with men of secrets, he came of a place of action and movement, where the ocean was at once a lover and an enemy, and her dangers were more honest than those of men. That was who he really was, and he offered to share all of it with her. The freedom of the waters, of a greater world than she had ever known.

She had to give him something in return. But what? What could she have to offer to him that could ever compare to what he already gave her? In his arms, his kiss, she found an exhilaration, a joy she had thought long extinguished. He already had riches, esteem, strength.

Her gaze drifted to the shelf of precious books above her head. Priceless volumes she carried so carefully from Milan, a legacy of her mother and grandmother she fought to preserve, no matter the cost. The wisdom of centuries was contained there, hers to master. Hers to share.

Julietta stood and reached for a slim, green leatherbound book. The binding was new, but the contents, faded black ink on yellowing parchment, were very old. It was one of her grandmother's last gifts to her, pressed into Julietta's hands as the old Frenchwoman lay on her deathbed.

"The recipes written here are very ancient, *petite,*" Grandmère had whispered. "And very, very dangerous. You should never have need of them, but then one never knows in life. Take it, and guard it well."

And, indeed, Julietta never did need these recipes. She was not a warrior, and these were battle secrets from Greece, Rome, Egypt, Mesopotamia. Gruesome, effective methods of dispatching one's enemies, they were used at Troy and Thermopylae, though less so now in Venice, where the enemies were gossip and jealousy. She kept the book, even though she never used it. As her grandmother said in life, one never knows.

She held the volume carefully between her hands, the leather cool and smooth against her skin, and remembered the thin scar along the hull of the *Elena*

Maria. Marc was fortunate in his encounter with the pirates. Luck and nature were on his side that day. They might not be next time.

Julietta sifted through the pages, past sketches of intricate siege engines, diagrams of scorpion bombs, recipes for poison arrows, until she found what she wanted. Yes, this could help him in his next battle, if he had need of it.

Yet she could not take the chance of brewing it here. Her shop was too near other structures, and she did not even have the proper ingredients in her workshop. If something went wrong...

She shuddered to think of *that*. But surely it would not happen. She knew the precautions to take. Still, a person could not be too careful when dealing with such powerful matters. She would take it to her farm on the mainland, the one Ermano Grattiano seemed to so covet. The villa there was empty since the caretaker and his wife elected to live in their own cottage on the grounds. She would have quiet, privacy and space to perfect her gift.

Julietta reached for two other books, and searched through her various chests and boxes until she found the herbs and utensils she would need. They were all neatly bundled together, a linen-wrapped parcel that could be her doom if it was found.

Bianca could look after the shop when she returned, and surely Julietta would be back by tomorrow night. Just in time for her rendezvous with Marc.

Chapter Seventeen

"Signor Velazquez!" A fusillade of knocks cracked at Marc's door, sharp and preemptory, brooking no argument or resistance. "Signor Velazquez, we require entrance."

Marc slid over in his rented bed, brushing his hair back from his bleary eyes. He had only just sunk into sleep as the sun peered over the horizon, his rest broken by erotic dreams of Julietta. What was the meaning of this new interruption?

He squinted towards the window, noting the intensity of the light. It was past noon, surely, but there was no bustle from the walkway outside, no hum of crowds hurrying along, shouts of greeting, the song of peddlers. It was silent, except for the pounding at his door.

Marc frowned, remembering how this very room had been secretly searched, his perfume bottle tampered with. He remembered the Doge's Palace, the watchful eyes, the careful questions.

"Julietta," he whispered, his chest suddenly tight, his skin chilled. He snatched up his bedrobe and rolled from the bed, sliding the brocade over his naked shoulders.

He unlatched the door and threw it open, unsure of what he might find. An arrest warrant? Julietta's head on a pike? A company of *bravos* sent to cripple him? His fingers closed over the plain hilt of a dagger hidden in the folds of his robe, but all he saw on his threshold was one slight man, clad in a rich purple-velvet cloak. The noise of the knocks seemed all out of proportion to his size, and long, thin strands of pale hair straggled from beneath a red velvet cap, which was pinned with the gold brooch of some office. Behind him were two taller guardsmen, clad in the white-and-gold livery of the Doge.

"Yes?" Marc said coldly.

The small man fell back a step, as if surprised by the abrupt opening of the door, but he quickly recovered. His shoulders lifted, and he drew the folds of his cloak tighter around himself. "Signor Velazquez?"

"I am he."

"I am sent to summon you to the Doge's Palace for an audience with his Excellency. It is of the utmost importance."

Marc's gaze skimmed over the impassive guards, the narrowness of the stairwell behind them. There was a single, shadowy figure lingering there, his landlady in her apron and kerchief, watching the proceedings with a scowl. Surely he would soon need to seek new lodgings, if he was not provided them free of charge in the Leads prison.

What would the charges against him be? he wondered. Loving a woman with such a foolish intensity that he lost sight of his old errand? Failing to protect her—or himself—as he should?

"When?" he asked the messenger.

"As soon as you are dressed," the small man answered. "His Excellency emphasised the need for haste."

Marc glanced again at the two guards, who bore slender, steel-tipped pikes in their gauntleted hands.

"We will escort you to the Palace," the messenger said stoutly.

Marc nodded briefly, before stepping back into the room and shutting the door behind him, right in the guards' faces. As he shed his robe and reached for the basin of cold wash water, he remembered last night, remembered the haven of his ship, the beckoning welcome of the open sea. He remembered Julietta's naked body in his arms, the jasmine smell of her hair, the press of her warm skin, the humid, sultry heaviness of their passion mingled with the salty ocean.

He should have kept her there, Marc thought wryly as he splashed water over his face and chest. Should have sailed away with the morning tide, left Venice far behind and damned the consequences. Before it was too late.

For a summons to the Doge's Palace, sudden and

surprising in the middle of the day, could only bode
ill. But he would protect Julietta, however he could.

Marc was not led to the same audience chamber he
was in before, with its echoing marble floors, and
palatial tapestries to muffle all sound and close out the
clamouring world. The antechamber, where he had
encountered the angry, black-swathed Signora
Landucci, was not crowded as before. Only a few
servants hurried quietly along its length, going about
their errands with silent efficiency.

Marc observed that silence, the curious absence of
activity. He shifted the folds of his short velvet cloak
closer, and felt the reassuring length of a hidden
dagger, strapped tight beneath his dagger sleeve.

"This way, *signor,*" the messenger said, leading the
way up the gleaming white staircase. The two guards
fell back, posing with their pikes at the foot of the
steps, soundless as the stone beneath their feet.

The corridor was even more deserted than the
antechamber, with nary a soul to be seen along its length.
Candles flickered in their brass candelabra, casting
living shadows on the frescoed walls. The only sound
was the click of their boot heels, the rustling of fabric.

At the end of the corridor, the messenger gently
pushed open a door and stepped back. "If you would
please to wait here, *signor,*" he said.

Marc gave a short nod, and slid past the man into
the room. The very air around him, pleasantly warm
in the corridor, seemed to chill, cold and clammy with

foreboding. Yet he felt strangely detached from the whole scene, as if he dreamed it from the berth of his ship. He knew very well that his errand in Venice was a dangerous one, that he might not escape from it alive, and he was always prepared to pay that price. At least—he had been before.

Now, he saw Julietta's dark eyes in his mind, felt the crackle of magic in her smile. He was not alone in this any longer. He *had* to protect her.

The door slid shut soundlessly behind him, and he stood alone in the small room. The light was so dim that at first he could not make out the curtains, the contents of the chamber. The one window was heavily muffled in brocade curtain, and the fire in the small grate was very low and smouldering. The air smelled of woodsmoke and a faint, tangy stuffiness.

Marc blinked, waiting for his eyes to adjust to the gloom. What would he find, then? Instruments of torture, primed for their next victim? The boot, the rack, the scavenger's daughter?

No such thing. Once some of the darkness cleared, he saw only ordinary furniture, chairs, a long table, a cushioned stool. And one man, who sat silently at the far end of the room. As Marc watched, unmoving, waiting to snatch his dagger, the man rose and made his way closer to the fire.

The low flames illuminated the face of Ermano Grattiano.

Marc gazed at him steadily, carefully keeping all expression from his face, pressing down all emotion beneath an impenetrable sheet of ice. Now was not the time to let the heat of passionate hatred get the best of him, to let the rage of years bubble over. Now was the time for cold calculation. Later—if he survived—would be the moment.

Ermano's elaborate finery was gone today, Marc noted. No fine satins or jewels. He wore only a black robe, sombre in the half-light, his face above it pale and expressionless.

"You did not expect to see me, Signor Velazquez?" Ermano said quietly.

"I was told I was coming here to meet with the Doge," Marc answered.

"I act as the Doge's emissary today." Ermano held up a narrow scroll, hung with wax seals and ribbons. "I have his authority."

"His authority for what?"

"The Republic has an errand for you—*Il leone*. A most important errand, one whose successful outcome could earn you much gratitude. And reward."

Marc leaned back lightly against the door, his gaze never wavering from Ermano's face. "And an unsuccessful outcome?"

Ermano shrugged. "You never fail at your endeavours. Do you?"

"I do not." The words were brief, truthful.

"Well, then. But come, sit. Our conversation may be a long one," Ermano said, gesturing towards a pair of chairs by the fire. "Would you care for wine?"

"Nay, *grazie*." Marc strolled warily towards the

proffered chair, watching Ermano all the while. He had never trusted the count's hearty affability; he trusted this quiet assurance even less.

A tiny smile touched the corner of Ermano's lips as he poured out a measure of wine into a goblet and sipped at it. "Of course. You are a man of war, are you not, a man of caution? Not one to stand on social protocol. But you really should try the wine. It is excellent."

Ermano seated himself in the chair across from Marc, the goblet loosely clasped in his fingers. He watched Marc steadily, just as Marc examined him, letting the moments lengthen in silence.

"No doubt you will want to hear of this errand," Ermano said at last.

Marc allowed himself a quick grin. "If you wish to tell me of it. I would just as soon return to my warm bed, from which I was so rudely awakened."

A glint, as of a flash of steel, glowed in the depths of Ermano's eyes. "No doubt you would. But this matter is of vital importance."

"To whom?"

"To the entire city." Ermano sat back in his chair, laying aside the goblet to take up the scroll again. "You know Signora Bassano, of course."

So now it came. Julietta *was* involved. Marc pressed the tips of his fingers together, examining the steeple they formed as if his heart had not seized in his chest. As if he had all the leisure in the world. "You know that I do."

"Indeed. And you know she is not Venetian born, not a part of our hierarchy."

"Neither fish nor fowl?"

Ermano gave Marc a sharp glance at this flippant tone. "She comes from a noble family in Milan, yet she chooses to be a shopkeeper. We have permitted her residence here as a courtesy to her late husband's family and because her shop provides a valuable service. However, now developments have suddenly come to light."

Marc slowly lowered his hands, curling his fingers around the hard wooden arms of the chair. "Developments?"

"Yes." Ermano tapped the scroll against his palm. "Signora Bassano's parents were prominent people in Milan, long in the service of the Sforzas. Her mother's mother, though, was French, of a minor branch of the royal family. Her father died soon after Signora Bassano's marriage to Giovanni Bassano, but her half-French mother died a long time before that. Of natural causes, it was supposed."

Marc frowned. "And this was not so?"

"Perhaps not. You see, recent inquiries have turned up a fact that Signora Bassano's family have worked very hard to conceal. Her mother was arrested for suspicion of witchcraft. Though she was released after only a few days, she died soon after at one of the family's country villas. It was rumoured that the devil came to claim his own at last."

Marc repressed a cold shiver. *Witchcraft?* He knew very well she was not as other women. But—communion with the devil? No. That was not what Julietta was about. He knew that of her as well as he knew his own name.

But the merest whisper of sorcery could get her killed. Could be the end of them both.

"What are the charges against Signora Bassano?" he asked tightly.

Ermano was silent for a long moment, his mouth drawn into a tight line. "You know of the poisonings that have lately plagued certain of the Doge's counsellors?"

Marc nodded shortly. "I have heard tell of it."

"As you know, our investigations have turned up one link between them, outside that of their work. Their wives and mistresses are all faithful patrons of Signora Bassano's shop."

Marc drew in a deep, careful breath. "Surely the nature of their work, so trusted by the Doge, so vital to the city, would be far more likely to hold a clue to their murders than their ladies' shopping habits?"

"Signor Landucci's mother does not think so."

"His mother?"

"I believe you met her on your last visit here. She is most insistent. And her word has no little influence. Her late husband served as an officer of the Quaranta Criminale. She says her son was poisoned by his wife via perfume from Signora Bassano."

"What does the wife say?" Marc asked.

"Ah, now, young Signora Landucci is not without influence of her own. Her father has sent his daughter off to the mainland to recover from her—grief. It is rumoured he is arranging a new marriage for her, with a member of a great family in Rome. We have been unable to question her."

Marc gave a doubtful snort, leaning back leisurely in his chair as if this entire conversation could hold only the mildest interest for him. "The suspicions of a grieving mother seem a flimsy basis for conviction of poisoning and witchcraft. In Spain—"

"We are not in Spain," Ermano interrupted. "This is Venice. And we have our own way of doing things, as you have no doubt learned in your time with us. Signora Bassano's shop will be searched, and, if the vile poison is found there, she must be taken care of."

Marc's hands tightened on the chair arms, until the thickly carved wood creaked. Every instinct urged him to leap on Ermano, to stab his dagger down into the count's black heart and watch his blood stain the pale stone floor. Yet that would not save Julietta. Cold calculation plotted her downfall; only equally careful plotting could redeem her. Redeem them both.

"Taken care of?" he said slowly.

"Yes. Surely even in Spain there are individuals who become liabilities. Obstacles. Signora Bassano still has distant relations in Milan who could successfully protest if she was publicly arrested, could demand that she be returned to them. Then justice would be lost. That is where you come in, *Il leone.*"

Marc's gaze narrowed. "Me?"

"Of course. You will help us avenge these deaths. You will kill Signora Bassano." Ermano held up his scroll. "On the Doge's orders. And if you choose not to listen to our request, remember—we have your ship under watch. And your first mate is our guest in the Leads."

The sunlight was sharp and sparkling, piercing into Marc's eyes as he stepped out of the palace into the crowded piazza. He drew the brim of his cap down to shield his face, closing his eyes for a mere instant.

The noise of the piazza crescendoed around him, the shouts of merchants, the whine of beggars, children's laughter, the strains of a distant lute. The music of every day, the mundane and familiar of any city. It was foreign now, jangling and discordant in Marc's ears.

He was to kill Julietta.

Ermano's words rang in his head, echoing as if from the distant reaches of Dante's hell. She was a "liability" to the government of Venice—she had to be eliminated, but quietly, deceptively, as if in a lovers' quarrel. It would never do to attract unwanted attention from Milan. This was Marc's assignment, a task he must fulfil to prove his own loyalty to the city that had given him such adulation, so many riches. To save his ship, his men, himself.

Marc stared up at the stone lion, crouching high above the crowds, its paw firm on its open book. Perhaps it was the book of destiny, where the ends of all humans were written. Where a mere slash of blood-red ink could sign the end of fleeting, unlooked-for happiness.

A passing pedestrian, hurrying towards the basilica, jostled Marc's arm, pulling him from his musings. Marc edged back into the shadows of the portal, hurrying away from the palace even though he was not sure where he would go. Where he could escape the sinister reach of politics.

Marc left the piazza and turned on to a narrow walkway that ran along the Grand Canal before edging on to a deserted alleyway. The noise of the crowds was muffled here, a mere echo on high stucco walls, distorted and strange. The harsh sunlight was blocked by overhanging balconies, and the air was chilly. Only a single stray cat, balanced on a beam high above, signalled that there was still real life. The dark, deserted space echoed well the black fury of his heart.

A rustle of cloth, a shuffle of boots on flagstone, sounded at the entrance to the alleyway, and Marc ducked behind tall wine barrel, peering out to watch the men go by. They wore black cloaks over their white-and-gold livery, but, still, Marc knew them. They were the guards who escorted him from his rooms to the palace.

The men paused for a moment, squinting into the dimness. Marc held his breath, reaching slowly inside his sleeve for the dagger still strapped to his forearm. There was no need for bloodshed yet, as the guards finally shook their heads and went on their way, looking for him elsewhere. Those men would not be alone, though. Marc knew this well. Venice was filled with spies, including the one who betrayed his affair with Julietta to Ermano.

Ermano did not say this, of course. He never mentioned his own feelings for Julietta at all, or the "favour" he once asked of Marc to watch her for him. How quickly the man's desires had changed! There were no harsh gestures at all, only a calm recitation of the charges against Julietta, and what Marc must do about them. Only that cold, steel-sharp glint in Ermano's eyes told Marc the truth. The count knew what had happened between Marc and Julietta, knew they were lovers in truth, and this was to be Marc's punishment. To destroy the woman who divided them. And then, surely, his own death to follow. Pain and grief unending.

It was an apt punishment, indeed. Not even Ermano could know how much so.

Marc leaned his head back against the rough wall, feeling the bumps and waves of the uneven stucco against his skull, pressing his back through the cloak. Around him, the world went on, but elongated and distorted, as if underwater or a dream. The fragment of sky above him was impossibly blue, a wedge of sea glass, mocking him with its distant, crystalline freedom. Had he not, just last night, promised Julietta he would protect her? Promised her that his ship was always ready to carry her away to the open sea? Now that ship was under watch, their freedom curtailed.

Were they now to be caught in this gilded fisherman's net Ermano cast for them? Thrashing like flounder in the light.

Marc gave a harsh laugh. Not if he could help it! Had

he not learned much from his father, the wiliest merchant-sailor of all the oceans? Had he not escaped such traps countless times, beginning when he was a mere child and saw his mother slain before his eyes? Her murderer would have killed him, too, yet Marc escaped, a boy alone in the world. Escaped and prospered.

Not much had changed in all these years, he saw that now. He was still battling those old demons, still evading their curse. Yet now he was not alone. He had his black-haired enchantress, the jewel he must protect. And he had his secret weapon.

When had that happened? When had his mission, an errand he planned and trained for all these years, become eclipsed by *her?* He could not remember when his need for her powers, for the secrets she wielded, became this all-encompassing desire for her. For this strange, harsh, beautiful woman, full of her own secrets and lies, who held him enthralled as surely as if she had truly cast a magical spell on him. The burning need for revenge evaporated in the face of her danger.

He could not name the moment; perhaps it was when he first saw her in her shop, tall and black-veiled, behind her counter. Or when he kissed her amid the smoke and wine of Nicolai's party, made love to her in her dark room. Saw the wonder glow on her face as she stared through his porthole to the sea beyond. Whenever it was, he was caught like a knight in an old song of courtly, enchanted love, and he would not be easily freed.

He did not even want to be free. Not now. Not of her. But how could they escape this new trap laid for them?

Marc glanced back towards the mouth of the alley. It was empty now, yet he remembered the guards who peered down it only moments before. They would not be alone; others would be out there, close on Marc's trail. He could evade them now, but not easily. Not in bright daylight. He could not just go to Julietta's shop and snatch her up to carry her away to safety.

There had to be another way. Marc pushed away from the wall, tore a rough woollen cloak down from a clothesline, replacing it with his own velvet mantle. Thus disguised, he strode silently to the edge of the alleyway, staying carefully to the shadows as he peered out. Only a few people lingered there to chat before they entered the piazza, an old man in rusty black robes, two young ladies with market baskets over their arms, a whispering couple. He hurried past them, his cloak drawn up close to his jaw, turning not back to the *piazza* but towards the narrow, shabby streets of a less exalted neighbourhood.

Only one friend could help him now—Nicolai. It was time to call in a favour or two.

Chapter Eighteen

Julietta drew back the shutters, waving away the billows of dust released from the painted slats. The motes danced in the broken rays of sunlight, glittering as insect wings before sinking to join the soft gray drifts on the wooden floor. A heady rush of clean air flowed into the stuffy room, bringing with it the cool scents of grass and dirt, the bleaching freshness of country sunshine.

It was obvious that her caretaker, Paolo, and his wife, Rosa, who lived in their own cottage on the grounds and were meant to look after the villa itself, did not consider housecleaning a high priority. The room, a sunny solar set at the top of the house, held only a few pieces of furniture, a long table and some chairs, a crooked sideboard, and they were all dusty. The dark blue draperies were faded, the tapestry cushions set in the window seats threadbare. No fire was lit in the grate, no paintings hung on the whitewashed walls. Still, it was a welcoming room, quiet and isolated, comfortable enough, and it would suit her needs very well.

If it was an untidy dwelling, it was her fault, as well as the stewards'. She neglected this little farm and its villa, spending all her time in her Venetian shop. She was a city-bred woman; what did she know of barley and grapes, of the bounty of the soil, of quiet days ruled by nature? This property had been part of her widow's portion, part of her bribe from Giovanni's family to leave Milan quietly and never return.

Still, there was something now about its earthy peace that appealed to her. Julietta leaned against the window frame, unmindful of the dust on her apron, and stared out over the fallow fields, the distant twists of brown, gnarled grapevines on the slope of a hill. The silence seemed magical, serene, not ominous as quiet moments were in the city. The air was clear, unpolluted by the sickly waters, the crush of people trying to live side by side.

She loved Venice, loved the way a person could hide there, could become someone else entirely. The way one's true nature never needed to be revealed— not even to oneself. But she was not as young as she once was, not as adept at walking the tightrope of an always-deceptive life. This seemed a spot where she could let the mask drop into the dust and breathe free, even if only for a moment.

Or perhaps affection and lust had mellowed her heart?

Julietta laughed to think of it, to think of how Marc Velazquez had crept so stealthily beneath her skin, invading her thoughts and senses as if she was a giddy girl again. How strange it was to laugh about it, when only days ago it would have been horrifying! It was difficult to think or care about anything else, even her work. She could not trust these feelings, didn't even entirely like them, but they would not be banished. Marc was too firmly ensconced now in her senses. He would never be easily dislodged.

So, she would deal with it in the only way she knew. In work. In magic.

Brushing off her hands, Julietta moved to the next set of windows, unlatching the shutters and opening them wide. The chilly, clean light curled in, clearing the last of the gloom and the damp. A wide couch was revealed in the corner, an elaborate, heavy wrought iron creation very different from the plain wooden tables and chairs. There were no coverlets or cushions there now, but Julietta could imagine it piled high with rich blankets and soft sheets. Could imagine her body tangled with Marc's, her hair trailing over his bare chest as their low laughter drifted on the breeze. They would be truly alone here, their passion free to take wing…

Julietta shook her head ruefully, turning away from the bare couch. So, her fantasies followed her everywhere now! Marc would surely never come to this place with her. He would be long gone when next she returned here, back to his beloved sea. Better to have at least one place that would not resonate with his memory. Where she would not be haunted by the echoes of lustful cries, incoherent love words.

She went to the table, where her old, battered travel cases already sat, waiting for her. Their brass latches gleamed dully as she unlocked them and lifted the lids, peering inside. Her bowls and mortar and pestle, her bottles and spoons, her packets of herbs, all sat nestled neatly in their places, waiting for her touch them, to awaken them to their true purpose.

Marc might sail away, but not entirely alone. He would carry her gift with him. Her gift of protection.

"Signora! Signora, are you in there?"

The knocking at the solar door awakened Julietta with startling abruptness. She sat straight up, groaning at the sudden ache of her neck and shoulder. She had fallen asleep at the table, slumped over her crossed arms.

Rubbing at the cramped shoulder, Julietta gazed down at her clutter, at the open book and the tangle of ingredients before her. The light from outside was darker now, tinged with a grayish pink. It grew very late in the day, then.

She hastily closed the book and pushed it into one of the open cases, locking the clasp. It would never do for anyone to see the volume, to guess at what she was about. A glance at her strange ingredients would only lead a casual observer to think she was working on a new perfume. If they could read, though…

"Signora!" The knock came again. "Are you there?"

"*Sì*, I am here." Julietta rose from the table and crossed the room, shaking the wrinkles out of her skirt.

The steward's wife, Rosa, stood there, her white apron stained with traces of whatever she was preparing for supper, a few strands of faded brown hair escaping from her kerchief. Her gaze darted past Julietta into the room, as if to see what was going on there.

Julietta crossed her arms, staying firmly in the doorway. "What is it, Rosa?" she asked.

"You have visitors."

"Visitors?" Julietta frowned. Her nearest neighbours were miles away, and she scarcely knew them. No one would be likely to follow her from Venice, unless—no. It could *not* be Ermano.

A sudden pain twinged in Julietta's temple, and she pressed her numb fingertips to the throbbing spot. This was the property Ermano had wanted to buy, hiding whatever his true purpose was behind land acquisitions. But surely he would not follow her here, now? To what reason?

Not that Ermano ever needed a reason.

"Who are these visitors?" she asked.

Rosa shrugged. "Two men, dressed as wandering players. They are waiting outside. Unless you want Paolo to send them away?"

Travelling players? The only player she knew was Nicolai Ostrovsky, and surely *he* would not be in the country during Carnival. Puzzled, Julietta went to the open window and peered out, careful to stay hidden from view. Below was a curving pathway of crushed shells and gravel, wide enough for horses or even a carriage, but overgrown now with a tangle of wild vegetation. Two horses waited there, their bay hides glistening as if they had galloped a fair distance. Their riders stood on the cracked marble of the front steps, but they wore dark, hooded cloaks, and she could make little of them in the twilight, players or not. Neither of them were wide enough to be Ermano.

Whoever it was, it was obvious they wouldn't leave until their errand was accomplished, not after riding such a distance. Perhaps they were really no one to do with her at all, just travellers seeking direction or sustenance before riding on their way.

She could only hope so.

Julietta drew back into the room, closing the window. "Very well, Rosa. I will go down and see what they want."

After the woman left, Julietta took her travel cloak down from the hook where she had left it and removed her dagger from its hidden pocket. She slid it beneath her tightly tied sleeve, grateful for its slender, reassuring weight. Even in the countryside sanctuary a blade offered its own comfort.

Rosa had left the front door ajar, a mere crack, but through it Julietta could hear the whistle of the wind, the soft rise and fall of murmuring voices. One was rough, too low to make out, but one was tinged with Slavic music.

Julietta dashed forwards to swing the door all the

way open. "Nicolai!" she cried, facing the golden-haired actor. He grinned at her from beneath the shadow of his cloak as the other man turned to face her.

"Marc," she breathed, longing to fall into his arms, to feel his kisses on her skin. It seemed an eternity—and yet only a second—since they had parted in that swaying boat. She did not run to him, though, clutching instead at the edge of the splintered door. His face was so harsh, so solemn in the gathering darkness.

Her gaze travelled over them, noting the brightly striped hose and beribboned doublets hidden by their cloaks, the gilded masks dangling by their strings. Travelling players, indeed. "What are you two doing here?" she asked quietly. This was surely no romantic rendezvous.

"We bring news," Nicolai said. Despite his greeting smile, even his voice was solemn, low and quiet. No Arlechino tonight.

"How did you find me?" she asked.

"Your maid, Bianca, gave me your direction," Nicolai answered. Marc just watched her closely.

Julietta shivered as the night breeze blew over her. "She was not supposed to tell anyone where I went."

"You must not blame her," Nicolai said. "She did not want to divulge your location at first."

"But you were—persuasive. Yes." Julietta stepped back, drawing the door wide. "You had best come in and tell me your news, since you have ridden so far."

They followed her through the silent, empty corridors to a small chamber at the back of the house. Paolo and Rosa sometimes used this room so it was better furnished than the others, with cushioned chairs and stools and a neatly swept floor. A ewer of wine and cluster of goblets sat on a table by the closed window, and that was where Julietta went. Fussing with the familiar motions of pouring and arranging wine helped her gather some calmness, still the shaking of her hands. *News.* No one rode so far, so fast, in disguise, with glad tidings.

"I am sorry there is no supper yet," she said, her voice unsteady even to her own ears. Their news, surely of no good, could wait. "But perhaps some wine will help clear the dust of the road."

A soft touch fell on her arm, stilling her jerky movements. Julietta glanced up to find that Marc had come silently to her side, regarding her with solemn eyes, midnight blue in the half-gloom.

She had seen him teasing, laughing, passionate, angry, silent with a hidden longing. Seen flashes of the warrior feared by pirates, courted by the great. Never before had she glimpsed such quiet sombreness in him, such watchful tenderness. It reminded her a bit of her old Scottish nursemaid, who had tried so hard to comfort Julietta when her mother was snatched away before her very eyes.

And that was the most frightening thing. The careful tenderness.

"Let me pour," he said quietly. "You sit by the fire. The night is cold."

Julietta bit her lip, her gaze sliding away from him to find that Nicolai stood beside the stone grate, holding out a chair for her. His smile steadied her a bit. Surely no witch-baiter could find her with two such men at her side! They were not as her weak father had been. And she—well, she did not have her mother's innate powers, but hopefully she inherited some of her defiant spirit.

Julietta straightened her shoulders and tilted back her chin, turning towards the waiting warmth of the fire. "Thank you, Marc," she said, settling into the chair. Nicolai seated himself across from her, and they waited in careful silence until Marc joined them, handing around the goblets of rich, spicy wine.

Julietta took a long sip before saying, "Very well. What is this news that has brought you all the way here? What could not await my return to the city?"

Marc and Nicolai exchanged a glance, and Julietta felt an ember of anger catch deep inside of her. She set her goblet down on the nearest table with a sharp clatter, the liquid sloshing against the metal sides. "I am not a child who needs coddling!" she cried. "Tell me now, so I may know how to deal with matters. What? Did my shop burn down? Did someone steal all my supplies?"

"Nothing like that, Julietta," Marc answered. "But I fear you are in great danger."

Danger? Julietta leaned back in her chair. She had been in danger since the day she was born. It was simply who she was, her heritage as a Montcrecy woman. Yet in Venice she had hoped that she had found a small measure of peace.

Until she met Marc, and discovered how fragile that illusion of peace was.

"Tell me," she said shortly.

"I have been asked—nay, ordered to kill you. For the good of the Republic," Marc answered flatly, as if he inquired what they were to have for supper or stated that the sky was blue. He watched her carefully, but did not reach out for her, which was just as well.

Julietta feared she would shatter at a touch, for it felt as if her skin turned to ice. Burning ice. A low buzzing sounded in her brain, enclosing her in a cocoon of unreality. She crossed her arms tight over her abdomen, feeling the sharp press of the hidden dagger.

"You have come here to kill me?" she murmured.

Marc's brows drew down in a fierce frown. "Of course not, Julietta! I have come here to make plans with you. My ship is being watched, my first mate held as hostage. We cannot just run. So, we must devise a means whereby Ermano—and all of Venice—will *think* you are dead."

"A play, you see," Nicolai said. "A scene within a scene. And we will all be the players."

Julietta glanced warily between the two men, that dreamlike sense only increasing. She knew not what they spoke of, what new web enclosed her. She reached out blindly for her goblet and drank deeply of the wine, until the heady brew cleared away some of the shadows. "I think you had best tell me the whole tale."

And it was a long tale, indeed. Night crept over the countryside, shadows lengthening in their little room until Rosa came to light the rest of the candles. Julietta sent her away, performing the task herself as Marc and Nicolai spoke. The flickers of candlelight cast an even more hallucinatory air over the room, an edge of gold and rose that half convinced Julietta she must soon awaken in her own bed, finding all of this nothing but an illusion.

Even Marc must surely be a figure of a dream—him most of all. He sat by the fire, half in shadow, the sharp planes of his face outlined in gold like a saint in the basilica. His hair, pushed carelessly back from his brow, fell to his shoulders in a tumbled river of brown and amber. He looked just as an angel should; an angel who brought strange and terrible tidings.

"I was summoned to the Doge's Palace this morning, where Ermano Grattiano waited for me," he said. "He gave me this—task himself."

"Ermano?" Julietta asked sharply. Of course. She should have known. With all the wealth and power she saw flaunted at his banquet, a shop owner, even one as prosperous as she was, would be a mere fly beneath his jewelled heel. Quick. Easy. Yet painful for the fly.

"He is a bad enemy to have," Marc said simply.

Julietta snorted. "Indeed, he is. Everyone in Venice knows this well. And yet I thought *you* were his friend, *Il leone*."

Marc's mouth tightened. "I was never that man's *friend*."

"You merely played a game, then. A dangerous game."

"And one of very long standing."

"One you think you can win?"

A ghost of a smile whispered across Marc's face, easing the tension. "Obviously not. We are both now trapped, are we not?"

"It would seem so," Julietta said, her gaze never wavering from his face. Marc was an enigma, an onion hidden beneath hundreds of iridescent layers, if she could make so unromantic an analogy. She had seen glimpses of his soul before, especially aboard the *Elena Maria,* yet they were always veiled. Now, she sensed she was closer than ever before to seeing the exposed core of him.

Dared she unmask her own heart? No, not yet. Not quite yet.

"What makes him your enemy?" Marc asked.

Julietta shrugged. "He wished to buy this property, as you know. He came to me last year with an offer. It was not a bad price, but I have no desire to sell. I find this place convenient at times. I refused, and thought it was an end to it. Yet still he kept returning."

Marc leaned closer to her, the bells on his player's doublet jangling discordantly. Nicolai watched them, yet said nothing. "He kept coming back for this land?"

"It is not much, I know. It has grown wild under my lax care, yet a careful steward could make it profitable. Mainland farms are always of use to rich Venetians," Julietta answered. "I always knew there was more to his request, though. There always is with men like Ermano. But I did not know for sure what his true aim was until a few days ago. The afternoon before we went to your ship."

"He wished to have you for his mistress?" Marc asked softly.

Julietta stared at him. His face was still as impassive as those golden saints, but his eyes glowed sea-blue. "He wished to marry me. Was most insistent upon it, in fact. And he was not best pleased when I refused." She paused, her thoughts and memories whirling until she feared she would scream out from it all. She pressed her fingertips to her temples. "And this is his answer. I would not do as he wished, so I must be eliminated. I do not understand why he would give the task to *you*, Marc. Why not simply have me charged with witchcraft and hauled out to be burned, like—" She broke off, unable to go on. Unable even to think it.

"Like your mother?" Marc said softly.

Julietta closed her eyes tightly. "So, you know."

"It was one of the things Ermano told me, when I was summoned to the Doge's Palace and given my— task."

Julietta nodded, greatly weary. Her mother's sad fate, Julietta's own screams as she was torn from her arms, haunted her still. Echoed inside of her every day. Later, she would have to tell Marc of that horrible night, of the sizzling torches, the soldiers' leering faces, her mother's pale, unshakeable dignity. But not this moment. For now, Marc knew all he needed to.

Nicolai spoke at last, breaking into the tense silence. "That would not be subtle enough for the illustrious count, I think. A lurid trial, a burning, much gossip. *Nyet.* I believe he knows the two of you are lovers, and this is his way of eliminating you both. Of taking his secret revenge."

"Revenge," Marc spat out, as if that single word, so essential and ever present in their world, was a foul oath.

"Nicolai is right," Julietta said. "Ermano has spies everywhere. I should have known to take more care, but I just—" And again she broke off, her voice choking. How could she speak of that hot rush of need, of oblivious passion she felt when Marc touched her? The need that crackled between them and made care meaningless and impossible.

"*We* should have been more careful," Marc said tightly. "But we were not, and now we must plan our counter-attack."

Julietta tapped her fingertips on the arm of her chair, regarding Marc steadily. This was how he must have looked as he watched the pirate ship approach in the mist, narrow-eyed, calculating, coolly gauging the strength of his foe's guns compared to his. Ermano's "guns" were formidable, indeed—the backing of the Doge, great power and wealth.

But Julietta would not like to be the one caught in Marc's cold blue gaze, even backed by money and power.

She herself was not completely without resources, either. Was she not her mother's daughter? Her *grand-mère's* grandchild? She would not dishonour their legacy.

"Where is my murder to take place?" she asked.

Marc reached inside his beribonned player's doublet and withdrew a small, tightly furled scroll. The Doge's seal gleamed in the flicker of the candles.

"At the Doge's ball. We are to have a lovers' quarrel in the midst of the dance, and then I am to stab you to death." He watched her steadily, one brow crooked teasingly. "An intriguing game, is it not, *querida?*"

Chapter Nineteen

Marc's tale was interrupted by Rosa announcing that supper was ready, and Julietta discovered, much to her surprise, that she was famished. Plotting developed quite an appetite, after all. After a simple, hearty country repast of bread, cheese, olives, and a stew of sausage and boiled vegetables, she led Marc and Nicolai out to the garden, where they could speak without any fear of being overheard.

The moon was still low in the sky, lighting their way with a pale, silver-green glow. The gardens were tangled and overgrown, but the pathways wound their white way around the twisted beds and ragged mazes, past tilting, cracked urns and marble cupids, a dry, empty fountain. The bare limbs of the trees overhead, interlocking like skeletal fingers that rattled in the chilly wind.

Julietta shivered, and tugged the edge of her cloak closer about her throat. She paused beside an old statue, a chipped torso of some Roman goddess. Her limbs and head were long gone, leaving only perfect breasts, a sloping abdomen, the tops of smooth thighs. Julietta leaned against the ancient hunk of marble, half fearing that such mutilation might soon be her own fate.

Yet the unfortunate goddess lacked something Julietta possessed—two strong warriors at her back, bent on keeping her, and themselves, intact. They paused with her, two tall, thickly cloaked figures limned in moonlight.

"So," she said, picking up the threads of their abandoned conversation as if they had never been interrupted, "you are to stab me at the Doge's grand ball?"

Marc nodded. He smoothed his palm over the goddess's shattered shoulder. Julietta watched, mesmerised. "In a fit of lover's jealousy."

"But then what happens to you, when I am lying dead on the Doge's marble floor?" she asked.

Marc gave a bitter laugh. "I am seized and carried off to prison, of course. Borne over the Bridge of Sighs, never to be seen again."

"It seems poor recompense for delivering the city from a plague of pirates."

"According to this little scroll, it will only *seem* I am being taken to prison. I will actually be taken to my ship, along with my freed first mate, free to sail away, yet banned from Venetian ports. In return, I will be paid a fortune in Grattiano gold."

"Yet we both know that Ermano is not best known

for keeping his promises," Julietta said quietly, taking just a step closer to Marc in the cold night. Why, oh, why had she wasted her studies in useless alchemical experiments, in making perfumes and lotions for vain women? She would have been better served in learning dark spells, in becoming a witch in truth. Then she could weave an enchantment to carry them all out of this place, and leave Ermano Grattiano and his cursed whelp Balthazar smoking in their wake.

But, alas, she had not. She had no magic to offer now when it was most needed.

"Accidents do happen, though," Marc said wryly. "Especially on the way to prison."

"How shall we devise our way out?"

"Ah, now," Nicolai interrupted. "That is where I come in, *doushka*."

Julietta swung towards him. He could barely be seen, yet starlight glimmered on his golden hair. He seemed an elvish creature then, emerged from a spell-bound forest to save them. Or lead them astray, as mischievous elves so often did. "How so?"

He held out his hands, palms up. "Am I not the leader of a troupe of players, *signora*? This will be our greatest moment, though no one shall ever know it but ourselves."

"What do you mean?" Julietta asked, intrigued. Yes, he was definitely sent to lead them astray.

"Ermano Grattiano wants a masque to play out at the grand ball. Very well—he shall have one. Just not quite the one he requested. Here is my idea..."

* * *

The country quiet was perfect, absolute. And terribly disquieting.

Julietta leaned out of her bedchamber window, staring at the deserted garden below. A cloud skittered in front of the moon, bathing everything in a grayish mist, blanketing all in silence. In the city, there was seldom true quiet. There was always someone talking, laughing, shouting, always the creak of wood and stone, the bubble of fountains, the toll of church bells. Here, there was nothing. Even the wind was still now.

The only sound came from the room behind her. Julietta drew back into the fire-warmed chamber and turned to face Marc. He stood by the bed, his gaudy doublet tossed over the clothes chest, the lacings of his white linen shirt loosened to reveal a vee of glistening bronze chest. The ends of his hair were damp from the quick splash of water he had tossed over his face.

He rested one hand flat on the carved wooden post of the bed, regarding her with a silent stillness that rivalled the night outside. His lips did not curve in any reassuring smile, yet neither did they arc in a frown. His face was smooth and perfect as a Carnival mask, his eyes deep wells of blue-black emotion.

Julietta curled her own hand into a tight fist, feeling the weight of the ruby ring on her finger. *Send me the ring if you have need of me, and I will come to you,* he had said. It appeared she *did* have need of him, of his strength and sword. She, who never needed anyone. Who knew the folly of relying too much on anyone else. She needed him for more than his warrior strength, too. Far more.

Julietta frowned at the thought, dropping her gaze from the enticing sight of him waiting in the firelight. Their bodies had been as intimate as two beings of flesh and blood *could* be, so close that not even a whisper of air could come between them. Yet she never felt as dangerously close to him—to anyone—as she did at this moment, with the length of a silent room stretching from her heart to his. Their secrets seemed to hover over them, ready to crash to the floor in a fiery explosion, and change all with a word.

He knew of her mother, of what had happened to her, yet he did not know it all. Julietta did not think she even had the words for the truth any more.

A soft rustle of movement broke into her thoughts, and her gaze flew back to Marc. He seated himself on the clothes chest at the foot of the bed, his long legs in their black hose stretched out before him. He leaned back on his flattened palms, still watching her. His shoulders were stiff, as if he was as wary as she. As if she was an approaching ship, too far for colours to be discerned and he knew not if she was friend or foe.

They could not be foes. Not now. If they could not stand together they would surely fall, for they had only each other now.

Julietta closed and locked the shutters, and came into the chamber to perch on the edge of the bed. She could only see Marc from the corner of her eyes, but she heard his breathing, sensed every ripple of the fine linen across his body.

"Is Nicolai truly a travelling player?" she asked.

Marc crossed his booted ankles, slowly, as if considering his reply. "Among other things," he said slowly.

"What sort of things?"

"Ah, now, those are his own secrets to tell. And even I do not know the whole tale of Nicolai Ostrovsky."

"But he will really help us?"

"I would stake my life on it."

"You trust him that much?" Julietta said doubtfully.

Marc nodded, his curtain of hair falling forward to shield his expression. Julietta longed to sweep it back, to sift the silken strands in her fingers, to cup his face in her palms and absorb some of his warm life into her cold soul. She stayed where she was, though, tucking her hands beneath her woollen skirts. Right now, she needed some answers even more than she needed the consolation of Marc's body.

"Yes, I do," Marc answered firmly. "He has saved my life many times."

"He says you have done the same for him."

"So I have."

"Why?"

"Is that not what friends do? Pull each other from the fire when needed?" A faint amusement touched the edge of Marc's voice.

Is that not what friends do? Julietta pressed her hand to her bodice, feeling a strange, sharp pang in the region of her heart. Had she ever truly possessed such a friend? Her mother and grandmother had loved her, but they were her teachers, her protectors, not her confidantes. Bianca, maybe, though Julietta held so many secrets from the Turkish maid that they could never truly be close. She had a feeling Bianca held plenty of secrets of her own.

Julietta glanced at Marc, who had turned towards her, gazing at her in careful silence. Marc was her lover, yet was he her friend? Did he, too, have hidden interests that would one day clash with hers, bringing them both to grief? In her experience, that was ever what happened. "Friendship" was a shifting matter. And yet here he was—pulling her from the fire when he could have taken to his heels and fled.

"So, Nicolai will help us, even though his own secrets cannot be divulged," she murmured.

"They are not my secrets to tell," Marc answered. "You will have to ask him for yourself."

Julietta tilted her head, studying him carefully. "And what of you, Marc Velazquez? What are *your* secrets to tell?"

A shadow passed over his face, casting a darkness over the edges of his cheekbones, his glorious eyes. He tilted his head, giving her a considering glance. "I have many, *querida,* just as you do. Which would you like to hear first?"

Julietta thought of the tarot cards—*you must let go of fears, move into the future free of chains.* Did she want to know, truly? Nay, not *want.* She *had* to know.

That was all. "Who are you, really? Why did you come to Venice? It was not truly to chase pirates, I think."

Marc laughed, a harsh, humourless sound, far older than his years. "The pirates were just a fortuitous happenstance. As to who I really am—well, as you know, I was not born Marc Antonio Velazquez. For the first six years of my life, I was Marco Rinaldi, the son of Veronica Rinaldi. And the son of Ermano Grattiano."

Chapter Twenty

Julietta stared at Marc, her ears ringing. Had she truly heard him aright? He was...

"Ermano's son?" she whispered, horrified.

Marc nodded, still watching her, his face impassive. She could see nothing of the count in the harsh, beautiful angles of his face, in his turquoise eyes. He was only the masculine shadow of his lovely mother. Yet there was something deeper, some kind of ruthlessness that was his father.

"I have long planned to return to my birthplace, to find my father again," he said.

Julietta stared at him, confused. "But why? You had a fine family in Spain, parents who cared for you, a prosperous life. Why would you leave it behind to find Ermano? Or did you not know of his true nature before?"

Marc's eyes gleamed coldly. "Oh, I knew."

"Then..." Julietta shook her head, puzzlement

slowly clearing like clouds after a storm, leaving only a cold certainty. She should have known, have guessed, when he told her of his mother, of how she died at Ca Grattiano. "You came to have your revenge on him."

"Yes," Marc answered simply. "He murdered my mother."

Julietta swallowed hard past the painful, icy lump in her throat. She saw the scene all too well in her mind, the palatial room, the small boy cowering in fear. The flash of a blade, or perhaps the soft slither of a garrotting scarf, a woman's scream abruptly cut off. She longed to reach out to Marc, to take him in her arms and soothe away the wounds of the past, the dangers of the present. But in truth, she had never been terribly good at soothing; any ministrations beyond the practical always seemed to end so badly for her. And Marc's face was so closed, so expressionless, his shoulders defensively stiff. The solitary warrior.

"And you saw it happen," she said softly.

"I did," Marc answered. "They had been quarrelling all evening, over what I knew not. Perhaps one of my mother's admirers. Ermano was ever a jealous man. He still is, as we know well. There was a banquet that night, and we were to stay at Ca Grattiano after. My father liked to keep my mother close, you see, and he had not yet wed Balthazar's mother, so there was no lady of the house to gainsay him. I was allowed to watch the beginning of the party, to hear the music and filch a sweetmeat or two. Then, my nurse put me to bed."

"But you did not stay there," Julietta said.

He turned his steady, cool gaze onto her. "I did for a time. I was only six, and the banquet was very exciting. Luckily, I did not remain in oblivious sleep for long."

"Luckily?"

"If I had not wakened when I did, saw what I did, I would not be here now, would I? I would be dead, or, worse, one of Ermano's minions, scurrying about Venice to do his dirty deeds. Like Balthazar."

"Or you would be heir to his great fortune." Somehow, that prospect, so glittering and enticing to so many, made Julietta shiver. Marc did not belong at the head of Ermano's bountiful table, lord of the cold, dead rooms of that palazzo. He belonged on his ship, with the waves and the wind. Free.

Sometimes God was so strangely merciful.

Marc laughed bitterly. "I will leave poor, young Balthazar to that. I want only one thing from Ermano."

"His blood."

"How perceptive you are, Julietta. If you had known my mother, seen what happened that night…"

Julietta had *not* been there, and yet she would rejoice at the end of Ermano Grattiano. He had planned for her the same fate as her own mother, as Marc's mother, and schemed to use her lover as the instrument of her downfall. All because she, a free woman, would not give in to his wild demands. She left her perch on the bed and went to Marc's side, holding out her hand to him.

"Tell me about what happened," she whispered.

Marc stared at her hand for a long, silent moment before suddenly reaching out to clasp it hard. His fingers tightened on hers, and he tugged her down to sit beside him on the chest. The wooden surface was not wide and they were pressed close, shoulder to shoulder, her thigh tight to his. He still held her hand, yet she could sense he was not entirely with her. That he was trapped in a moment that happened years ago.

"I was awakened by something—a movement outside my door, perhaps servants whispering. I could not go back to sleep," he said, staring down at their entwined fingers. "So, I got out of bed and crept out into the corridor. My chamber was not far from that room where I found you at Ermano's banquet."

"The one we escaped from," Julietta said, remembering how he carried her out that window and down those narrow stone steps, rescuing her from Ermano and his suffocating banquet.

"Yes. It was very late, all the guests had gone home. It was dark and silent. Then, suddenly, I heard a sound, voices, coming from the *sala*. They rose sharply, sounding so angry. My parents. I knew they would be even more angry if they found me out of my room— the one rule of my young life was never to interrupt my mother when she was with a man. Especially my father. I turned back towards my chamber, but then I heard a scream." His voice, so distant and cool, deepened. Cracked.

"And you ran down there." Julietta could see it all.

Even as a six-year-old, her gallant lion would not leave a person in distress unprotected. Look how he was trying to rescue *her,* when he could be long gone from Venice.

"The door was ajar, so I slipped inside and hid behind a carved screen, which is no longer there. It used to be in the corner by the fireplace. There are no hiding places now in that house, I suppose. My parents had argued many times before, of course. They would part in great flames of acrimony, only to come back together again. This seemed somehow different, though. It was a hot night, and blood seemed stirred by the heat. I did not understand half of what they said. What are wild accusations of faithlessness to a child? But I did understand the dagger my father drew."

Julietta could not breathe. Her chest felt tight, her skin cold. She tightened her hand in Marc's, ready to pull him back into the present, if only she could. Still, she persisted. She had to. "He stabbed her."

"Slit her throat, like a pig in the market. And he dropped her to the marble floor and left the room, slamming the doors behind him." Marc's voice was toneless, quiet. But Julietta knew what it was to be young and helpless, to have the person you loved best torn from you, suddenly, cruelly. She knew the meagre shreds of emotional armour a child learned to gather around their heart. How that armour hardened and grew.

"I ran to her," he went on, "called her name, but she was dead. Her blood spread on that cold floor. I heard my father out in the corridor, calling for a servant to fetch Claude Gonzago. Saying there had been a robbery, a foul murder. I knew I did not have much time. I took the ring from her finger and put it on my own." He unfurled his hand to balance Julietta's on his palm, displaying the blood-red ruby. "And I ran, fled out of that room you and I escaped from. I was convinced that if my father knew what I had seen, he would kill me, too."

Julietta gazed down at the ring, its magnificence mocking in the firelight. Still, she knew she could never take it off. It represented the bravery of a slain woman, and that courage she passed on to her son. The heart of a lion.

"Did he never look for you?" she asked, curling her fingers tightly around his.

Marc shrugged. "I do not know. By the time he thought of me at all I was probably halfway to Spain."

"To a new life."

"Aye. I love the Velazquezes with all my heart, Julietta. They are my true parents in so many ways, and I owe them my very existence. But I made a vow over my mother's body that I would avenge her, no matter how long it took. No matter what I had to do. Who I had to use."

He stared at her steadily, and Julietta knew what he meant. He had tried to use *her*. That was why he first appeared in her shop. Yet look where they were now— hunted, trapped, outcast. Yet hardly outmanoeuvred. It had come close to full circle on them.

She almost laughed at it all, the absurdity, but the choked chuckle turned to a sob.

"Do you think I'm a monster?" Marc asked fiercely. "A creature with Ermano's tainted blood in my veins?"

"Do you think *I* am a witch?" she retorted.

A grin twisted his lips, and he reached up to touch her cold cheek. "You have certainly enchanted me."

"No more so than you have me, *Il leone.* We are a lovely pair, are we not? A witch with no powers, a monster beset with chivalry. What shall we do?"

"Carry out Nicolai's plan, of course. It is our only hope. We are followed too closely, my ship watched too fully for us to flee now. I have run before—I will not run this day."

"And what of your revenge? If our scheme succeeds, it will be left undone."

Marc was silent for a long moment, the quiet stretching out before them in a shimmering strand. At last, he said, "Do you not think that simply being Ermano is enough punishment for anyone?"

Julietta gave a startled laugh. "It is not a fate I would wish on anyone, not even a stray cat. Yet he has his money, his power."

"What has it gained him? I came back to Venice expecting to beard a lion in his den, but I could not find what I looked for. He does have his riches and his power, true. All of the great patricians bow to him. But he is not satisfied. He is like an engorged spider caught in his own web, twisting with his own bitterness, his own frustrated longings. Look how he has pursued you. Look how he treats his own son and heir."

"Twisted, indeed," she murmured, remembering

Ermano's eyes as he grabbed for her in her shop, insisting that she be his wife. Crazed. Caught up in a vision only *he* could see.

Julietta could understand that. Did she not pursue her own vision in the face of all obstacles and opposition? But her skin crawled at the memory of Ermano's touch.

"Leaving this place is of the greatest importance," Marc said. "But I don't think we will leave Ermano completely unpunished. There are depths to young Balthazar that I think have not yet seen their full realisation. He will take his own back from his father with a ruthlessness not even Ermano can match. There is a light in his eyes I have only seen before in those of a pirate before he engages in battle."

"And he is your brother," Julietta said.

Marc looked surprised by this, as if he had not thought of that before. "So he is."

"Perhaps he will one day learn to emulate you, and set his anger aside for a different course."

"Venice will be all the better for it, if he can. I am not sure I have the strength for it."

"You are the strongest man I have ever known," Julietta said. She reached up with her free hand, gently tracing the clean, handsome line of his nose and chin, the sharp sweep of his cheekbone. A strand of his hair caught on her skin, tangling as if to hold her there. "I wish…"

"What do you wish?" He covered her hand with his, pressing her skin to his.

Julietta shook her head, dizzy with all she had learned tonight. How could Ermano have wanted to marry her? Intrigue exhausted her. And Venice would always be filled with plot and counterplot, never resting. She wanted only peace at this moment, a long, dreamless sleep in the haven of this man's arms. They still had a journey ahead of them, one fraught with dangers, but tonight—tonight was theirs. And it was still young.

She lowered her lips to his, featherlight, soft. Gentle. The feel of him, the taste of him, salty and sweet at the same time, intoxicating as the finest wine, was familiar now, yet she still craved it. *Needed* it. Needed him, Marc.

The old, welling sense of fear rose up inside of her, but she pressed it down. Marc was not Giovanni, or Ermano; he was not like anyone else at all. It was not so very dangerous to be vulnerable with him, to let herself open to him, as he had to her.

Her lips brushed his again, and she felt him groan deeply against her, felt his hands clasp her hips, pulling her closer. Her tongue plunged past his lips, seeking his dark, sweet depths as he dragged her skirts higher. Cool air brushed against her bare thighs, but it was swiftly erased by the heat of his touch, rough and urgent on her skin.

He stood up, still holding her close, their mouths still fused, and tumbled them back on the bed. Julietta's legs spread, welcoming his body into the soft cradle of her femininity. His hose was in her way, and she reached out to tug at the lacings, ripping the thin cloth in her need.

Marc rose up, tearing his lips from hers to stare down at her. His hair tumbled back from his face, loose and tangled; his skin glistened in the candlelight. Her pirate, her lion—her love.

"Do I not disgust you?" he whispered roughly. "Now you know where I came from."

Julietta fell back against the pillows, breathless, aching. *Disgust* her? How could he? He was the most beautiful thing she had ever seen. She hardly knew where to find the words to tell him the full depth of her feelings. Were there the words in all the world?

"Do *I* disgust *you?*" she said. "Since you know I am descended from French witches, that my husband's family cast me off? Do you not want to search for Satan's mark on my body?"

Marc gave a dismissive snort. "Julietta! Even if your mother *was* a witch, which I scarcely believe— nay, even if she was the devil's mistress incarnate, you are not her. You are yourself, your own person entirely. Answerable only for your own actions."

"As are you!" Julietta cried. "You are not your father, not a manifestation of his sins. You are a victim of them, as your mother was. You are Marc, that is all. Just Marc."

He went willingly into her embrace, his lips seeking out the curve of her neck, leaving a trail of flames in the wake of his kisses. He nibbled at her earlobe, and her thoughts turned blurry. Soon, she would have no coherent mind at all, only quivering need. And she welcomed that sweet oblivion, turning her head to give him free access to her flesh.

"For tonight," he whispered. "For tonight, then, I am only Marc, a man who loves Julietta."

Julietta's eyes fluttered closed, and she purred with deepest contentment. He *loved* her! Right now, that was all that mattered. That was everything. "And I am only Julietta. But…" She pushed him away, reaching up between their bodies to teasingly tug free the edge of her bodice lacing, slowly revealing one pale breast. One aching, peaked pink nipple. "Are you certain you won't reconsider that search for the devil's mark? I am sure I must have one here some place."

Marc growled and fell upon her, his mouth covering that hard, inviting nipple, until she cried out at the cresting sensations. Thought vanished entirely, given over to sensations, feelings, *needs*. His hand slid up her torso, drawing down her loosened bodice, her dampened chemise, until he could cup her breast, rolling her sensitive nipple with his fingertips. Her back arched, begging for more, for everything.

Slowly, the wet heat of his mouth trailed away, and he blew lightly over the pebbled flesh. Julietta groaned out incoherent words, tangling her fingers in his hair to try to draw him back.

He resisted, leaning up to draw away her gown entirely, tossing it to the floor. His own garments swiftly joined them, and they were pressed skin to skin.

"*Do* you love me, Julietta?" he moaned. "For tonight?"

"For always," she answered. Her eyes opened and she stared up into his beautiful, desperate face, at the eyes that glowed like sapphires. And with those words she knew the past, her horrible marriage, her lonely widowhood, was gone. "For always."

That seemed all he needed. He lowered himself between her welcoming legs, his heavy, engorged penis probing at the edge of her damp, hot cleft. Julietta gasped as all her nerve endings contracted, and she lifted herself up to draw him fully inside. He plunged deep, touching her womb, her very soul. They were as one, and no plots could separate them, no schemes or secrets or lies or even the shadow of death that hung over them.

Julietta threw her head back, straining with him as their bodies lunged and heaved in an ancient rhythm. Her eyes closed so she could feel him, all of him, the slide of his manhood, the clinging dampness of their skin, the humid smell of their sweat and passion. She wanted it all, every bit of it, for ever. She wanted to never forget it.

But then *everything* was forgotten in a vast explosion, a blast of thunder. A shower of hot stars, blue, red, purple, silver, shooting up into the black sky, and then collapsing over her whole body. She tightened her legs even more around him, sobbing, crying, as he shouted out above her.

"Julietta!" he roared. Then, softer, infinitely tender, as he collapsed against her shoulder. "Julietta *querida*."

"Marc. My wonderful pirate," she whispered. She reached up weakly to caress the damp, tangled length of his hair, the strands sifting through her fingers. His weight on her, bearing them down together into the mattress, was glorious. They were joined, truly joined, floating in the midst of those stars that proclaimed the night was theirs. Theirs alone.

Chapter Twenty-One

The shop was still locked up and dark when Julietta returned from the countryside, even though it was past midday and business should have commenced long ago. The other merchants around the square sported open windows, swinging signs, patrons bustling in and out with their baskets over their arms. Servants scooped water from the fountain, their gossip and teasing laughter echoing from the stucco walls.

Julietta frowned at the blue-painted boards of the closed door at her perfumerie. Bianca was usually so very reliable, careful in her management of the shop when Julietta was away. Could she be ill? Or perhaps Ermano had tired of his cat-and-mouse game, and raided the place already, carrying off the maid in place of the mistress.

A sense of disquiet, of foreboding, making her shiver, Julietta reached inside her cloak pocket to retrieve the key. Fortunately, the door was not barred, and the iron lock scraped easily apart. Julietta pushed open the door and slipped inside, her mind and nerves taut.

She wasn't sure what she expected, but the room was swept clean, the counter polished, the bottles and pots all in their places. There was no scatter of broken glass carpeting the floor, no torn upholstery or gouged walls. The building was silent, echoingly so. Even the everyday noises from outside were muffled, distorted, as if they came from another world.

"Bianca?" Julietta called softly. Her own voice reflected back to her. She put her case on the counter and went up the stairs, her footfalls gentle on the floorboards. The chamber was as empty as the shop, the bed neatly made up, the gown she changed from before she left still draped over the chair. Bianca's truckle bed in the corridor was also carefully in its place.

Julietta stood in the corridor, her gaze scanning the empty corners as if surely there must be some clue there. Bianca had been such a loyal servant, a friend even, since she came to Julietta's shop so long ago! Something must have happened. But what?

She went back into the bedchamber and edged open one of the shutters, peering cautiously on to the square below. The ebb and flow of commerce and socialising went on, and there was no Bianca to be seen anywhere. There was, however, one figure who did not belong in the colourful mosaic of everyday life. A tall, burly man in a brown leather jerkin stood near the arched entrance, his plain wool cap pulled low over his brow. He pretended to pare his nails with the tip of a slim dagger, yet it was obvious he watched her shop. Even a pert, pretty maidservant in a cherry-coloured skirt sashaying past could not gain his attention.

Really, Ermano, how clumsy of you to choose such a guard, Julietta thought. He was usually more subtle in his spies. But then, perhaps this lack of subtlety was part of his plan. Perhaps he wanted to show her that he had her neatly cornered.

She tilted back her chin, staring down at the man. Ermano would never have her cornered, not if she could help it. She had her own plans. In the meantime, she might as well give the bored guard something to observe and herself a way to wile away the long day, before she went crazy with the waiting. She would just open the shop herself, albeit a bit late, and wait for the patrons to come.

She spun around and dashed down the stairs, shedding her travel cloak and reaching for an apron, instead. She still wore her plain woollen gown, but that could not be helped. There was no time to change into her usual black-and-white attire. Her customers would just have to accept her as she was today. Besides, if all went as planned, she would not have to worry about business in Venice much longer.

As Julietta reached up to open the shutters in the shop, she at last heard a noise that was not of her own making. A small sound of tinkling, shattering glass from the store-room.

Julietta froze, her fingers convulsing on the latch. Why had she not thought to look in the store-room before? She glanced back over her shoulder at the tightly closed door behind the counter. Was that a ray of candlelight she saw passing fleetingly under the threshold?

"Who is there?" she called, loosening the dagger beneath her sleeve. The heft of the hilt was reassuring in her grasp.

There was no answer, just a soft shuffle that was well nigh undetectable. Julietta crept to the door, leaning closer to listen. Perhaps it was only the strange events of the last few days making her imagination too keen, but she would vow she heard a breath. Her skin prickled with suppressed fear.

Julietta suddenly threw open the store-room door, brandishing her dagger high as she cried out, "Show yourself, villain!"

Bianca threw up her arm, cowering back against the wall. A sack fell from her grasp, landing on the flagstone floor with a muffled crash. "No, *madonna,* please! 'Tis only me, Bianca."

Julietta lowered the blade, but still held the hilt firmly curled in her fingers. Her lungs ached as she tried to breathe again. There was something so very odd about this whole scene, something that made the very hair on the back of her neck tingle. "Bianca? What are you doing in here? Why did you not answer when I called out?"

Bianca gave a choked sob, pressing her hand to her mouth. She had lost her cap, and the thick tumble of her matte-black curls fell to her shoulders. She wore a heavy brown cloak over her striped skirts and pink bodice.

"I—I did not hear you," Bianca said, her voice hoarse. "I thought you were still in the country."

Julietta thought it unlikely Bianca had not heard her come in. The store-room door was not very stout, so that patrons could be heard entering the shop. Her gaze darted from the maid to the sack on the floor, to the dishevelled mess along one wall. The shelf had been pulled away, dislodging many of the ceramic containers of oils and lotions to reveal a small cabinet, turned on its side and empty but for a few powdery grains. Julietta had never seen it before.

"What is this?" she said slowly.

Bianca gave a cry and lunged past Julietta, only to be brought up short when Julietta grabbed her arm, holding it tightly. She kicked at the dropped bag until its loosely bound opening gaped, spilling out part of its contents. There were coins, a mingled hoard of gold and silver, mixed with the remains of broken glass bottles. A white powder like that in the jar fluttered along the flagstones, releasing a sharp, herbal smell Julietta knew all too well.

She had smelled it in the dregs of Cosima Landucci's perfume bottle, the night they found her husband poisoned in his bed. Cold, harsh anger swept over her.

Still holding tight to a squirming Bianca's arm, Julietta knelt down to peer closer into the sack. More bottles, cracked yet still intact; a few sheets of paper, closely scribbled in a childish hand; and even some jewels, including a diamond brooch Julietta recognised. She last saw it pinned in Ermano Grattiano's cap the day of the Marriage of the Sea.

So, Ermano *had* been more subtle. And very patient. He must have been working against her for a long time, using her own servant to trap her in a maze of poison. Julietta had to give him credit for stealth, and had to chastise herself for her own naïveté. Never once had she suspected what was right beneath her nose, despite all the hard lessons of her youth in the folly of trust. Bravo to Ermano, then. He had taken the battle. But who would take the war?

Still bound in that icy fury, Julietta reached out with the tip of her dagger and stabbed it into one of the papers, drawing it closer until she could read the words. The writing was not neat; after all, Bianca was only slowly gaining literacy under Julietta's tutelage. She could just make it out, though. It was her own recipe for rose lotion. And the one beneath it was a tonic of lavender and rosemary. All her own concoctions, passed down from her grandmother. "The little traitor," she murmured.

"Nay!" Bianca cried. "I never meant to harm you, *madonna*. I wanted only to help…"

She squirmed harder, twisting in Julietta's iron grasp. The maid was wiry, but Julietta's anger gave her strength. She straightened to her full height, shaking Bianca hard. "To help who, Bianca? Our patrons who wished to be rid of their inconvenient husbands? Or yourself?"

"You don't understand!"

"Then, pray, explain. Explain how you took my generosity, my friendship, all I gave you, and then sold me to Ermano Grattiano," Julietta said, softly, without heat. She stared down at Bianca, yet truly it was as if the white-faced, wild-eyed woman she held fast was not the same cheerful girl she worked beside every day, lived with under this very roof. She was a stranger.

"It is my brother," Bianca sobbed. "He has been released from the Leads, but he is not in good health, though Ermano forced him to work at Ca Grattiano as a servant. My brother, he wants to escape, wants me to go with him back to Constantinople, and I thought I could support us there by opening a perfume shop like this one. I needed these recipes to help me get started."

"I would have given you any of these recipes you wanted, had you but asked!" Julietta said. A cold, soulless feeling took hold of her, slowly freezing out the sudden flash of red-hot anger. She feared she might cry, and it made her shake Bianca all the harder.

"Would you, *madonna?*" Bianca said doubtfully.

"Of course." Just perhaps not *all* of them. Never all of them.

"Could you have given us the money to go back to our home, to buy supplies, lease an establishment?" Bianca's brown eyes, usually so bright and eager, were dull now, echoing Julietta's own bitter regret. Her round face was set in weary, determined lines. She stood still in Julietta's grasp, no longer fighting.

"I would have given you what I could," Julietta said.

"I needed more. Coin for a physician for my

brother, to make a fine business that all the lords and ladies would patronise." She edged the sack with her toe, making the coins and jewels clink. "When the count came to me, he offered such riches! Enough to build a glorious new life, for all my family. And just for watching you and telling him what you did. Your life was so quiet, *madonna,* I thought there could not be anything he could ever use against you."

"To watch me—and to commit murder. Was it he who sent Cosima Landucci and the others to you?"

Bianca shook her head. "I do not know why they came to me! They just made inquiries. After you helped them heal their injuries when their husbands were— unhappy with them. Their husbands were such cruel men, I wanted only to help them! I thought you would do the same, after—well, after your own husband."

And perhaps she would have, at that. Julietta's head was spinning. She hardly knew up from down any longer. "And if they chose to reward you generously, and it pleased Ermano at the same time, so much the better. Eh, Bianca?"

"It was not like that," Bianca said again, sobbing.

"Then why are you running away so secretly?" Julietta demanded.

"I have had enough of the count, of this whole putrid city. I know they will close in soon, that something terrible will happen. I saw the man watching the shop this morning—he is the same man who often came for my messages. My brother is at last able to travel now, so we must go." Bianca leaned closer, her eyes shining suddenly with a flood of tears. "You should flee, too, *madonna,* while you still can."

Julietta shook her arm. "It is too late, Bianca! What you helped to set in motion can no longer be stopped, or even slowed."

Bianca's face hardened. "I am truly sorry for it, though I know you will not believe me. I am grateful for all you have done, *madonna;* I would help you, if I could. But I cannot." Bianca suddenly lashed out with her booted foot, catching Julietta in the knees and making her fall back a step. Bianca wrenched herself free, fleeing the store-room. The front door slammed heavily behind her.

Julietta could have gone in pursuit, could have chased the maid through the *calles* and easily caught her. Yet the weariness, the infinite sadness, was too heavy, and she had no desire to drag Bianca back into the sordid drama they were all forced to play out now. Bianca had done what was best for her and her own family, or at least what she perceived to be best. That was all that could be expected of mere mortals.

Julietta even hoped Bianca might make good her escape, and open her new shop in the teeming souks of Constantinople. Perhaps one day she and Marc would appear on that doorstep, and this would all come full circle. And Ermano would pay for making yet another victim of a poor woman.

But Julietta could not think of that now. She had important work to do, and not much time left at all.

Chapter Twenty-Two

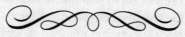

The sunset before the Doge's ball was brilliant and clear, a burst of bright orange and gold that seemed to presage the gaudy gaiety that lay ahead.

Julietta stood in her silent bedchamber, already dressed in her gypsy costume of a full, red, ribbon-bedecked skirt and tight black bodice over a full-sleeved white chemise. The small, hard lump of the sack tied tightly to her waist could hardly be seen, thankfully. Her hair fell loose down her back, a black river entwined with more multi-coloured ribbons. An easy costume to slip into without the assistance of a maid; a deceptive change from her usual sombre black and white. All that remained was to pick up her red mask, and be off to the Doge's Palace.

But not until nightfall. Only when darkness shielded the deceptions of the night would Marc come for her. Until then, she was alone with her thoughts. Her fears.

Julietta sat down on the edge of her bed and rested her red-slippered feet on the small trunk she had so carefully packed that morning. All of her mother's books were there, neatly wrapped in linen chemises; a few gowns, a few of her favourite perfume bottles. That was all she would take from this life.

What the days ahead could hold, she did not know. Could not even begin to fathom. Whatever it was, this part of her life was over. Her time in Venice—her refuge in these watery streets, her place of independent livelihood—was drawing to a close with that sunset. Bianca's betrayal, her defection, only underscored the fact that Julietta no longer belonged here, any more than she had belonged in Milan. Maybe she never truly had. And that knowledge was as bittersweet as anything she ever faced. Ermano had caused this, and he would surely pay in the end. But would he be the only one?

She held out her hand, watching in fascination as the rays of light caught on her ruby ring, shooting out sparks of fire. The ring bound her to Marc, stronger than any nuptial bond in a church. Their hearts, their fates, were entwined now, for good or ill. And, next to it, a new purchase—an assurance in case of emergency. A thick gold band set with a large green stone, hiding a tiny, secret poisonous compartment. A trick her *grandmère* taught her.

Julietta curled her hand tightly over the rings, holding them close. "Oh, Maman," she whispered, "if I have even an ounce of your magic inside me, help me to find it now. I need every aid I can find."

But her mother was silent. Julietta was alone. Still holding her ring close, she lay slowly on her side among the neatly stacked pillows. Her eyes fluttered closed against the blazing light and her weary body sank into a dreamless, weary sleep.

"Julietta? Julietta, *querida,* wake up."

"Ermph," Julietta muttered, trying to sink deeper into the bed, away from the hand that shook her shoulder, the voice that called out her name.

"It grows late. *Andiamo!*"

And she was pulled upright from her cosy nest, held close in hard, warm arms so she could not fall back again.

Disgruntled, she opened her eyes, blinking at the candlelight that had suddenly replaced the sun. The haloed glow was disorienting for a moment, and she thought she dreamed again. Then she suddenly remembered—the ball!

She jerked into cold wakefulness, and her gaze shot up to the man who held her. Marc. A wild joy rose up in her at seeing him again, as if they had been parted for years rather than days.

He, too, wore gypsy garb, close-fitting black hose, a wide red sash, an embroidered vest over a half-laced white shirt. His hair fell loose to his shoulders in wind-blown waves, his pearl earring replaced by a small gold hoop. But his casual, festive appearance was belied by his eyes, which were narrow with concern as they focused on her.

She caught at his shoulders, balancing herself on his strength as she came fully awake. "What time is it? Have we missed…"

"No, no," he assured her. "I came here early. We have enough time."

"Va bene." Julietta drew back a bit, reaching up to smooth her hair. The ribbons entwined there had become tangled, and she set about unravelling them. The small, mundane task soothed her, bringing her slowly back into the present moment.

"All is in readiness here, as you can see," she said, gesturing towards her packed trunk, the tidy chamber.

"Have you not been sleeping, Julietta?" he asked gently. He brushed aside her hands, taking over the ribbon task himself. His fingers were as careful as hers, but his touch was *not* soothing! Julietta trembled, her body bending into the heat of his as a flower sought the sun. They had been too many days apart; too many hours she spent without his touch, the sound of his voice. She tried to run her shop, to act as if nothing had changed, but she thought of him far too often. Wondered what he was doing, craved his caress, his whispered words.

Marc Velazquez was far too addictive.

And now that he was here, she could hardly turn her thoughts to the night ahead. To what had to be done. She drew in a deep breath, and his clean, seawater scent filled all her senses.

"Sleeping?" she murmured. "Nay, not well. Not since Bianca left."

"Your maid left? Why?"

Of course he did not know. Their only communication in the last two days was by a short, hasty note passed by Nicolai's Columbine when she visited the shop. There was no space to explain Bianca's betrayal in that message.

She leaned back against him, his arm about her waist, and she told him all. Everything Bianca confessed before she dashed away into the past.

Marc's body was still and wary against her back, his arm tightening around her. "So, the maid was Ermano's spy."

"Indeed," Julietta said tautly. She still did not like to speak of it, to remember her foolish blindness.

"And did he pay her to sell that poison? Tell her who to give it to?" Marc asked.

Julietta frowned. She had not really thought of such details. Not closely. "Perhaps. He certainly paid her to spy on me, as he meant to do with you, and I'm sure her...er...patrons paid handsomely for those doses. Anyway, the details hardly matter now. Bianca is gone. She will get no information from me now, and surely no more money from Ermano."

"She will be fortunate if she doesn't get a dagger in the ribs from him," Marc muttered. "But I am sorry *you* were hurt, *querida*."

"It does not signify. What is past is past. We must think only of the future now." Julietta turned in his arms, looping her hands about his neck as she stared up at him, her gypsy-pirate. In that moment, her heart was so full of love that there was scarcely room for anything else. No betrayal, no fear.

He reached up to smooth her hair back, cradling her face tenderly as his gaze memorised her every feature.

"Is all in readiness?" she whispered.

He nodded. "Nicolai and his players wait for us."

Julietta bit her lip, that old surge of excitement and dread and foolish hope rising up inside her. "Is this like facing pirates?"

Marc smiled wryly. "It's worse, *querida*. At least with pirates you see their guns, their steel. They face you honestly across the open water. With men such as this, the swords are hidden behind silks and etiquette." He held up his black leather mask, tied with red ribbons. "And behind these."

Julietta kissed him, hard and fast, savouring the taste of him on her lips. "Don't worry, my lion. We'll see the steel before the night is out—and answer it with our own."

The Doge's Palace was aglow, like a fairy abode set to welcome all its glittering guests. The blue skies of the day and the golden sunset were vanished, eclipsed by a thick, shimmering fog moving in off the water. It blanketed the *piazza,* cleared of the usual detritus of peddlers and ragged booths, in iridescent silver clouds. Only the windows of the palace shone through, beckoning to the fantastical figures emerging from the mist. Cloaks and masks muffled figures and features, giving mere glimpses of glittering satins and jewels beneath, increasing the mystery and unreality, the sinister quality of the scene.

Julietta held on to Marc's arm as they paused near the basilica, watching the ebb and flow of the crowd. The faintest strains of music emanated from the open doors, a strange, almost Byzantine song that evoked such sad longings, such a yearning for what could be and yet might never be seen. It mingled with the tinkling of hidden bells sewn on costumes, the muffled rise of voices, of sudden bursts of laughter. She and Marc, though, seemed surrounded by their own magic halo of silence.

She glanced up to find his eyes sharp and sparkling through the slits of his mask, his gaze scanning the scene as if he stood on the deck of his ship.

At last he glanced down at her and smiled, a grin filled with bizarre humour, martial anticipation. This was to be a battle, the greatest of their lives, and he was ready for it. Ready to rush out and meet whatever came.

She had to be ready, as well. Her stomach tightened in a flutter of excitement.

"Shall we go in?" he said. "It would be rude to be the last to arrive."

Julietta nodded, and held his arm as they merged with the river of costumed revellers streaming towards the entrance to the palazzo. The crowd was thick, and soon they were pressed on all sides, hemmed in by the mingled scents of rich perfumes and warm bodies, by the rising tide of laughter, the tinkle of bells, the rustle of stiff silks and flutter of airy gauze. All she could see through the eyeholes of her mask was a swirl of colour—reds, blues, greens, gold and silver—all blurred together like stained glass.

But the merriment was strangely subdued. This was the Doge's Palace, after all, the centre of power in Venice, not a wild revel in some hidden taverna. Every move was watched, every word weighted.

Every step precarious.

The only reality, the only anchor that tied Julietta to sanity, was Marc's arm. The feeling of his strength under her clasp. They moved slowly up the grand staircase, past the looming statues of Mars and Neptune, the still forms of the guards in their shining white livery with their equally shining pikes and swords. Julietta followed the train of the woman ahead of her, an iridescent, snakelike twist of green-and-gold brocade, as they moved along the curved steps. It was easier to concentrate on that sinuous movement than on what lay ahead.

At last, the tight cord of humanity loosened, floating free into a vast ballroom. Even by daylight, empty of the throngs, it would surely be an impressive space. Frescoes covered the high, arching ceilings, the long expanse of the walls, classical scenes of gods and goddesses plotting the fates of humans from their Olympian perch. Nymphs cavorted amid fountains and columns with their flutes and lyres, echoing the music of earthly musicians half-hidden behind a gilded screen. Pointed arches curved over the crowd, laden with greenery and silver ribbons, turning the area into an enchanted forest.

High above those manmade arches was an even greater wonder—acrobats balanced on high wires, twisting in graceful leaps and jumps. A woman in a short, spangled blue gown and glittering gauze wings flew along on a trapeze, flashing and graceful as a butterfly.

Dancers were forming long lines along the length of the marble floor, moving into a slow, stately pavane as the music swirled around them. Despite the chilly night, the air was thick and warm, heavy as a velvet cloak. Julietta flicked her hair back off her neck, seeking relief, a cool flow of air, a clear breath.

There was none to be had. Though she and Marc turned away from the dance, looking for an open space near the wall, the crush of people was too great and their progress painfully slow.

Julietta craned her neck, searching for a familiar face. Every visage was masked, though, concealed behind painted leather and ribbons. She did not see Nicolai's tall, lean figure, nor his Columbine's slender quickness. At the far end of the room the Doge sat on a dais, a figure of dignity in his white-and-gold robes upon his thronelike chair, surrounded by his black-clad counsellors. His strong, creased features and white beard were an indistinct blur, but the gold corno on his head sparkled. In his hands he held a strange, plain wooden coffer. Julietta glanced away swiftly before she could be caught staring.

Marc took two goblets from a passing servant and

handed her one. The sweet wine was cold on her aching throat, easing some of her tension.

"When will it happen?" she whispered anxiously.

Behind his mask, Marc's gaze was sharp and clear as he scanned the crowd. "Not yet. I told you, *querida*—we must wait for Nicolai's signal. Come, let us dance."

"Dance?" Julietta was not sure she could even remember the steps, not with such nervous excitement humming in her veins.

Marc threw back his head, swallowing the last of his wine. "We should try to get closer to the dais, so the Doge and his counsellors have a good view of all the drama. No?"

Julietta laughed humourlessly, and finished her own wine before giving the empty glass to another servant. "Quite right. It will be no good if no one can even see us."

They eased their way around the knots and clumps of people, who were growing louder, more full of ease and laughter as the wine and the music did their work. The *pavane* had moved into a livelier *galliard*.

"I do not see Ermano," she murmured.

"I'm sure he is not far away," Marc answered. "No doubt he is just waiting to make his grand entrance."

His arm slid around her waist, swirling her into the dance. She found she *could* remember the steps. The pattern was burned into her feet, and she turned and leapt and twirled, clasping Marc's arm for the high lifts, even as she searched for Ermano. This entire

farce was of his own making—would he abandon
it now?

Of course he would not. When had Ermano ever
abandoned a scheme? As the figures of the dance moved
forward, carrying Julietta and Marc ever closer to the
dais, Ermano at last appeared at the Doge's side. He, too,
wore a black robe of state, but beneath, revealed by the
loose fastenings, was a white satin doublet, heavily embroidered with jewels and silver thread. He glittered
and sparkled, a malevolent, bright peacock. As he
leaned down to whisper in the Doge's ear, Julietta saw
Andrea Gritti smooth his gnarled palm over the coffer
he held. What was in the box, so incongruously plain in
this shining cavern? What was going to happen in only
a moment? The tension was nigh unbearable, stretching at Julietta's spine until she feared she would snap.

Marc twirled her again, one step ever closer. As she
spun, a shower of shimmering ribbons suddenly descended on their heads. Julietta glanced up to see the
woman on the trapeze swooping away from them,
confetti trailing from her fingers. There was only a
glimpse of the pale, heart-shaped face of Nicolai's
Columbine, half revealed by the blue-and-pink silk of
her butterfly mask.

"Now!" Marc growled. He shook his sleeve to
loosen the hilt of a dagger, and yanked Julietta out of
the dance, towards a small space directly in front of the
high dais. Julietta gasped, pressing her hand to her
abdomen to feel the small, heavy sack tied under her
skirt. Was that sack enough to save her?

"Scream, damn it all!" Marc whispered fiercely. He gave her a rough shake, and pulled hard at the length of her hair, making her scalp sting, her brain rattle.

Instinct took over. Julietta screamed, reaching out to slap Marc's face as hard—as loudly—as she could. *"Bastardo!"* she shrieked. "I never looked at that man, never kissed him."

"Liar!" Marc shouted back. "Whore! I saw you with him in that gondola. After all I gave you. Ungrateful *puta!*"

Julietta kicked out at him, but her skirts got in the way and his grasp on her hair tightened, and she saw more of that shining dagger appear from his gypsy sleeve. It was as if she observed the scene from a great height, as if she was not a participant at all. She was vaguely aware of the gasping, deliciously titillated crowd around them, of their avid eyes and tense silence. Of Ermano suddenly looming mere feet away. But it all seemed a sort of bizarre, hazy dream.

If nothing else, surely they could abandon ships and perfumeries and turn to acting. Everyone seemed completely fooled.

"I hate you!" she sobbed. "How could you turn against me like this?"

The dagger came fully free, balanced on Marc's palm, and Julietta tensed, bracing for the blow that would pierce the sack of pig's blood and send her collapsing to the floor. Then Nicolai and his players, in their garb of hooded pallbearers, would carry her away, and then…

Then she had no idea what would happen. If their whole ridiculous scheme would hold together.

The dagger came down in a gleaming arc, piercing through her skirt to the bag beneath and releasing a heavy, hot flood of blood. Julietta had no need to fake her shocked scream; the blood felt disgusting, and the force of the stab was hard enough to bruise her stomach. She fell to the floor, screams and pandemonium erupting around her. Footsteps thundered as revellers fled, their beautiful gala turned to a bloodbath.

Julietta closed her eyes, willing her breath to slow, to become so shallow it was undetectable, as Nicolai had shown her. The marble floor under her head amplified everything, turning their words and screams to a cacophony.

"Murderer!" she heard Ermano shout. "Vile traitor. Seize him!"

There was the clang of swords and pikes as guards rushed towards Marc, the harsh rustle of fabric as the Doge and his ministers hurried to the edge of the dais. Any minute now, Nicolai and his players would appear and carry her off in their coffin, free of this place, dead to all of Venice. Then they would rescue Marc and his first mate, with the help of those high wires, and flee for ever. Any minute now…

Her entire body screamed at her to jump up, to run like everyone else, to escape this horrible nightmare. At least to open her eyes and see what was happening. But she forced herself to lie limp, still, blind.

Even when she heard Ermano leap down from the

dais and land a heavy blow to Marc's stomach. Marc gasped, stumbling back a step into the guards' grasp as Ermano yelled, "After everything Venice has given you, this is how you repay her, with murder in the Doge's Palace. Take him to the Leads."

Julietta tensed, ready to leap up to defend Marc, to use her hidden poison ring. *Now, Nicolai! Now.* She cracked her eyes open, peering into the crowd around her.

Marc lunged forward, dragging at his captor's confining grip, but it was too late. Ermano had already spun around to see Julietta's half-open eyes. His jaw slackened and his ice-green eyes were filled with something Julietta never saw there before—fear.

"You *are* a witch," he whispered. "You can raise yourself from the dead."

"No…" Julietta began, panic rising inside her like icy flames.

But it was too late. Ermano dove forward and seized Julietta's arm, yanking her to her feet, his clasp frozen, implacable. Julietta cried out at the sensations that flooded through her at his touch, the rush of fear, fury, madness that flowed from him into her own being. He seemed imbued with an iron strength. Her gift of perception had never been more a curse than this moment. Terrified, she instinctively lashed out, scraping his hand with her lethal ring.

Ermano's clasp tightened, as he stared down at the thin line of blood welling on his skin, the flecks of white powder. "What…"

Julietta shook her head, shocked by her own rash

actions. "All the world will soon know of your evil, Ermano," she whispered. "But I fear you will not be here to see it. You have made a murderer of me."

Ermano wrenched her hand upwards to display the ring, its green stone turned inward, the tiny compartment empty. "Poison," he said, his face turning even whiter. "You have killed me. But, no! You saved yourself, witch. You can save *me*. You can give me the antidote to this vile concoction," he said hoarsely, shaking her arm as she cried helplessly, darkness closing around her like a mist.

Julietta twisted and fought, but the emotions she felt from him weighted her down, making her muscles ache. She could not break free. He dragged her through the now-empty room, towards a half-open door in the frescoed panelling. A secret escape hatch.

"Seize that woman!" the Doge called. Ermano, though, had already pulled her through the door, bolting it against the onrush of guards who were now completely befuddled by the tragedy around them.

"Let me go!" Julietta cried, reaching out to tear at his hair, kick at his legs. Anything to escape from the web of his dark emotions, from the tangle that dragged her down inexorably to the depths. She thought of Marc, of all he suffered for her sake, and fought ever harder.

"Enough!" Ermano roared. "I can't think with all this shrieking. We have to get out of here."

She saw a shadow of movement as he brought up his fist. Then there was a hard thud, a sharp pain at the back of her head—and complete darkness.

* * *

"We must go after them!" Marc shouted, struggling in the grip of his guards. It did no good; they just tightened their clasp, their faces set and grim. It took four of them to subdue him.

After Ermano fled with Julietta, disappearing in the walls of the palace before anyone even realised what was happening in the crush of pandemonium, the Doge hastily retreated to this small, windowless antechamber. A few of his counsellors went with him, and he had gestured for the guards to bring Marc, as well. Nicolai and his players tried to follow, but the iron-bound door was shut in their faces. Now, after the clamour and screams and blood, everything was encased in an eerie, icy silence.

Except for Marc's heart. It howled in fear and protest, screaming at him to run, to find Ermano, to save Julietta! Every second that passed was precious. But the men around him were impassive, expressionless. The Doge watched him with a cool, cynical gaze, as if in his long lifetime he had seen such things many times before and it would take far more than a murder, a suicide and a kidnapping, all in less than five minutes, to affect him.

"Be at peace, Signor Velazquez," the Doge said, seating himself in a straight-backed chair, balancing a small wooden coffer in his hands. "She will be found. Very soon."

"Your Excellency, I beg you," Marc choked out. "Before you take me to prison, let me search for them.

If you will just let me retrieve Julietta, I shall gladly go to the darkest dungeon…"

The Doge just laughed. "Signor Velazquez! Who said anything about prison?"

Marc stilled in his guards' hold, staring at the man in utter disbelief. "*You* did, your Excellency. Is that not what this whole night was about?"

Andrea Gritti shook his head, the corno of power sparkling dully. "I have been Doge of this city for a few years now. Before that I was a soldier, a simple man really who understood guns, swords, strategy, perhaps all too well. Yet I did not always understand people, not as the Doge should. Must." He smoothed his palm over that coffer. "I sometimes listened to counsel that was—erroneous. Perhaps even dangerous."

Marc's very skin ached with impatience. What good would *talk* do, when Julietta was in Ermano's clutches? Vanishing into the foggy night? "Your Excellency…"

"I know. But hear me out. Today I received a visit from Balthazar Grattiano, who was most insistent he be admitted for an audience. He had information that was of exceeding interest." The Doge lifted the lid of the coffer to reveal a small, neat stack of letters. Sealed with the dark green Grattiano wax.

"Balthazar gave me these messages, sent between his father and yet another corrupt counsellor. Young Balthazar has been most useful to me," the Doge said. "He also told me of a conversation he overheard in his father's home, where they plotted to accuse Signora

Bassano of poisoning and bring you, Signor Velazquez, down with her. All for their own gain, to the det-
riment of the Republic. Disgusting."

The Doge steepled his fingers beneath his chin, regarding Marc steadily over their tips. "A message was
sent to you, Signor Velazquez, cancelling your instructions. I take it you never received it."

Marc shook his head. "Nay, your Excellency. That
was why we concocted the idea of the fake murder, the
funeral pallbearers."

"Ah, I see." Andrea Gritti did not appear surprised
at the wild scheme. No doubt he had seen far worse in
his times as Doge. "The missing cancellation is no
doubt Ermano's doing. He does have his spies everywhere. Or rather—he did. You are free to go, Signor
Velazquez, with the Republic's apologies. Go and find
your undead lady. If you can. And *we* will later deal
with Grattiano and his usurpation of the authority that
belongs only to the Doge. His actions will mean his
doom."

His head whirling, his senses on fire, Marc bowed
quickly to the Doge and rushed out of the room,
leaving the man to his flock of counsellors and the de-
predations of politics. Marc had had enough of both.
Enough of the hasty swirl of treachery and retribution
and blood. He had only one thought now, one burning
need, so that he was barely aware of Nicolai and Balthazar Grattiano falling into step behind him.

He had to find Julietta. Before it was too late.

Chapter Twenty-Three

Consciousness slowly pierced Julietta's mind, like a sliver of bright white sun on a gray day, unexpected and sudden and painful. She felt as if she swam up from the depths of the ocean, her limbs turned to marble, the water thick and viscous around her, pulling her back down to the depths. She longed for those depths, for the soft oblivion they held out so temptingly. Yet she somehow knew, in some primitive, instinctual way, that she must not surrender to that lure. Must fight against it, or she would be lost.

Julietta grasped desperately for that shred of reality, seemingly so far above her. She strained for it, summoning every ounce of strength until finally she could pry her eyes open and let that ray of light break through. Marc's face flashed through her mind, his brilliant blue eyes. *You must get up, survive,* her mind screamed. *For him!*

"Ugh," she groaned. Every muscle in her body

ached, stiff and painful. Her head throbbed as if gypsy drummers took up residence behind her eyes. To drown in that warm ocean of sleep sounded better than ever, yet she still struggled against it. There was something she needed to know, to remember. It seemed so vitally urgent…

What had happened? She could hardly recall. Her mind was so soft, like fluffy lambswool where only flashes of images could shine through.

Julietta slowly edged on to her side, forcing her eyes to stay open until she could focus on her surroundings. She lay on a bed, a rumpled, worn velvet counterpane beneath her. Directly across was a window, half unshuttered in a haphazard fashion that let in that dagger of light. The quality of the sun was buttery, muted, as if it grew late in the day. But what day was it?

She pressed her palm hard to her brow, dragging in deep, ragged breaths of stale air. Once some of the fuzziness cleared, she slowly sat up, pushing herself back against the carved headboard of the bed. Her gaze took in the bedposts, a cushioned chair by the empty fireplace, a clothes chest at the foot of the bed…

Of course! She was at her own country villa, her own bedchamber. Yet she was alone, not like when she left here only a few days ago and Marc was with her in this very bed. The bed they'd shared in such glorious passion.

It all came back to her now, a tumble of pain-filled images. The ball, where all their foolish plans seemed to be coming together so well, despite all her doubts and hidden fears. Then disaster in only an instant. A nightmare haze of people rushing upon them, screams, shouts, sobs. The ring; the livid scratch on Ermano's hand. Marc, so far away from her. An eternity away.

Julietta pressed her fingers to her mouth, holding back a cry as the truth of her situation descended on her. She felt again the bruising, inhuman force of Ermano's imprisoning grasp on her wrist, his insane emotions flowing through her. He dragged her from the chaos, stifling her screams with a silken scarf. Not that anyone could have heard her in that barbaric cacophony that took over the palatial palace. Not that anyone would even notice her struggles in the midst of their own.

Her fingers slid to the back of her neck, and she felt the telltale lump rising there beneath her hairline, sticky with matted blood. She remembered her fight with Ermano, remembered stumbling on a flagstone, his fist coming down, and then—nothing.

And then he brought her here, to her own house. Far from the city, from anyone who might search for her after the riot subsided.

Julietta eased her way to the side of the bed, moving her sore limbs carefully. Her muscles creaked in protest, but she pressed on. She could not just stay here, lying in bed as she waited for whatever Ermano planned. Waited for her doom. She had to *do* something.

She slid down from the high mattress until her toes touched the uneven planks of the floor. Her shoes were gone and her stockings were snagged and filthy. Her entire costume was in disarray, the ribbons wrinkled and torn, the white chemise streaked with dirt, a long tear in the red skirt that was stiff with dried pig's blood. Yet at least she was still clothed, and she could detect no signs that Ermano had tried to get those sons he raved about on her unconscious body.

Clinging to the bedpost, she stood upright, swaying as if she stood in a whirling storm. The blow to her head had affected her more than she thought, then. What she wouldn't give for one of her grandmother's healing possets.

As the room tilted upright around her, Julietta was able to push away from the bed. The chamber was cold without a fire, but the chill helped clear her head. She made her slow way to the window and eased the shutter open another inch. If Ermano or one of his men lurked below, she didn't want them to see she was awake. But there was no one. The pathways and shadowed groves were empty and silent. Not even a bird sang. The sun hung in a pale pink orb just above the horizon, poised in the hour before sunset.

No Ermano, then. Where were Paolo and Rosa, the servants? Hopefully they had been merely forced from their dwelling, and did not meet a sad end. And neither would she.

Her stomach suddenly seized in a painful spasm, and she lunged for a basin just as she lost the meagre contents of her stomach. As the sour nausea subsided, so did some of her body's soreness, the raw edge of her nerves. There was half a ewer of wine left on the chest from her night with Marc, and she rinsed her mouth with its sour sharpness. She felt hungry, yet there was no food to be had. If she had only thought to store some bread or apples in that chest!

Julietta laughed at her whimsical thoughts. How could she have known she would be trapped here by a madman, in need of secret sustenance? Even going over her situation now, it seemed absurd. She always knew Ermano was determined, self-centred, spoiled by his power and unwilling to be refused. Yet who would ever have imagined he would go so far?

She finished the wine and opened up the clothes chest. There was nothing there to change into, but there was a moth-eaten shawl she could wrap around her shoulders for extra warmth and a pair of worn leather slippers. At least she would not have to pad around practically barefoot. She tied her hair back with a ribbon torn from her skirt, and felt halfway human again. But was she strong enough to escape?

The door was locked, as she expected. Firmly bolted from the outside. She rattled at the latch for a moment, futilely turning it this way and that. Finally, she gave up and went back to the window. It was much too far to jump, of course, but could she fashion a rope and lower herself to the ground?

She peered down at the walkway below, so disconcertingly far. Even if she did get down there, how long would it be before Ermano came up here looking for

her? How long did she have to flee? She had probably
been locked up here for hours already.

She must try, though. She knew that. It was un-
thinkable to stay in this room, trapped in a deserted,
isolated house with a madman. Surely Marc was
looking for her, but it could take hours, days, before
he discovered her whereabouts. And that was if he
was even still alive, amid that wild mêlée at the palace.
At the very least he was surely in the Leads.

No! No, she would not even think of that. Julietta
hastily crossed herself. Marc could not be dead.
Surely, after everything they had been to each other,
she would feel it if he was gone. Her heart thudded
hard in her chest, yet there was no aching hollowness,
no void that signalled her love's absence.

"He will come for me," she whispered. She knew
that, as surely as she knew that soon darkness would
fall. But how long would it take? She could not wait,
like some princess in an ice tower. She had to get away
from here, to find Marc so they could flee together. It
was the only way.

And she had to hurry.

Julietta spun back towards the bed, drawing away
the counterpane so she could strip off the linens. Using
the sharp corner of the clothes chest, she tore away the
edges and proceeded to rip them into long, thick ropes,
twisting the strips together. Her hands trembled, but
still she worked on. The light outside was turning pink,
and there was so little time.

She had barely finished tying off the last section of

her makeshift rope when she heard the sound she dreaded—the scrape of the lock being drawn back from the door. She had been so busy she hadn't sensed footsteps in the corridor! Julietta hastily stuffed the sheets into the chest and clambered on to the bed, pulling the counterpane up around her shoulders to cover the lack of sheets.

Let it just be a servant bringing food, she prayed. *Or—or...*

Her prayers were not to be answered. Ermano himself stood there as the door swung slowly, creakingly open. He held a branch of candles high as he peered into the chamber, his figure ringed in light like a creature from Dante's hell. His jewelled satin finery was as dishevelled as her own attire, streaked with dust and grime, the shoulder of his doublet torn away to reveal the shirt beneath. His white hair stood on end, his skin was gray and clammy. For once, he looked every year of his age. An old lion cornered in his rich den.

And along his hand snaked the fatal scratch, livid and bright red now, thick with crusted blood.

"So, you're awake," he said, his voice scratchy. He made no move towards her yet, just stared at her with burning green eyes. His free hand curled around the door-frame, clinging tightly as he swayed.

How could this man have ever produced her Marc?

"I am, and I'm hungry," Julietta said, stiffening her shoulders and putting as much hauteur as she could into her tone. She had never let herself be intimidated by Ermano before; she would not start now. No matter how mad he grew. "Where are the servants?"

"We're the only ones here, *bella* Julietta," he answered. He advanced slowly into the room, setting his candles down on the mantel. Their glow blended with the now-fiery sunset, gilding the corners in a surreal glow. The night of love she spent here with Marc seemed so far away now. The whole house was encompassed in an insane nightmare.

Ermano ran his hand through his hair, leaving it in ever greater disarray. As he turned to look at her, his expression was heavy, sad. "Oh, Julietta. Why have you made me do this? Why have you brought us to this state? I offered you everything—wealth, jewels, a place of honour. A place as the mother of my children. The woman who read my tarot cards told me it would be so, it was our destiny. Why did you spurn that, choosing *this,* instead?"

Julietta's jaw tightened. She had refused Ermano again and again, refused him her property, her body, everything, in no uncertain terms. Yet there was no reasoning with a lunatic. There never had been. "I love another," she said simply.

Ermano's gray face suffused with a dull red fire. "Marc Velazquez? He is *nothing.* He is my creature, my spy! He can give you nothing."

"Marc is no one's *creature,*" Julietta said quietly. Her calmness seemed only to anger him further; his hands tightened into fists at his side. His shoulders coiled, as if he would lunge for her, strangle her.

Julietta felt only cold, numb. There was no fear, no pity. Nothing.

"He merely used you," she added. "As you tried to use him."

"That is a lie!" Ermano shouted. "How could he use me? A mere ship's captain!"

Julietta turned her face away, unable to bear the sight of him. Unable to bear for a moment longer the sordidness of this man, the harsh truth of Marc's story. Ermano wanted strong sons, did he? Offspring of ruthless steel, beautiful men of intelligence and shrewdness. Well, he had gained more than he ever bargained for, but the harsh irony of that made her feel nauseous all over again.

"Marc Velazquez is twenty times the man you could ever be," she said, facing Ermano again. Her gaze travelled pointedly to his codpiece. "In every way."

With a low, feral growl, Ermano lunged across the room and grabbed her arm in a bruising grasp. He dragged her from the bed, yanking her upright when she could not yet get her numb legs beneath her feet fast enough. Her back gave a painful, protesting spasm, her body instinctively curled away from him.

"He is as good as dead!" Ermano hissed, snakelike, between his teeth. His breath was foul with decay. "And you are mine. The tarot cards promised that!"

"The cards can always lie, you know," Julietta said, straining against his hold, twisting and writhing to break free. "Or the person who reads them can. I belong to no one, least of all you, Ermano Grattiano! You are loathsome, a worm in the canals, a woman killer—"

"Shut up, whore!" He slapped her hard across the face, snapping her head back in a shower of painful, sparkling stars. Julietta's breath whooshed from her lungs, her mind reeling in fresh waves of agony. She would have tumbled to the floor if his iron grip had not held her upright.

Julietta stared up at Ermano dizzily. A drop of spittle glistened at the corner of his pale, cracked lips, and sweat beaded on his brow. He leaned even closer to her, and her nostrils filled with a faint, bittersweet herbal smell. That was when she saw the truth. The poison truly worked, and fast.

Ermano's eyes narrowed and he went very, very still, his fingers tightening on her arm until she felt bruises raise their black forms on her skin. "Yes. You see your vile work now."

"You are doomed, Ermano," Julietta answered dispassionately. "Why did you bother to bring me here at all?"

"You will save me," he said, his voice rising desperately. "Now!"

Julietta shook her head. "What, did the cards tell you *that*? Nay, it is too far along. These streaks show that the poison has spread."

"You are a witch! You rose from the dead!" he shrieked. All his smooth charm, his vast power, was utterly vanished now. He was only a desperate man facing death—the same death he dealt out to so many others over the years. "You know how to poison. Surely you know how to cure. You raised yourself from the dead!"

She *did* know how to poison, true. She even knew a few antidotes, had read about them in her mother's books. But… "I do not know exactly what substance was in the ring. It is impossible to know if there is a cure, or what treatment might work."

Ermano just dragged her towards the door, her feet barely touching the floor. For a sick man, he had a sturdy strength, his grasp powerful with grief and fury.

But Julietta possessed an anger to equal his. She envisioned Marc's beautiful mother, her throat slit, her terrified child watching her die. Julietta dug in her heels, twisting hard.

"Nay!" she cried. "Even if I knew the antidote, I would not help you."

"You will!" Ermano yanked his dagger from his belt, holding it against her neck, the steel cold and unyielding. Julietta went still, breathless as she felt the sharp prick of the knife's tip, the heat of a drop of her own blood.

"Unless you never want to see your lover again," Ermano whispered in her ear. "Unless you want to join me in hell this night, you will do as I say. You will only live as long as I do."

Julietta swallowed hard, feeling anew the press of that dagger. She stared up into Ermano's face. His eyes were clearer now, his skin white beneath the gray pallor, and she read the truth of his threat writ large there. He *would* kill her, just as he had Veronica Rinaldi. She had to play along, to be as clever in her deceptions as Nicolai Ostrovsky always was.

Yet time was surely on her side. The poison would do its work, or perhaps Nicolai had managed to escape, to look for her. She had to survive, to rescue Marc. If she could just convince Ermano.

And if she could just lead him to the solar, where her experiment waited patiently

"Very well," she said slowly, softly, as if reasoning with a wild animal, a recalcitrant child. "I will help you, Ermano, if I can. But we have to go to my work-room. All of my tools are there."

He steadied her carefully, eyes wary, as if gauging the truth of her words. Finally, he nodded. "We will go to this work-room of yours," he said. "But my dagger is always ready, Julietta. And any potion you produce, *you* will taste first. I will be watching you."

"Of course," Julietta murmured. She wouldn't have it any other way.

Marc stood on the ridge of a hill above Julietta's villa, peering down past tangled, dead grape vines at the dwelling. The sun had vanished long before as they made their way out of the city, leaving only milky streaks of moonlight to limn the scene. The house appeared shuttered and deserted, aside from one patch of warm candlelight glowing from what Marc knew to be Julietta's bedchamber window.

The scene was silent, eerily so. No nightingales sang. No breeze creaked at the branches. It had a haunted quality, as if ghosts watched over them all tonight. As if spectral death gathered all around them.

Marc glanced over his shoulder to where Nicolai and Balthazar waited, watching just as warily as he did. Surely they were exhausted, after aiding him in his search for all these long hours, but they had the alert, tense air of men about to plunge into battle.

"You are sure they're here?" Marc asked quietly.

Balthazar gave a curt nod. In the moonlight, his eyes were flat, opaque, his face hard and expressionless, years beyond his youth. Marc's brother had surely become a man this night, one with many disillusionments to face. Demons to slay. Marc only hoped Balthazar would be fortunate enough to find his own Julietta to help mend those scars. And that he would prove trustworthy.

"Ermano often spoke about this place," Balthazar said, shifting his beautifully carved Irish bow higher on his shoulder. "There is no place nearer where he could have taken refuge. I think it is our best guess."

"Stay here," Marc told Balthazar and Nicolai, quietly. He drew his sword, balancing the plain, leather-wrapped hilt on his gloved palm. Moonlight sparked on the shining length of finest Toledo steel.

"You can't go in there alone, Marc," Nicolai protested.

Marc shook his head. "If Ermano is in there with Julietta, I can surprise him more easily alone. His actions of this night prove how unbalanced his mind has become; we can't frighten or startle him. He would fight back, hurt Julietta." If she was not hurt already. But those words went unspoken in the cold night.

Nicolai understood. They had stood shoulder to shoulder in many past battles. There were some, though, that had to be fought alone. Nicolai nodded and melted back into the night's shadows, his hood drawn up over his bright hair. He would be near; that, Marc understood.

Balthazar half turned to follow. He paused, gazing back at Marc with his hard, dead green eyes. "Will you kill him, Signor Velazquez?"

Signor Velazquez—so formal between brothers. But Balthazar had only just discovered this fact, a truth Marc had lived with alone for so many years. They were brothers by blood, not in truth. This night would surely do little to change that.

Marc nodded shortly. "If I must. I'll do anything to save Julietta."

"Good," was all Balthazar said. He eased into the darkness, and Marc was alone.

Or nearly so. Alongside the ridge of the hill ran a row of spindly, gnarled olive trees, their branches skeletal against the moon. They stood silent in the windless night, but as Nicolai and Balthazar vanished he heard a muffled sound from that grove. A low sob, a whisper.

Clutching at his sword, Marc crept closer, ready for anything in such a dark, wild hour. Ghosts, bandits— an insane Ermano, crouched over his victims' bodies as he had over that of Veronica Rinaldi so long ago. It was nothing of the sort, though. Merely the old house-keeper, Rosa, and her steward husband, Paolo. They sat together under one of the trees, huddled as one beneath a worn blanket. The woman was sobbing, dry, low sounds as her husband whispered, trying to soothe her.

Marc's booted foot landed on branch, sending a sharp crackle into the hushed, haunted world. The woman gasped, and her husband thrust her behind him, brandishing a dull eating knife.

"Who goes there?" Paolo cried hoarsely.

"Marc Velazquez," Marc answered, moving carefully closer. "I met you a few days ago, with Signora Bassano."

The knife lowered a bit, but there was no easing of the man's posture, no lessening of his wife's sobs. "We remember. You have come for her, then?"

"She is in there? In the villa?"

"He carried her in!" Rosa said suddenly. "And then he—he…"

"He made us leave," Paolo said. "They are alone in there."

"Are either of you hurt?" Marc asked.

Paolo shook his grizzled head. "Rosa is just frightened, *signor.*"

"The *signora,* she was unconscious!" Rosa burst out. "She was so still…"

Marc's blood froze. An image flashed in his head, Julietta unmoving and pale, her dark eyes closed for ever. "Dead?"

"I don't think so," Rosa said. "He was carrying her, but her hand moved. There is not much time, *signor!*"

No time. After all his long years of planning, his schemes, it had all run out in an instant.

"Do not fear," he answered, "I will go to her."

"There is a tunnel, a cellar near the kitchen," Paolo said. "The trap door is near the fountain in the garden. It will lead you into the house."

Marc nodded, and spun around to make his way down the slope to the villa's tangled gardens. The house remained silent, but there was still that light in the window, beckoning him ever closer.

If only Julietta was still alive.

Chapter Twenty-Four

Julietta bent over her work-table, stirring carefully at the cauldron before her. The mixture down in the depths bubbled, heated by the tiny spirit light beneath. Its flame glowed; the thick, dangerous liquid was dark. It wasn't ready, not quite. Soon.

Julietta eased away, holding a scrap of linen torn from her chemise over her nose against the fumes. Ermano refused to let her open the window, and the room was close. Yet he seemed not to notice the smell, the soft sound of the bubbles. He just sat in the corner, watching her with his scalding gaze, a sword balanced in his hands. The scar on his hand shone bright red on his clammy flesh.

"Is the potion ready?" he gasped.

"Not yet," she said, keeping her voice quiet. "You must not take it until it's at its full potency. If you do, it will not work and you will die all the sooner."

He laughed, a harsh sound that held only an echo

of the old charm that held Venice's patricians in thrall. "So, I must rely on you, Julietta Bassano. Yet again. That I, a Grattiano, should be brought to this!"

Julietta leaned against the rough edge of the table, still a bit dizzy from the fumes and Ermano's abuse. "When have you ever 'relied' on me, Ermano? I am nothing in Venice. You said so yourself."

"I needed you. You were my hope. That is what the card reader said. Yet I could have given you so much in return."

"In return for what?" Julietta peered down at the cauldron again. The bubbles were larger now, revealing under-colours of gray and sickly green. She had to keep him distracted. Keep him talking.

"For sons!" he barked, as if that was obvious to all. "Strong sons to carry my name into the future."

"You have a son. Balthazar."

Ermano spit contemptuously on the floor. "Balthazar! He is weak, useless. He has too much of his mother's blood. He wants only to spend my coin, waste my wealth on whores and scholars' books. He has no fire in him, no steel. When I am gone my kingdom will vanish. I have told you all this before, yet still you do not see!"

"Hmm," Julietta murmured, poking at the mixture with a long-handled spoon. "Balthazar *is* a bit sullen, I'll admit, yet certainly no more so than the other wealthy youths of Venice. I'm sure he will soon grow out of it."

"You do not know what you speak of! Balthazar is nothing to what our own sons could have been."

Julietta peered at him sadly. What a wreck he had made of himself, of all of them. Destroying all their lives for some foolish prophecy of the cards. Why did he even believe them? She shook her head, silent. She had no words for him, only a weary longing, a desire, to fly free of this hot, stinking room of madness.

But her silence only inflamed his anger. He stumbled to his feet, lurching towards her like a wounded bear. Julietta dropped the spoon, feinting to one side, stumbling over her hem as he grasped her sleeve, ripping it. Her bare skin prickled in the room's toxic heat. "No more talking! Finish the potion now!"

"What are you doing?" she screamed, arching away. Ermano's sword came up, its blade whistling, aimed towards her breast. She managed to dodge, reaching out for the cauldron as the blade slashed out again. One of her frayed ribbons fluttered to the floor, severed, and Ermano howled in frustration, in bloodlust. If she could just reach the cauldron!

Suddenly, the door flew open, cracking as it hit the wall. Julietta flattened herself against the edge of the fireplace, gasping for breath as Ermano's crazed attention swung to the intruder.

It was Marc, poised in the shadowed doorway, his sword outstretched. Unlike Ermano's, *his* blade was steady, a shining beacon of revenge. His hair was tied back from his face, revealing the stark, beautiful angles of his face; he wore only his black hose and white linen shirt, all disguise and artifice vanished. His turquoise gaze flickered over Julietta, assuring himself she was safe before focusing intently on Ermano.

"Velazquez?" Ermano croaked, disbelieving. "What are you…"

"Will you kill another woman, then?" Marc said, quiet and steady. Deadly. "As you did Veronica Rinaldi?"

Ermano stared at Marc, Julietta seemingly forgotten. His sword hung heavy, slack from his fingers, and, if possible, his flesh turned even whiter. "How do you know of Veronica?" he whispered.

Julietta was reminded of scenes in plays, when the sinner is confronted by the ghost of his victim and dies of the shock. Ermano shook all over, his eyes wild, as if Veronica Rinaldi herself had just risen from her tomb.

Julietta took advantage of the moment to edge away from Ermano and his erratic blade, melting silently into the dark corner.

"How do you know of Veronica?" Ermano said again. He took a step towards Marc, but stumbled and went still.

"Do you not know me?" Marc answered. "It has been a long time, I know, and I have changed very much. You, however, are still exactly the same. Vermin who will attack only the helpless. Well, Ermano, *I* am not helpless. Not any longer." He moved closer, his sword raised, steady and lethal. His face was as smooth as cold marble. "Will you attack me now?"

Ermano shook his head. "Tell me who you are!"

"Once, long ago, I was known as Marco Rinaldi."
Marc's steps finally halted, the very tip of his sword
resting on Ermano's heaving chest. "So, we meet
again—Father."

"Nay," Ermano protested, the one word a mere
whisper of sound on his lips. He shook his head again,
but even Julietta in her corner could see the light of realisation in his eyes. He stared at Marc, swaying back
and forth, obviously torn between fear, fury—and joy.
Here, at last, was a son to be proud of.

Too bad Marc was going to kill him. Julietta just
knew it.

"Nay!" Ermano cried, his voice stronger. "Marco
died."

"Oh, did I? Is that what your *bravos* told you, when
you sent them to hunt me down? I fled then, and was
found by my true father. A man of strength and integ-
rity and honour—things you know nothing of,
Ermano. It was a fortunate day for me. But a most
unlucky one for you."

Ermano tried to step forward, but Marc's blade held
him where he was. "How can you say that, Marco? I
searched everywhere for you! You were my son, a
strong and handsome child who I knew would become
a great man—as you have. I would have raised you to
be the most powerful lord in Venice, would have given
you all I have. I thought you lost!"

"And so I was. Until now. I promised my mother
she could rest quiet in her grave because I would one
day return to Venice and avenge her. That I would ruin

you in this city and watch your downfall, that I would kill you." Marc pressed the blade ever closer, until the shining tip pierced the dusty satin of Ermano's doublet. "It will not happen quite the way I planned—public humiliation, the revelation of all your sins to the world. You brought yourself down with your own greed, even as you schemed to destroy me through the woman I love. And now I'm going to kill you with honour. As I promised so long ago."

"Marco, how can you say that?" Ermano groaned. "If I had known you were my son..."

Marc merely stepped back, raising his sword in a flashing arc. *"En garde."*

Ermano's eyes widened, his back stiffening as he took in Marc's cold expression, the perfect stillness of his sword arm, and realised that his lost son was in terrible earnest. It was the last act of a play he had not even realised was in progress, and he didn't know what to do when he was not the one who had composed the plot. "So—you are like your mother after all. Turning your back on all I offer."

Even Julietta trembled, watching in horrified fascination. The tension was nightmarishly unbearable, and she could do naught. Nothing but watch, and wait. This was Marc's revenge, his destiny. Not hers. Yet she had never been adept at waiting. She pressed her back even tighter to the corner, staring on as Ermano at last realised the terrible truth of his situation.

He had the son he dreamed of, a warrior of ruthless desires and strength, of great honour. Yet his dream was his downfall—unless he could destroy Marc first. Ermano's own sword came up in a clumsy swing, none of Marc's light grace about the movement. Marc met the blow easily, his blade tangling with Ermano's in a metallic clash that drove the older man back.

Ermano soon recovered, though, years of reflexes rescuing him from a quick end. He pushed himself away from the wall, lashing out in a heavy rain of blows. Marc warded them off, twisting one way then the other, his body a blur.

Ermano growled, using both hands to bring his sword down again and again. Marc was quick and skilled, as light on his feet as the lion he was called. Ermano had little of that flexibility, but he did have bulk, and he also had little to lose. He attacked desperately, like a creature in a bear pit, striking blindly but boldly against his foe. Against the son who, like Julietta, refused all the tainted riches he offered.

It was not a quick fight. Ermano pressed on, driven by poisoned fury, following as Marc evaded him. Marc's blade pierced his shoulder, evincing howls of anger, yet still the bloodlust prevailed. Marc's light movements grew a bit heavier, a bit slower. He had surely been awake for a long night and day, searching for her, and even Julietta could see his strength slowly ebbing from him.

Do something now! her mind screamed. She could not huddle in the corner like a terrified damsel, any longer, not after how hard they had fought and schemed to come together! It wouldn't end like this. It could not.

No one was coming to their rescue. No armies of warriors. They were alone. But together they were surely a force to be reckoned with.

Julietta shook her head hard, trying desperately to clear her dizziness and confusion. The room was dim, the candles burned low and only fragments of moonlight were coming in through the closed windows. The clash of swords, grunts and cries filled every corner, and the air was thick with the tang of sweat, the coppery tang of blood—and something else. Something sharp and hot.

Julietta's gaze shot over to her work-table, where her cauldron bubbled and snapped. The mixture was boiling now, rising to the black edge of the pot. If she could just reach it...

She turned to see Marc and Ermano still locked in mortal combat near the splintered door. Marc was wounded, a slash on his thigh that matted his black hose with blood, yet still he fought on fiercely. Ermano's blade crashed down clumsily, and Marc met it with a huge clang. His movements were even slower now. There was not much time.

Julietta dashed from her corner, keeping to the wall, far from the tangling combatants. The smell of the fight clung to her, a miasma of fear and sweat and doom.

She reached out for one of the sputtering candles, staring into the tiny, beckoning flame. This could mean the death of them all, but she had no choice. She had no blade of her own, and they blocked the doorway. If she could just be careful, and manage things in the proper proportions, she could distract Ermano while she and Marc escaped. If not...

"Whore!" she suddenly heard Ermano roar. While she was distracted, he had looked to her, turning from Marc just as she raised the flame to the cauldron. He swung his sword at her, all movement seemingly slowed in the fog of the room. Marc lunged towards him, his blade arcing towards Ermano's arm, but it was too late. Ermano overturned the table, spilling out the heavy contents of the cauldron, and Julietta dropped the candle.

The flame caught, racing up the length of the viscous liquid like a band of hellfire. Gagging at the stench of the greasy smoke, Julietta dodged away. She accomplished one thing she had set out to do—Ermano was distracted. He stared at the growing wall of fire, horribly mesmerised, as Julietta grabbed Marc's hand and dragged him out the door. "Hurry! It is no ordinary fire."

Marc asked no questions, made no protests, as they ran out of the house. The heat seemed to chase them, licking at their heels in a white rush, ever closer. He clung to his sword with one hand and caught her around the waist with the other, half carrying her out into the night just as the windows blew out in a fiery blast.

"What is happening?" Julietta heard a breathless, heavily accented shout—Nicolai. "Has Ermano..."

They landed at his feet in a heap near the cracked garden fountain, under the shelter of an open trap door, gasping in the clear night air. Even here, the heat singed, yet it barely touched them, as if they were beyond its range. The villa behind them smoked and smouldered, more windows cracking inward.

"By all the saints, Julietta," Marc panted, "what *was* that?"

Julietta laid back on the pathway, staring up at the black, clear bowl of the sky. The air was sweet, and they were alive. *Alive!* A quiet exultation overtook the blind panic, drowning out the fear at last, and she laughed. "Greek fire," she said. "An ancient and very dangerous recipe, one that belonged to my grandmother. Its main ingredient is naphtha, which is very hard to find, plus quicksilver, sulphur, turpentine, saltpetre, a little wax for thickener. It was invented by Kallinikos in about 668 BC…"

Marc stopped her words with a sudden kiss, grabbing her up against him and holding her in a hard, desperate grasp, as if he would never let her go. He tasted of smoke, of blood, yet he was so sweet to her. Precious. She clutched at his shoulders, returning his kiss with all the love and fear in her heart. Behind them, the house crackled and roared, consumed by the flames of her own making, yet she cared not. Everything she wanted was here, in her arms.

"Confounded woman," he growled, drawing back to rest his forehead against hers. "Who else in all of Italy would possess Greek fire exactly when it is most needed!"

"I was making it for you," she said, closing her eyes. She was so very weary suddenly, all her strength ebbing away in a great rush.

"For me?"

"To protect you from pirates. The sea is so dangerous."

"Obviously not as dangerous as dry land, *querida*," he said, gesturing towards the soaring flames. The excitement of their flight ebbed, and he sank slowly back to the ground.

"Perhaps not." Julietta stared as the roof collapsed inward, and she thought of the sea, cool and blue, an endless, mysterious expanse. "Oh, Marc. Let's go to the sea now, to the *Elena Maria*. I wish so much—"

But her wishes were drowned in a shout, a roar that rose above even the harsh crack of flames. Julietta twisted around to see a vision straight from hell—a hell she herself had created. Ermano stood on the pathway, outlined by the red-orange glow of the fire. The ends of his hair were singed, his face and clothes black with smoke, but he was alive. Obviously escaped from the flames with the help of some destructive imp of evil.

He raised up his blackened blade. "I would have welcomed you to my palazzo, Marco," he shouted, in a shredded voice. "Given you all that I had. But you turned against me, just as your mother did. Now, you and your whore will die!"

Marc lurched to his feet, raising his sword, but Julietta was so shocked she could not let go of his hand. They were weakened, unprotected. She released Marc, scrambling in the light of the flames for a sharp rock to throw, for *anything*.

As her hand closed on a chunk of marble fallen from the old fountain, a strange, eerie sound pierced the chaos of the night—a high-pitched whine that arced over the snap of flames and ended with a dull thump in Ermano's chest.

Julietta stared as Ermano staggered back a step. An arrow vibrated above his heart, its fletching iridescent in the light. Thin, elegant, lethal as Marc's sword and her fire had not been. Ermano collapsed on to the pathway, a solid, unmoving mass. Dead at last.

Clinging to her marble, Julietta stumbled to her feet and saw Balthazar Grattiano. He stood a long distance away, yet she knew who it was. He had the same height and slender, powerful grace of his brother, his hair a silken tumble over the shoulders of his black cloak. He looked like an ascetic, avenging angel, a man of bitter honour and infinite years. A spoiled young noble no longer.

Balthazar slowly lowered his bow. "This was a gift from an Irish merchant when I was a child," he said musingly, as if in some distant dream. "I practised it secretly until my fingers bled, until I mastered the art of killing at two hundred yards. Yet another example of my 'unworthiness' to be a true Grattiano—a sword is the true weapon of a nobleman, not a lowly bow and arrow." He gave them a salute. "It is done now, brother."

Then he was gone, vanishing back into the night. And they were left with a house in flames, Ermano's crumpled body.

Julietta clasped Marc's arm, holding tightly as a wave of dizziness washed over her.

"Is it?" she heard Nicolai murmur. "Is it really ever done?"

Chapter Twenty-Five

It was nearly dusk when Marc emerged from below-decks, leaving Julietta sleeping peacefully in his cabin. The sky was streaked with indigo and violet, shimmering gold at the edges that reflected on the calm waters. The wavelets lapping at the *Elena Maria* glimmered the palest blue, capped with purest, foaming white. All around was quiet, broken only by the murmurs of the men as they ate their supper, the splash of those waves, the shrill cawing of a sea-bird wheeling high overhead.

Marc shielded his eyes, peering up into the rigging. The ropes and furled sails lay silent, and the lookout up in the crow's nest waved down to him. It was a rare hour of peace aboard ship, simple and rough. An entirely different world than the palatial deceptions of Venice. The city seemed so very far away.

Except for one small piece of its gilding that had broken away and landed on the deck of the *Elena*

Maria. Balthazar Grattiano stood by the railing with the newly freed first mate, Mendoza, listening intently as the sailor explained the mariner's astrolabe. Marc remembered Ermano's words, that Balthazar spent all his coin on scholars and scientists. And whores.

Yet even Balthazar was not as he was before. Marc had seen him as a silent, sullen boy, desperate for his father's tainted attention; as a hardened warrior, ruthless with his bow. Today, his face was alight with curiosity, his eyes glowing with a fierce, awakening intelligence. A new independence.

Marc recalled that day, so long ago, when Juan Velazquez first took him around a ship very like this one, showing him its mechanics, its inner workings. Opening up an entirely new world. Could Marc do that now, for his brother? Could the sea help wash away Balthazar's sorrows and guilts, as it had Marc's?

Marc made his way along the railing to where Balthazar stood, still absorbed in the mariner's astrolabe. When Balthazar noticed Marc's presence, he turned to him with an oddly shy smile.

"Good evening to you both," Marc said.

"Good eve, Signor Velazquez," Balthazar answered. "Signor Mendoza was just demonstrating the use of this mariner's astrolabe. It's fascinating, how this small thing can determine the latitude of a ship, or the meridian altitude of a star!"

"You are interested in navigation?" asked Marc, leaning his forearms on the railing. Far below, the sea lapped at the hull, as if impatient to draw them out into the open water again.

Balthazar shrugged carelessly, yet, still, Marc could see that glow in his green eyes. "I have read De Kaert vander Zee and Astronomicum Caesareum. And, of course, Signor Polo's chronicles of his voyages."

"The lad knows more than I do of the stars, I would vow," Mendoza said.

Balthazar laughed. "Not at all! I know so little, and I have had no chance to truly study the intricacies of navigation, the topography of foreign lands. But, living in Venice, one does have to know the waters."

One of the other men hailed Mendoza then, and he departed with the astrolabe, leaving Marc and Balthazar alone. Balthazar sat down on a coiled pile of rope, leaning back on his elbows to stare out at the darkening horizon. "You are a fortunate man, Signor Velazquez."

Marc turned to watch his brother, crossing his arms over his chest. Balthazar was clad in a rough sailor's smock, his hair tied carelessly back—far from the satin-clad patrician. His thin face was stark in the faint light, and he seemed both younger and years older than could be fathomed.

And Marc owed him his own life, as well as the infinitely more precious life of Julietta.

"I know I am fortunate in many ways," Marc answered carefully. "Yet, compared to a powerful Venetian I have naught. No fine palazzo, no place at the Doge's court."

"And that is where your greatest fortune lies," Balthazar said. "You have this ship, your freedom. A woman who loves you."

"You can have all of that, as well."

Balthazar shook his head. "I murdered my own father. And I am not sorry for it."

"No one knows the truth of what happened at the villa, no one but myself, Julietta, and Nicolai," Marc protested. "None of us will ever speak of it."

"I will know the truth." Balthazar fell silent for a moment, his brow creasing in a frown as he watched that beckoning horizon. "All my life, I wanted only to possess all my father had—his home, his riches, his place in society. I wanted his approval, his acceptance, yet it never came. My mother said it was my birthright, and I believed her. I saw it all slipping away, and I was willing to do anything to keep it."

"Anything?" Marc asked quietly.

A bitter little grin twisted at Balthazar's lips. "I betrayed you and Signora Bassano, did I not? Even knowing it could mean your deaths. And look what has happened."

"In the end you saw your error. You made it right."

"With yet more bloodshed. My father's methods."

"You are not like your father, Balthazar," Marc protested. "You have the power to make amends."

"I am not like him any longer. Because I refuse to be. I want to be more like you—or at least try to be."

"Like *me?*" Marc laughed ruefully, not believing what he heard. "I have done my own share of plotting and betraying. I am just an old sea-dog. You have the means to be much more, to be a ruler."

"Those were my father's dreams. They are not my own. Not now."

"Then what are your own dreams?"

"To find a place on a ship like this one. To work honestly, to see other lands. I cannot go back to Venice."

"I'm sure you will have no difficulties finding a place on a ship," Marc said. "Navigational skills, even rudimentary ones, are always welcome. There may even be a spot here on the *Elena Maria*. What of your father's properties, though? His palazzo, his business ventures, his money?"

"They can fall into the canal for all I care. I won't be tainted by them the way he was." Balthazar paused, his gaze sharpening as he focused suddenly on Marc. "Or why don't you take them?"

Marc laughed. He—become a Venetian grandee? Surely Balthazar jested! "Nay."

"Of course! It makes sense, does it not? You are Ermano's son as much as I. The wrongs he did to you and your mother far outweigh any he did to me and mine. You should take the palazzo and the other properties and run them as you see fit."

"I am a ship's captain," Marc protested. "I know little of republics and kingdoms."

"You know as much of them as I know of ships. And yet you are willing to give me a place here." Balthazar pushed himself to his feet. "Take Ermano's property or not, strip the palazzo of its treasures, throw his jewels

into the sea. It matters naught. I gift it into your hands
from this moment on. And now I want my supper."

He turned and strolled away, humming a light
madrigal as if all his worldly cares had dropped away.
As, indeed, they had, right on to Marc's head.

Marc faced the sea, staring out at the same horizon
that beckoned Balthazar, the horizon that had formed
the ever-shifting edge of his world for so many years.
Once, not so long ago, the offer of assuming his
father's kingdom would have been all he could ask for.
All he desired. To have Ermano gone; to possess all his
mother would have said he was entitled to.

Now Ermano *was* gone, but his riches were hollow,
his kingdom a force of empty wealth, fatal power.
Even a young, brash man like Balthazar had the
wisdom to walk away from it.

Did Marc?

He braced his hands on the polished railing, feeling
the edges of the smooth wood under his palms. The
splinters of battle had been sanded until it was once
again smooth as Murano glass. The wounds of the
Elena Maria were healed. As were his own. The anger,
the hatred he had held in his heart since childhood
were vanished, burned away under the heat of Julietta
Bassano's passion.

You are not your father, she had insisted, holding
him in her arms. In her eyes, he was only Marc, a man
of goodness and honour.

Honour. He thought not. No true man of honour
would have tried to use a woman as he had set out to

use Julietta. But one thing she said was true—he was
not his father. Not a true Grattiano. And he no longer
wanted any part of that man's world, not even his
wealth. Marc possessed something of infinitely more
worth—he had her love. That meant he could leave this
place without accomplishing all he planned so carefully, but with no regrets. Not a single one.

Surely a new life waited beyond that alluring
horizon. A life to be shared.

A board creaked behind him, and he turned to see
Julietta standing there. She was wrapped in one of his
cloaks, her black hair loose over her shoulders, her
eyes clear and alight as he had never seen them before.
His beautiful sorceress. His lady of fire.

She gave him a gentle smile. "What do you think
of so intently, *signor?*"

"I think of you," he answered honestly. "Always."

One dark brow arched. "Do you, indeed?" She
moved closer, her arm sliding about his waist as she
gazed down at the waves. The water was deep blue
now, opaque as ink as night set in around them. It was
as mysterious as her eyes, and he saw that was what
first drew him to her. She was so like his first love, the
sea. Deep, gloriously beautiful, full of strange secrets,
unyielding, ever changing. Their life together would
surely be a stormy, ecstatic, ever-shifting journey, and
he would trade it all for nothing else. Not even the
richest palazzo in all Venice. Not if she refused to
share it with him.

"You told me once that a ship, that the sea, meant

freedom," she said, leaning against him, her arms sliding about his waist. He could smell the sweet jasmine in her freshly washed hair, feel the heat of her body curling around him, capturing him for ever.

"So it has always been for me," he answered, pressing a kiss to the top of her head. Her hair was satin under his lips.

"And you offered it all to me. Does that freedom belong to both of us now?"

"It does. We can sail away with the morning tide, if you like. Let the waves carry us out of this lagoon to wherever you desire. Paris, London, Amsterdam." He drew her even closer. "Unless you would rather be a grand lady of Venice. A wife of a courtier, mistress of your own grand palazzo."

Julietta pulled away from him, frowning. "What do you mean? Surely Venice is done for us."

"Balthazar wishes to find a place on a ship, to become a navigator," Marc told her. "He wants to give all Ermano's property over to me."

"To administer for him?"

"To keep. Own. Be master of."

Julietta glanced away, tucking her arms tightly in the shelter of her cloak. Her face was as pale and unreadable as a Grecian statue, but her eyes glittered like the stars blinking on above their heads. "Is that what you desire, my love? To stay in Venice? After all that has happened?"

Marc shook his head. "Surely you know me too well to think that is what I would want. A narrow, restricted life. But if we are to be married, you have a say in our life, as well. If you would like to have that security…"

"Fool!" Julietta suddenly burst out, her statue façade cracking away to reveal the woman he loved beneath. She threw herself against him, locking her arms about his neck as if she would never let go. "Look where the *security* of Venice got us! Almost killed. I would die if I lost you, Marc, and I surely *would* lose you if you took up Ermano's mantle. You would suffocate away from the sea, locked up in a black robe at the Doge's court, and I would wither with you. I say we take our chances out in the wide world. Always."

Marc laughed, lifting her off her feet and twirling her about until she laughed, too, both of them giddy as children freed from the schoolroom. "And so we shall! Together."

Julietta leaned against him as he lowered her to the deck. She held up her hand, moonlight glinting on his ruby ring. "When you gave me this, Marc, you said I should send it to you if I had need of you, and you would come to my side."

Marc clasped her hand, holding it against his heart. "So I shall."

"Nay! It will never be off my finger, for we will always be together. Facing whatever comes. We won't be parted again."

"I have your solemn promise on that?" he said, drawing her closer for a scalding, branding kiss, sealing their bargain for all time. "The word of a sorceress?"

She smiled up at him, a smile with all their future in it. "It's the very best kind, *Il leone*. The word of a sorceress in love."

* * * * *

Here is a sneak preview of Nicolai's story in

A SINFUL ALLIANCE

Coming April 2010 from
Mills & Boon Super Historical…

Prologue

⤜∼⤛

Venice, 1525

Her quarry was within her sight.

Marguerite peered through the tiny peephole, leaning close to the rough wooden wall as she examined the scene below. The brothel was not one of the finest in the Serene City, those velvet havens purveying the best wines and sweetmeats, the loveliest, cleanest women—for the steepest prices, of course. But neither was this place a dirty stew where a man should watch his purse and his privy parts, lest one or the other be lopped off. It was just a simple, noisy, colourful whorehouse, thick with the scent of dust, ale and sweat, redolent with shrieks of laughter and moans of pleasure, real or feigned. A place for men of the artisan classes, or travelling actors here for Carnival. A place where the proprietor was easily bribed by women with ulterior motives.

She had certainly been in far worse.

Marguerite narrowed her gaze, focusing in on her prey. It was him, it must be. He matched the careful description, the sketch. He was the man she had seen in the Piazza San Marco. He did not look like her vision of a coarse Russian, she would give him that. Were they not supposed to be built like bears, and just as hairy? Just as stinking? Everyone in France knew that these Muscovites had no manners, that they lived in a dark, ancient world where it was quite acceptable to grow one's beard to one's knees, to toss food on to the floor and blow one's nose on the tablecloth.

Marguerite wrinkled her nose. *Disgusting.* But then, what could be expected from people who lived encased in ice and snow? Who were deprived of the elegance and civility of France?

And it was France that brought her here tonight, to this Venetian brothel. She had to do her duty for her king, her home.

A bit of a pity, though, she thought as she watched the Russian. He was such a beauty.

He had no beard at all, but was clean shaven, the sharp, elegant angles of his face revealed to the flickering, smoking torchlight. The orange glow of the flames played over his high cheekbones, his sensual lips. His hair, the rich gold of an old coin, fell loose halfway down his back, a shimmering length of silk that beckoned for a woman's touch. The two doxies in his lap seemed to agree, for they kept running their fingers through the bright strands, cooing and giggling, nibbling at his ear and his neck.

Other women hovered at his shoulder, neglecting their other customers to bask in his golden glow, in the richness of his laughter, the incandescence of his skin and eyes.

And he did not seem to mind. Indeed, he appeared to take it all as his due, leaning back in his chair indolently like some spoiled Eastern lord, his head thrown back in abandoned laughter. He had shed his doublet and his white shirt was unlaced, hanging open to reveal a smooth, muscular chest, glimmering with a light sheen of sweat. The thin linen hung off one shoulder, revealing its broad strength.

No lumbering Russian bear, then, but a sleek cat, its power concealed by its grace.

Oui, a pity to destroy such handsomeness. But it had to be done. He and his Moscow friends, not to mention the Spanish and Venetian traders he consorted with, stood in the way of French interests with their proposed new trade routes from Moscow to Persia, along their great River Volga and the Caspian Sea. It would interfere with the French trade in silks, spices, furs—and that could never be. It was even more vital now, after the king's humiliating defeat at Pavia. So, Nicolai Ostrovsky would have to die.

After one last lingering glance at that bare, golden skin, Marguerite turned away, letting the peephole cover fall into place. She had her task; she had done such things for France before, she had done worse. She could not hesitate now, just because the mark was pretty. She was the Emerald Lily. She could not fail.

There was a small looking glass hanging on the rough wall of her small room, illuminated by candles and the one window. She gazed into it to find a stranger looking back. Her disguises often took many turns—gnarled peasant women, old Jewish merchants, milkmaids, duchesses. She had never tried a harlot before, though. It was quite interesting.

Her silvery blonde hair, usually a shimmering length of smooth waves, longer even than the Russian's, was frizzed and curled, pinned in a knot at the back and puffed out at the sides. Her complexion, the roses and lilies so prized in Paris, was covered with pale rice powder, two bright circles of rouge on each cheek and kohl heavily lining her green eyes.

She was not herself now, not Marguerite Dumas of the French Court. Nor the lady who had strolled, modestly veiled and cloaked, through the Piazza San Marco in the bright light of day, watching Nicolai Ostrovsky in his guise as an actor. An acrobat, who juggled and jested and feinted, always hiding his true self behind a smile and the jangle of bells. Just as she did, in her own way.

Voila, now she was Bella, a simple Italian whore, come to Venice to make a few ducats during Carnival. But hopefully a whore who could catch Nicolai's eye, even as he was the centre of attention for every woman in the place.

Marguerite stepped back until she could examine

her garb in the glass. It was scarlet silk, bought that afternoon from a dealer in second-hand garments. It must have once belonged to a grand courtesan, but now the gold embroidery was slightly tarnished, the hem frayed and seams faded. It was still pretty, though, and it suited her small, slender frame. She tugged the neckline lower, until it hung from her shoulders and bared one breast.

Hmm, she thought, examining that pale appendage. Her bosom was good, she knew that; the bubbies were not too large or small, perfectly formed and very white. Perhaps they were meant to compensate for her rather short legs, the old scars on her stomach. But they seemed a little plain, compared to the other whores'. Marguerite reached for her pot of rouge and smeared some of the red cream around the exposed nipple. There. Very eye-catching. For good measure, she added some to her lips, and dabbed jasmine perfume behind her ears. Heavy and exotic, very different from her usual essence of lilies.

Now she was ready. Marguerite lifted up her voluminous skirts, checking to see that her dagger was still strapped to her thigh, its point honed to perfect sharpness.

She smoothed the gown back into place and slipped out of the small room. The corridor outside was narrow, running behind the main rooms of the house, the ceiling so low she had to duck her head. It was also deserted. But even here she could detect the sounds of laughter and moaning, the clink of pottery goblets, the whistle of a whip for those with more exotic tastes. Marguerite hoped that was not a Russian vice. Baring her backside for the lash would surely reveal the dagger.

She turned down a small, steep flight of stairs, careful on her high-heeled shoes. The low door at the foot of the steps led out of the secret warren into the large, noisy public room.

It was like tumbling into a new world. Noises here were no longer muffled, but loud and clear, echoing off the low, darkened ceiling. Smoke from the hearth was thick, acrid, blending with the perfumes of the women, the smell of flesh and sex and spilled ale. The wooden floor beneath her feet was sticky and pock-marked.

Marguerite stood for a moment in the doorway, her careful gaze sweeping over the entire scene. Card games and dice went on by the hearth, serious play to judge by the great piles of coins on each table, the intent expressions on the players' faces. There was drink and food, plain fare of bread, cheese and prosciutto. But whores were the first commodity, any sort a man could fancy. Short, tall, fat, thin, blonde, brunette. There was even a young man clad in an elaborate blue satin gown. He was quite good, too, with smooth skin and silky, black hair. 'Twas a shame he couldn't do something about that Adam's apple.

Marguerite surveyed them dispassionately, her competition for this one night. She knew she was beautiful, had known it since she was a child, taken to Court by her father. She was not vain about it. It was merely an asset to her work, particularly at times like this. She was fairer than any of the others here, even the boy in blue. Therefore she should be able to catch Nicolai's attention.

Her competition was less now, anyway. Many of the women who had clustered around him were scattered, sent by the proprietor to see to the other patrons. There were just the two on his lap, half-dressed in their *camicias,* wriggling and giggling. Marguerite straightened her shoulders, displaying her bosom in its red silk frame, held her head high, and sauntered slowly past the Russian and his harem. She let her train trail over his boots, let him smell her perfume, glimpse her white breast, her half-smile. Once past him, she glanced back and winked. Then she went on her way, seeking a cup of ale.

Now—well, now she waited. In her experience, a touch of mystery worked better than fawning attention, which he obviously got enough of anyway. She sipped at her ale, carefully examining the room behind her in an old, cracked looking glass hanging on the wall. The two whores were still on his lap, but she could tell his full attention was no longer on their full-blown charms. He sat forward on his chair, watching *her,* a small frown on his brow. She turned slightly toward him, her pretty profile displayed. A slight impatience made her fingers tighten on the cup. He had to come to her before anyone else did! She flicked lightly at her lips with her tongue, and tossed her head back.

Whatever the secret charm, it worked. She turned away again, and in a few moments she felt him close to her side. How warm he was, yet not in a heated, lascivious, overpowering way, as most men were. More like the summer sun in her childhood home of Champagne, touching her skin with light fingers, beckoning her ever closer. He smelled like the summer, too, of some green, herbal soap behind the salty tang of sweat and skin. Of pure man.

She swivelled toward him, smiling flirtatiously. He had eased his shirt back over his shoulders but his chest was still bare, and he stood near enough that she could see the faint sprinkling of wiry blond hair against his skin. Gold on gold.

"Good evening, *signor,*" she said, every hint of a French accent carefully banished.

"Good evening, *signora,*" he answered, giving her a low bow, as if they were in the Doge's palace and not a smoky brothel. His eyes were blue, she noticed. A clear, sky-like expanse where anything, any wish or desire or fear, could be written.

And they watched her very carefully. The laughter he shared with the other women was still there, but lurking in the background. He was a wary one, then. She would have to be doubly cautious.

For an instant, as that blue gaze met hers steadily, unblinking, she felt a prickle of unease. A wish that she had worn a mask, which was ridiculous. The heavy make-up was disguise enough, and he would not see her after tonight.

Marguerite shoved away that unease. There was no time for it. She had to do her task and be gone.

"I have not seen you here before," he said.

"I am new. Bella is my name, I have just arrived from my village on the mainland to work for Carnival," she answered, gesturing for more ale. "Do you come here often, then?"

"Often enough, when I am in Venice."

She laughed. "I would wager! A virile man like yourself, I'm sure the pale, choosy courtesans of the grand palazzos could never keep you satisfied." The ale arrived, and she handed him one of the goblets. "Salute."

"*Na zdorovie,*" he answered, and tossed back the sour drink. "Venice is truly filled with the most beautiful of women, *signora*. Lovelier than any I have ever seen, and I have travelled to many lands. But I do prefer company more like—myself."

Marguerite glanced toward the boy in blue. "Yourself, *signor?*"

He laughed, and she was again reminded of summer and home, of the warm, sparkling wine of Champagne. "Not in that way, *signora*. Closer to the earth." She must have looked puzzled, for he smiled down at her. "'Tis a saying from my homeland."

"You are not from here, either."

"Nay. I can see where you might mistake me, though, given my excellent Italian," he said, giving her a teasing grin. "I am from Moscow, though many years removed from that place."

"Ah, that explains it, then."

"Explains what, *signora?*"

"The virility. For is Moscow not snowbound for

much of the year? Much time to spend in front of the fire. Or in a warm bed."

"Very true, *signora*." His arm suddenly snaked out, catching her around the waist and pulling her close. For one flashing instant, Marguerite was caught by surprise and instinctively stiffened. She forced herself to go limp, pliant, arching back against his arm.

Through her skirts and his hose she felt the press of his erection, hard and heavy. "No ice tonight, I see, *signor*."

"The Italian sun has melted it away—almost."

She smiled teasingly up at him, twining her arms about his neck. His hair was like satin spilling over her fingers, cool and alluring. She tangled her clasp in its clinging strands, inhaling that clean, warm scent of him. "I'm sure *this* Italian sun could finish the job completely, *signor*. You would never feel the touch of ice again."

In answer he kissed her, his lips swooping down on hers so quickly she had no time for thought. She could only react, respond. His kiss was not harsh and bruising, but soft, gentle, nibbling at her lips, luring her to follow him into that sunshine and forget all. For a moment, she *did* forget. She was not Marguerite Dumas, not the Emerald Lily. She was just a woman being kissed by a handsome man, a man who ensnared her with a blurry, humid heat, with his scent, his strong arms, his talented lips. She pressed closer to him, so close the edges of her being melted into his and she couldn't tell where she ended and he began. His tongue pressed into her mouth, presaging an even more profound joining.

Overwhelmed, Marguerite eased back. She needed her own ice now, the cold thoughts, precise actions. Not this, this—*lust*. This need. The Emerald Lily did not have needs, especially not carnal ones. Nicolai Ostrovsky was a task, nothing more.

Why, then, was it so very hard to remember that as she stared up into his pale blue eyes?

She made herself smile. "You *are* hot tonight, *signor.*"

"I told you the Italian sun has made me so."

"Then come with me, *signor,* and I'll cool you off— eventually." She untangled her clasp from his hair, reaching down to take his hand. His fingers held hers tightly, holding her prisoner as she led him toward that small doorway she earlier emerged from.

They climbed the narrow stairs, Nicolai ducking to avoid the rafters overhead. The quiet enclosed them again, the loud, bright world shut away, and Marguerite felt her heart thud in her chest, felt her skin grow chilled. The time was almost upon her.

At the entrance to her little room, Nicolai suddenly reeled her close to him, spinning her lightly around to press her to the wall. Marguerite's heartbeat quickened—had he discovered her, then? Was she caught in a trap of his own?

He did not slit her throat, though. He merely held her there, pressed against her in the half-light, staring down at her with those otherworldly eyes as if he could see into her soul. Her sin-riddled soul.

"Where did you come from, Bella?" he said softly. His accent was more pronounced now, the edges of his words touched with some icy Russian music.

Marguerite smiled at him. "I told you, from the mainland. This is our most profitable time of year, but one has to be in Venice to make the coin."

"Have you been a whore long, then, *dorogaya?*"

She laughed. "Oh, yes. Decades, it seems."

"Miraculous, then. For you still have your teeth, your clear eyes…" He reached down to trace the underside of her naked breast, the soft, puckered flesh. His thumb flicked lightly at the rouged nipple, making her shiver deeply. "Your smooth skin."

"I was born under a lucky star, *signor.* My father always said so," she said, still trembling. And that was one true thing she said tonight. Her father *had* told her that when she was a child, holding her up on his shoulder so she could see the clear, bright stars in the Champagne sky.

But then her star faded, and here she was in a Venetian brothel. Bound up with this beautiful puzzle of a man.

"A lucky star on the mainland," he said.

"Just so. You must have been born under an auspicious sign yourself, to be so handsome." She spoke teasingly, but it was also true. Such beauty and charm should belong to no ordinary mortal. He was blessed. Until tonight.

This was a fateful hour for them both, then.

"If we are both so fortunate, then, Signora Bella, why are we *here?*" he murmured, as if he truly could read her thoughts. "A whore and an actor, who must both sing for their supper. Can we even afford each other?"

"I am not so expensive as all that," Marguerite said. She went up on tiptoe and whispered in his ear, "Not for you. I think we are alike, you and I, whores and actors both in one. And we do love our homelands, though we don't want to admit it."

He pulled back, staring at her as if surprised by her words, but she wouldn't let him go. She caught him closer, kissing him with every secret passion of her heart.

"You didn't come from any human land," he muttered roughly against her neck, his lips trailing a fiery ribbon of kisses along her throat, her shoulder. "You come from an enchanted fairy realm, and you'll surely vanish back there at the dawn."

"'Tis hours until then," Marguerite gasped. "We have to make the most of the night."

Nicolai captured her breast in his kiss, laving the pebbled, rouged tip with his tongue until she added her hoarse moans to the others of the house. That hazy, hot passion descended on her again like a grey cloud, and she felt so weak, so warm and yet shivering. Through that fog, she felt him reach down and grasp her hem, drawing her skirt up.

The cold draught on her bare leg brought sanity crashing down around her. *Non!* He could not see her dagger, or all would be lost. She pulled away, laughing. "I said we had all night, *signor!* We don't have to rut against the wall." She drew him toward the small cot tucked beneath the room's one window. Later, when her task was done, she would escape through that portal, vanishing over the rooftops of Venice. Not to any fairy kingdom, but to a curtained gondola where "Bella" would disappear for ever.

She lightly pushed Nicolai, unresisting, on to the sheets, standing above him for a moment, studying him in the moonlight. His golden hair spilled around him on the rumpled, dingy linen. *So handsome—so unreal.* He smiled wickedly up at her, a fallen angel.

"So, we can rut on a bed like civilised beings?" he said.

"Exactly so." She leaned over him, tracing the muscled contours of his chest with her fingertips. The arc of his ribs, the flat, puckered discs of his nipples. So glorious, like a map of some exotic, undiscovered country. She felt the pace of his heartbeat, racing under her caress. "We can savour each moment. Each— single—touch." She kissed his nipple, tugging its hardness between her teeth, tasting the salt of his skin.

Nicolai shivered, and she felt the pull of his fingers in her hair, the shift of his body under hers. He was so hard against her hip, his whole body taut as a bow string. *Oui,* he was under the spell of desire now. She couldn't let herself fall prey to it, too.

"How much will this cost me?" he said tightly.

Marguerite eased up his body until she lay prone atop him, pressed close. "Your soul," she whispered.

Then she acted, as she had before. As she was

trained to do. She drew up her skirts and snatched the dagger, in the same smooth motion rising up from his chest and lifting the blade high. She had a quick impression of his eyes, silver in the moonlight, his body laid bare for her to claim. She had only to plunge the dagger down into that heartbeat, and an enemy of France would be gone.

But those eyes—those inhuman, all-seeing eyes. They watched her steadily, not even startled, and she was captured by their sea-like depths.

Only for an instant, one quicksilver flash, but it was enough to lose her the advantage. Nicolai seized her wrist in a bruising grip, tightening until her wrist bone creaked and she cried out. Her fingers opened convulsively, and the dagger clattered to the floor. He swung her beneath him, pinning her to the bed. No lazy, debauched, lustful actor now, but a swift, pitiless predator. Just as she was.

Marguerite was well trained in swordplay and the use of daggers and bows, in courtly fencing and rough street brawling. She knew tricks and dupes to compensate for her small size and feminine weakness. Yet she also knew when she was truly defeated, and that was now. She knew what it was she saw in those eyes. It was doom.

As she stared up at him now, she felt strangely calm, as if she was already hovering above her body, watching the scene from the rafters. Her victim became her murderer, and it was no less than she deserved for her sins. This day had been long in coming. If only she could not die unshriven! She would never meet her mother in heaven now.

But she *did* see her avenging angel, rising above her in the darkness. He scooped up her dagger, examining the blade while he held her firmly down with his other hand, his strong body. She felt the full force of that lean strength; the smooth, supple muscles that held him on a tightrope or in a backflip now held her easily in place.

He stared at the dagger, so thin and perfectly balanced. So lethal. The small emerald embedded in the hilt gleamed. "Why me?" he said roughly. "Why try to kill a poor actor?"

"You are not a poor actor, Monsieur Ostrovsky, and we both know it," she said in French. "You have secrets to equal my own."

"What *are* your secrets, *mademoiselle?*" he answered in the same language.

Marguerite laughed bitterly. "It hardly matters. I have failed in my task, but I take my secrets to the grave."

"Do you, indeed? Well, that might be a long time from now, *mademoiselle.* I have the feeling that fairies, like cats, have many lives. You are young; I'm sure you have some to go."

Marguerite stared up at him, baffled, but his face gave nothing away. He was as beautiful, as cold, as the marble statues in the piazza. Her passionate lover was gone. "What do you mean?"

"I mean, *mademoiselle* whatever-your-name-is, that this is not your night to die. Nor mine, though you would have had it otherwise." The dagger arced down, but not into her heart. It sliced into her skirt, cutting away thick strips of silk. Holding the blade between his teeth like a corsair, he bound her hands and feet tightly, with expert knots.

"What are you doing?" Marguerite cried, bewildered. This was not how the game was meant to be played! "I would have killed you! Do you mean you won't kill me? You won't take your revenge?"

"Oh, I will take my revenge, *mademoiselle,* but not on this night." He tied off the final knot around her wrists, so firm she could not even wriggle her fingers. "It will be some day when you least expect it."

Once she was trussed up like a banquet goose, he leaned down and pressed one gentle kiss to her lips. He still tasted of herbs, ale and her own waxen rouge. And he still smelled of an alluring summer day. *Quel con!*

"I just can't bring myself to destroy such rare beauty," he whispered. "Not after your fine services, incomplete though they were. *Adieu, mademoiselle*—for now."

He tied the last strip of silk over her mouth, and opened the very window Marguerite had planned for her escape. As she stared, infuriated, he gave her a wink, and with one graceful movement leaped through the casement and was gone.

Marguerite screamed through her gag. She arched her back and kicked her legs, all to no avail. She was bound fast, caught in her own scheme. And the *cochon* didn't even have the decency to kill her! To follow the code all spies and assassins adhered to. At least French ones.

"Have his revenge," would he, the beautiful, arrogant Russian pig? Never! She would find him first, and finish this task; no matter what. No matter how far she had to go, even to the frozen wastes of his Russia itself.

For the Emerald Lily never failed.

Chapter One

~~~~~~~

The Palace of Fontainebleau, January 1527

Marguerite Dumas walked slowly down the corridor, gaze straight ahead, hands folded at her waist, her face carefully blank as she ignored the whispers of the courtiers loitering about. In her fingers she clutched the summons of the king.

She had known this day would come. A new assignment. A new mission for the Emerald Lily. If only this one ended better than the last, that night in Venice!

Marguerite paused at the end of the corridor, where a shadowed landing became a narrow staircase. Here, there was no one to see her, and she closed her eyes against the spasm of pain in her head. It was no illness, but the memory of Venice, the thought of the handsome Russian *encule*. The coppery, bitter taste of humiliation and failure.

The king had said nothing when she returned to Paris with her report of the Russian's escape. He had said nothing when he sent her back to her "legitimate" duties as *fille d'honneur* to Princess Madeleine, her ostensible reason for being at Court in the first place. There she had languished for months, walking with the other ladies in the gardens, reading to the princess, dancing at banquets. Fending off the advances of useless, arrogant courtiers.

They could do her no good, those perfumed popinjays who pressed their kisses on her in the shadows. Only one man was useful here, King François himself. And he maintained his distant politeness, merely nodding to her when they happened to pass in the garden or the banquet hall.

Marguerite knew the whispers, that she and the king had been lovers who were estranged now that he was involved with the Duchesse de Vendôme. If they only knew the truth! They would never believe it. Not of her.

She scarcely believed it herself, in these days of quiet leisure in the princess's apartments. Had she truly ever been sent to the far corners of Europe, to defeat the enemies of France? Had she once used her wits, her hard-learned skills, to find a secret victory over those who would defy the king? It did not seem possible.

Yet at night, alone in her curtained bed, she knew it was true. Once, she had had adventures. She had won a place for herself in the wider world. Had one mistake, one instant's miscalculation, cost her all she worked for?

It had made no sense to her that she would be dismissed in only a moment, when now more than ever her special skills were needed. Since the king's humiliating defeat against the forces of the Holy Roman Emperor at Pavia, since his two sons were sent to Madrid as hostages, dark days had descended on France. Her enemies were becoming ever bolder.

Marguerite *knew* she could be of use in these new, dangerous games. Why, then, was she relegated to dancing and card playing? All because of the Russian, damn his unearthly blue eyes!

But those days seemed to be at an end. She held the king's note in her hand, so tightly the parchment pressed her rings into her skin. It was time for her to redeem herself.

As she climbed the narrow, privy staircase, the sounds of hammering and sawing grew louder, more distinct, shouting of the king's new mania for building. Since his return from Spain in defeat, François had thrown himself into a frenzy of remodelling, of making his palaces ever grander.

Fontainebleau, one of his favourite castles thanks to the seventeen-thousand hectares of forest ripe with deer for hunting, was his latest focus. Since the Christmas festivities, so muted without the presence of the Dauphin and his brother, work was begun in earnest. The old keep of St Louis and Philipe le Beau was being demolished, replaced by something vast and modern.

Marguerite lifted the hem of her velvet skirt as she

stepped over a pile of rubbish. A shower of stone dust from above nearly coated her headdress, and she hurried to the relative safety of the great gallery.

This was one of the few rooms in the place to be almost finished. A long, echoing expanse of polished parquet floor swept up to walls of pale stuccowork, inlaid dark wood in the panels of the *boiserie*. A few of the many planned flourishes of floral motifs, gods and goddesses, fat little Cupids, were in place, with blank spaces just waiting to be filled.

At the far end of the gallery, leaning over a table covered with sketches, was King François himself. He was consulting with one of the Italian artists brought in to take charge of all this splendour, Signor Fiorentino, and for the moment did not see her. Marguerite slowed her steps, studying him carefully for any sign of his thoughts and intentions. Any hint that she was truly forgiven.

François was very tall, towering over her own petite frame, and was all an imposing king should be, with abundant dark hair and a fashionable pointed beard. His brown eyes were sharp and clear above his hooked Valois nose, missing nothing. After Pavia and his captivity, he seemed leaner, more wary, his always athletic body thin and wiry.

But his famous sense of fashion had not deserted him. Even on a quiet day like this, he wore a crimson velvet doublet embroidered with gold and silver and festooned with garnet buttons, a sleeveless surcoat of purple trimmed with silver fox fur to keep the chill away. A crimson cap sewn with pearls and more garnets covered his head, concealing his gaze as he bent over the drawings.

"There will be twelve in all, your Majesty," Fiorentino said, gesturing toward the empty spaces on the gallery walls. "All scenes from mythology, of course, to illustrate your Majesty's enlightened governance."

"Hmm, yes, I see," Francois said. Without glancing up, he called, "Ah, Mademoiselle Dumas! You surely have the finest eye for beauty of any lady in my kingdom. What do you think of Signor Fiorentino's plans?"

Marguerite came closer, peering down at the sketches as she tucked the king's note into her tight undersleeve. The first drawing was a scene of Danaë, more a stylish lady of the French Court in a drapery of blue-tinted silk and an elaborate headdress than a woman of the classical world. But her surroundings— broken columns and twisted olive trees, her attendants of fat cherubs and even more fashionable ladies— were very skilfully drawn, the scene most elegant.

"It is lovely," she said. "And surely the dimensions, the way the scene is framed by these columns, make it perfect for that space there, where the afternoon sunlight will make Danaë's robe shimmer like a summer sky. You will use cobalt, *signor,* and flecks of gilt?"

"You are quite right, your Majesty! The *mademoiselle* has a most discerning eye for beauty," Fiorentino said happily, clapping his paint-stained hands. Perhaps he was just glad he wouldn't waste expensive cobalt.

"*Bien, signor,*" the king said. "The Danaë stays. You may commence at once."

As the artist hurried away, his assistants scurrying after him, François smiled at Marguerite. Try as she did to gauge his thoughts, she could see nothing beyond his courtly smile, the opaque light of his eyes. He was even better at concealing his true self than Marguerite herself.

"Shall we stroll in the gardens, Mademoiselle Dumas?" he asked lightly. "It is a bit warmer, I think, and I should like your opinion on the new fountain I have commissioned. It is the goddess Diana, a great warrior and hunter. A favourite of yours, I believe?"

"I would be honoured to walk with you, your Majesty," Marguerite answered. "Yet I fear I know little of fountains."

"Egremont will loan you his cloak," he said, gesturing to one of his attendants, who immediately presented her with his fur-lined wrap. "We would not want you to catch a chill. You have such important work, *mademoiselle.*"

Important work? Was this truly a new task, then? A chance for the Emerald Lily to emerge from hiding? Marguerite was careful not to show her eagerness, settling the cloak over her shoulders. "Indeed, your Majesty?"

"*Oui.* For does my daughter not depend on you, since the death of her sainted mother? You are her favourite attendant."

"I, too, am very fond of the princess," Marguerite

answered, and she was. Princess Madeleine was a lovely child, charming and quick-minded. But she was hardly a challenge. She could not offer the kind of advancement Marguerite's ambition craved. The kind she needed for her own security. She thought of the stash of coins hidden beneath her bed, and how they were not yet enough to gain her a vineyard, a life, of her own.

"Indeed?" François led her down the stairs and out into the gardens, now slumbering under the winter frost. They, like the palace itself, were in the midst of upheaval, their old flowerbeds being torn up to be replaced by new plantings, a more modern design. For now, though, everything was caught in a moment of stasis, frozen in place, overlaid by sparkling white like an enchanted castle in a story.

François waved away his attendants, and led her down a narrow walkway. The air was cold but still, holding the echo of the abandoned courtiers' voices as they lingered by the wall.

"It is most sad, then, that my daughter will have to do without your company for a time," the king said.

"Will she?"

"Yes, for I fear you must journey to England, *mademoiselle*. And the Emerald Lily must go with you."

England. So the rumours were true. François sought a new alliance with King Henry, a new bulwark against the power of the Emperor.

"I am ready, your Majesty," she said.

François smiled. "*Ma chère* Marguerite—always so eager to serve us."

"I am a Frenchwoman," she answered simply. "I do what I can for my country."

"And you do it well. Usually."

"I will not fail you. I vow this."

"I trust that is true. For this mission is of vital importance. I am sending a delegation to negotiate a treaty of alliance with King Henry, and to organise a marriage between his daughter Princess Mary and my Henri."

Marguerite considered this. Despite flirting with English alliances in the past, including the long-ago Field of the Cloth of Gold, which was so spectacular it was still much talked of, naught had come of it all. Thanks to the English queen, Katherine of Aragon, aunt of the Emperor, England always drifted back to Spain. Little Princess Mary, only eleven years old, had already been betrothed to numerous Spanish grandees as well as the Emperor Charles himself, or so they said.

"What of the Spanish?" Marguerite asked quietly.

"I have heard tell that Henry and his queen are not as—united as they once were," François answered. "Katherine grows old, and Henry's gaze has perhaps turned to a young lady who was once resident of the French Court, Mademoiselle Anne Boleyn. Katherine may no longer have so much influence on English policy. Since the formation of the League of Cognac, Henry seems inclined to a more Gallic way of seeing things. I will be most gratified if this treaty comes to completion."

Marguerite nodded. An alliance with England could certainly mean the beginning of brighter days for France. Yet she had dealt with the Spanish before. For all their seeming piety and austerity, they were just as fierce in defending their interests as the French, perhaps even more so. It was said that in their religious fervour they often employed the hair shirt and the scourge, and it seemed to sour their spirits, made them ill humoured and dangerous as serpents.

"The Spanish—and Queen Katherine—will not let go of their advantage so easily as that," Marguerite said. "I have heard Katherine seeks a new Spanish match for her daughter."

"That is why I am sending you," François answered. "I have assigned Gabriel de Grammont, the Bishop of Tarbes, to head the delegation, and I am sure he will do very well. As will his men. But women can see things a man cannot, go places a man cannot, especially one as well trained as my Lily. Keep an eye on the queen, and especially on the Spanish ambassador, Don Diego de Mendoza. It is entirely possible they have plans of their own, of which Henry is not aware."

"And if they do?"

François scowled, gazing out over his frozen gardens. "Then you know what to do." He drew a small scroll from inside his surcoat and handed it to her. "Here are your instructions. You depart in two weeks. I will have dressmakers sent to you this evening—you must order all that you require for a stay of several weeks."

With that, he turned and left her, rejoining his waiting attendants. They all disappeared inside the château, leaving Marguerite alone in the cold afternoon. There were no birds, no bustle of gardeners or cool splash of fountains, only the lonely whistle of the wind as she unfurled the scroll.

The words were brief. The king's kinsman, the Comte de Calonne, was to be part of the delegation, along with his wife Claudine. Marguerite was ostensibly to serve as companion to Claudine, to accompany her when she called on Queen Katherine and attended banquets and tournaments.

But Marguerite knew well what was *not* written there. At those banquets, she was to flirt with the English courtiers when they were in their cups, draw secrets from them they were not even aware they were sharing. To watch the queen and the Spanish ambassador. To watch King Henry, and make sure the notoriously changeable monarch did not waver. To watch this Anne Boleyn, see if she had real influence, if she could be turned to the French cause.

And, if anyone stood in France's path, she was to remove them. Quickly and neatly.

It was surely the most important task she had ever received, a test of all her skills. The culmination of all she had learned. If she did well, if the treaty was safely signed and the betrothal of Princess Mary and the Duc d'Orléans sealed, she would be handsomely rewarded. Perhaps she would even be given leave to travel, to seek out the one man who had ever defeated her and thus finally have her revenge.

The Russian. Nicolai Ostrovsky.

The soft crackle of a footstep on the pathway behind her startled her, and she spun around, her knees bending and hands forward in a defensive position.

It was Pierre LeBeque, a young priest in the employ of Bishop Grammont. His eyes narrowed when she turned on him, and he fell back a step, watching her warily.

Marguerite dropped her hands to her sides, but still stood poised to dash away if need be. She did not often see Father Pierre, for he was usually scurrying about the Court on errands for the bishop, but when she did encounter him she didn't care for the sensations he evoked. That prickling feeling at the back of her neck that so often warned her of "danger."

What danger a solemn young priest, tall but as thin as a blade of grass, could hold she was not sure. He seemed to bear nothing but dutiful piety on his bony shoulders. Yet he always watched her so closely, and not as others did, in admiration and awe of her beauty—it was as if he was trying to see all her secrets.

And she well knew how often appearances were deceiving.

"Father Pierre," she said calmly, drawing her borrowed cloak closer around her. "What brings you out on such a chilly day?"

He did not smile, just stared solemnly. His face, white as the frost, was set in stony lines too old for his youthful years. "I am carrying a message to the king from Bishop Grammont, *mademoiselle*."

"Indeed? Such industrious loyalty you possess, coming out on such a day, when everyone else is tucked up by their fires."

"You are not," he pointed out.

"I felt the need for some fresh air. But I am returning to my warm apartment now."

"Allow me to escort you back to the palace, then."

Marguerite could think of no graceful way to decline his company, so she merely nodded and turned on the pathway. Pierre fell into step beside her, the hem of his black robes whispering over the swept gravel.

"I understand from the bishop that you are to join our voyage to England," he said tonelessly.

Alors, but news did travel fast! Marguerite herself had only just learned of her assignment, and here this glorified clerk already knew.

What else did he know?

"Indeed I am. The Comtesse de Calonne requires a companion, and I am honoured that my services have been requested."

"You are very brave then, *mademoiselle*. They say the English Court is coarse and dirty."

"I have certainly heard of worse."

"Have you?"

"*Oui*. The Turks, for one. And the Russians. I have heard that the Muscovites grow their beards so very long, and so tangled and matted, that rats live in the hair with their human owners none the wiser."

Father Pierre frowned doubtfully. "Truly?"

Marguerite shrugged. "So I have heard. I have seldom met a Russian myself, except for the ambassadors who sometimes visit Paris. Their fur robes are antique, but their grooming is fine." And there was one, who had no beard at all, but hair as golden and soft as a summer's day. One who always popped into her mind at the most inconvenient moments. "Surely the English cannot be as crude as rats in beards. I am certain our weeks there will be most pleasant."

"Nevertheless, we will be in a foreign Court, with ways we may not always understand. I hope that you will feel free to come to me for any—counsel you might require, Mademoiselle Dumas."

Counsel? As if she would ever need advice from him! Marguerite curtsied politely and said, "It is a comfort to know there is always a French priest ready to hear my confession if needs be. Good day, Father Pierre."

"Good day, *mademoiselle.*"

She left him at the foot of the grand staircase, now a bare expanse of marble waiting to be refurbished, reborn. As she made her way up, dodging workmen and stone dust, she could feel the priest's cold stare on her back.

Tiens! Marguerite rolled her eyes in exasperation. Would she have to avoid that strange man the whole time they were in England, in addition to all her other duties? It was sure to be a most challenging few weeks indeed.

On sale 5th March 2010

ON THE WINGS OF LOVE
by Elizabeth Lane

The last thing Alexandra Bromley wanted was a colourless marriage like her parents…

Alex was all about adventure, and that's exactly what she got when dashing pilot Rafe Garrick crashed – quite literally – into her life!

The chemistry between them undeniable, Rafe couldn't ignore the courageous spirit that matched his own. Or the fact that Alex was soon carrying his child…

Now forced to wed, Rafe must find a way to give his adored new bride the freedom she so desperately craves!

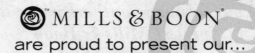

millsandboon.co.uk Community

Join Us!

The Community is the perfect place to meet and chat to kindred spirits who love books and reading as much as you do, but it's also the place to:

- Get the inside scoop from authors about their latest books
- Learn how to write a romance book with advice from our editors
- Help us to continue publishing the best in women's fiction
- Share your thoughts on the books we publish
- Befriend other users

Forums: Interact with each other as well as authors, editors and a whole host of other users worldwide.

Blogs: Every registered community member has their own blog to tell the world what they're up to and what's on their mind.

Book Challenge: We're aiming to read 5,000 books and have joined forces with The Reading Agency in our inaugural Book Challenge.

Profile Page: Showcase yourself and keep a record of your recent community activity.

Social Networking: We've added buttons at the end of every post to share via digg, Facebook, Google, Yahoo, technorati and de.licio.us.

www.millsandboon.co.uk